THE LAST NAZI

Also by Stan Pottinger

A Slow Burning

The Fourth Procedure

STAN POTTINGER

THE LAST NAZI

Hodder & Stoughton

Copyright © 2004 by Stan Pottinger

First published in Great Britain in 2004 by Hodder & Stoughton
Published simultaneously in paperback by Hodder & Stoughton
A division of Hodder Headline

The right of Stan Pottinger to be identified as the Author
of the Work has been asserted by him in accordance with the
Copyright, Designs and Patents Act 1988.

1 3 5 7 9 10 8 6 4 2

A CIP catalogue record for this title is available from the British Library

Hardback ISBN 0 340 77099 6
Trade Paperback ISBN 0 340 77100 3

Typeset in Kis by
Phoenix Typesetting, Burley-in-Wharfedale, West Yorkshire

Printed and bound in Great Britain by
Mackays of Chatham plc, Chatham, Kent

Hodder & Stoughton
A division of Hodder Headline
338 Euston Road
London NW1 3BH

For Zoe

Christmas Eve, 1944

Auschwitz-Birkenau
Concentration Camp
Poland

HE HEARD A SOFT VOICE, a little girl's voice, singing quietly in the operating room. When it stopped, Adalwolf told her to keep singing, there was no need to be afraid, everything was going to be fine.

Twelve-year-old Benjamin Ben-Zevi didn't need to guess what was going on in there. He knew.

Sitting in the darkened anteroom outside the OR, young Ben stared out the frosted windows, anxiously awaiting a kapo to come and take him back to his barracks. It was ten o'clock at night, and a blanket of snow had turned the camp unusually quiet. The boilers in the clinic had been turned off, leaving it bone-chilling cold, and Crematorium V was working at reduced capacity so that more SS officers could be home with their families. Ben wondered why Adalwolf, the sixteen-year-old foster son of Dr. Mengele, wasn't one of them, but apparently this was where he preferred to be. This was his Christmas present to himself.

Ben nervously fingered an ivory pendant hanging on a chain around his neck, then unwrapped a piece of chocolate from his pocket and held it lightly on his fingertips to keep it from melting. The door to the operating room was slightly ajar, casting a shard of light across the anteroom floor. He could hear Adalwolf still trying to convince the little girl that everything was fine, but to no avail. And no wonder: that was Ben's job. Lacking the warmth to tell a comforting lie, Adalwolf had conscripted him as an aide to calm the small children who were about to undergo one of Dr. Mengele's procedures. Sometimes Ben did it by teaching them a song;

sometimes by giving them a piece of chocolate or a toy that Dr. Mengele had made available. Regardless of the method, he knew what to do – so why hadn't Adalwolf asked him to do it? Why bring him here if he wasn't going to use him?

He ran his hand through his dirty hair.

Maybe Adalwolf was waiting for Ben to knock. But then he remembered rule number one: *Don't volunteer. For anything. Ever.*

He wiggled his toes nervously in his soggy leather shoes. He'd been there for nearly half an hour. Where was that kapo?

The snowflakes were coming down harder now, blanketing the muddy paths and powdering the trees in the Little Wood. Ben wondered if he'd ever see another snowfall in his home town of Vakhnovka. He wondered if anyone in his family was still alive. He wondered about many things until he remembered it was better not to wonder.

He lifted the ivory pendant and kissed it for good luck even though he didn't believe in luck any more. Survival didn't depend on good fortune, hard work, or any of the virtues he'd been taught as a boy. Survival depended on one thing: obedience. Calming frightened children was simply a matter of doing what he'd been told. And it was a good deed at that. If ever he was in their shoes, he hoped someone would do the same for him.

He let out a resigned sigh, then stood up and crept over to the operating room door, careful not to touch it for fear of making it creak. He'd been inside the room too many times not to know what was inside: the holding cots, the operating tables, the metal autopsy islands, the countertops with bell-shaped jars and stainless steel tools, the formaldehyde, the gooseneck lamps lighting bare walls. And the children.

He peeked through the crack and saw the little girl sitting on a sheet-covered stretcher, her eyes blindfolded with swaths of gauze wrapped around her head, her body naked from the waist up, shivering and scrawny from rations of stale bread, margarine, and black coffee. In her hands was a red and silver Christmas tree ornament that reminded Ben of a fishing pole bobber about to be dropped into a summer pond. A summer in a different life, a pond in a forgotten world.

Adalwolf's white lab coat moved in front of the opening, blocking Ben's view. Even though he was only sixteen, Adalwolf's uniform and chiseled face gave him the bearing of a real Nazi doctor – if 'doctor' was the right word for the people who worked in that room.

'Sing to me,' Adalwolf said, prompting the girl with a few bars of *Silent Night*.

Instead, she began crying.

'Come, come, Rochele,' Adalwolf said. 'If you sing everything will be fine.' He held her hand and, after a little more cajoling, she stopped sniffling and tried again.

'*Stille Nacht . . . Heilige Nacht . . .*'

The little girl kept singing softly, clutching the Christmas tree ornament against her belly.

'*Alles schläft, einsam wacht . . .*'

Ben heard the hiss of a bottle being opened. As he craned his neck to see where Adalwolf had gone, tears filled his eyes, some from the chemical fumes, some from the ache in his heart. He squeezed the pendant through his shirt and stuffed it into his mouth. The aroma of melted chocolate on his fingers mingled with the smell of chloroform.

The little girl was singing the last stanza now: '*Schlafe in himm-lischer Ruh*.' Ben held his breath, closed his eyes and waited for what was to happen next.

It didn't happen.

The door opened abruptly, bumping Ben's shoulder and jolting open his eyes. Adalwolf stood in the doorway looking down at him, a chloroform-filled syringe held in one rubber-gloved hand while the other reached for Ben's chocolate-covered fist. He pried the boy's fingers off the pendant, lifted it from around his neck, and held it up between them.

'You shouldn't have taken it, Ben,' he said, dropping it into his lab coat pocket.

Ben volunteered nothing. His flushed cheeks did it for him.

'Don't worry,' Adalwolf said, 'your punishment will fit the crime.' He grabbed Ben's shoulder and pushed him into the room.

Fifty-eight years later
December, 2002
Atlantic City, New Jersey

THE FBI AGENTS CLIMBED the grimy wooden stairwell smoothly, five sylphs in rubber-soled boots, black Ninja suits, Kevlar vests and helmets with visors lowered. Their MAC-10s were loaded, their gloved fingers inside the trigger guards.

Melissa Gale followed them up the steps at a short distance, her sneakers, turtleneck, and bulletproof vest suddenly feeling inadequate. But it didn't matter. She wanted this guy so much it made her mouth dry. 'Come on, Adalwolf,' she said in a soft whisper, 'be inside that room.' She had a habit of talking to herself when the pressure was on.

The SWAT team leader reached the top of the stair and put his back to the wall next to the door while the other agents moved silently into postion. Next to the leader was a nervous rookie holding a Maglite the size of a night stick, and on the other side of the door was a veteran African-American agent from the Washington field office named Harris Johnson. In front of the door were two more agents with a battering ram.

Melissa climbed the steps until her eyes reached floor level beneath the wooden banister. It was rare for a prosecutor to join the FBI on an arrest – in addition to the danger, it could make her a witness – but there were unusual circumstances in this case. She was closer to the action than she was supposed to be, but the agents were too focused to notice. She rested her double-gloved hands on the banister's lower rail, at eye level, and looked at the bottom of the door. The crack revealed the flickering blue light of a TV set.

He was in there. Seventy-five-year old Adalwolf – Josef

Mengele's teenage lab assistant at Auschwitz, the last Nazi on her list – was watching television in a rooming house in Atlantic City's run-down Inlet section.

Melissa's heart felt fuel-injected. Since she'd gotten word five years earlier that he was living in the United States, capturing him had been like trying to grab smoke. Twice they'd broken down doors where he was supposed to be only to find nothing. As a lawyer for OSI, the Justice Department's Office of Special Investigations – the 'Nazi hunters' – she had arrested eight former Nazis living in the U.S. and deported them by court order, but none of them were like this. This one wasn't a toothless old geezer hiding out as a retired car salesman in Des Moines; this one was still active, still a menace. Although she couldn't prove it yet, she was sure he'd killed three people with a deadly virus called NTX. The FBI's digital tracing program, called BackFire, had located him in this flophouse three hours earlier when he'd sent Melissa one of his taunting e-mails.

This time, he didn't know they were coming.

The SWAT team leader from the Newark field office raised his hand, signaling his men to get ready.

Melissa patted her pocket and felt the search warrant. She'd never set eyes on Adalwolf, didn't even have a photograph of him except for one taken in 1944 when he was the acolyte of the 'Butcher of Auschwitz.' But she knew how to identify him. Two death camp survivors had testified that he had a black *Totenkopf* – the SS death's head – tattooed on his upper left arm. The judge's warrant required her to see it as a condition of arrest. In addition, Adalwolf had no voice box, which she knew because she'd talked to him many times on the telephone. If they arrested him and got him to speak through his electrolarynx, she'd recognize his voice in a second.

The team leader counted down: three fingers, two fingers, one. When the last digit disappeared, the agents with the ram smashed in the door with one swing, knocking it off its hinges.

HARRIS JOHNSON AND THE team leader went through the door with their submachine guns in hand yelling, 'FBI! Don't move!' followed by two agents on their flanks, automatics at eye level. The rookie shone a beam of light into the subject's face.

Watching from the stair, Melissa caught a glimpse of an old man sitting in a worn club chair, his grizzled face stunned and confused, his eyes squinting at the Maglite and guns. Harris Johnson, whom she'd been working with on the case, put the muzzle of his weapon against the old man's head and said, 'We can't prone him out, he's hooked up!'

Another agent said, 'I say we put him down anyway!'

The team leader said, 'Everybody hold what you got!'

Ordinarily they would have put their subject face down on the floor and cuffed his hands behind his back, but there was an IV pole standing next to him with a plastic bag of fluid at the top and a clear tube running down to his arm. She heard the team leader yell from beneath his lowered visor, 'Harris, you've got the controls.'

Harris Johnson looked at the old man a moment, then yelled, 'Okay, Gale! We're ready to make an ID!'

Melissa Gale pulled her industrial mask over her nose and mouth, adjusted the elastic straps behind her head, and climbed the remaining steps toward the open door. Entering the room, she saw an old man in gray sweatpants and a dirty T-shirt sitting upright with his arms resting on tattered armrests, his feet on the floor, his head wobbling but proud and erect. She thought he looked more like a dying old athlete than a killer.

She looked around the room and saw his ratty slippers, an unmade Murphy bed, magazines and junk strewn around, a grimy window at the back wall, a Styrofoam coffee cup, and a TV set still flickering with a *Seinfeld* rerun. To her right was a kitchenette with dirty pots in the sink, a Formica table with a laptop computer on it, lid up, screen dark. On the wall was a movie poster of *Saving Private Ryan*.

She stepped up to the subject and looked into a pair of watery eyes. Could this old coot with salt-and-pepper stubble and a Zane Grey paperback on his lap still be killing people? Yes, he could. Evil didn't look like Freddy Kruger, evil looked ordinary. Banal. Like him.

'He looks doped up.'

'Don't take anything for granted!' Harris Johnson said.

'Maybe he caught his own virus,' the team leader said. 'He looks like he's got the flu.'

Melissa stepped in closer.

Harris Johnson said, 'Come on, Melissa, we need positive ID.'

She stooped down with her face level with his. 'Who are you?' she said through her mask. He didn't speak. 'Blink if you are Adalwolf.' He didn't blink. She stood up and reached toward him slowly. He stared at her through bleary eyes as she rolled up the sleeve of his T-shirt.

It was right where it was supposed to be: a faded black tattoo of a human skull – the *Totenkopf* – the symbol of the Nazi SS.

She turned to Harris and nodded. He looked at it and agreed. She stooped in front of the old man again and pulled her mask down around her neck, revealing her face.

'Hello, Adalwolf,' she said. 'It's me. Melissa Gale.'

He stared at her a moment, then, as if he finally understood what was happening, slowly raised his right hand from the armrest. When it was a few inches off the fabric she could see an object taped to his palm – something dark and metallic – something resembling a—

'*Gun!*' an agent yelled.

WEAPONS CLACKED AND Harris Johnson pushed his MAC-10 hard against the old man's skull.

Without warning, the rookie rammed the large end of the flashlight into the old man's chest, knocking spit out of his mouth.

'Easy!' Melissa said angrily. 'It's not a gun, it's a microphone!'

The team leader yanked the rookie's hands back, but the old man's wind was already gone. As much as Melissa hated him, she didn't like seeing him bashed in the chest. He wheezed, his face red, the veins on his neck prominent. Then his eyes glinted and the muscles in his arms rippled and a warrior's spirit inside him came alive. This, Melissa thought, was more like the Adalwolf she expected. He let out a phlegmy cough.

'Put your mask on,' Harris Johnson told her.

She pulled the white shell over her mouth and pinched the frame onto the bridge of her nose. His eyes were watering and his lips dry. He raised the microphone another inch, and she thought, *That's strange*. His fingertips were wrapped in wet gauze.

The old man's hand stopped moving to let them see that he was holding an amplifier, not a weapon, then continued rising slowly. Despite the drugs or fever that clouded his mind, he understood that there were loaded guns pointed at his head. When his hand was about a foot away from his stoma – the hole at the base of his neck where his larynx used to be – Melissa noticed that the plastic IV line was dangling next to his elbow, unattached to his arm. And the liquid medicine wasn't draining out.

His hand-held electrolarynx continued approaching the base of his neck. He opened his lips to speak. Melissa's eyelids widened at the sight of a silver glint running up inside the clear plastic tubing.

'Wait!' she said—

But he didn't wait. He pressed the transmit button to talk – she heard the click of the battery-driven speaker and his first two electronic words – '*You are*—' The transmission sent an electrical charge up the silver wire into an explosive cap at the base of the IV bag, igniting a liter of liquid naphtha masquerading as medication.

Boom-whooooosh!

THE BAG BURST INTO A blazing sun and dropped onto the old man's head, shoulders, and lap, splashing in all directions like spilled milk, engulfing everything in its path. Melissa and the agents leapt away with their hands shielding their faces as Adalwolf lit up like a self-immolating Buddhist monk. A bonfire swirled around him with a roar, turning his face into black silhouette behind a veil of orange.

Harris: 'Keep it off your clothes!'

The team leader: 'Over there!' Pointing.

Two agents yanked a braided rug from under a coffee table and threw it over Adalwolf's head. Flames licked out and joined the burning liquid on the floor.

'Water coming!' one of the agents yelled from the kitchenette. He had the faucet at the sink running full blast into a pot which he grabbed and threw toward the burning chair. Another agent stamped his feet on the flames; yet another beat them away from an agent's burning legs. Smoke and hot gases and the stench of burned flesh filled the room. Everyone was coughing.

'Get everybody out of the building!'

Three agents hustled through the open door and moved past tenants who were already standing on the stair to see what was going on. Agents ran up and down the stairwell yelling and knocking on doors, entering rooms, pulling residents out.

Harris Johnson and the rookie wrapped Adalwolf in the rug and carried his body down the steps. Melissa backed up to the door, looking at the flames creeping toward the walls. The full-throated wail of a fire truck sounded in the distance.

She saw the laptop on the table.

She ran between the licking spikes, grabbed the computer, and dashed to the door through a wall of fire. When she reached the stair she looked down at her legs and saw smoke drifting up from the soles of her shoes, but no flames. She jogged down and met Harris coming up.

'Is everyone out?' he shouted as he passed her.

'I don't know,' she said.

Out on the sidewalk she stood looking up at smoke billowing from one of the old man's windows that had shattered from the heat. A wet December snow was falling with the ash.

The first fire truck arrived and the firemen jumped off just as Harris and the team leader came out the door. Everyone was out of the building, Harris said, and walked to an emergency medical van that sat idling with its rear doors open, about to receive Adalwolf's rug-covered body on a gurney. Harris and Melissa looked at his smoldering remains. Harris expressed his sentiments in a low voice: 'Fuck.'

Melissa carried the laptop to the hood of the ambulance, lifted the top, and hit the function key. The screen lit up.

If you are reading this, Melissa, take no satisfaction from my death. You and your jackboot friends – at least the ones who survived   are going to miss me. But enough is enough. My work is done, and I choose to depart on my terms, not yours.

Joseph Goebbels wrote the Third Reich's epitaph in Hitler's bunker shortly before the end: 'When we depart, let the earth tremble.' The world has waited fifty years for that to happen, and now the time has come.

Look to a child to complete the Führer's work, Melissa. The Final Solution isn't over, it's just begun.

A.

P.S. The butter cookies in the round tin are terrific.

She closed the laptop and picked it up and found Harris.

'You okay?' he said.

She nodded and shivered. The wet cold was going to the bone.

'Bastard almost nailed us,' Harris said. 'We've got two agents with burns.'

Melissa looked over and saw them lifted into an ambulance. 'How bad?'

Harris shrugged. They stared at each other.

'What?' Harris said.

'I don't understand why he killed himself,' she said.

Harris yelled at an agent, 'Jim – ride with the EMS, okay?' To Melissa he replied, 'He knew his days were numbered and he wanted to take a few of us out before he went.'

Melissa knew Adalwolf was capable of killing himself if he had good reason, but was trying to kill some FBI agents good enough? She didn't think so. His suicide was a sideshow to cover up something else. And why do it with fire? He hated fire. He'd once said in an e-mail to her, *'Fire is for ovens, and ovens are for Jews.'*

Watching Harris walk over to a cluster of FBI agents, she held up the laptop to show him she had it, then headed for the FBI van.

Adalwolf loved the game. How had he won it by losing?

'DAVID?' NO ANSWER.

Entering her Alexandria, Virginia, townhouse apartment, Melissa called out to her husband before the door closed. 'Honey, you home?' She'd telephoned him as she was boarding the FBI helicopter to tell him she was all right but the bust had gone bad, she'd explain when she got home. Apparently he wasn't back yet. He'd been in Baltimore working on a story for the *Times*, but said he'd be home if at all possible.

She went into the bathroom and took off her clothes, trying to rid herself of the smell of smoke and human cremation.

Standing naked in front of the full length mirror on the back of the door, she caught a glimpse of the tiny pearl studs she was still wearing. She couldn't believe she'd forgotten to take them off before the bust. She faced the mirror and leveled her head and looked at them straight on. As usual, they were noticeably uneven, the one on the left ear higher than the one on the right. 'That's what you get when you let your junior high girlfriend use a kilt pin as a piercing needle,' she said. Leaning forward, she removed the studs and set them down on the sink.

She turned on the bath water – ran it hot – then took another look at herself in the full length mirror. Her cheekbones were still pink, but her face looked tired. She never wore mascara; it made her naturally full lashes so long they brushed against the insides of her sunglasses. In fact, except for the occasional use of lipstick, she rarely wore any makeup at all. People thought she was being politically correct, but basically, she was just too lazy to mess with it. David said she didn't need it anyway. Lovely David, still blinded by love.

With the bath water running, she stepped back from the mirror and turned sideways, in profile, to examine her belly. She stood up straight and put her hands on her stomach and drew it in hard, accentuating her rib cage – then let it go, pooching it out as far as possible to imagine what she'd look like pregnant. There wasn't enough there to get the idea, not even when she slumped her shoulders forward. Jane, her pregnant assistant, said she'd kill for Melissa's figure, but Melissa would have swapped it for hers in a second.

She turned on the bath and opened the medicine cabinet and took a swig of Mylanta from a turquoise-colored bottle. After swallowing a gulp – it made her shudder – she hung her head over the sink and breathed deeply. When the queasiness subsided, she lifted her husband's robe off the back of the door, pulled it on, and walked down the hall to the kitchen.

The message light was blinking on her answering machine. She hit the play button and pulled a carton of orange juice from the refrigerator and set it on the table to take the chill off before drinking. The first message was from her boss, Barry Sherer, the second from Janet Wayward, the Justice Department public information officer who dealt with the press.

Evidently the fun had already begun.

She lifted the phone, then set it back on the cradle and drank some juice. Adalwolf had left the investigation in a shambles. Without interrogating him, how would they know what he'd done? What virus he'd used? Who else might be infected? What scheme he was pursuing?

She told herself to relax and be glad he was gone.

Waiting for the tub to fill, she looked out the window at the yellow lights lining the Potomac on the Washington side of the river. If she craned her neck she could see the edge of the Lincoln Memorial with its white marble walls glowing under the spotlights. They lived in a renovated town house in Old Town Alexandria, a cozy spot for young married couples. Not that they were all that young – she was thirty-eight, David forty – and not that they were all that cozy, either, at least not in the last few months. They said their work schedules were the problem, but she knew that wasn't true. When two people wanted a child they couldn't have, the price of disappointment was distance.

Being childless was a bad-luck roll of the biological dice, and yet it felt like a personal failing to her and compromised manhood to him. Finding it increasingly annoying to talk about, increasingly they didn't. They both had a thousand excuses.

She put the orange juice away. God, she wished he was home. It was a strange time to be thinking about sex, but she was sure she was ovulating. Sometimes she could tell. The doctors said it didn't matter; the scars on her uterus made implantation nearly impossible. But it was the 'nearly' in that diagnosis that gave her hope.

Picking up her keys, she took a second look at the thumb-sized, red plastic sneaker dangling from the chain, her souvenir of the moment they fell in love. It was on their third date, a restaurant in Washington that had unexpectedly closed, David claiming to know where they could find fresh oysters and, two hours later, eating Blue Points and Belons in Rehoboth Beach, Delaware.

After dinner they'd walked to a carnival with the usual gaudy lights, pop guns, and merry-go-round calliopes and he'd offered a reckless bet: You pick the game, and whoever wins a teddy bear first gets whatever he or she wants.

'Anything?' she said.

'Anything,' he said.

She chose to throw baseballs at lead milk bottles. 'Now that we shook on it,' she said, 'you should know I played softball in high school.'

'And I played baseball in college,' he said.

'You didn't tell me that.'

'You didn't ask. Chickening out?'

'Hand me the damn baseballs.'

Six games later Melissa had won a teddy bear and David had won a key chain with a red plastic sneaker. He said it was too late to drive back to Washington, they'd had too many martinis, it'd be *very* dangerous. Climbing the steps to a beachside B & B, she swapped the teddy bear for the key chain, which meant now he could redeem it for whatever *he* wanted. Which was fine with her, because what he wanted was the same thing she wanted. She'd carried the keychain ever since.

ASHERMAN'S SYNDROME WAS the name of the problem. She'd acquired the scars in her uterus from a rare case of tuberculosis when she was fifteen. Since the diagnosis, she'd read so much about it her fertility specialist said she understood the disease better than most doctors.

The specialist was Dr. Eric Brandt, director of the Myrna Ben-Zevi Memorial Fertility Clinic in Miami and one of the top specialists in the field. Professor Ben-Zevi – 'Ben' to everyone who knew him – was the semi-retired chairman of the clinic and the widower of the woman for whom it was named. As long as these two men continued treating her, she had hope.

Ben in particular inspired confidence. He'd met Melissa's grandmother, Esther, at Auschwitz when he worked as a conscript in Dr. Josef Mengele's clinic. After the war, he migrated to Israel for a brief stay, converted his European name 'Wolfson', to its Hebrew counterpart 'Ben-Z'ev', then came to the United States to complete his medical eduction. Grandma Esther was instrumental in bringing him to New York where he eventually became the family doctor. Years later, when Melissa joined OSI, he testified for her as an expert witness in one of her Nazi deportation cases, and later helped put her on to Adalwolf's trail. He was more than a doctor and friend; he was family. Except for David, the only family she had left.

She looked at the calendar on the refrigerator. Six weeks earlier she'd undergone a high-risk surgical procedure to see if enough healthy uterine tissue could be restored to hold a fertilized egg. A few more days and she'd know. For that matter, the operation might have been successful and she was ready to conceive right now. Her hormones were calling and her eggs were waiting. All she needed was David.

She finished her glass of juice, put away the carton, turned off the kitchen light and headed for the bathroom where she washed her hair and soaked in the tub. After drying off, she went to the bedroom and lowered the shades and crawled between the sheets. They felt cool and clean against her naked skin. She was setting the alarm on the night stand when the phone rang. At this hour, it had to be David.

'Hi, baby,' she answered.

'Uh, Melissa, this is Janet Wayward at Justice. Sorry to be calling so late, but I'm getting press calls about Atlantic City.'

Melissa sat up and told her what had happened and answered her questions. When they were done, Wayward said she wanted Melissa to do an interview on CNN first thing in the morning. 'The Attorney General doesn't even want a whiff of Ruby Ridge, which means we need to tell the world what happened and tell it fast.'

'Why not get somebody from the Bureau?' Melissa said.

'Don't worry, nobody's out to savage you. Everybody knows this Nazi killed himself. Good riddance.'

'But . . .'

'The AG wants it, Melissa. It's tag, and you're it.'

Melissa took down the address of CNN's Washington studio and turned out the light on her side of the bed, leaving the lamp on David's side. She slept better that way.

She didn't know what time he would get in. As a reporter with the Washington bureau of *The New York Times*, his day was dictated by events, not the sun. But that was okay with her, she worked long hours herself. 'Live with it,' she said out loud as she turned off the phone ringer. Then, 'I gotta stop talking to myself.' She lay back and burrowed into the covers and closed her eyes.

HER EYES OPENED IN darkness. David had turned out the light and was crawling into bed quietly, trying not to wake her. She turned toward him and touched his shoulder through the sheet. His hand found her naked thigh and squeezed it the way he always did. She cozied up behind him, a spoon in a spoon, but it was too late: The mess in Atlantic City came pouring in.

'He fooled us again,' she said.

David reached across his chest and found her hand. 'What happened?'

'He set us up with a booby trap and we fell for it.'

He rubbed her hand sympathetically.

She said, 'He burned to death. There's going to be a lot of flak.'

David stopped rubbing her hand and turned onto his back. 'I'm glad the bastard is dead.'

'I think I'm ovulating,' she said.

She felt him prop himself on an elbow above her and stroke her hair. He leaned down and kissed her – missed her lips in the dark, found her nose, then her lips – and began massaging her breasts, down to her belly, around to her back and down her buttocks, down to the back of her thigh. He had a gentle hand that made the dough rise slowly, but tonight foreplay only made her impatient. When his hand rolled over onto the top of her thigh, she spread her legs an inch. It was the only signal he needed.

He mounted her gracefully, pulling her legs up, guiding himself into her easily, taking her hands in his and pinning them high above her head. She squeezed them hard and curled her legs around his calves.

'Don't wait, baby,' she whispered.

His hips began moving with a slow camshaft motion.

A film of ambient light crept into the room around the edges of the night shades, putting him in silhouette. He let go of her hands and raised his torso above her and loomed over her like a warm shadow. She put her hands on his back and buttocks and felt the rhythm of their motion. Except for the rustle of sheets and an occasional murmur, they made love silently. He seemed more driven than usual, and she felt like a woman on a mission, the last two people on earth, desperate to conceive.

She said, 'It's going to happen, I can feel it.'

She could feel heat starting to tingle on the soles of her feet, running up her legs . . . up her back and into her face . . . all around her in a full-body aura.

'I'm almost there!' she whispered. 'Come with me!'

She felt the aura start to implode. She was so close . . . so ready . . . 'Don't stop!' she whispered and dug her nails his hands. 'Don't stop, don't stop . . . '

He stopped. Almost, it seemed, on purpose.

'Honey?' she said. She reached up to touch his face, but he grabbed her wrists to stop her. 'What's wrong?' she said.

He held her wrists tight and made a guttural sound she'd never heard before.

'David, what is it?' She was wildly confused, her legs still spread. She tried to pull her wrists free but he wouldn't let go. Another guttural sound came from deep in his chest.

I know that sound.

She wrenched her wrists from his hand, but it happened slowly, like trudging through a muddy field. She reached for the lamp next to the bed but he pulled her arm back down. She tried to reach it again. 'David, you're hurting me!' She finally found the switch – fingers fumbling – and turned it on.

Above her was the sagging face of an old man with beady eyes and mottled, gray skin. Icy revulsion swept through her. He put his hand over her mouth and grinned a hideous grin. She tried to scream but couldn't; she was panicked from being pinned down. He kneeled between her legs and without warning burst into flames. Terror welled up in her and a silent shudder ruptured her dream.

When she woke, heart was racing like a small bird's and one of her arms was still suspended in midair, reaching for the bedside lamp. But the light was still on, David's side of the bed still empty. He hadn't come home yet.

'Good God.'

She got up and went to the bathroom and splashed cool water over her face. It was two-thirty in the morning, the perfect time for gut-wrenching witchcraft.

She looked into the mirror. *Come on, Adalwolf, let go*. He was still in her head, still powerful enough to climb into her bed and fuck her. The show was over but the music lingered on.

She dried her face and returned to the bedroom with a glass of water. On the bedside table was half an Ambien. She washed it down and got into bed and waited for the chemistry to kick in. She felt like a marathoner who'd stopped running before she hit the tape. All that work and still no victory. So frustrating. *Relax and be glad he's dead. The rest will take care of itself.*

She rolled onto her side and tried to sleep again. When her grandmother, Esther, had come out of Auschwitz she was pregnant with Melissa's mother and had died at age twenty-five, long before Melissa was born. Who had fathered her mother had remained a family mystery until a year after her death, when Ben – having promised he would tell no one during her mother's lifetime – revealed to Melissa that the man who had made her mother pregnant had been an SS captain. Melissa's grandfather had literally been the enemy.

It hadn't come as a surprise to Melissa. The way her mother had

clammed up over the subject made Melissa wonder if her biological grandfather might have been a fellow concentration camp
prisoner, or a kapo, or maybe an SS officer. While the possibilities
were nothing to celebrate, neither did she feel a sense of shame
about them. Regardless of the awful circumstances, her grandmother's pregnancy had saved her own life and given Melissa a
loving mother. Besides, Melissa didn't believe in genetic determi-
nation. Even Hitler, she assumed, had relatives who were decent.

She pictured Adalwolf sitting in his chair with fire floating
around him on transparent film. For some reason she began to cry,
and soon she was crying hard. When she was finished, she thought:
How about that. It's finally over.

She laid the damp tissue on the bed next to her and closed her
eyes. A moment later she was starting to drift, her breathing deep
and her heartbeat soft and regular. Down, down, down . . . down
like a ball of unraveling twine. When the last inch unfurled, sitting
before her in neon lights was Adalwolf's e-mail on her laptop: *'Fire
is for ovens . . . and ovens are for Jews.'* The words morphed into the
question she'd asked Harris earlier: *Why would he kill himself with
fire?*

She sat bolt upright, her eyes open and her mind clear despite
the sleeping pill. A phantom had poked her awake and disappeared
around the corner. She lay back and exhaled. His death may have
left unanswered questions, but she didn't have to be the one to
answer them. For her it was over.

Except it wasn't. There was still something unsettled that kept
nudging her, keeping her awake. Not only did she not know the
answer, she didn't even know the question.

Yet.

THE SIX O'CLOCK MORNING news was blaring on the bedroom TV when Melissa got out of the shower and grabbed a towel. David had called to say good morning and tell her how sorry he was he wasn't there and ask her what happened last night, but she didn't have time to give him more than a quick outline. They gave each other verbal kisses and hung up.

Drying off, she heard the words 'Atlantic City' on the television set and looked through the bathroom door. Over the TV anchor's shoulder was a picture of a swastika on fire.

'The FBI attempted to arrest a World War II Nazi in a tenement house in Atlantic City, New Jersey, last night,' the anchor said, 'but as they were taking the man into custody he apparently killed himself.'

She saw videotape of a sheet-covered body on a stretcher being pushed toward the back of an emergency medical van.

'According to a Justice Department spokeswoman,' the anchor's voice said behind the pictures, 'the suspect, known only by the name Adalwolf, left a suicide note and rigged a booby-trap that exploded shortly after the FBI entered the room. The seventy-five-year-old Nazi had been sought for nearly five years as a suspected SS Officer at Auschwitz.'

Now firemen were walking into a tenement house cordoned off by yellow plastic tape.

'Two FBI agents were hospitalized with burns in the fiery raid.'

There was nothing about three suspected Jewish victims of Adalwolf, nothing about a deadly virus, no panic in the streets. The press had got the gist of it, and that was enough. She got dressed wondering how long it would stay that way.

SOMEONE PINNED A MICROPHONE to her white silk blouse; someone else straightened the crease in her slacks and said, 'Would you rather cross your legs or leave both feet on the floor?' Someone else patted her forehead and nose with a powder puff. Melissa sat there feeling like a mannequin.

She looked behind the cameras at the crew and saw ordinary people like the ones she'd grown up with – so why did she feel like they were preparing an execution? All those cables and all this electricity, that's why. Not a word had been spoken, not an accusation made, and yet she felt guilty.

'Hello,' the familiar voice said, 'I'm Dee Dee Donovan.' A perky blonde gave Melissa a big smile, and Melissa thought, Hey, she's fine, relax. Dee Dee Donovan said, 'Did you get some coffee in the green room?' Putting her at ease.

'Are you doing the interview?' Melissa said.

'No, no, you're being interviewed by Paula in New York. Split screen. Just look into that camera right there. She'll see you, but you won't be able to see her.'

'Listen, I—'

Donovan held up a finger and pressed her earpiece to her head. Her face turned serious. She repositioned her mouthpiece and said, 'I haven't seen it,' to the voice talking to her. A pause and a glance at Melissa. 'She's right here, ready to go.' Another pause. 'I'd be happy to show it to her, but I haven't got it.'

Got what? Show what? Melissa felt a meat hook tugging at her back.

The man next to the camera said, 'Thirty seconds.'

Dee Dee Donovan turned toward a girl with earphones and electronic gear approaching with a bright yellow piece of paper in her hand. Donovan took it and read fast. After finishing, she looked up at Melissa and was about to say something when the man by the camera counted down softly, 'Five, four, three . . .' They were live.

Melissa heard Paula Zahn's voice, as smooth as Sunday morning.

'Most of the Nazis responsible for the unspeakable atrocities of the Holocaust are dead by now,' Zahn said, 'but not all. A few who were young SS guards are still living in the United States with their crimes unknown even to their friends and neighbors. But if they think they're home free, they haven't met Melissa Gale, a Nazi hunter with the Justice Department who has located and prosecuted seven men and one woman involved in death camp atrocities.' She spoke to Melissa. 'Welcome.'

Melissa gave her a dimpled smile and said, 'Good morning.'

'Last night you were part of an FBI team that tried to arrest a Nazi named Adalwolf,' Zahn said, 'but before you could take him into custody he died in a fire. What happened?'

'When we were making the arrest he set off a fire bomb.'

'To kill your team?'

'And himself, apparently.'

'So he knew you were coming?'

'I'm sure he suspected it, we've been pursuing him for years.'

'You wouldn't think a man in his mid-seventies would be so dangerous,' Zahn said.

'This one was unusual,' Melissa said.

'So I gather. What, exactly, does a Nazi hunter do?' Zahn asked.

'There are different kinds,' Melissa said. 'I work for the Office of Special Investigations which has authority to deport Nazis who lied on their immigration forms when they entered the United States.'

'You don't put them in jail?'

'Not for lying, no. The most we can do is deport them – unless they've also committed other crimes, in which case they can be prosecuted for those.'

'Nobody likes Nazis,' Zahn said, 'but when someone dies in a raid there are always going to be questions, aren't there?'

'Routinely,' Melissa said.

'Do you expect accusations of official misconduct?' Zahn said.

'No,' Melissa said. 'We tried to take him peacefully.'

'I'm sure the videotape will back you up.'

Videotape? The word was an icicle in her chest.

Zahn looked at the camera and said, 'We have a piece of video-tape that just arrived at our studio. I understand parts of it are very graphic, so you might want to make sure the kids aren't watching.'

Melissa felt her heart pound. On a monitor off to the side, near the camera, she saw a replay of the events of the night before.

Oh, shit.

ADALWOLF HAD MOUNTED A hidden camera in the kitchen cupboard high on the right. Melissa watched what it had recorded.

She saw him sitting in his club chair staring forward in the general direction of a TV set, the IV pole at his side, his head bobbing as he fought to overcome the sedative he'd given himself.

'Does this look like the room?' Zahn asked.

'Yes,' Melissa said. Nothing like seeing yourself on national TV.

The tape showed the door crashing in and flattening at Adalwolf's feet. He was so drugged he didn't blink.

Three agents in black Ninja gear entered with guns drawn and took positions around the subject. He looked overwhelmed. The sound on the videotape was bad but distinguishable.

There was Harris and the team leader saying, 'FBI! Don't move!'

Adalwolf squinting at the guns and flashlight.

Harris saying, 'We can't prone him out, he's hooked up!'

Another saying, 'I say we put him down anyway!'

Melissa wanted the videotape to self-destruct, but it didn't. It showed her entering the room with her protective mask on.

'Is that you?' Zahn said.

'Uh, looks like it . . .'

An agent could be heard saying, 'He looks doped up.'

And another saying, 'Maybe he caught his own virus.'

Oh, Christ now the virus is out there.

The videotape showed Melissa checking Adalwolf's tattoo . . .

pulling down her mask and stooping in front of him to speak
... Adalwolf raising his hand with the electrolarynx. It showed the
rookie slamming the head of his Maglite into Adalwolf's chest.
Melissa winced again. It looked uglier than she remembered.

Paula Zahn said, 'What is happening to make the FBI hit an old
man like that?'

Melissa said, 'The agent thought he had a gun.'

It showed the team leader yanking the flashlight away.
Adalwolf's hand rising slowly, Melissa and the agents watching.
Adalwolf placing the electronic speech device at the stoma in his
neck and clicking on the device to speak. Melissa yelling, 'Wait!'

The bag of naphtha exploding.

The brightness turned the videotape white. When the picture
returned there was a Niagara of fire, but only for a split second.
The show's director apparently saw no reason to put a barbeque
on America's breakfast tables.

Melissa sat there feeling burned, too. *It wasn't the fire department
that sent them this tape.*

Paula Zahn said, 'I'm told he was holding a voice amplifier, not
a gun.'

Melissa said, 'As it turned out it wasn't a gun, but the agents had
only a split second to determine what it was.' *It wasn't a CNN
reporter who found the tape, either.*

Zahn said, 'What virus was the FBI agent talking about?'

Here we go. 'As I recall,' Melissa said, 'the next thing he said was,
"He looks like he's got the flu."' Hoping Paula would assume it was
the flu.

'So we're not talking about the spread of a disease like smallpox
or anthrax or some other nine-eleven deadly virus?'

How could Melissa answer that? 'I certainly wouldn't want to
leave that impression.' Like a lawyer, that's how: technically
truthful and generally misleading. 'I'd like to say more about this,
but since it's an open investigation, I'm afraid I can't.' *The FBI didn't
leak this tape either.*

'Why do you suppose he made a videotape of his arrest, Ms. Gale?'

'I don't know. He was an angry, dangerous man.' *Only one person could have done it.* 'Despite the pyrotechnics, the arrest was in order. We have two FBI agents in the hospital as a result of this man's actions.'

Melissa saw the floor producer run his hand in a small circle, telling Dee Dee Donovan they were about to cut to a commercial.

Paula Zahn said, 'I'm sorry we didn't have more time to talk about your marvelous career.'

'Oh, you didn't miss much. Thanks for having me,' Melissa said.

Zahn said, 'We'll be right back.'

Only one person could have sent the tape to CNN. Only one person wanted to get me and Harris thrown off the case. Adalwolf.

He's still alive.

MELISSA SAT IN A WINDOWLESS room in WFO – the Washington Field Office of the FBI – staring at cardboard boxes filled with the charred remains of Adalwolf's room. Everything smelled of smoke, burned fabric, and an occasional whiff of something worse. She stuffed two pieces of rolled-up Kleenex into her nostrils but it didn't help, so she took them out.

She'd live with it.

Her cell phone rang. She lifted it and recognized the caller's number: Janet Wayward, Justice PIO. Even the tone of the ringer sounded desperate. She decided not to answer until she had more information. She needed facts and she needed them fast.

She pulled on a pair of latex gloves and turned to the boxes. Opening one at random, she found the remains of Adalwolf's kitchenette – old pots, a George Foreman minigrill, utensils. She went through three more boxes but found nothing helpful. In the next box she found a jar of pennies, more papers, books.

Then, beneath them all, paydirt: a video camera burned to a crisp, blackened cables still connecting it to a charcoaled modem, a burned telephone line dangling from its port.

She picked them up and was staring at them when the door opened and Harris Johnson stepped inside. Wearing a dark blue suit and a crisp white shirt against his coffee-colored skin, he looked more like Michael Jordan than a G-man. He closed the door without speaking. Obviously, he'd seen *American Morning* with Paula Zahn.

Melissa lifted the burned camera and modem and cables. Harris pulled on a pair of latex gloves and took the scorched items from her.

'He set us up,' she said. 'Videotaped the whole thing by modem and sent the tape to CNN.' Her cell phone again. Seeing the number was her husband's, this time she answered. 'Hi, David,' she said. 'You see the interview?'

'I did.'

'What'd you think?'

'You did the best you could.'

'It was a disaster,' she said. 'I'll call you later, I'm up against it right now. Love you.'

Harris turned the blackened camera and modem over to inspect them, then dropped them into the cardboard box. 'Far as I'm concerned the only thing he caught on tape was his own suicide and an attempt to kill some FBI agents.'

She heard him but wasn't buying it.

Harris said, 'If he wasn't the guy in that chair last night, who was?'

'Good question,' she said, 'but that's not the way it's going to be asked. It's gonna be, Who was the guy the FBI torched?'

Harris pulled off his gloves. 'It was Adalwolf, and we didn't torch him, he torched himself.'

'I don't think it was him. He wants us to think it was so we'll close the case.'

'Then why send a videotape to CNN?'

'I don't know.'

'It was him, Melissa. You made the ID yourself. His age, the SS tattoo, the electrolarynx, the Backfire e-mail trace to his room – who else could it be?' He removed a box from a swivel chair and sat down.

'Look at this.' She tapped away on Adalwolf's laptop and opened an e-mail he'd sent her months before. *Me go to hell? Never. Fire is for ovens, and ovens are for Jews.* She looked up. 'Why would someone who hates fire use fire to kill himself?'

'That's why he drugged himself,' Harris said.

She pushed her caster chair over to a box and pulled out a biography of Lincoln, a Zane Grey paperback, the short stories of Jack London. 'These aren't the kind of books Adalwolf would have read,' she said, stacking them.

He watched her a moment, then got off his chair and sat on the table.

'We always try to take the bad guys alive, Melissa, but sometimes they do the world a favor.'

She sat back in her chair. 'If I don't answer some of these frantic calls, the Department's going to come after me.'

'With who, the FBI?'

She reached for a phone and opened her notebook, turned to a marked page, dialed a number. A few seconds later she was talking to the medical examiner for Atlantic County, New Jersey, Dr. Carol Reed. Melissa didn't have to say much to explain why she was calling. She put the call on the speaker, introduced Harris, and said, 'We need an expedited autopsy. Can you help?'

'Am I looking for something in particular?'

'The subject looked like he may have been on drugs,' Melissa said.

'We don't do toxicology here, but I'll stat it to the lab in Newark.'

'He had a tattoo on his upper left arm. Could it have survived the fire?'

'Depends on how badly he was burned. Tattoos are subcutaneous. Do you know what it looks like?'

'It's a skull with two bones behind it. Probably been there for decades.'

'You want a microscope of the tissue? Newark has a gas chromatograph and a mass spectrometer that will tell you how old it is.'

'Right now I just need you to eyeball it, okay?'

'Okay.'

Harris said, 'Take a look for a small tattoo under his left arm, too. Letters indicating his blood type.' It was a common tattoo of the SS.

An assistant entered the room and handed Melissa a pink telephone slip. She took it and said into the phone, 'Let me ask you something else. Does a virus survive a burned body?'

'What kind of virus?'

'Does it matter?' She started reading the message on the slip.

'It might,' Dr. Reed said. 'If it's a serum virus we should be able to find it unless his blood got so hot it boiled. If it's a virus that resides in tissue, like respiratory syncitial virus, it might have burned up. We'd have to look with an electron microscope.'

Melissa finished reading the message and said, 'I'll know more about it later today.'

'That must have been quite a scene last night,' Dr. Reed said.

'Afraid so,' Melissa said. 'Listen, thanks for the help.' She hung up and read the pink telephone slip again. 'Can you go to Atlantic City?' she said to Harris.

'What's in Atlantic City?'

'If the autopsy reveals what I think, you're the only one who can handle the fallout.' She was on her feet.

'What do you think it'll show?'

'I'll tell you on the phone. Right now, I gotta get to Atlanta.' She pulled her bag onto her shoulder and reached for her cell phone. 'EIS called.' That was the Epidemiology Intelligence Service of the Center for Disease Control in Atlanta. 'Somebody else has come down with an NTX hemorrhagic fever.' Telephone to her ear, hearing it ring.

'Where?'

'Their own backyard. A twenty-five-year-old male, son of a federal judge.'

She headed for the door with Harris saying 'Call me!'

'HI, SWEETHEART,' MELISSA said. 'It's me.'

She talked into the airplane telephone with one hand over her ear, trying to filter out the noise of the jet engines.

David said, 'Hi, baby, where are you?'

'On my way to Atlanta. Where are you?'

'Back in Washington.'

'Send in the clowns,' she said.

'What's going on?'

'CDC called. Something's up.'

'What happened last night? I'm getting more from CNN than I am from you.'

'I'll give you the rest of the picture tonight, okay?' She'd been on the phone with Janet Wayward during the first half hour of the flight and didn't have time to go over the same ground again. The AG was out of town for the day but Wayward said wherever he was the press would be hounding him about the videotape. He needed information and he needed it now. The AG was always the first to be asked about public disasters and the last to know. Melissa understood.

David said, 'I'm really sorry I couldn't get back last night.'

'I haven't seen you in three days.'

'Two, but I'm no happier about it than you are.'

She slouched in her seat and talked quietly. 'What kind of marriage is it when work is more important than seeing each other?'

'It's not right, that's for sure. We'll talk about it tonight.'

There was a significant silence.

'When are we going to do our shopping?' she said.

'How many shopping days left?'

'No idea.' Another silence. 'Tell me something good.'

'I miss you.'

'That sounded lame.'

'That I miss you?'

'That sounded better.'

'That's what I just said.'

Silence.

'You still there?' she said.

'Just reading some e-mail,' he said. 'Holy shit. Are you sitting down?'

'Seat twenty-four C.'

'Listen to this. Dear Melissa and David.'

The phone cut out.

'David, I can't hear you.'

More static. '. . . an e-mail from the clinic in Miami. Dr. Brandt says you shouldn't . . . get pregnant.'

Shouldn't get pregnant? Her heart sank. 'David – say again, you're breaking up.'

He came back shouting, as if volume were the problem: 'Eric Brandt says you *shouldn't – wait – too – long – to – get – pregnant.*'

'He says I can get *pregnant*?' Two heads in front of her turned.

'They think the operation was a success!' David said. 'Eric and Ben both see normal tissue in the uterus. They think they can do an *in vitro*!'

'Are you serious?'

'Would I kid you about this?'

'Oh, my God! You have to come home tonight!' She felt a small tingle in her stomach. 'We'll try it our way first. Drinks, candles, whatever it takes!'

'It takes a Petri dish.'

'This is the first good news I've had all week.'

Suddenly all was forgiven. She hung up and thought about nothing else all the way to Atlanta.

Until the plane landed.

'YOU GOT A MINUTE?'

David Gale stuck his head inside the door of the chief's office at the Washington bureau of *The New York Times*. He'd just come back from two days in Baltimore and wanted to get something off his chest. His boss, Joe Jacoby, was on the telephone but waved him in. There was a chair, but David preferred to stand.

Jacoby hung up. 'What's up?' he said, picking up a draft story someone had laid in his basket. He pushed up his glasses and started reading as if David wasn't there.

'Joe, put down the copy, okay?'

Jacoby looked over the top of his glasses. 'Don't tell me you're going to sit down.'

'I need to see more of my wife.'

'David, I don't need slow pitches this early in the morning.'

'I need more time at home.'

Jacoby saw it was something serious. 'You want a leave of absence?'

'No, I just want to get off the road every night.'

'That sounds reasonable.' His expression said otherwise.

'Just think about it, okay?' David said. He headed for the door. 'And don't be thinking, How can I punish this son-of-a-bitch for asking?'

'Never crossed my mind.'

'Like hell.'

'Tell you what,' Jacoby said. 'You go back to Baltimore and

finish the Container Tech story and I'll make you an offer you can't refuse.'

'Finish it *today*?'

'This just came in,' he said, waving a piece of paper. 'The president of the company will talk to you if you get to him before he hops a plane to Paris.'

David stepped back into the room. 'This is what I love about you, Joe. I come in here asking for a little consideration toward my marriage and you ask me to dump it for a story.'

'Sit down.'

'Huh?'

'Go ahead, sit down.'

David sat down and they talked. Jacoby even waved off a couple of intruders. David said he would rather be an investigative reporter than a rock star, but he loved his wife and missed her and wasn't going to screw up his marriage for anybody, not even Mom and Pop Pulitzer. Melissa had just gone through hell with the Adalwolf arrest, and on top of that, she was trying to have a baby. They'd both be trying if he ever got home.

Really, Jacoby said. Tell me about that.

David told him about the operation.

Jacoby listened and outlined a possible solution. David thought, if he can pull that off, he's right, it's an offer I can't refuse. Neither could Melissa.

MELISSA HAD ALWAYS wondered what she'd look like as an astronaut. Staring at herself in a full-length mirror, she saw a white biohazard suit with full head cover and a large plastic window in front of her face. The technician who'd helped her into it ran his hands down the Velcro seams covering the zippers on her hips and torso, begging her pardon; this was Atlanta and gentlemen were still afoot. When the seams were closed he tested the suit with an air hose in a port on her right side. No leaks. Every surface and opening on her body – pores, eyes, and mucus membranes – were insulated from the outside world, impervious to microorganisms of every kind, even the harmless pollen she'd been breathing a few minutes before.

She was ready to see the NTX virus.

Dr. Otto Heller stood next to her in the anteroom undergoing the same procedure. Looking like an aging Gary Cooper, he was a tall man in his mid-seventies with a gray buzz-cut and pale skin from spending too much time in the lab. The immigrant son of a German laborer, he was a brilliant virologist with expertise in emerging viral pathogens, the study of newly discovered infectious agents. At one time the head of the CDC's elite Epidemiology Intelligence Service, he'd retired ten years earlier to teach part-time at Florida State in Tallahassee and consult with the Florida State Health Agency, which was part of the CDC network of health agencies. He'd been called by CDC to work the Adalwolf case because no one understood incipient epidemics better.

Finding no leaks in his own biocontainment suit, he turned to Melissa. 'Ready?'

'What if I get an itch on my face?' she asked.

'I wouldn't break your seals to scratch it,' he said. 'This isn't a class five virus – at least not yet – but we're putting it under quarantine until we know what we're dealing with. Are you comfortable?'

Melissa felt like a pig in a blanket. 'No problem.' The words bounced off the Plexiglas shield and back into her face in warm puffs.

'Okay,' Heller said, 'let's go.'

The technician exited the anteroom and closed the door behind him, latching it with a heavy *clunk*. A few seconds later a rush of air swirled around the room, then a green light appeared over the opposite door. Heller turned the lever and the door swung open smoothly. Three steps forward and they were into the repository of the most dangerous infectious particles on earth.

The lab looked similar to the way she'd pictured it. There were rows of black bench tops, chrome fixtures, gray metal cabinets, and glass hoods with stainless steel interiors bathed in the eerie glow of purple ultraviolet light. But no windows. They were deep underground.

Heller sat in front of a large apparatus. 'This is a transmission electron microscope.' He began to manipulate the controls.

Melissa said, 'I just realized I don't know exactly what a virus is.'

'Do you want the medical model or the comic book model?'

'Comic book,' she said. When it came to technical jargon, doctors were harder to understand than lawyers.

The microscope was still warming up. 'A virus is an infectious particle so small most of them can't be seen with a regular microscope. They don't smell, taste, or take up any noticeable space inside the body. Basically, they're nothing but tiny sacks of protein and chemicals that exist for only one reason: to make more viruses like themselves.'

'Darwin's dream,' she said.

'Or nightmare, depending.' He faced her so she could see his smile. 'Most of them are harmless. You've got millions in you right now and don't even know it.'

'Really.' She made a mental note to clean the apartment.

'Since we're going to see a flu virus, let's talk about that.' He stood and walked a short distance to a whiteboard, picked up a colored marker, and began to draw. 'Picture these two wormy brothers we'll call the Enza twins – Flu and Influ.' He drew two stick figures with hats, mustaches, bandit eye masks, and a bag of tools. 'Let's say they're floating along on a droplet of moisture from someone's sneeze, okay? The first twin, Flu, lands on an un-suspecting person's cheek and looks for a cell he can plunder, but unfortunately for him cheek cells are hard to penetrate, and all that light and oxygen make the place a desert. He dries up and gets washed away at bedtime.'

He drew an X over Flu.

'His brother, Influ, gets sucked into the same person's nose during an inhale and lands where it's dark, warm, and moist. He thinks, wow, look at all these epithelial cells. This is fertile terri-tory almost as good as a bloodstream.'

He drew a smile on Influ Enza's face.

'He wiggles along looking for a cell to invade and comes to a security guard named Sergeant Antibody who got his training at Camp Immune System. If this is the first time the cell has been exposed to Influ or one of his clones, Sergeant Antibody won't recognize him as a bandit and will probably let him inside.'

'So the immune system isn't perfect,' she said.

'If it were, there'd be no infectious diseases and I'd be out of a job. It takes time to train the immune system to recognize the enemy, and it's during this time that infection can happen. Influ knows if he doesn't get past the guard, he's finished. He won't have the energy to go door to door, and besides, if Sergeant Antibody does recognize him, there's a good chance the other guards will recognize him, too, since they talk over lunch and share most-wanted posters.'

'So does he get in?'

'So far so good. His mustache and straw hat fool Sergeant Antibody, who lets him proceed to the factory door. You see, guards don't actually open the door for viruses, they only let them go to the door to try entering on their own. If Influ doesn't have the right key he won't get in, which is another security precaution.'

He drew a door on the cell.

'Influ goes up to the door and reaches into his bag and takes out a key. In front of him are thousands of keyholes, but he goes through them like lightning, and sure enough, the key fits one and he gets in.'

'And does what?'

'He goes straight for the office marked "nucleus" and takes control of the factory's central computer, called DNA. It holds the blueprints of the cell and runs the manufacturing process by which it makes more cells identical to its own. As fast as he can, he reprograms the computer and tells it to stop making healthy, normal cells and start making viruses identical to himself.'

'And that's it? He wins?'

'Not yet. Once he starts fiddling with the computer it alerts the troops at Camp Immune System, and soon they're in their rafts floating down the bloodstream to the virus factory. The minute they get there, they blow it up.'

'The whole cell? Not just Influ?'

'They can't kill Influ without destroying the whole cell, but that's not so bad. Chances are, by the time they got there Influ has already turned the cell into a virus factory anyway.'

'What happens to Influ?'

'He and the cell both become a form of refuse commonly known as snot.'

'Huh?'

'That's what a runny nose is, the body washing away dead cells killed by the immune system.'

'So how do the viruses win?'

'Fortunately, most of the time they don't. You may get sick and miss a day of work now and then, but eventually the good guys prevail and you get well.'

'But not always.'

'No, not always. Some viruses are craftier than others. HIV sneaks in through your dendritic cells and sets up shop in the lymphocytes that help eradicate viral infections. In effect, it knocks out the computer's alarm system and makes billions of copies of itself before the troops even know it's there.'

'Like moles.'

'Exactly. Ebola is just the opposite. It takes over cells and converts them to virus factories so fast, by the time the immune system responds, the patient has been ravaged. Herpes hibernates until something like cracked skin wakes it up and it decides to make trouble.'

'And the flu?'

'Depends on the strain. If it's mild, the immune system wins. If not, it doesn't. The Spanish flu of nineteen-eighteen spread so fast it killed twenty to fifty million people worldwide in a matter of months. Half a million were Americans, which is more than died in World War Two. And that's what worries me about your NTX virus.' An amber light appeared on the microscope, indicating that it was ready to process an image. 'I'll show you what I mean.'

'WHEN WE FIRST SAW AN NTX death two years ago we rounded up the usual suspects: Lassa, Ebola, Marburg, Rift Valley, Congo-Crimean, hanta, dengue – every virus that causes quick and violent death through a hemorrhagic fever. Turned out it was none of them.'

He fiddled with the controls a moment, then removed a small box labeled with an orange biohazard warning from a locked cabinet nearby. Lifting the lid, he took out a small glass rectangle and placed it in a chamber in the microscope. An image came into focus on the screen. Melissa saw five iridescent objects reminding her of a loud paisley tie.

'I'm going to give you the chronology in reverse order,' Heller said. 'This is your present-day run-of-the-mill orthomyxovirus, otherwise known as Influenza-A. It came from lung tissue at a local hospital here in Atlanta. No big deal.'

'How large is it?' Melissa said.

'A strand of your hair is one hundred microns across. This virus is five.' He loaded another slide. 'What you're looking at here is the H5N1 virus from Hong Kong, summer of nineteen ninety-seven. It started in chickens, which usually carry a strain of flu harmless to humans.'

'There's such a thing as harmless flu?'

'Lots. This was benign until it shifted into the one you're seeing here. Once that happened, normal, healthy adults died in a matter of days after coming into contact with it.'

'Eating it?'

'Breathing it. If it's cooked, it dies.' He placed the two viruses side by side on the screen. 'See how similar they are?'

'Hard to tell the difference.'

'Let's add another one.' He loaded another slide, and up came a paisley worm with spikes all over its body like a bug in medieval armor.

'That's our baby,' he said. 'Adalwolf's pet scorpion, NTX.'

Melissa felt her face flush. It looked ugly. She pictured someone convulsing with hemorrhagic fever, bleeding from the eyes and nose before dying in three days.

'Now,' Dr. Heller said, 'here's what's interesting. We canvassed all known viruses in our data bank looking for something with a similar molecular structure to NTX. We've got a big inventory of viruses – even bigger since nine-eleven – but we still came up empty.'

He took out the slide.

'I went back to data banks in university labs and state health departments around the United States, Europe, and Asia and asked for a search. This is what I came up with.' He put in another slide. What appeared was a virus that looked like a bent fortune cookie with a fuzzy outer coating and dim stripes inside.

'What's that?'

'It's a virus from USAMRIID, the Army's Medical Research Institute for Infectious Diseases.'

'Where'd they get it?'

'It came from the lungs of a Russian soldier who died of a fast-killing flu virus at the end of World War Two. He and sixteen members of his platoon.'

'Do you know where they contracted it?'

'They were with the Red Army unit that liberated Auschwitz in January nineteen forty-five. According to the records, twelve of the seventeen men who died came into contact with one of the camp's medical laboratories. The Russians called it the Auschwitz flu.'

Melissa stared at it. 'What kind of laboratory?'

'I don't know.'

She pictured Josef Mengele and his lab assistant Adalwolf. 'Does it appear anywhere again?'

'Not that we know of. But look at this.'

He brought up the fourth virus that looked similar to the bent fortune cookie. 'By doing a molecular comparison we came up with a virus that's the kissing cousin of the Auschwitz flu. See how similar it is?'

They looked almost identical. 'Where did that come from?'

'That's the nineteen-eighteen Spanish flu I told you about, one of the worst epidemics in history. We found these samples in the tissue of American soldiers who died in army camps at the time.' Another slide. 'This one, which is identical, was found in the lungs of an Alaskan woman preserved in permafrost.'

A lethal worldwide epidemic in 1918, influenza deaths at Auschwitz in 1945, three deaths from NTX in Florida, and now a young man in a coma in Atlanta. All from the same family of viruses.

'Could Adalwolf have kept the Auschwitz virus all these years and used it to make NTX?'

'Maybe.'

'A virologist with the right knowledge and equipment could mutate a virus into something new?'

'Sure, it's done all the time. Pharmaceutical and university labs are trying to engineer viruses to attack degenerative diseases like multiple sclerosis and Parkinson's disease.'

He set down his marker.

'By the way,' he said, 'the fact that the NTX virus isn't identical to the Auschwitz or Spanish flu is a good thing. So far, there's been no documented evidence of person-to-person transmission.'

Melissa imagined a new problem. Had Adalwolf infected himself with the virus – deliberately or by accident – and used his own death to start an epidemic? The SWAT team leader's words rolled across her mind: *'Maybe he caught his own virus. He looks like he's got the flu.'*

She told Heller what she was thinking. 'Maybe I caught the disease last night,' she said. 'Maybe all of us on the SWAT team did. Maybe we're carriers right now and don't know it.'

'Did you wear a mask?'

'Most of the time.' But she'd pulled it down to talk to Adalwolf. Stupid!

'How do you feel?' he asked.

'Fine.'

'It's not likely you got it,' he said. 'We know from the first three deaths that the incubation period is somewhere between ten and twelve hours.' He reached for a speaker phone and dialed. 'Still, it's not a bad idea to check out everyone who came into contact with him last night.' A voice answered and he put a follow-up study in motion.

They backed out of the cubicle and entered the anteroom. Heller locked the doors and a moment later they were bathed in a shower of germicidal soap. 'Send me a list of the SWAT team that entered his room, would you?' he said.

'Will do,' she said.

'Include any paramedics who picked him up and the people at the morgue where they took him. Is he still on ice?'

'I think he's undergoing an autopsy,' she said.

'Now?'

'If it's on schedule.'

'If he's got the disease, the medical examiner is at risk.'

They reached the decontamination area where they removed their biohazard suits. Melissa said, 'What do you make of the fact that the four known cases of NTX have occurred so close to home?'

'Home?'

'Here in Atlanta. Near the CDC.'

Heller opened the door. 'Everything has to be considered,' he said.

That felt like an inadequate answer, but Heller was already moving down the hall at a fast clip, his long legs putting Melissa at a disadvantage. For some reason, she had an eerie feeling about Heller. Something about him felt . . . creepy. But then she reminded herself that she was looking at dangerous viruses in a containment room in the bowels of the CDC, so she dismissed it. There was nothing wrong with him, she told herself. The whole scene was weird.

That's all.

'DR. CAROL REED, PLEASE. Melissa Gale calling.'

Melissa sat on a leather sofa in Heller's office, her knee jiggling impatiently, a pad of paper on her lap, waiting for the Atlantic County medical examiner to come on the line. Heller sat at his desk listening in on an extension.

'This is Carol Reed.'

'Carol, it's Melissa Gale on the line with Dr. Otto Heller at EIS in Atlanta. Have you autopsied Adalwolf yet?'

'I finished the physical exam a couple of hours ago and picked up a fax of the toxicology report when I heard you were on the phone. Let's see what it says.'

'Before you do that,' Heller said, 'I need to let you know there's a possibility the body was infected with a serious pathogen.'

'Really? Like what?'

'An influenza-like virus. How do you feel?'

'A little tired, but that's from doing five autopsies a day.'

'No fever, sore throat, lymphadenopathy, myalgias?'

'Nothing.'

'Good, but you're still in the incubation period. Just to be safe, you should quarantine yourself for the next ten hours.'

She sighed. 'I have a dance class at five. I never make it.'

'Afraid you'll have to miss it again,' Heller said. 'I'm going to have an EIS team pick up the body and ship it to CDC right away.'

'I've never been in a containment procedure before,' Carol Reed said.

'I'm sure you're fine. Just a precaution.'

'What did the autopsy show?' Melissa asked.

'Caucasian male, mid-seventies, died of asphyxiation and shock from severe third-degree burns.' She spoke flatly, preoccupied with the information she was reading, no sign of panic in her voice.

'What else?' Melissa said.

'He had a laryngectomy and only one kidney which was in bad shape. Let's see. He was on dialysis. There were AV fistulas in both arms, and the left one was clotted off. This is interesting. The tox screen shows lorazepam.'

'What's that?'

'A sedative related to Valium.'

'A prescription drug?' Melissa said.

'Well, sure. It's used by anesthesiologists.'

'What about the gauze taped to the ends of his fingers?'

'I can't say why they were there, but his fingerprint had been burned off.'

Melissa saw all the arrows pointing in the same direction. 'What about the tattoo?'

'I'm afraid I've got bad news on that,' Reed said.

'What's wrong?'

'It wasn't there.'

'You mean it was burned off?'

'I mean it wasn't there before the fire.'

Melissa felt herself sinking into her chair. 'But I saw it.'

'You saw something you *thought* was a tattoo. I saw it, too. But there was no dermal pigment, so it couldn't have been a real tattoo.'

'What was it?'

'Indelible ink, probably drawn on with a Sharpie. What was left of it came off with an alcohol swab.'

That cinched it. The man who died in the fire wasn't Adalwolf. It took Melissa a moment to accept it even though some part of her had known it the night before.

WHILE CAROL REED AND Otto Heller continued to talk about containment procedures, Melissa hung up and called Harris Johnson.

'The tattoo on the dead man's arm was ink,' she said. 'Not tattoo ink, just ink, like from a pen.'

Harris didn't answer.

'It wasn't Adalwolf, Harris.'

'Are you sure?'

'Yeah. Are you in Atlantic City?'

'Got here an hour ago,' he said. 'How do we know Adalwolf even had a tattoo? We've never seen it.'

'Two survivors described it, and so did Adalwolf in one of his phone calls.'

No response.

'Harris, it wasn't *him*. That's why he taped gauze on the victim's fingertips, to burn off the man's fingerprints.'

Harris said, 'What about the suicide note?'

'Pure smoke. How do you feel?'

'Pissed.'

'I mean physically.'

'Fine, why?'

'Adalwolf might have spread the NTX virus. A doctor named Otto Heller from CDC will be calling to check you out and get the names of the rest of the SWAT team.'

'Great.'

'How badly did we screw up?' she said.

'You mean by not securing the suspect, or by not checking for a booby trap?'

'Both.'

'We did what was right under the circumstances.'

'I told everyone to stand back and let him use his electrolarynx,' she said.

'That wasn't unreasonable.'

'Then why did one of your guys tell him not to move, and another said to put him down?'

Harris's silence said, *So maybe we screwed up a little.*

'If we killed Adalwolf,' she said, 'no one will care because he's a Nazi killer himself, but if we killed someone else . . .' Now she turned silent. 'We need to find out who it was, Harris.'

'What have we got to work with?'

'According to the ME the victim had severe kidney failure, which means we're looking for somebody in his seventies who's been on dialysis and has no voice box. How many people in Atlantic City fit that profile?'

'I'd be surprised to find one.'

'That should make it easy. I'll be back in Washington at six-thirty.'

'I'll meet you at Charlie's Bar and Grill. Melissa?'

'Yeah?'

'Just so you know, I'm gonna try to prove you wrong on this.'

'Just so *you* know, nothing would make me happier.'

THE DOCTOR TURNED OFF the pump and slowly withdrew the sonic probe from the vagina of a thirty-five-year-old home maker from downstate Illinois who'd traveled to Miami for the procedure. A nurse unscrewed the tube at the base of the cannula and capped it, then carried it to a pass-through window at the side of the room and handed it to a lab assistant waiting on the other side.

From there the woman's eggs would be put in an incubator for less than an hour, transferred carefully to a Petri dish, and joined with her husband's semen. If fertilization occurred, it would happen in a matter of hours. The embryo would then be gently lifted from the dish, placed on the end of a cannula, and inserted into her womb to implant itself in the endometrium – or not implant itself, which was usually the case. Pregnancy happened thirty percent of the time in circumstances like hers, a little more often under better conditions, a little less in worse. It was what they did at the Myrna Ben-Zevi Memorial Fertility Clinic in Miami Beach, Florida.

Even before the woman's feet were removed from the stirrups, the surgeon was off his stool, removing his mask and gloves as he walked toward the door. One of the nurses looked up and caught the eye of another nurse, saying, He really is a hunk, isn't he? With straight blond hair, blue eyes, and chiseled cheekbones, Dr. Eric Brandt, the clinic's forty-four-year-old director and chief endocrinological surgeon, was at the top of his game. He had a touch of the European manner about him – sophisticated, serious, a little mysterious – the kind of man who'd offer a light to a woman in a spider-net veil on the Orient Express. Best of all, he had great hands, a pianist's fingers. 'Hunk' was the wrong word. 'Cool' was more like it. Streamlined, elegant, and cool.

He moved smoothly down the hallway, his eyes set on a distant point, and disappeared into his office.

HARRIS JOHNSON WAS already sitting in a booth at Charlie's Bar and Grill when Melissa came in and slipped into the seat opposite his. He'd ordered her a black-and-tan with lots of head and positioned a plate of bite-sized pizzas in the middle of the table. She picked one up – it was cold, the cheese congealed – and gobbled it down, realizing that she hadn't eaten since breakfast. He waited while she passed over her beer and drank some water and set her glass on the table.

'Okay, I'm ready,' she said.

'His name is Harry Sherwood,' Harris said. 'It's all right here.' He tapped a manila envelope next to him.

'You going to make me read it?'

'The first thing you'll find is a copy of his honorable discharge.'

'From whose army?'

'The United States of America.'

Good God. They'd killed a former G.I.?

Harris said, 'He was a sergeant with the 45th Infantry, the Thunderbird Division. Do you know what they did in World War II?'

'No idea.'

'Hold that thought. Next you'll find his file from the Military Records Service Center in St. Louis including a letter of commendation from his commanding officer. I stuck it in because it's so eloquent. There's also a file from the VFW, the American Legion, and a real dandy from the Association of the Purple Heart.'

'He had a *Purple Heart*?'

'Oh, yeah, but don't get so excited, he also had a Silver Star.'
She stared at him. 'For what?'

He pointed at the envelope. 'It's all laid out in a July seventh nineteen forty-five article from his hometown newspaper in Flint, Michigan. Sergeant Harry Sherwood was a member of the Thunderbird Division that liberated Dachau.'

She started to say something but he held up his hand and stopped her.

'You asked how he got his medals. When his brigade liberated the camp he captured three SS guards who were trying to escape posing as prisoners. One of them shot him up and wrecked his kidneys.'

'I don't believe this.'

'We didn't just torch a war hero, Melissa. We torched a Nazi hunter.'

'How in God's name did Adalwolf do it?'

'Actually, it wasn't that difficult. He got access to the VA Hospital computer, searched for a World War Two vet with a lost voice box, and came up with two guys: Sgt. Harry Sherwood of Atlantic City, New Jersey, and an eighty-year-old man in Sacramento. He chose Sherwood, took a room in a tenement house two blocks from where he lived, befriended him, drugged him, tattooed him with a pen, rigged him up to a bag of naphtha, and e-mailed us to come and get him.'

'And we went for it.'

Harris gulped down his beer and set the empty glass on the table, his eyes watering from drinking too fast. 'Hannibal had us for lunch, Clarice.'

'Who has access to the VA computer?'

'Who doesn't? Pharmaceutical contractors, civil servants Medical people from CDC to Fiji.'

'Damn, he's good,' Melissa said. 'He wins if we fall for his suicide act and close the file, and he wins if he ties us up with an internal investigation into how we got the wrong man.' She pushed her glass of water from, side to side. 'Anybody know about this yet?'

'Just you and me.'

They stared at the dead pizza. She looked at Harris and said, 'You can have my beer.'

He shook his head. 'This going to be a full-blown scandal?'

'I don't know.' She looked at her watch and slid out of the banquette.

'Since when do you pass up a black-and-tan?' Harris said.

She sat down again and asked him with her finger, Is this between the two of us?

He nodded of course.

'No more alcohol for me. I may be getting pregnant soon.'

He looked surprised, then smiled and reached out with his fist and bumped her knuckles. 'Fantastic.'

She leaned forward on the table. 'We've got to collar this guy fast, Harris. As of now this case is messing with my personal life.'

'Not to mention my job.'

She opened her notebook and returned the call to Dr. Otto Heller at CDC. It was late, so she left a message saying she'd try him the next day. When she was done, she laid her phone in her bag and stood up to go. 'See you at the meeting,' she said, starting for the door.

'What meeting?' Harris said.

'The one they're going to call when the shit hits the fan.'

THEY CALLED IT FOR eight a.m.

The Attorney General's conference room had the air of a funeral parlor: wood-paneled walls, neatly arranged flowers near an ornamental fireplace, a sense of mourning for the recently departed Sergeant Harry Sherwood and for those who'd be suspended because of a screw-up. When this sort of thing happened, somebody had to drink the Kool-Aid, and everyone knew it.

Melissa arrived with her boss, Barry Sherer, and took a seat next to him four chairs away from the AG's seat at the head of the conference table. The Big Man wasn't there yet, but the other participants were. Canvassing the room, she remembered that the first rule of high-level meetings was that where you sat revealed where you stood, and nobody had better standing with the AG than Marshall Moffitt, known in the hallways as his *consigliere*. Sitting next to the AG's chair, Moffitt was the AG's chief trouble-shooter, which meant he attended meetings only when there was trouble that needed to be shot. With his rumpled unbuttoned coat and his briefcase spilling papers, he reminded Melissa of a paunchy Colombo, but she knew better than to underestimate him. Beneath the gentle demeanor was a tough-minded, take-no-prisoners, former president of the *Harvard Law Review*. Every cabinet officer needed a Marshall Moffitt, but only the AG had him.

In the seat next to Moffitt's, sporting neatly combed hair and a grim face, was the fifty-something Assistant Attorney General of the Criminal Division, Henry Jergens. He kept his eyes on a pencil he twirled in his fingers, an excuse not to talk to the others at the table. Next to him was Melissa's boss, Barry, then Melissa.

On the other side of the table, closest to the AG's chair, was the sandy-haired, ruddy-faced Deputy Director of the FBI, Felix Maltby, and next to him, Melissa's friend and cohort, Harris Johnson. She was glad he was there despite the circumstances. In the third chair, wearing a snappy dark blue suit and an efficient face, was Janet Wayward, the Department's spokesperson. Next to her, directly across from Melissa, was George Calvin, an investigator from the Office of Professional Responsibility, a nice-sounding name for the FBI's internal investigators, otherwise known as the Gestapo. She wasn't surprised to see him even though he gave her the willies.

It was a small group for such a large room, which raised rule number two in Washington: the fewer the people, the more serious the meeting. Firing squads at the Department of Justice were never large.

The door to the Attorney General's office opened and in walked the chief himself: John Armstrong – known from his days as a senator from South Carolina as 'Jack Armstrong, the all-American boy.' He was in his late fifties now and looked good the way distinguished southern politicians did: silver-haired, a bit too coifed, and not a trace of beard on a rugged, tawny face. Lean, muscular, and smelling of a hint of Bay Rum cologne, he gave the impression he worked as a railroad engineer by day and a maître d' by night. You misjudged the man at your peril.

Marshal Moffitt took off his glasses and looked up, then placed the memo he was reading in front of the AG's chair. The Attorney General unbuttoned his suit coat and took his seat.

'Good morning,' he said, looking at the memo and putting on elegant antelope horn glasses. 'I have read both briefing memos but I'd like to start by hearing what happened.' He looked up and found the Deputy Director of the FBI on his right. 'Felix?'

Note that he called him 'Felix,' not 'Mr. Maltby.' They probably play golf together at a club where you can't even caddy.

Damn it, she'd forgotten to read her horoscope this morning.

FELIX MALTBY SPOKE with ease. 'We've been chasing this guy Adalwolf for five years, General. We nearly caught him twice, but both times he slipped away. This time we thought we had him with our new BackFire software that allows us to trace modem-generated e-mail.'

The AG said, 'Why is a criminal suspect sending e-mail to the Department of Justice?'

Felix Maltby turned toward Barry Sherer and raised a hand as if to say, You want to field that one?

Barry said, 'That's a good question, sir.'

'Most of mine are,' Jack Armstrong said.

Barry flushed. 'He knows we're looking for him, so he communicates with us to try to get information about our investigation. We engage him to see if we can get a lead on his whereabouts.'

'So far, I'd say he's getting the better end of the deal,' Armstrong said. 'What do we know about this guy?'

'He was born seventy-five years ago,' Barry said, 'in September nineteen twenty-eight, the same month as Elie Wiesel.'

'What a lovely coincidence,' the AG said.

'He came to work in Mengele's lab in nineteen forty-three at age fifteen and stayed until the camp was liberated by the Russians in January nineteen forty-five.'

'Where'd he come from?'

'That's not clear,' Barry said. 'According to survivor accounts he was Josef Mengele's adopted son, but there's nothing in the record to indicate Mengele ever adopted anyone, at least not formally.'

'We're told he had a French accent,' Felix Maltby said. 'One story claims he was born out of wedlock and grew up in a French orphanage. How he made his way to Auschwitz isn't known.'

'Does he still speak with an accent?' Moffitt asked.

'Not that we can tell,' Barry said. 'He talks with an electronic device.'

Armstrong said, 'So I noticed on CNN. And this device is what led your men to think he had a gun, right?'

Harris Johnson said, 'Sir, if I may address that.' The AG looked up at him over his glasses. Harris continued, 'If you saw the videotape, you probably noticed that when he raised his hand, it looked like this.' Harris drew a gun-metal gray electrolarynx from nowhere and aimed it across the table at AAG Henry Jergens, who flinched. It was a cheap but effective shot. If the smile on Marshal Moffit's face was any indication, it was also amusing.

'I noticed on the videotape that you held your fire,' the Attorney General said.

'Yes, sir.'

'And when he touched the transmit button to speak, it set off an explosion.'

'Yes, sir.'

The Attorney General said, 'Was the punch in the chest with the flashlight necessary?'

'In retrospect, no, sir. At the time, it was more prudent than shooting him.'

Reading the memo, the Attorney General mumbled, 'I'm not so sure. If you'd shot him there wouldn't have been an explosion.'

Harris kept his eyes on the AG.

The Attorney General said, 'You understand where I'm going with this, right, Mr. Johnson? There's going to be an internal investigation, but frankly, that's not my problem. My problem is catching this guy, and keeping the public from panicking over this NTX virus, and containing the press before they turn this thing into another Ruby Ridge.'

'In my opinion we didn't violate procedures, sir,' Harris said.

'That may be true but it doesn't solve any of my problems. Now that it's all over the news, we have to cope with the image of an

American war hero who lost his kidneys in the service of his country sitting quietly watching a *Seinfeld* rerun in his room with an IV drip when the FBI bashes down his door and turns him into a cinder.'

Silence filled the funeral parlor.

THE AG SAID, 'WHEN THE cameras start rolling at my press conference, I don't want to look like a hayseed, understand? I want the facts before I read them on the front page of the *Washington Post*.' His eyes hit every other pair at the table. 'Ms. Gale,' he said, 'I gather this is your case?'

'Yes, sir.'

'You have quite a record with OSI.'

'Thank you.'

'Don't misunderstand me, Ms. Gale. I want to root out the last decrepit old Nazi as much as you do, but why are we doing it with a SWAT team?'

'If I may,' Melissa said, 'Adalwolf is not a decrepit old Nazi, sir. He is a very energetic killer. Three people have died of a virus the CDC has been unable to identify, and another one is badly infected. We think Adalwolf is responsible.'

'How do you get that?'

'The three people who died were in northern Florida, and the latest victim is in Atlanta, which is roughly in the same area. The CDC epidemiologists look for traits in common, and other than geographical proximity, they've found only one.'

'What was it?'

'They were all Jews.'

Moffit looked skeptical. 'There are six million Jews in the United States, Ms. Gale.'

'Yes, sir, but out of two hundred and eighty million Americans that's still a small number. The CDC's Epidemiology Intelligence

Service examined the virus and did a work up on it. They labeled it NTX and said although it resembles a flu virus, it isn't on all fours.'

She had the AG's attention.

'A few days ago, a young man named Jeremy Friedman who lives in Atlanta came down with flu-like symptoms that have gotten progressively worse with each passing hour. When he developed a hemorrhagic fever, the hospital quarantined him and the state sent blood samples to CDC, which identified the disease as NTX. The young man's father is Warren Friedman, a federal judge in Atlanta. Whether by coincidence or not, he's also the judge who presided over the Herman and Gerta Spengler trial, the Nazi couple we deported to Germany in nineteen ninety-five.'

The AG shifted in his chair. 'Are you saying this guy Adalwolf infected Judge Friedman's son?'

'I don't know. In any event, the CDC sent an investigator to interview Mr. Friedman about every move he'd made in the period leading up to his illness.'

The AG had his chin in his hand.

'It turns out that he leads a boy's choir that was invited to Poland during the holiday break, which meant he had to undergo a routine physical arranged at a public health facility. The examining doctor gave him a nose inhaler and showed him how he and the choir boys were to use it in case their ears got stopped up on the plane. Mr. Friedman inhaled in both nostrils. CDC thinks that's how the virus was transmitted.'

'And what makes you think Adalwolf had something to do with it?'

'He said the doctor was an old man who talked through a hand-held microphone.'

The AG leaned back in his chair.

'Who is this guy, a one-man revival of the Third Reich?'

Melissa said, 'Something like that, yes, sir.'

'Where's young Mr. Friedman now?'

'He's in a coma.'

'Good God.' The AG turned to Felix Maltby. 'What's it take to catch this guy?'

'We're trying, John.'

The AG looked down at the affidavit Melissa filed with the court in support of the search warrant. 'Tell me how you managed to get from Mr. Friedman to a tenement house in Atlantic City.'

'As Barry said, Adalwolf has been in touch with me for the last five years.'

'By e-mail.'

'And cell phone.'

'Never in person?'

'No, sir. He knows if he tried that he'd be caught. Except for a fifty-year-old photograph, we've never seen him.'

'So how did you identify him in the first place?'

'In nineteen ninety-four a college student writing a paper on Josef Mengele dusted off some files in the World Jewish Congress archives. One of them contained survivors' eyewitness accounts of a teenage lab assistant known as Adalwolf.'

'No other name?'

'I'm sure he has one, but we don't know what it is.'

'What did a lab assistant to Josef Mengele do?'

'His job was to kill children for autopsy. Twins, mostly.'

The Attorney General's jaw muscles rippled.

'He was also involved in a project involving pregnant women and sterilization as a way of killing Jews more efficiently. We don't know much about the details, only that he worked with a Dr. Schumann who headed the program.'

She took a drink of water and continued.

'In nineteen ninety-four the World Jewish Congress profiled Adalwolf in one of its newsletters. At that point he would have been about sixty-six years old. A few months later they received a letter from a woman in Toronto saying she was the widow of an Auschwitz survivor who'd told her about Adalwolf. Her husband even had a photograph of him which she sent us. May I?'

Melissa got up and walked to the head of the table. By the time she reached the AG's chair he was examining a black-and-white photo of five concentration camp prisoners about ten-to-twelve years of age.

Melissa said, 'The photograph was taken in front of what appears to be Block Nineteen, the location of Mengele's lab. Children inmates like the ones you see here were required to help Mengele with a variety of jobs until they were killed.' She pointed at the photo. 'The widow from Toronto said this boy here, named Adam, later became her husband. He was working in the lab with the other assistants when the Russians liberated the camp in January nineteen forty-five. Eventually he made his way to Canada and met his wife. She said he had no idea what became of the other people in the picture.'

'Did you interview her?'

'Only by telephone. She was too ill to see us, but I showed the photograph to someone else who knew Adalwolf at Auschwitz, a life-long acquaintance of mine named Dr. Benjamin Ben-Zevi. He's a retired professor at the University of Miami. When he was twelve years old he worked as a conscript in Mengele's lab.'

'As a twelve-year-old?'

'Yes, sir. This is him right here, the one kneeling down in the center. He was from a family of six, five of whom were gassed.'

'How did he survive?'

'He was lucky during what was known as "the selection." After getting off the train men and women were separated into two lines. Mengele or another high-ranking SS officer stood at the head of the columns and pointed left or right as the prisoners marched forward. To the left meant to the gas chamber, to the right meant the labor camp. Old people, the sick and the injured were killed without exception. People who looked strong enough to work might be sent to the camps until they became too weak and were killed within hours. Girls who were pretty sometimes escaped death as long as they were . . . useful. Twins and dwarfs were routinely saved for Mengele's experiments. Parents who heard about that often tried to pass their children off as twins. Sometimes it worked, sometimes it didn't. It did for Benjamin Ben-Zevi and his sister.'

'What happened to her?'

'She was never seen again.'

The AG was silent. Marshal Moffitt slid a pencil through his fingers.

Melissa returned to her seat. 'Ben-Zevi emigrated to New York City in nineteen fifty when he was eighteen. My grandmother, Esther, who'd met him in the camp, was helpful in bringing him over. After graduating from City College, he studied medicine at Cornell and eventually became a professor of endocrinology at Columbia Medical School. In the late eighties he and his wife, Myrna, retired to Florida. She died a few years ago, but he's still in good health. I know him well because he was our family doctor who delivered me. We showed him the photograph and he was able to identify three people in it – himself, the little boy Adam who eventually married the woman who gave us the picture, and Adalwolf.'

She held up her copy of the photo and pointed.

'ADALWOLF IS THE ONE standing off to the side wearing a lab smock.' Melissa waited as the AG and Marshal Moffitt examined the picture in the folders.

'He looks like a midwestern farm boy,' the AG said.

'He was tall for a teenager,' she said. She laid her photo on the table. Adalwolf's hair was dark and cut short, and he had high, gaunt cheekbones. His expression was so plain and earnest, if he'd been wearing stripes he could have passed for one of the prisoners.

Marshal Moffitt said, 'He could have been on my high school basketball team. What do you think he looks like now?'

'That's hard to say,' Melissa said. 'He might still be thin or he might have put on weight. The FBI digitized his face and aged it, but they say fifty years can do a lot to your features.'

'Tell me about it,' the AG said, stroking his cheeks. Everyone waited for him to look up from the photo. 'What about the missing voice box and the tattoo, Ms. Gale? You put a lot of weight on them in your affidavit.'

'That's because they are distinctive identifying traits.'

'And they are based on what record?'

'I can hear his electronic voice on the telephone.'

'How did he lose his voice?'

'According to him it was cancer. I'm not sure.'

'You can use an electrolarynx if you still have a voice?'

'Yes, sir.'

'What about the tattoo?' Marshall Moffit said, staring at the photograph, 'In the picture his sleeve is covering his upper arm.'

'Professor Ben-Zevi saw it on Adalwolf's arm while he was working in the lab, and so did the husband of the widow in Toronto.'

'It's hearsay,' Moffitt said, 'but I guess that works for a warrant. What does the tattoo look like?'

'It's the *Totenkopf*. The SS death head.'

'Sounds like a Hell's Angels thing,' the AG said.

'I'm told it was highly unusual for the SS to decorate themselves with tattoos. They were proud of a small one under their left arm that indicated their blood type and entitled them to priority medical treatment. Maybe he did it because he was a teenager.'

'How old did you have to be to join the SS?' Marshal Moffitt said.

'Eighteen.'

'So he was too young to join.'

Felix Maltby of the FBI said, 'You were supposed to be eighteen
to join the U.S. Army in those days, but kids lied and got in
anyway.'

'That would have been difficult to do with the SS,' Melissa said.
'They made a thorough background check of their candidates to be
sure they had no Jewish blood. Frankly, I wish they *had* bent the
rules and let him in because then we could have looked him up in
their records, which are excellent.'

'You've done a search of first names?' Marshal Moffitt said.

'Yes, sir. There are a few Adalwolfs, but none that could be him.'

The AG said, 'Surely there can't be that many old Germans
with death head tattoos and missing voice boxes.'

'That was our thinking when we entered that room in Atlantic
City and found a man fitting that exact description.' The smile on
Harris's face said, *Nice job, Melissa, you nailed it*.

The AG said, 'Sounds prudent to me. So he set you up to arrest
the wrong man, who was rigged up to a bomb.' He looked up at
Felix Maltby. 'Don't your guys check for booby-traps?'

Melissa spoke up. 'I'd like to address that, if I may.' She
wanted to explain that she was the one who'd asked the agents to
stand by and let the old man speak, but before she could start
Marshal Moffitt held up his hand to stop her and leaned over to
whisper into the Attorney General's ear. When he finished, the AG
spoke.

'Mr. Moffitt has reminded me that because there's going to be
an investigation that could result in grand jury proceedings, it's
inappropriate for potential witnesses – or subjects – to make admis-
sions without having an opportunity to consult counsel.'

Melissa felt her cheeks turn scarlet. An internal investigation she
understood, but a grand jury? Potential subjects? What was that
all about? She didn't want to consult a lawyer, she wanted to clear
the air.

'Sir, if I may,' she said. 'This was my case, and whatever

occurred was my responsibility. I'd like to waive counsel and explain what happened.'

'I'm sorry, Ms. Gale, but I can't let you do that,' the AG said. He turned a page. 'I'd like to finish up with how we're going to handle the press on this and minimize the political fallout.'

WHEN MELISSA FELT frustrated she usually did one of two things: ate ice cream or went for a jog. Today she'd do both.

It was midmorning and she was running on the mall with the Capitol in front of her and the Washington Monument behind. The cherry trees were mere skeletons in the December rain. She could see her breath and feel the goosebumps on her legs. She wore black-and-white running shoes, school-bus yellow gym shorts, and a dark blue pullover that said MICHIGAN – David's alma mater – on the back. The bill of her baseball cap peeked out from under her pulled-up hood. She wore no makeup, but the pink in her cheeks and her amber-tinted rain glasses gave her face a peaches-and-cream glow. She looked good and felt like shit.

She'd run forty-five minutes and was cooling down now, watching tourists and civil servants with umbrellas crossing the mall, their holiday packages in hand, thinking that with only three shopping days left she should have been one of them. She walked to a black metal railing behind the red-brick Smithsonian Institution and put her heel on the middle bar to stretch her hamstrings. She was hating the pain when her cell phone played the Lone Ranger's favorite four bars. She unzipped her fanny pack and pulled out the phone.

'Hello?'

'Where are you?' David said.

'Just finished jogging.'

'How'd the meeting go?'

'They're doing an internal investigation and maybe a grand jury.'

'A grand jury?'

'A criminal investigation.'

'That's bullshit.'

'You know how it is.' She changed legs and leaned forward. Changed ears with the phone, too. 'What's happening with your story?'

'I've got one more interview and then I'm done.'

'In Baltimore?'

'Don't know yet.'

'That means in Baltimore at an undisclosed location at midnight, which means you won't be home tonight.'

'Not a chance, baby, I'm coming home. Hang on a sec, the other phone's ringing.' He put her on hold.

She extended her left foot forward and stretched her right calf. David came back on and said, 'It's Joe Jacoby calling about Miami. I'll call you back in two seconds.'

'What about Miami?'

'Tell you when I call back.'

She stuck the phone into the fanny pack and continued stretching. When she was done, she took out a bottle of water and drank it too fast, sending rivulets down her neck. She tossed the empty into a waste can and began walking up the sidewalk toward the reflecting pool. A few yards away a baby in a knit cap was being pushed along in a stroller. Melissa jogged to catch up.

'Hey, there, sweetie,' she said, bending down. The baby had red hair and brown eyes and reached for Melissa with outstretched fingers. Melissa wanted to kidnap her on the spot.

'Say hi, Lily,' the girl's mother said in a baby voice. 'Say hi.' The little girl frowned and whacked her hand on the carriage tray. Her mother picked her up. Melissa rubbed the baby's cold cheek with her finger.

'Hi, there, Lily. What are you wearing these days, Nike or Adidas?'

The baby stared at Melissa's mouth and tried to put her fingers inside. When Melissa blew raspberries on her palm she squealed, so Melissa did it again.

'She likes you,' the girl's mother said.

'I'm hoping to have one of my own soon,' Melissa said. She loved this feeling.

Her phone rang. She pulled it out of her fanny pack and watched the stroller roll away. Waving goodbye, she hit the talk button. 'That was fast,' she said. No answer. 'David?' No voice, no static. 'Can you hear me?' She'd lost the connection. She was about to punch the end call button when she heard a voice colder than the December rain.

'Hello, Melissa.'

IT WAS HIM. A VOICE OF buzzing metal so eerie it tightened every muscle in her back.

'Adalwolf,' she said. 'What a surprise.'

'Congratulations. I thought in your eagerness to incinerate a Nazi you might have overlooked who you really killed.'

Hit the pager. She fumbled for a transmitter in her fanny pack, found it, and pressed the SEND button. If the FBI received her signal, they'd start a trace on the call in a matter of seconds.

'You almost pulled it off,' she said.

'How does the government feel about killing an American war hero?'

'Government officials are not big on irony, Adalwolf.'

She heard an electronic chuckle. *'You have to admit it was effective.'*

Always the heartless bottom line. 'If killing an innocent man and burning two FBI agents was your goal, yes, it was effective.'

'Your jackboot friends are expendable. So was Sergeant Sherwood.'

She looked at her pager. The moment the Bureau traced his call, a line of pound signs would flash in her message window telling her they had him. She had to keep him on the phone until she saw them. From prior experience Adalwolf thought it would take them at least eight minutes to trace his call, but the Bureau's new BackFire program could do it in five.

'If you were trying to fool us into closing the case, you lose,' she said.

'It doesn't matter. I can still get you off the case.'

She hit the transmit button again. *Were they on him yet?* 'Even if I quit, the FBI would still come after you.'

'I can handle them. It's you I care about.'

Keep the clock running. 'Strange way to care. You got me in big trouble.'

'Quit and go home, Melissa. Bake cookies and be a good wife. Have a baby.'

Hearing him tell her to do something she already wanted to do pissed her off. 'My personal life is none of your business,' she said.

'Your personal life is my only business.'

That sent a fresh chill down her legs. She hit the transmit button on her pager again for good measure. *Come on, guys, come on.* 'I have no idea what you're talking about.'

'You never have. But you will soon. It's time.'

She checked her watch. Two minutes had passed. She had to vamp another three. 'Why don't you educate me?'

There was silence on the other end. Was she losing him?

'Tell me something, Melissa. Why are you a Nazi hunter?'

'Isn't it obvious?'

'I'm not interested in sentimental claptrap about the Holocaust. I want the personal reason.'

'To me the Holocaust *is* personal.'

'Please. All these maudlin tales from whiny survivors. It's so tiresome.'

'You can always turn off your TV set.'

'Doesn't help. Jews own everything now – radio, television, newspapers. If their movies aren't "Saving Private Ryan" one minute, they're crying about some poor little Jews in "The Pianist" the next.'

'But you know those things really happened, you were there.'

'I am not a Holocaust denier and never have been. As a matter of fact, why Jews get all worked up over the yokels who spew that nonsense is a complete mystery to me.'

'They're mildly irritating.'

'Jewish paranoia.' He coughed. *'My complaint isn't that the Holocaust didn't exist, Melissa. My complaint is that it didn't finish the job.'*

Another shiver. 'I'm afraid I can't help you with that one.'

'Oh, but you can.'

'I don't think so.'

'You still don't get it.'

'Maybe I would if you told me.'

'The more I want you off the case, the more you want to stay with it, but there's something more important you have to do.'

She wanted to dismiss this as bullshit, but his voice wouldn't let her.

'Look inside yourself and answer my question. Why are you a Nazi hunter?'

She checked her pager. *Come on, tell me you got a bead on him!* 'Why wouldn't I be? I'm a Jew, isn't that enough?'

'You see, that's precisely the kind of self-delusion I was talking about. You're not a Nazi hunter because you're a Jew. American Jews like you don't care about their roots. You're not like the European Jews we sent to the ovens. Now they really cared about being Jews, I have to give them that.'

Take his crap and keep talking. 'You know nothing about what makes a Jew.'

'I know better than you think.'

She felt her pulse in her neck.

'Let me guess where you are. You're sitting at your desk writing a report on how you didn't mean to kill poor Sergeant Sherwood.'

'You don't even know what city I'm in.' She checked the clock on her pager. Three and a half minutes had elapsed.

'I know you are in Washington.'

'What makes you think so?'

'I can hear the bells in the Smithsonian tower.'

She turned and looked up at them.

'I love church bells. Reminds me of my childhood. "Maxima debetur puero reverentia".'

He also loved Latin phrases. 'Translation, please?' she said.

'Are you walking on the mall to calm your nerves, or are you looking under more beds in search of another pathetic old Nazi? Catch a Kraut, win a case. Does that make you feel good, about yourself?'

'I'm just doing my job, Adalwolf.'

'*It means nothing. Your purpose in life isn't to hunt down the little men who cleaned Mengele's boots.*'

'What is it then?'

'*It's me. You've been searching for me all your life. Not to deport me, but for something far more important.*'

'Like arresting you for murder.'

'*Much more important than that.*'

So damned irritating. 'Why are you killing them, Adalwolf?'

'*Killing who?*'

Her clock said almost four and a half minutes. *Hold him!* 'We've identified the virus that killed three victims and infected a fourth.'

'*Is that supposed to mean something to me?*'

'Jeremy Friedman is still alive, Adalwolf. He can identify you.'

'*Oh, I'm shitting my pants.*'

Only thirty seconds to go. 'The virus you're using is a derivative of the H5N1 virus the Russians found at Auschwitz in nineteen forty-five. Do you know what that means?' She told herself she was going too far.

'*No, what does that mean?*'

'I'll tell you if you meet me.'

'*Some day. I promise.*'

'When?'

'*Melissa, Melissa. My little do-gooder.*'

Come on, guys, he's signing off!

'*I have to run now. Quit the case and you'll be fine. Otherwise . . .*'

'Now *you're* the one who doesn't get it. I'm not quitting until I put you behind bars.'

'*What a pity. I guess killing Sergeant Sherwood wasn't enough to make the point.*'

Six minutes had passed. Where was the sign they'd found him?

'*Okay, my little liebchen, the stakes just got higher. Don't say I didn't warn you.*'

Why didn't they have him?

'*Oh, yes. You asked what "Maxima debetur puero reverentia" means.*'

'I'm afraid my Latin's a little rusty,' she said.

'It means, The greatest respect is owed to a child. Keep that in mind, Melissa. The day will come when you'll live by it. Au revoir.'

She looked at the message window. No pound marks. *Damn it! I gave him too much information and got nothing back!*

WALKING DOWN THE HALL at Justice, Melissa muttered to herself about how much she hated holding the short end of the stick. Turning the corner, she saw Harris. He smiled as if nothing was wrong.

'The press is having a field day,' he said.

She felt herself melting into the marble. 'What's the department's line?'

'They're telling everybody it was a booby trap we couldn't do anything about.'

'But that's true.'

He rolled his eyes. 'It's not a bad place to start.'

She said, 'Are you getting press calls?'

'Yeah, but I'm not answering them.'

'What's the AG's state of mind?'

'He's pissed about being blindsided by the videotape and seeing an FBI agent slam an American hero in the chest with a Maglite. Oh, by the way, if you didn't see enough of that you can catch it on the news every twenty minutes or so. Personally, I think he's miffed that the press told the world about a deadly virus before he did. Yeah, I'd say that's it. For some reason he doesn't like getting calls comparing a new virus to anthrax and asking why the government didn't inform the public.'

'Should I stop by my office to say goodbye or go straight to hell?'

'Go to your office. You have to be crucified first.'

'What'd they do to you?'

'The Assistant Director told me to take some vacation time and hit the beach until the dust settles. No formal suspension, which means I get to keep my credentials and gun. But I'm off the case.'

'Jesus, Harris.'

'It's not that bad. I'll get to see Sherrie and kids for a change. Which reminds me.' He looked at his watch. 'Gotta run, she's picking me up for lunch and Christmas shopping. According to her, there's a whole world out there waiting.' They stopped in front of her door.

'I'm really sorry, Harris.'

He stopped. 'Don't be. You may need to save some of that for yourself.' He turned and said, 'Don't be a stranger,' as he went down the hall.

Melissa walked into her office. If the news was bad, her assistant, Jane, would tell her to go to Barry Sherer's office ASAP. And if it was *really* bad, Barry would be waiting in her office.

Jane pointed at the door to Melissa's room and said, 'He's waiting.'

MELISSA PULLED INTO THE parking lot at Georgetown Law School feeling a strange, new-found sense of freedom. The conversation she'd had with Barry Sherer was brief: there might be a grand jury, he said, then again, maybe not. She might be cleared by OPR, then again, it all depended. The one thing he was clear about was her job: like Harris, she'd been placed on administrative leave and taken off the case, which, of course, was exactly what Adalwolf wanted. Recognizing that, Barry said he hoped she'd continue working the case anyway, *sub rosa*, because no one knew Adalwolf better than she and Harris. She said she'd think about it, then left to do her Christmas shopping.

It was ten after six when she entered the classroom and took off her raincoat and tossed it onto the back of a chair. 'Hello, every-body, sorry I'm late.' She took a drink of water as she sat on the edge of the desk. Her law students – all seven of them – were always hungry and a bit restless at this hour.

'When we broke last week,' she said, 'we were in the middle of debating whether it's ever justifiable to violate the law in order to accomplish a greater good. Can civilized society achieve justice at the expense of the rules it lives by? Jerry?'

'The only way the men of the *Mignonette* survived in their lifeboat was by killing and eating one of their fellow sailors. Wasn't that better than dying?'

'You tell me.'

Jerry looked surprised. 'It was if you were a survivor.'

A young woman named Kathleen said, 'Martin Luther King,

Junior violated the segregation rules and went to jail for it, but he created a more just society as a result.'

'The laws he was protesting were constructed to perpetuate an injustice,' Melissa said. 'What about so-called natural laws that all societies agree on? Laws prohibiting theft, assault, and murder?'

'Isn't executing people a form of murder?' Kathleen said.

'By definition, no, because it's not outside the law. But the evidentiary mistakes and uneven application of the punishment are often unjust.'

A student named Aaron said, 'How about Adolf Eichmann?'

'Instead of hanging him, I would have put him in a cell and studied him,' Melissa said.

'And Hitler?'

'Same thing. How about you?'

'I would have put Hitler in a crematorium and roasted him like an onion until every layer of his skin came off.'

A few students laughed and clapped. A female student said, 'Such a male point of view.'

'You know what I would have done?' another guy said.

Melissa said, 'No, and I don't want to know. This is a class on ethics and the law, not the Marquis de Sade. Torture is no more justified than killing.'

'What about people like Osama bin Laden?' a student asked. 'Would you kill them if you had the chance?'

'Not if I could try them first.'

Some of them looked convinced, some didn't.

'Look, guys,' Melissa said, 'I don't want to spout clichés about the majesty of the law, but when it comes to the big stuff it's hard to think of situations where going outside the law is better than staying within it. Sure, civil disobedience is a legitimate way of changing things, but note that it's *civil* disobedience we're talking about, not murder or mayhem.'

The student said, 'I don't think it's that easy.'

'I didn't say it was easy, I said it was clear. The more that's at stake, the more the law needs to be respected.'

They discussed the proposition until class ended and everyone left. Melissa was gathering up the papers on her desk when a shy young woman named Maria Tressler stopped by to say something. 'I'm afraid you underestimate the healing effect an execution can have on the victims of a violent crime.'

'Are you sure it's really healing or just a temporary emotional release?'

'In my case it was healing,' she said.

Melissa knew what she was referring to. As a twelve-year-old girl, Tressler had been tied up by an escaped convict in Tyler, Texas and raped along with her mother. Her father had been mutilated and left to die and her mother had been forced to drink a fatal dose of Clorox. The killer had been executed only a few months ago. Melissa had wanted to talk to Maria about it, but only if she raised it. Now that she had, Melissa didn't know what to say.

'Some killers' crimes,' the young woman said, 'are so outrageous, letting them live actually perpetuates the crime over and over and magnifies the survivors' pain. Survivors may be weak and unsophisticated for not being able to forgive and forget, but the burden of doing that shouldn't be theirs. Not if it eats them alive. The killer's life isn't worth it.' She headed for the door. 'As for torture being no better than killing, I just hope you never have to face the choice.'

Melissa turned out the lights and walked down the hall toward the parking lot, thinking less about executions and torture than being placed on leave pending the outcome of the Department's investigation. Never had she felt the need to be with David more. She opened her purse and searched for her red sneaker key chain. When she turned the corner, she saw roses first, then the man who was holding them.

'I know I'm late,' David said, 'but my homework ate the dog.'

She raised her arms to him, and he wrapped his around her.

'I'm so glad to see you,' she said.

THERE WAS SOFT MUSIC and lighting, fresh flowers next to the maître d's podium, a carpet that quieted the dining room. A tall candle sat in the middle of their table, just off center. Melissa positioned her cranberry juice and soda to catch the light and spread a warm halo on the linen tablecloth.

'In the last three days,' she said to her husband, 'we whacked around an American war hero and burned him alive, leaked the existence of a deadly virus we'd been trying to keep secret until we knew what it was, missed catching a serial killer for the third time, put two agents in the hospital with second degree burns, maybe ruined Harris's career, put the FBI and the Department of Justice in line for this year's Waco Memorial Award, and managed to get yours truly suspended without pay until the outcome of an OPR investigation or a grand jury indictment, whichever comes first. And how was your day, my love?'

David lifted his martini and took a sip. 'They're crazy to take you off the case.'

'Well, you see, there's the catch. I'm *officially* off the case, but I'm still working it from home, which means now I get to do what I did before without the help of the FBI, my files, or a paycheck.'

'What a deal,' David said.

She lifted her soda and juice. 'Truth is, I want Adalwolf now more than ever. No way is he taking me off this thing.' Another cooling drink. 'By the way, I told Barry the news about the operation and said if I get pregnant, I'll have to take it easy. I hope you don't mind.'

'Not at all.'

They ordered dinner and talked about his story on shipping industry corruption. When they'd finished, it was the usual after-dinner routine: coffee but no dessert for him, dessert but no coffee for her.

'Maybe there's a good reason I got suspended,' she said.

'No, there isn't. It's politics.'

She didn't argue the point. David would never fully understand her power of intuition any more than she would fully appreciate his angular logic. But together, one and one made three.

'Now that you're suspended, you can do whatever you want,' he said.

'Like what?' she said.

'Instead of flying back and forth to Miami you can stay there and do the fertility procedure and get a tan.'

'Sounds great, but how am I going to get pregnant without you?'

'I'll phone it in.'

'You've been away too long, dear heart.'

'Must be some way to solve this.' He took a drink. 'How about this: I'll leave Washington and come to Miami with you.'

She nodded, yeah, sure. When he said nothing, she said, 'You're kidding, aren't you?'

'Not really. The *Times* has agreed to assign me to Miami for a year. If you want to go, we can.'

'David!'

'We could live there while we try to have a kid.'

'Oh, sweetheart.'

They leaned across the table and kissed until the heat from the candle got to them. Sitting back, they found their napkins and stole glances at people who were stealing glances at them. The whole world loved a pair of lovers.

David said, 'It's time you forgot about Adalwolf and the FBI and the Department of Justice for a while.'

What a great move. She adored him.

'We'll need to find a place to rent,' he said.

'I'll call Linda in the morning.' Linda Gonzales was a real estate broker Benjamin Ben-Zevi had introduced to Melissa. 'Ben will let us stay at his house till we find something.' He had a beautiful house with a large guest room on Granada Boulevard in Coral Gables. She and David had stayed there before, most recently when she underwent the uterine scar removal.

They finished dinner and went back to their apartment. David found a radio station with soft music, lit a scented candle, and dimmed the lights. They came to bed in terrycloth robes and nothing else. He massaged her feet – the gateway to her heart – and she let herself relax. He said he was going to make up for every night he'd been gone in the last two weeks. She asked him how. He said he'd rather show than tell, and soon they were two people in search of one experience.

'You said on the phone . . . I'd tell you I love you,' she said.

'You gonna come through . . . for me?' he said.

'Depends on what . . . you've got to offer . . . '

They locked fingers and stopped talking. They were moving beyond words now, communicating with breath and movement and nerve endings that spoke far more eloquently. They knew each other so well they could time their climaxes as they wanted, separately or together.

Tonight they stuck together.

THEY GOT THROUGH THE holidays just fine: no horrible mistakes with the gifts, no shoes thrown at holiday specials on TV, no fake New Year's resolutions. The season seemed to be behind them before it ever got started. They were looking ahead to Miami. When January third arrived Melissa was on a plane a day ahead of David. She couldn't wait.

She stepped out of the air-conditioned terminal and felt a blast of Florida's balmy air.

Miami was a different world from Washington, full of Cuban music and tanned retirees and Puerto Rican high energy. Even the sun was different down here, closer to the earth and more coppery in tone. Despite the glass office buildings and fancy condominiums, the city felt natural and fertile and ripe, the perfect place to get pregnant.

She found a taxi at the airport and drove to the clinic located on Alton Road, near the Mt. Sinai Medical Center. Pulling her suitcase, she entered a palm-lined building that could have been a medical facility anywhere in the world: air-conditioned air, leather chairs in the waiting room, a stack of outdated magazines. She checked in with the receptionist on the fourth floor and sat down, but before she had time to get nervous the door opened and in walked Dr. Eric Brandt, smiling, his hand extended.

'Hello, Melissa!'

She stood up and shook his hand warmly, feeling instantly in his care.

'It's so great to be here,' she said. 'I love Miami.'

He ushered her through the door and down a hall to his office, which was neater than most. She sat in a soft chair. He sat behind his desk and leaned back with his hands behind his head.

'I missed your interview on CNN,' he said. 'I hear you did a good job under the circumstances.'

'Under the circumstances.'

'The world's a better place because of what you do, you know,' he said.

She thought, what a lovely thing to say. Doctors' opinions always seemed authoritative no matter what they were talking about. 'And how are you?' she said.

'Nothing's changed since you were here six weeks ago. You, on the other hand, are another story.' He stood up and clicked on a light board. A set of MRI photos taken of her womb before the uterine scraping appeared. Scar tissue showed up as white; it was all they could see.

He put a second set of photos on the board. 'Here are the pictures from two weeks ago.' She'd had a hysterosalpingogram – an x-ray of the uterus while it's filled with radioactive dye – which was done in Washington and sent to the clinic. After seeing it, he'd written her saying he thought she could get pregnant, and now she saw why: there were splotches of darkness indicating the absence of scar tissue in her womb. He pointed at them with a pencil. 'Pretty nice, huh?'

'Gorgeous.' A fly on the wall would have thought they were nuts.

'I think it's time to take another look at your uterus,' he said.

'An MRI?'

'Yes, but we'll do a pelvic examination first.'

He showed her to an examining room and said he'd be back in a minute. She closed the door and sat on the edge of an examining table and prayed for good luck, then began undressing. When she finished she weighed herself on a true-weight scale – one-twenty, same as six weeks earlier – then put on a hospital gown, tied the string in back, and sat down and waited for Dr. Brandt to return. She trusted him.

So did David, despite an inevitable touch of jealousy. After her first visit he asked if Eric had used rubber gloves during her pelvic exam. No, she said, he wore railroad engineer gloves that came up to the elbows. David smiled and said he hoped they were made of asbestos. Male stuff like that, nothing serious.

Six weeks earlier she'd come to the clinic and put on a gown, climbed into a pair of stirrups, been anesthetized from the waist down, and had the operation. David had paced nervously in the waiting room for two hours while Dr. Brandt removed the scar tissue with micro scissors. Despite the high intensity light and loupes, the delicacy of his touch was crucial. If he cut too deeply into the womb's scarred lining it wouldn't hold an embryo, but if he cut too lightly, he'd leave the offending synechial scars intact. When he finished, he placed a balloon inside her womb to keep the surfaces from adhering to each other and waited for her to heal. Today she'd get the definitive results.

A nurse knocked on the door and told her to follow. The sound of Melissa's paper slippers filled the hallway as she walked to the OR and entered a room full of bright lights and equipment. She said hello to the scrub nurse who called Melissa a TV star. Melissa rolled her eyes and climbed onto the examining table without being told. See stirrups waiting, place feet inside. Pavlov must have been laughing. David had wanted her to wait until he got to Miami and joined her, but the thought of his waiting in the reception room only made her nervous. She said she'd call him the minute she had news.

Dr. Brandt entered from the scrub room, hands gloved, mask up, his blond hair covered by a surgeon's cap. Seeing nothing but his eyes gave her the impression he was someone menacing, but only for a moment. She knew it was really him by the light blue irises that matched his gown and the familiar loupes around his neck. He told her to relax, this wasn't going to be nearly as difficult as the operation. She'd feel some 'discomfort,' he said, but nothing serious. God, how doctors loved that word. It included everything that hurt from level one to nine, with only ten meriting the word 'pain.'

All those teenagers wanting *not* to get pregnant and doing nothing about it, and all us thirty-eight-year-olds trying to get pregnant no matter what it took: hormone injections, stainless steel stirrups, superstitious prayers to the goddess of fertility. There was no justice.

'Lie back and relax,' the nurse said, and raised a privacy curtain between Melissa's face and her midsection. The lower half of her body belonged to them now, but that was okay. *I trust him.*

'Sorry to be so formal,' Dr. Brandt said, 'but I don't want to take any chances of post-op infection.' An enormous speculum caught Melissa's attention just before the curtain blocked it out. The indignity of it all.

Mother Nature wasn't a sister, she was a mother, and that was only half the word.

SITTING ON A SOFA reading a *Sports Illustrated*, Harris Johnson lifted his feet off the carpet to make room for the vacuum cleaner. His wife, Sherrie, yelled over the roar.

'You've got to get out of the house, Harris, you're driving me crazy!'

He kept reading. She tapped his shins, telling him he could put his feet down now. He lowered them without looking up. When the noise moved away he set the magazine down and sat listlessly. She was right. Two weeks off the job and he was driving himself nuts, too.

He patted his shirt, found his pen, and pulled the cap off with his teeth. Writing over an article about the LA Lakers, he listed what he and Melissa knew about Adalwolf, then the questions that needed to be answered. The two columns looked like this:

What we know:

German. SS.
Hitler fan.
Nazi.
Smart.
Technically educated.
Auschwitz.
Mengele's lab.
Worked with children.
Worked on pregnant women.

Twins experiments.
Eugenics nut.
Handles viruses.
Uses Latin phrases.
'Maxima debetur puero reverentia.' = 'The greatest respect is owed to
*   a child.'*
Uses French phrases occasionally, like 'Au Revoir.'

In the column of unknowns was this:

What skills needed to develop NTX virus?
Virologogy?
Chemistry?
Biology?
Pharmacology?

'Honey?' his wife said.
'Yes, love?' he answered.
'If you're looking for something to do, the banister needs fixing.'
'Yes, love. In a minute.'

Has access to laboratory?
Learned something from Mengele?
From the Auschwitz female sterilization project?
How'd he get to Auschwitz as a boy?
How's he stay undetected?

One thing professional investigators like Harris understood was that, even with a host of identifying characteristics, finding a crafty killer was difficult. Son of Sam killed for months without detection. Ted Bundy for years. Jack the Ripper was never caught, and the D.C. Snipers shot people from fifty yards away without detection. Harris and Melissa had talked to the FBI team investigating the dissemination of post 9-11 Anthrax and learned that even though the culprit had to come from a small group of candidates having access to the pathogen, he was next to impossible to find.

Adalwolf had to have rare knowledge of the virus and how to use it, which shrunk the size of the haystack, but still left him as a very small needle.

Harris picked up the telephone and dialed Melissa's cell phone number. He didn't know where she was, but he had to talk to her.

MELISSA WAS IN A recovery room waiting for a verdict. The anesthesia was almost worn off now, and she was sore in tender places. The female reproductive system seemed to be a testament to the shortcomings of evolution's grand scheme. Why not a sliding door or a detachable pod? A removable chip you could put into a computer and just print out your baby? Nine seconds later instead of nine months? All these tubes, wombs, eggs, scars, sperm, periods, douches – you could have them all. Well, maybe not the sex. That she'd put up with a little longer.

Her cell phone rang. She fished it out of her bag and recognized the caller in the window.

'Hi, Harris.'

'Where have I got you?' he asked.

'In a recovery room at the clinic. Where are you?'

'Home. Are you okay? You sound a little dopey.'

'I'm just a little hung over from some anesthesia.'

'Adalwolf's Latin phrase, The Greatest Respect is Owed to a Child. Who would use that as a motto?'

'First thing that comes to mind is a hospital,' she said.

'I've got that on the list.'

'How about a baby food company?'

'Okay.' Mumbling to himself, he said, 'You got babies on your mind.'

'A school or an orphanage,' she said. 'A pharmaceutical company specializing in children's medicine.'

'Wait a sec, I'm still on school or orphanage.'

'A Lamaze class,' she said.

'Wait, wait.'

'Let's see. A clinic or a hospital. Did I say that?'

'You want to call me back when your head's clear?'

'No, I need to wake up.'

'So far, I like a school,' he said. 'I'm picturing a German orphanage.'

'I'm seeing a French day school,' she said.

'How about a Polish church school?' he said.

'A Hitler Youth school.'

Harris said, 'Maybe.'

'If he knows Latin he must have had a good education,' she said. 'How many schools in Europe taught Latin during World War Two?'

'No idea.'

The door to the recovery room opened and someone stepped inside. 'I'll call you back,' Melissa said, and hit the end-call button.

SHE TURNED AND SAW DR. Brandt come into the room. She wanted to check his eyes for a hint of the outcome, but he was reading a report. Not good. When a jury had bad news for a defendant it didn't look at him. He sat on a countertop.

'It looks good,' he said.

'It does?'

'Most of the scarring is gone and the tissue looks healthy. We're not home free, but it's time to try for an impregnation.'

'Oh, my God.' She felt a cool wind beneath her wings. 'Tell me the truth, Eric. What are my chances?'

'I'd say thirty percent.'

The wind stopped blowing. 'That's all?'

'That's all? That's remarkable. Until the scar removal, it was virtually zero.'

All right, she'd accept that. Thirty percent would have to be good enough. Her horoscope that morning had said *Take that high risk to get that high reward.* Not that she took horoscopes seriously, but she did read them. 'What do we do next?' she said.

He picked up her chart. 'You should be ovulating in about eleven days. We'll do a sonogram this afternoon and take a look at your follicles. If they look promising I'll put you on ten days of Pergonal and then harvest the best eggs you've got. We'll put them in a Petri dish, add David's semen, and see if we can create some healthy embryos. If we get what we need, we'll do an implant. If the implant doesn't spontaneously abort, we'll look for a viable pregnancy about ten days after that.'

It all sounded so plausible. 'Should David and I stop having sex?'

'No reason to. You might even conceive naturally, although it's unlikely given where you are in your cycle. But I'm concerned about new scar tissue forming as you heal, so sure, go for it, the sooner you get pregnant the better.'

'How do you extract the eggs?' Melissa said.

'With a laparoscope. You won't feel any pain, just a little discomfort.'

Ah, yes. Discomfort. 'And David?'

'He'll donate his sperm when we extract the eggs from your tubes. Ginny will give you both the instructions you need. Let me check your abdomen.'

She climbed onto an examining table while he called Ginny to come to the room and washed up. After the nurse entered, he stood next to Melissa and moved his hand on top of her gown. 'What's going on with your work?' he said. 'Or are you on vacation?'

'Oh, I'm still working,' she said. 'The FBI agent on the case just called.'

'I thought I read that he was suspended.'

'He was, but he can't give up on the case any more than I can. Do you know Latin?'

'Just medical school stuff. Does that hurt?'

'No.'

'That?'

'No.'

He continued pressing with his fingers. 'Why Latin?'

'Someone used a phrase on the telephone the other day that means The Greatest Respect is Owed to a Child. Have you ever heard it?'

He didn't answer, just kept palpating her.

She said, 'I'm trying to figure out where the caller might have picked it up. Someplace like a hospital or a clinic or a school.'

Eric finished. 'You feel fine. You can do the usual things, but take it easy, okay? You're not planning to travel, are you?'

'No, why?'

'We'll need you here for tests until we complete the program.'

Melissa stood up as Ginny left. 'No problem, that's why I'm in Miami.'

He gave her a reassuring smile and started for the door.

'Eric?' she said, stopping him. 'Regardless of how this turns out, I can't thank you enough.'

MELISSA SLIPPED INTO A cotton sundress and a pair of sandals and finished unpacking. The guest room in Ben-Zevi's house was spacious and quiet. She hung her clothes in the closet and opened a dresser to put away the rest of her things, including a small wooden box with a lock.

Becoming distracted the way unpackers do, she opened the box with a key she carried on her red sneaker key chain. Inside were mementos of her family history: a photograph of her mother and herself at Coney Island eating ice cream; a picture of her father carrying her on his shoulders, her hands covering his eyes as she held on for dear life. It was taken when she was six, a few months before he died in a construction accident. Her mother died ten years later of tuberculosis – the same strain that had attacked Melissa and scarred her uterus. Melissa had one gossamer-like, black-and-white photograph of her grandmother posing for a portrait shot. Despite the overdone hair and serious smile, she was beautiful, and Melissa wished she had more pictures of her, especially a color shot that showed her red hair. She closed the box and laid it in the top dresser drawer.

It was time for her first dose of pills and her first hormone shot.

Dr. Brandt's nurse, Ginny, had taught her how to do it. She poked a large diameter needle through a rubber diaphragm covering the mouth of a bottle of Clomid and drew out the cc's she needed. Then she removed the large needle and attached a smaller gauged one for injection. After removing air from the syringe, she was ready.

Her head felt warm and her cheeks perspired. She started talking to herself. 'Okay, this is no big deal.'

She put her hand on her abdomen and pinched some fatty skin between her left thumb and forefinger. 'Don't do it slowly, do it fast.'

She couldn't do it at all. After wiping her forehead, she started over.

'One . . . two . . . three.' She stuck it in, pushed in the plunger, and withdrew the needle, whispering, 'Holy shit.' She laid back on the bed until her lightheadedness passed, then got up and disposed of the needle in a plastic box.

Once a day, every day. She'd have to get used to it.

She returned to her room and plugged in her laptop and turned it on to check her e-mail. There were two messages waiting: one from David saying he was finishing his story, hope the doctor's appointment went well, miss you badly, can't wait to see you tomorrow in Miami, xox, and one from Harris telling her to call when she could. The one she was looking for – the one from Adalwolf – wasn't there. His silence pissed her off.

She sent an e-mail to Harris saying she'd call later, then closed her laptop and carried it down the hall. The house was large and homey with terrazzo floors and vaulted ceilings, a seldom-used fireplace in the living room, plump sofas with pillows rarely moved.

She entered Ben's study with its cherry paneling and cherry shutters that allowed enough sunlight to bring the wood to life. There was a heavy desk befitting a professor, and on it were piles of medical reports, pharmaceutical samples, and a plastic model of a uterus. Standing prominently near the center was a silver-framed photograph of Ben and his wife Myrna walking arm-in-arm on the beach. The room was a comfortable place to work or read.

Ben had left a house key in the usual place and written her a note saying he'd be back around seven-thirty to take her to dinner, and so make herself at home. She attached a cable from her computer to a LaserJet printer he seldom used and began printing out e-mails and records from the Adalwolf case file so she could annotate them, a work habit she'd followed since law school.

She turned to a wall covered with the highlights of Ben's life: a photograph of him in black tie accepting an award; a ribbon-cutting ceremony with Myrna, opening the fertility clinic in Miami Beach. There were certificates, diplomas, and accolades. Behind the door was a copy of the photograph she'd received from the widow in Toronto showing twelve-year-old Ben standing in his striped prisoner's shirt with a group of inmates, including young Adam, the woman's eventual husband. Adalwolf, the lab technician, was off to the side. When she'd sent the photograph to Ben, his wife had framed it with a plain white mat that held no date or inscription or signature, as if to say Auschwitz was not just another ribbon-cutting ceremony. Melissa was examining it when she heard a knock on the doorjamb.

She turned and saw Ben standing in the doorway.

HIS BOW TIE WAS loosened and his coat unbuttoned, his arms outstretched, his smile big and slightly gap-toothed, like Ernest Borgnine's. Despite his age he had a full head of thick, salt-and-pepper hair, a trim beard, and modern horn-rimmed glasses. With his hunter green corduroy jacket and light blue, sea-island cotton shirt, he looked like the hip professor he was reputed to be.

'Melissa!'

She walked to him and fell into his embrace. 'Hello, Ben.' Of *course* she'd made him into a father figure, why wouldn't she? She'd hardly known her own. When they'd finished hugging, he excused himself a moment and came back into the room carrying a tray of tea – iced for her, a tall glass of hot tea for him – and *babka*, the apple cake he loved.

He gave her a glass and set the tray on an ottoman and sat back in his favorite leather chair, letting himself sink into it. After chatting a moment, he raised his glass.

'Eric told me the good news,' he said. 'Let's drink to it.'

'Are you sure that won't jinx it?' she said.

'If you're meant to be pregnant, you'll be pregnant.'

He took a bite of *babka* and downed it with a sip of tea.

'So, tell me everything,' he said. 'How's David?'

'You'll see for yourself. He's coming down tomorrow.'

'I saw your CNN interview.'

'Yeah, how about that. Adalwolf did it to us again.'

'To hell with Adalwolf,' he said. 'He'll be meeting the Malach ha-Mavet soon anyway.'

'The who?'

'The Angel of Death who comes for the wicked.'

'Adalwolf's going to make a lot of trouble before he dies,' she said, 'unless we catch him.'

'But you will,' he said.

'Somebody will, but not me. I've been suspended.'

'What?'

'Pending a grand jury investigation.'

'What a bunch of *putz*es you work for,' he said, sitting back in his chair.

The only Yiddish Melissa knew she'd learned from Ben, whose frequent use of it she thought slightly out of character for a man of his credentials and sophistication. When she said that to him, with a smile, he said, 'So better I should speak Chinese? You can call yourself a professor and live in a fancy house, *tsatskala*, but you can't change who you are.' He nodded toward the wall. 'Beneath those diplomas and fancy pictures is still a rabbi's son from the *shtetl*. Besides, some things you can say in Yiddish you can't say in American.'

'I'm going to work the case anyway,' she said. 'So's the FBI agent who was told to take a vacation.'

'Adalwolf is one of these modern bio-terrorists who use their ordinary appearance as camouflage,' he said. 'You could be close enough to touch him and still not know he's there.'

'That was true until a few days ago,' she said, 'but he may have finally slipped up.'

'How so?' Another bite of *babka*.

'He used a Latin phrase on the phone: *Maxima debetur puero reverentia.*'

'A large debt of respect is due to—' Ben smiled at himself. 'For an educated guy, my Latin stinks.'

'Mine, too. It means, 'The greatest respect is owed to a child.' We're trying to figure out where he picked it up.'

He took a drink of tea and wiped his fingers on a napkin. 'I'm telling you, they don't deserve you, Melissa. You're too good for them.'

'It's my life, Ben. I've wanted to track down Nazis since I was a little girl.' She waived off a piece of cake and drank some more tea. 'Why is that?'

His eyebrows rose in surprise. 'Your grandmother, what else?'

Although her grandmother had died before Melissa was born, when Melissa was a little girl she'd heard stories about her and had formed a clear image of who she was – not so much from the photographs she'd seen, but from a book of comic strips featuring Brenda Starr, the beautiful, daring reporter with blazing red hair, full lips, and sparkling brown eyes. That woman, Melissa knew in her bones, was the real Esther, and she wanted to be just like her. Ben's later stories about Esther in the camp – how she'd given him her pendant, and how he'd almost lost his life trying to save it – only reinforced Melissa's romantic childhood images of her grandmother.

She said, 'I'm looking for something I'm unaware of. Psychology, history, a hidden motivation.'

'Why hidden? Your grandmother suffered terribly in the camp, it's only natural you'd want to do something about that. What makes you ask?'

'Just curious.' Another sip of tea. 'Adalwolf said he knows why I'm a Nazi hunter even though I don't.'

'What a load of crap. You may have to listen to his *drerd* in order to catch him, but you don't have to let him get under your skin. He's a psychopath.'

He finished his tea in evident irritation and set his glass on the side table. Then, catching himself, he broke into a broad smile and smacked both chair arms with his palms. 'So – let's continue this over dinner. What would you like?'

'How about the News Cafe?'

'Whatever you say.'

They both stood and he gave her another hug before leaving to wash up. She watched him go out the door with his signature limp.

Why was she a Nazi hunter? Who cared? The only thing she wanted to hunt down now was a large stone crab.

'GOOD NIGHT, DADDY.'

'Good night, Sammy.' Harris Johnson reached for the light switch in his four-year-old son's room. His wife, Sherrie, stood at the door.

'Daddy?'

'What?'

'When can we go to a baseball game?'

'It's still basketball season.'

'I don't like basketball, I like baseball.'

'We'll go to a game this summer, I promise.'

'Daddy?'

'What, Sammy?'

'Will I see you before summer?'

'Of course you will. I'll see you tomorrow morning, little guy.'

'Will you take me to kindergarten?'

'There's no school tomorrow, it's Saturday.'

Sammy smiled at the news and pulled up the covers. Harris closed the door.

'I heard that,' Sherrie said as they walked down the hallway. 'The question is, did you?' She put her hand on the banister and shook it. It creaked and wiggled. She gave him a look.

'I'm fixing it tomorrow,' he said.

'A four year old needs his daddy,' she said.

'I see him all the time, Sherrie. Kobie too.' Kobie was their ten-year-old daughter.

'It's not just *seeing* the kids that matters, it's where your head is when you do.'

They came into the living room. 'Adalwolf is killing people, Sherrie. If he's not caught, the next thing you know he'll be killing children like ours.'

'You know I hope you catch the son-of-a-bitch,' she said. 'I just don't want you to make the world safe for other children at the expense of your own.'

Feeling unjustly accused, he sat on the sofa and began preparing his defense when it occurred to him that he'd never considered Sammy and Kobie to be *unsafe*. Given the job he held and the kind of people he pursued, maybe he should have. Sherrie asked him something about a TV show she was watching and, wanting to be attentive, he relaxed and put the kids out of his mind.

But not completely.

THEY SAT AT A TABLE outdoors overlooking Ocean Drive and Lummus Park, a grassy strip between the street and the beach. The weather was soothing and the people on the street were happy. It was good to be alive on a Friday night at the News Cafe. Melissa was already sinking emotional roots into Miami.

After ordering dinner, she told Ben the highlights of the Atlantic City debacle: how Adalwolf had found Sgt. Sherwood and drugged him and tattooed him with a pen and set him up for an awful death, and how she and the FBI had fallen for it. It was inevitable that she and Harris would be investigated, she said, although being taken off the case was worse than a public relations gimmick. It took the Department's attention off the hunted and placed it on the hunters, which was a coup for Adalwolf.

'That won't last long,' Ben said. 'The next time someone is infected with NTX the focus will be back on him.'

'You think there'll be a next time?'

'This guy isn't living out his golden years fly fishing. He's got a plan.'

Melissa toyed with her glass. 'There are simple things we could have done the night of the arrest, Ben. We could have held the subject's arms down, we could have inspected the IV pole. I could have licked my thumb and smudged the tattoo on his arm, for God's sake.'

'Why would you do that when it was obvious he was your man?'

'You can't take anything for granted. He was wearing a T-shirt. The tattoo was right in front of me.'

'Where was it?'

'Here.' She touched her upper arm, close to her shoulder.

'That's too high,' Ben said. He pushed up his short sleeve shirt revealing well-toned muscle. 'It was right here, between the bicep and the shoulder, where you usually see a vaccination scar.'

'Why would Adalwolf tattoo Sergeant Sherwood in the wrong place?'

Ben's shrug said he didn't know. 'It wasn't that far off. He probably assumed you didn't know the exact location.' He touched his shoulder in different places and looked at it, trying to recall. 'Maybe I'm wrong, it's been so many years.' He let go of his sleeve. 'Frankly, I'm glad you're out of the hunt.'

'I'll never be out of the hunt until he's caught.'

'As long as it doesn't interfere with getting pregnant, fine, but don't let him take you off course.'

'I can do both.'

'Yeah, I know. That's what all you girls say these days.'

She took a drink. 'Tell me about Eric.'

'He was one of my best students at Columbia. When Myrna and I came to Florida and started the clinic I put him on the staff, and when I retired as director two years ago he replaced me.'

'Why did you retire?'

'I'm seventy-two years old, my dear. Eric is forty-four and the best in his field. Are you relaxing yet?'

'I relaxed the minute I got off the plane.' She ate a fancy hors d'oeuvre the waiter had brought with their drinks.

Ben's eyes turned distant.

'He's under your skin, too, isn't he?' she said.

'Adalwolf? What makes you think so?'

'Come on,' she said. When he didn't argue, she said, 'Tell me what he did, Ben.'

Ben put his arms up and stretched. 'I already have, many times.'

That was true, but only up to a point. He'd told her Adalwolf had killed Mengele's subjects and prepared them for autopsy, but he'd never described how it was done.

'How did he do it, Ben?' she said.

'We're not going to talk about that over dinner,' he said.

'It wouldn't bother me,' she said.

'It would me.'

She looked at him sympathetically, sorry she'd asked. The waiter brought them their stone crabs, bibs they didn't wear, little picks and forks, fresh lemons, salad, beer and iced tea. They broke off the claws and peeled back the white shell and went to work. After her first mouthful, she said, 'Okay, now I know I'm in Miami.'

'COULD I HAVE THAT lemon?' Ben said. She handed it to him. He squeezed it, sending spurts all over the table. 'I became an endocrinologist because of a promise I made to myself in the camp. When the train stopped at Birkenau, I was in a state of disbelief like everyone else.' Birkenau was the gateway to Auschwitz. 'We'd heard stories about what was going on but we clung to our illusions that everything would turn out okay. The first person we saw was a kapo – a Jew chosen by the SS to keep fellow prisoners in line –'

'I know what kapos are.'

Ben nodded, of course. 'He opened the doors to our cattle car and told us we deserved to die because we were such naïve, dumb bastards. Even then I didn't get it. I just hung onto my father's hand and waited for him to make everything all right.'

He took a drink of beer.

'A guard blew a whistle and we got off the train. I remember it was dusk and the sky was deep blue with streaks of orange on the horizon. But then I noticed there was an orange glow in the east, too, from sparks flying out of the chimneys. Pretty soon the wind shifted and the smell was so strong you couldn't breathe.'

'And you knew.'

'Oh, yes. I knew.'

Melissa reached out and touched his hand.

'In the next year I saw everything you can imagine,' he said. 'Death and brutality, mindless inhumanity. I saw it all around me, up close, at a distance, everywhere. But you have to understand something, Melissa. The problem was . . . .' He took another drink.

'I didn't just *see* it.' He stared at her. 'Do you understand what I'm trying to say? I didn't just *see* it.' He waited for her to get it.

Now she took a drink. 'You don't need to say another word, Ben, I didn't mean to—'

'I survived by helping him, Melissa.'

He took out his handkerchief, removed his glasses, and wiped the perspiration off his forehead.

'Adalwolf wasn't just a killer of children,' he said, 'he had visions of a much larger plan. He said they'd never be able to eradicate all the Jews with gas and ovens because there were too many of them, they needed a more efficient way. Poison, perhaps. Radiation. Sterilization. He watched Dr. Schumann's experiments on pregnant women and thought it might be possible to breed Jews out of existence. You know, eugenics. Kill them in the womb.' He put his glasses back on.

'One day,' he said, 'they brought six women into the lab to be impregnated and tested. One of them was this beautiful eighteen-year-old redhead named Esther.' He spoke of her as if Melissa had never heard this part before, although she had.

'When it came time for Adalwolf to do the usual body search – oh, he loved that job, believe me – your grandmother Esther tried to pull him aside to tell him something in private, but he wouldn't listen. She finally gave up and did as she was told, of course. As she climbed onto the examining table she reached under her skirt and took a pendant from her most intimate place and slipped it to me.'

He took a drink.

'I knew I shouldn't take it but it happened so fast I didn't think. She was so beautiful, and I was so . . . young. I slipped it into my pocket and watched her lying there stony-faced and indignant while Adalwolf did his body search. I'd seen him search other women, but how he treated this one was noticeably different. His face was flushed and he actually made a clumsy effort to be respectful.'

He fingered his glass nervously.

'That night he sent a kapo to bring me to the clinic. I knew something strange was happening because it was Christmas Eve. Many of the guards were at home, and I thought Adalwolf should have been with the Mengeles, too, but here he was in the clinic with a little girl. Anyway, I was prepared to do my job and put the girl at ease, but for some reason he didn't ask me to.' He stared at his drink. 'I remember it was very peaceful outside, with fresh snow covering everything. I waited for the kapo to come get me, but he didn't come. I remember wondering how this could be happening on a night with snow falling and a child singing *Silent Night* and holding an ornament that must have come from Mengele's tree.'

He kept fingering his glass, staring at a thin layer of foam that swirled gently.

'He found me peeking through the door clutching the pendant your grandmother had given me. Keeping it was a terrible offense, and somehow he'd found out. He lifted it off my neck and brought me into the room and I thought I was dead. But he had something else in mind.'

She said nothing, waiting for him to continue.

'He took the gauze off the little girl's head. She'd been blinded in one eye when Mengele tried to change the color of her corneas. She was naked from the waist up, just sitting there quietly.' He stopped.

'What happened?' Melissa said softly.

'He handed me a syringe full of chloroform.'

Somehow, she didn't expect that.

He took off his glasses again. His eyes were red and teary. 'He made me kill her, Melissa. He made me kill a little girl.'

She wanted to say something comforting, like you did what you had to do, you were just a child yourself, you had no choice, no one who hasn't been in your shoes has the right to judge you. But she didn't. Everything she could imagine saying felt too trite. 'There's no need to say more, Ben,' she said.

'No, you asked and I want to tell you,' he said. 'The more you know about him the better your chances are of finding him. But I need to tell you in small doses.' He put his glasses back on. 'Anyway, that's why I became a doctor. Saving lives was not only my answer to Auschwitz, it was my answer to what I did.'

'Not did, Ben. Were made to do.'

His shrug said, That doesn't make it right.

'Why didn't he kill my grandmother?' she said.

'He was in love with her,' Ben said. 'He wanted to make her part of his pregnancy experiment so he could see her again.'

'But she was already pregnant with my mom, wasn't she?' Melissa said.

'Yes,' Ben said, 'but Adalwolf didn't know that. Only after the guards brought her back to the lab did she tell him. He was absolutely crushed when he found out, but she didn't stop there. She said she'd have nothing to do with his rotten experiment, and she'd have nothing to do with him. What's more, she wanted her pendant back.' He took a drink and remembered. 'Imagine a Jew talking to Mengele's foster son that way. Even with an SS captain protecting her, it was astounding.'

'Did he give her the pendant?'

'I don't know. The next time I saw her was at her funeral in nineteen fifty. I arrived at Coney Island the day after she died.'

Melissa knew that part of the story, too. After making his way to London after the war, Ben had enlisted the help of a survivors' organization that discovered Esther in Coney Island in 1948. The two of them corresponded for two years before he finally reached New York. He was only eighteen at the time and Esther only twenty-five, but the typhus she'd suffered in the camp had already taken its toll. The night before he arrived she collapsed during a late-night swim and drowned. Melissa's mother, five at the time, was raised by her aunt and uncle. Ben remained in New York after the funeral, completed his schooling, and eventually became the family doctor to Melissa and her mother. He never lost touch with them again.

Melissa looked out at the park. A small group of people was watching a man sculpt a huge sand castle. 'Looks pretty good, doesn't it?' she said.

'You teach a class in legal ethics at Georgetown Law School, don't you?'

'Yes.'

'I want to tell you something about ethics and the law.'

She waited.

'There are rules for everyone else,' he said, 'and then there are rules for monsters.'

She straightened her knife and spoon.

He said, 'There are some people who are not civilized, and if you treat them as if they are they'll use your respect to kill you. They feast on people who believe in the law. They're the kind of people who turned our children into ashes. If you ever come face-to-face with Adalwolf, keep this one thing in mind: there are rules for everyone else, and then there are rules for monsters.'

Melissa didn't want to argue the point, but she also didn't accept it. It was the law that allowed her to hunt down Nazis like Adalwolf and get rid of them. But to disagree with Ben now would have been unforgivable. He had been there and survived; he'd traveled a road she'd never even seen. She had to respect that even if his views weren't her own.

They finished their dinner and walked along the sidewalk past Johnny Rocket's, the Colony Hotel, and Mango's Tropical Café, taking in Miami's South Beach street life.

After a while they returned to Ben's house and said goodnight, and there was an emotional distance between them she hadn't felt before dinner. She had stirred the ashes of his past and driven him away. She regretted it, but she knew that after a good night's sleep, he'd be back. He always was.

'IT'S SATURDAY MORNING and I'm feeling good,' Melissa said into the phone. 'It's time to get back in gear.'

She was in Ben's study, her laptop screen up. Harris was on the other end of the phone on a squawk box at his desk in his Washington apartment. His computer was connected to the internet as was hers.

'You take Google, I'll take Yahoo,' Melissa said.

They entered the Latin phrase they were looking for: *Maxima debetur puero reverentia*. What they came up with were lists of various Latin state mottos, university maxims, sorority and fraternity mottos and slogans of clubs, churches, and schools. An hour later they decided to narrow their search and start over.

Harris took Germany, Melissa took France.

After another hour of surfing, they'd still found nothing. But she and Harris knew that investigations were like panning for gold: it was hard, tedious work with no shortcuts.

Melissa heard Sherrie enter Harris's room and say hello. The two of them caught up for a few minutes, then Sherrie said to Harris, 'Did you say you were going to fix the banister, or was I dreaming?'

'Soon as we're done here, baby,' he said. He plugged in another name and hit Enter.

Melissa heard the jangle of a toolbox being set on a table. 'Tell me you're going to do it before you leave for the game and I'll stop hounding you.'

'Deal,' Harris said.

Sherrie said goodbye to Melissa and left the room. Harris told Melissa he had tickets to see the Washington Wizards, Michael Jordan against the New York Knicks. An afternoon out with his pals.

Melissa said, 'It's time to hang it up for a while.'

Harris said, 'Don't quit on me, I'll have to fix the banister.'

They both continued clicking and reading.

An entry came up on Melissa's screen. Her mouse took her to a web site for the *Order of the Sisters of Mercy*. 'Click here for English, *cliquée ici pour français*. Easy choice.

She scrolled down the page searching for Latin expressions translated into English and found one on a church in Paris, but it was off the subject. She clicked 'Next' and found another on a religious retreat in Brittany, but again, it was off target. She clicked 'Next' for another twenty minutes with no results. She found one more search engine and leaned back and stretched while it loaded.

'You got any leads in Germany?' she said.

'Nothing,' he said.

'Okay, go fix the banister. We'll pick it up tomorrow.'

When the 'Search for a word or phrase' box appeared in her new search engine she entered the Latin axiom and hit 'Go.'

Same result. She was getting to know some of these French places pretty well. She hit the 'Go' button three more times like a gambler who couldn't stop.

A new name appeared, the *Couvent du Sacré Coeur*. She hit the 'Click here to see picture.' It took her to a Web site with a photograph of an old stone structure on a hillside in the Loire Valley, near Lyons. The description said it was a five-hundred-year-old French convent that had once been an orphanage, hence the Latin motto, *Maxima debetur puero reverentia*. The greatest respect is owed to a child.

She hit Print and saw a hard copy spill into the print tray.
'Harris?'

'What?'

'Forget the basketball game. We're playing bingo and you just hit the jackpot.'

LINDA GONZALES PULLED into the semi-circular driveway of Ben's house in her 1995 silver Mercedes with rust freckles dotting the hood. Rusty or not, a Mercedes was essential if you were going to show houses in Miami Beach. Melissa was inside, ending her call with Harris. She took her computer off-line, put it in sleep mode, grabbed her bag, and went out the door, sunglasses on. The door opened and she climbed into the passenger seat.

'Linda, how are you?' she said.

'Hi, Melissa. Gee, you're looking great.'

Melissa turned around and saw Linda's ten-year-old son Kevin sitting in the back seat reading a comic book. What a cutie pie, with his coal black lashes and Botticelli face. 'Hi, Kevin, how are you?'

'Fine,' he said without looking up.

'How's Armando?' Melissa asked as they drove toward the street.

'Working his usual twelve-hour day,' she said. Armando Gonzales was Linda's Cuban-born husband who built houses for a living. She looked in her rearview mirror and touched the part in her hair. '*Ay-yi-yi*, look at those roots!'

'What are you going to show me?' Melissa said.

'A beautiful house on Golden Beach,' she said. 'Ten rooms, a pool, a steam room, and a master bedroom to *die* for, if you know what I mean.'

'Good Lord, Linda, we can't afford that.

'Don't *worry* about it!' She changed lanes. 'It's a house-sitting

gig. I owe Ben a lot of favors, so when I told him about it, he
thought it was just perfect. The owners are in Europe for a year
while the house is getting rebuilt. Old man Butterfield was messing
with his barbeque and burned down the north wing. Freaked out
his wife and the maid. They asked me to look after it while they're
gone. Kevin, don't pick your nose.'

They drove up South Dixie Highway, took I-95 north to the
Julia Turtle Causeway, then Collins Avenue north to Golden
Beach, tooling along in the Florida sunshine. A few minutes later
they saw the pavilion entrance to the Beach. They drove past it up
Ocean Boulevard to the driveway of a modern house with large
windows and a red tile roof and graceful palms around the
property. At one end of the house were pieces of construction
equipment and piles of dirt. The rest of the house looked
untouched.

After parking near the front door, Linda turned and told Kevin
they wouldn't be long but he could come in when he finished his
comic book, okay?

Melissa got out of the car and stepped onto springy grass. Palm
fronds clattered in the afternoon breeze and the air was heavy with
the fragrance of sea water. Walking up the front steps, Linda took
a set of keys from her purse. 'Most rich people have no taste, but
this house is different,' she said.

She unlocked the door and they stepped inside. Beyond a foyer
was an elevated living room with high ceilings. The room was
tastefully decorated in light fabrics and sisal rugs and just enough
cane to say they were in Florida. They walked over to an enormous
picture window overlooking the water. Linda pushed a button and
a translucent gray shade rolled up revealing a beautiful beach with
tractor tracks from the morning cleanup. Across the way a colorful
umbrella stuck out of the sand like a mai-tai swizzle stick. Out on
the ocean two tankers looked like toys.

They walked to a white-tiled kitchen with skylights. The dining
room was clean and simple and lined with a grass wall covering.

Linda took her across the living room into a hallway leading to a back stair. Next to it was an automatic chair lift that ran from the garage breezeway, one floor below, and up to the bedroom wing a floor above.

'Mr. Butterfield uses it when he's not feeling well,' Linda said. She stepped onto the wheelchair platform, hit the on switch, and the two of them rode up. When they reached the top, they walked down a hallway past a study and two guest bedrooms – one for a baby, Melissa thought – to a master suite overlooking the beach. His and hers bathrooms, a large pop-up TV. Enough closet space to make Imelda Marcos blush. She and David could have lived in the bedroom alone. Linda was right: it was a romantic house and a great place for her and David to begin a new life.

'It's beautiful,' Melissa said.

Linda frowned. 'Too bad it's not for you.'

'Why not?'

'I want it myself.'

They walked down the main stair to the living room and continued to the ground floor. A game room with a pool table and large screen television opened onto a stone terrace facing the beach. In front of it was a wide patch of light green beach grass, and beyond that an exquisite expanse of beige sand and deep blue sea.

'Wait till I show you what's back here,' Linda said.

They walked down a short breezeway toward the garage. On one side was a sliding glass door to a wooden deck with an outdoor shower; on the other were his-and-her bathrooms, a massage room, and a steam room. Seeing it padlocked, Melissa cupped her hand and peered through a window in the door.

'It's locked for insurance reasons,' Linda said, moving through keys on a ring. She found the one she wanted, slid it into the padlock, and opened the shank. 'It's the brass one,' she said holding it up.

Unusually large, the room was lined in white tile with banquettes around the walls. In the center was a free-standing massage table with a white tile base and a redwood top. Linda spread her arms. 'So what do you think?'

'About the house? It's wonderful.'

'The Butterfields will *love* the idea of a Justice Department lawyer and a *New York Times* reporter house-sitting for them.'

'Will they mind a couple with a baby?'

'Are you pregnant?'

'Not yet.'

'We'll deal with that when the time comes.'

They stepped out of the steam room and Linda locked the door. Lifting a pile of white towels, she laid the key on a redwood bench outside the door and set the towels on top. From there they walked down the hall to a door to the garage. Linda opened it, showed Melissa the electric switch that raised and lowered the garage door, and handed her a remote control.

'If this works out, what can I do for you?' Melissa said.

'Lunch,' she said. 'That and keep the plants watered so I don't have to do it myself. What time is David getting in?'

Melissa checked her watch. 'About an hour.'

'Then we better scoot,' Linda said.

They climbed the stair to the living room and Linda lowered the sun shade, then they headed for the airport.

THE THIRD REICH HAD come to an end in Hitler's Berlin bunker. It was only fitting, Adalwolf thought, that its work should be resurrected in another bunker half a world away.

Adalwolf's laboratory had originally been built as an underground bomb shelter during the fifties, then, later, purchased by a small company he owned called Loring Pharmaceuticals and outfitted as a virology lab. If you were a researcher, it was a dream. If you were a killer, it was essential. If you were Adalwolf, it was both.

Sitting at his desk, he reached past his computer monitor to his stereo and chose a boys' choir recording of Joseph Haydn's *The Creation*, which he played loudly. No reason not to down here, you couldn't hear a bomb go off in this place. After closing his computer program, he got up, stretched, and checked his watch. Over the last few years he'd farmed out pieces of the research to three different laboratories using the cover story that he was developing a therapeutic virus to cure a disease. Over the last year, he'd pulled together what they'd developed, cutting out the good stuff and altering the DNA to create a virus of his own: NTX. Today was critical: he was testing whether it would make the genetic 'selection' it was designed to make. If it did, it would take care of more than a few cattle cars of Jews.

In ten minutes, he'd know.

He set a timer and walked past the sinks, Bunsen burners, and racks of acrylic test tubes to a red velvet curtain strung across a doorway at the side of the room. Behind the curtain was his lair: a spare room with a pipe frame bed made up with hospital-fold sheets and a wool blanket tight enough to bounce a quarter on it. Nearby was a clothes tree for his cardigan sweater, and next to the bed, a small table. Framed pictures hung on the wall.

He lifted a bottle of water from the table and looked at the photographs, interested that they told so much about his life. There was his mother in a sultry, Greta Garbo pose on a barstool, cigarette in hand. Next to that was a photograph of himself as a little boy at the convent with Mother Marie-Catherine at his side. There was a picture of Dr. Mengele and his wife standing in front of their house at Auschwitz, and the photo of himself and his lab assistants taken outside Block 19 in 1943 – the photo the Justice Department had. He never tired of seeing himself as a teenager in a white smock, or of seeing twelve-year-old Benjamin Ben-Zevi in his prisoner's stripes. It was the only photograph the Justice Department had of either of them, and he was proud that he himself had engineered that. They'd fallen for the so-called 'widow' in Toronto who'd supposedly sent the photo to Melissa after claiming to be too sick to be interviewed in person. That small deception still made him smile.

He checked his watch. Five more minutes to go.

There were more photographs in a large book that he lifted off the nightstand. Opening it in the middle, he found a shot of Melissa and David at their wedding, and next to it a telephoto shot of Melissa at a political rally on the Washington mall, totally oblivious that he'd taken it, totally oblivious that he was in her presence. He'd done that more than once.

Turning the page, he saw a portrait of Melissa's mother, and on the next page, the most prized photograph of the bunch: Melissa's grandmother, Esther, standing next to an empty stretcher in Mengele's clinic, unsmiling, bold and beautiful, a young Katharine Hepburn with a white pendant hanging around her neck. Even though the print was in black and white, he could still see her red hair, still remember his slight loss of breath when he saw her.

He took a drink of water without taking his eyes off the photograph, then wiped his mouth and screwed the cap back on. *It's been a long time, Esther, but all things come to him who waits. You still live in my heart and your granddaughter's flesh. The time is almost here.*

The timer sounded.

Adalwolf put his bottle down and walked into the laboratory, past the large, khaki machine that dried germs suspensions, past the books on viruses and genetics and the computer disks holding a slice of the genome, past the small centrifuges and the scanning electron microscope and freezers that hummed quietly. All these machines had been good soldiers in his lifelong battle to revive the Führer's dream, but now it was time to let them rest while he made a body count.

He entered a small room lit with a red lamp, like a darkroom. Against the wall were two cages filled with wood shavings and lab mice. He turned on a bright light over the first cage. Awakened, the mice wiggled their whiskers in search of food.

The first cage held only white mice, each with a numbered tab stapled through the soft spot in its ear. One of the mice lay on its side inertly, giving Adalwolf a start. He took a pencil and poked at him with the soft eraser and saw the mouse flip onto his feet and make a cheeping sound. What a relief: no catastrophe there. After making sure every mouse was alive and well, he turned off the light and moved to the second cage.

This one was filled with the same-sized mice, and they, too, had numbered tabs stapled through their ears. He turned on the light to see them. They looked identical to the mice in the other cage, except for two things:

They were gray instead of white.

They were all dead.

Adalwolf's heart nearly stopped. Could it be? He poked at each one through the wire mesh, and none of them moved. My God, it worked! The mice with the white hair genes were alive and well, while the ones with the gray hair genes were *all dead*. He'd finally engineered a virus that struck a deadly blow against one class of living organisms and left others completely alone. If you could do it with mice, you could do it with humans. If you could target genes that expressed the color of a mouse, you could target genes that expressed other traits as well. Ethnic traits. Not just hair color, but unseen ones.

He'd tried the NTX virus on four people, refined it, and made it ready to be incubated. Now all he needed was his incubator.

Melissa, dear Melissa. If only you knew the threshold of history you stand on today. But in time, you will. You most certainly will.

They called it NTX in Atlanta, but he had another designation for it: FSV for Final Solution Virus. *FSV – three letters the world will remember the way it remembers HIV, AIDS, TB, SARS, smallpox, and plague.*

He slapped his hands together in a moment of rare, unrestrained exuberance. The boys' chorus was booming in the background. He was *that close* to taking the final step.

He shut the door to the little side room, remembering what he'd said the night before: 'You can call yourself a professor and live in a fancy house, *tzatskala*, but you can't change who you are.'

No, but you can *hide* who you are. Rather easily, actually.

Adalwolf – better known to his friends, students, and Melissa Gale as Benjamin Ben-Zevi, the adult version of a twelve-year-old Jewish boy whose identity he'd stolen after killing him on Christmas Eve, 1944, shortly after making him kill a half-blind little girl – Adalwolf opened the file marked 'Jeremy Friedman: Virus Version 9.029' – and went back to work.

THE NURSE PUSHED A button on the intercom and yelled, 'He's dropped his pressure! Call a code!' She hustled over to the bed of Jeremy Friedman as fast as her biohazard 'space suit' allowed. The twenty-five-year-old man was in the critical stage of a viral hemorrhagic fever, blood oozing from his eyes and nostrils, his lips swollen and purple. The room was in Level 4 isolation, droplet- and respiratory-contained. Everyone who entered wore biohazard suits that prevented exposure to the virus, and the room had negative pressure that pulled in air from outside and expelled it with exhaust fans into decontamination devices.

A clear plastic tube ran from the patient's left nostril to a suction canister at the head of the bed, drawing black mucus into a container. A ventilator connected to another tube down the patient's trachea sighed every five seconds as it performed his breathing. His swollen eyelids were held closed with blood-stained tape, and his body, mottled with large bruises, was grotesquely bloated and spongy to the touch. And now, this. A rising fever. Falling blood pressure. A weakening heart.

A dying man.

The small room filled quickly with people who came to save Jeremy Friedman's life: three nurses, two pharmacists, an anesthesiologist, a critical care attending physician, a ventilator technician, an EKG technician, an x-ray technician, and a surgeon. All doing what they could, all at once.

'Another bolus of LR!'

'What's his last crit?'

'Twenty, forty-five minutes ago!'

'I got no pulse!'

'Hang another unit of PRBC!'

'What's his pulse?'

'I got no pulse!'

'Get that damned cooling blanket out of the way! Where's the Levophed?'

'Get those pads on, let's go!'

An intern holding the pads swung them around quickly, driving his elbow into the Plexiglas mask of a nurse, knocking it out of the frame.

'Jesus! Are you okay?'

'Somebody help Erin! Her shield's gone!'

'The pad – I need it now!'

'I don't feel a pulse!'

'He's in PEA!'

'EKG, let's go, let's go!'

'Erin's been exposed!'

'What's his rhythm now?'

'Looks like sinus.'

'Erin – get another mask on, fast!'

'Get me an echo, let's rule out an effusion.'

'No, no, give me an angiocath – that's how you do it.'

'He's flat line now! He's flat line!'

'Let's go with epitatropine and pace with the pads.'

'He's still flat line.'

'Where's his pulse?'

'I got no pulse.'

'Compressions, please!'

'He's flat line.'

It went on like this for forty-five minutes with everyone in the room except the grim reaper working at a feverish pitch. When it was over the notes documenting the team's efforts would run four pages long. The lead surgeon was the one who finally called it: 'Time of death, fourteen-forty-six.'

A resident had brought the nurse, Erin, another head protector even though she'd already been exposed to contaminated aerosols and would have to be quarantined. Another nurse straightened a bag of blood-filled urine that had been knocked over and was threatening to leak.

The attending physician drank half a cup of black coffee and headed for the lounge to tell Judge Warren Friedman and his wife what had happened to their son. Only then would he call CDC and give them the news.

MELISSA STOOD WAIST deep in the Atlantic Ocean looking at their temporary dream house. The glass walls reflecting light off the sand and water made the house seem to grow out of the beach, white and shimmering. At night, with soft lights and candles glowing in the windows, it would be stunning.

She dropped beneath the surface and let the cold water envelop her. When she ran out of breath she stood up and waded toward the beach. David's plane had arrived on time, and after picking up a leased BMW 325i convertible with a silver body and a black top, they drove to the beach house so he could see it. Linda had given her the keys and told them to spend the afternoon there.

The minute they drove up, David said it felt right, what a find. Melissa called Linda who said she'd already spoken to the Butterfields' attorney and everything was set. The house was theirs.

They drove over to Ben Ben-Zevi's house where Melissa packed up her things and left a note saying they'd found a house and would call him later to see if he'd join them for dinner. David brought her back to the beach house and went to a mall in Aventura to pick up soap and toothpaste while Melissa unpacked their bags and made herself familiar with the house. Waiting for him to return, she'd decided to take a swim.

She walked across the sand to the outdoor shower hidden by a sea grape tree at the north end of the ground floor, stripped off her bikini, and turned on the water. In a wooden caddy was a bottle of shampoo she used on her hair and body, enjoying the feel of the sand and salt sliding off her skin. She turned off the water and walked naked through the glass door to the stack of fluffy white towels on the redwood bench outside the steam room. It was one of those January days Floridians hated to admit existed: sixty-two degrees, partly cloudy, damp and cold. She shivered. The steam room beckoned.

Using the key under the towels, she unlocked the door and stepped inside, found the steam controls behind the door, hit the on button, and listened to the pipes clink to life. She stepped outside, picked up her cell phone, and dialed David.

'It's me,' she said. 'Where are you?'

'Just leaving the mall. What's going on?'

'Took a swim. How far away are you?'

'Fifteen minutes. Kinda cold to be swimming, isn't it?'

'Brisk. Hurry up.'

'What's cooking?'

'Me. I'll be in the steam room.'

'Anything you want me to bring?'

'Just your imagination.'

She hung up and laid the phone on her bag and felt the goose bumps rise. So many towels, so much luxury. She picked one up, then two more and walked to a console in the hallway that held a stereo system. There were CDs in a rack; she picked the first ones she saw – Madonna, k. d. lang, Tori Amos – and loaded them. A speaker switch said 'Hallway,' another 'Steam Room.' She selected both, touched 'Play,' adjusted the volume, and went back into the white-tiled chamber. After spreading a terrycloth towel over the redwood massage table, she climbed on and stretched out on her back.

The room was a cocoon. She exhaled grandly. It was the first time in weeks she felt contented. Washington, Justice, the FBI, Adalwolf, all seemed a million miles away. She loved this house. She pictured clambakes on the beach, the blue room for the baby. She laid her hands on her stomach. It felt firm and flat. If she was lucky it would be bulging soon. She wondered if she'd have stretch marks. She'd have to use some of the lotion Ben made for pregnant women, a combination of castor oil and lanolin.

She began worrying. Realistically, the odds were still against a pregnancy. Then she told herself to stop raining on her own parade. Positive signs were everywhere, even in her horoscope. *Spend today fantasizing about where you want to be, embrace your dream and it will show you the way.* She didn't believe in horoscopes, and yet . . .

She turned over. The room was getting hot. Her mind wandered to bedding. She wondered what color the sheets were in the master bedroom. *Where is he?* She checked her watch. Five minutes had passed since she'd called him.

She got up and turned the steam valve to Automatic Slow. A stream of vapor kept the room fogged and hot. She returned to the redwood slab and lay on her back again, her hands at her sides, a Mayan princess ready to be sacrificed. k. d. lang sang softly. Drums beat a steady rhythm in Melissa's head. Her skin glistened with beads of sweat and condensed steam. Her eyes closed. Her hand strayed. She was very ready.

SHE HEARD A NOISE outside and looked up to see the steam room door open. Through the mist she saw David pull the door handle behind him, forcing the pneumatic cylinder to close faster.

'Hi, there,' he said.

He was already undressed and carried a red plastic bucket in one hand, his beat-up leather briefcase, strangely, in the other. He set them on the floor next to the island she was lying on and leaned down and kissed her. His lips were cool. She closed her eyes.

He reached into his briefcase and pulled out a silk necktie with blue and red stripes. After laying it across her eyes, he tied it behind her head and lowered her gently back onto the surface. She heard him fumble in the briefcase, heard liquid expelled from a plastic bottle, then the clicking sound of lotion being rubbed between his palms.

He placed his hands on her neck and began massaging it, down to her shoulders, then her face. His fingers wound into her hair, onto her scalp, down her forehead, across the necktie and onto her temples. Fresh steam turned the room warm and cottony soft.

He lifted her arms from her sides and laid them above her head and massaged her from her hands down to her breasts. She heard him fumble in the plastic bucket, then felt the drip of ice water on her breasts . . . the touch of an ice cube in the hollow of her throat.

He let the cube melt a moment, then brought it down the center of her chest and drew figure eights around her nipples, making them hard before warming them with his tongue. She reached for him, but he put her arms back over her head. She was the female sacrifice, he was the Mayan chief.

She felt him sit on the bench next to her thighs and rub a pair of ice cubes across her midriff and down her sides, leaving cool traces on warm skin that tingled under the steam. She didn't know the path he was taking but she knew where he was headed. He was taking his time. He was taking *her* time.

He massaged her feet with oil, pressing his thumbs deep into her soles, squeezing her ankles in both hands, one after the other. She heard the bucket again and felt his hands return to her feet with more ice. They moved up her calves, across her knees, up the front of her thighs, moving in harmony with each other. She felt him massage her hips and outer thighs. Pressure from his hands spread her legs enough to massage her inner thighs.

She felt him get up from his sitting position and place his knees at her feet. Felt them work up between her legs. Felt ice again, this time on her belly, then again on her breasts. Felt his hardness against her thigh when he reached for it.

He drew the ice down her skin, down her abdomen to her silky hair, his cold fingertips lingering to make small, wet circles. His face was so close to her midsection now she could feel his breath on her skin, warm and steamy like the air, the stubble of his five o'clock shadow occasionally touching her. More ice and soft fingers between her legs. Melting ice trickling down crevices. There was madness in his method. She liked it.

He spread her legs a bit more and let his tongue chase the melting rivulets. She lowered her arms from above her head and wound her fingers into his hair. The ice had melted now. She felt his lips meet her nerve endings . . . felt herself swelling and rising, the center of her turning like the hands of a clock. *Don't stop . . . don't stop . . . even if the earth splits in two, don't stop.*

The soles of her feet turned hot. *Turn me into smoke and send me up to the gods. . . .* Then, the long, slow curve of a powerful, *Oh, yes.*

She lay still breathing hard, recovering. More steam entered the room, some of it, it seemed, from her body. They'd been together in Miami for only a few hours, but already life was good. The two of them hadn't been this close for a long time. She untied the knot on the blindfold, lifted it off, and pulled his face up to hers.

'I'm so glad we're here,' she said.

He kissed her neck and cheek and settled his lips on her ear. 'I love you, baby.'

'I love you, too,' she said.

He kissed her hair. She let her arms drop at her sides. He lay next to her on the damp towel. The temperature was perfect for naked bodies at rest. After a few minutes, he stirred to get up.

'Not so fast,' she said.

She rose to her elbow and was kissing his neck when they heard a voice – then two of them – a pair of men talking in the hallway outside the steam room. Workers here on Saturday? The door wasn't locked.

David put his hand on her shoulder, rolled off the platform, walked to the door and looked out the window. The men were gone, but now there was banging on pipes.

'They're working on the steam system,' he said, tossing her a towel.

She wrapped it around herself and came to the door. The coast was clear. She went out first.

'I owe you one,' she said.

THE CROWD GOT TO ITS feet and went wild after Michael Jordan made one of his tongue-out, signature baskets to tie the game. It was Saturday night, the Wizards were in contention, the beer was cold and the mustard yellow. Harris looked down at the seat next to him and saw his ten-year-old daughter, Kobie, reading *Harry Potter*. He sat down before his pals did.

'You're not having fun, are you?' he said to her.

'I'm not into basketball, Dad.' She turned a page.

The next basket was Harris's cue. He turned to his friend Leon, rolled his eyes toward Kobie, and said, 'We gotta go.' Leon patted Kobie on the back as she and her father worked their way toward the aisle. They walked through a cold rain to the parking lot with the sound of the crowd cheering behind them. Harris clicked open the doors on their Jeep. It was 8:30.

'Harry Potter, huh?' he said.

If they hurried, there was still time.

HARRIS LAID HIS microchip-embedded security card on the electronic reader and entered the J. Edgar Hoover Building with Kobie at his side. Hanging his ID around his neck, he led her into the elevator and to the third floor, down a wide hallway, and into the Bureau's central research room. Harris stooped down and spoke to Kobie. 'I want you to wait here.'

'Where are you going?'

'Just wait for me, okay?' He looked her in the eye. Would she freak out and tell him not to leave her alone, or would she handle it? She dug into her pocket, pulled out a piece of red licorice, and bit off a hunk. Harriet Potter at her best. He opened the door and walked to a desk half way across the room.

'What are *you* doing here?' the head clerk asked.

Harris pulled up a chair in front of her desk, sat down, and rested his ankle on his knee.

She said, 'After what happened in Atlantic City, I wasn't sure I'd ever see you again.'

Harris's foot started jiggling.

The head clerk looked up and said, 'What is it?'

'Archives B.'

She heaved a little sigh. 'Harris, you know I can't let you go in there.'

He leaned forward and spoke softly. 'What's the big deal? Everything in there is ancient history.'

'Harris.'

'Fifteen minutes, that's all.'

The woman's voice lowered. 'If you get caught, I'll be fired.'

'Nobody's there this time of day. Besides, I brought a lookout.'

'Who?'

'My daughter.'

He walked back to the door, opened it, brought Kobie inside and introduced her.

'Hello, Kobie,' the chief clerk said. 'Oh my, she looks just like you.'

The clerk was caving in, he could tell. She opened her top drawer, lifted a magnetic key card stamped *Authorized Access Only*, and slid it across the desk. Harris picked it up and returned the chair to its place.

'Fifteen minutes,' she said.

Harris and Kobie left and climbed the steps to the next floor, walked down a hallway, and found the room. He unlocked the door and entered. Washington's street lamps offered enough light to let him maneuver in the dark. 'I want you to sit by the door and listen carefully,' he said, closing the door. 'If you hear footsteps, let me know, okay?'

Kobie came alive with the thrill of a caper. She sat on the floor and hugged her knees, making herself small. 'We're being *bad*, aren't we?' she said happily.

'Hey, who's your daddy?'

'An FBI man.'

'And who's the FBI?'

'The good guys.' She had to revise her opinion. 'So we're being *sneaky*.'

'An FBI girl has to know how to sneak up on the bad guys,' he said.

She hunched her shoulders and laughed. He turned on the computer. *One thousand and one*, he told himself, waiting for the machine to boot up. If he got caught he'd do one year in Leavenworth and one thousand in hell for involving his daughter. His watch said they'd already lost four minutes. Come on, boot up.

The program finally beeped, signaling it was ready. He opened a search window and entered the phrase: *Maxima debetur puero reverentia*. He hit *Find* and got nothing. He entered the same phrase in English: 'The greatest respect is owed to a child.'

'**No Match Found.**'

He started over.

He tried the phrases in pieces: *Maxima*. Nothing. *Debetur*. Nothing. He went word-by-word through the phrase in Latin, each time receiving the same answer: '**No Match Found.**' It was almost nine. They were out of time.

He entered another phrase on a whim, knowing that whims were not whims but a combination of subconscious experience and logic. Luck, Leo Durocher once said, was the residue of the well prepared. He entered 'French Convent.' The computer gave him something he hadn't seen before. It said, **T-22**.

What was T-22?

He entered it and hit search. The only thing that came up was a equally cryptic: **File HG/OC**.

'Daddy!' Kobie whispered.

'What's wrong?'

'I hear footsteps!'

He put his finger to his lips.

She rested her chin on her knees and waited.

Harris could hear the footsteps himself now. They came to the door and stopped. After a moment, there was the sound of a key moving into the lock. Harris stood up from his chair and waited, knowing it was too late to turn off the computer and too late to find a good reason for being there. The door opened just far enough for someone to enter.

IT WAS THE HEAD CLERK. She stepped inside and closed the door behind her.

'You said fifteen minutes!' she whispered.

'Take a look at this,' Harris said.

'You've got to get out of here!'

'One look.'

She walked over to the monitor. 'What in the world are you into?'

'You tell me.'

'Harris—'

'What's T-22?'

The librarian examined the information. 'I don't know, probably a file.'

'What kind of file?'

'It could refer to subject matter, a person, or a case.' She looked again. 'In the old days T was the designation for a confidential informant. "T" for "Tattletale."'

'How about this?' He changed screens and pointed at **File HG/OC**.

'Good Lord, Harris. HG is Helen Gandy, Hoover's lifelong personal assistant, and OC means Official and Confidential.'

'We talking about J. Edgar's personal files?'

'Of course! Those were his blackmail files, the dirt he dug up on everybody from Warren Harding to Richard Nixon. There's stuff in there on presidents, senators, congressmen, judges, entertainers – everybody who was anybody.'

'I thought all of it was public now.'

'Most of it is. Now turn off the computer!'

He shut it down, made sure nothing was out of place, and went to the door.

'What do you mean, most of it?'

'When Hoover died Helen Gandy destroyed everything on the so-called "D list", packed up a few files she wanted to keep, and left the rest behind. What she took with her never got published.' She motioned for Kobie to leave first, then closed the door behind them.

'What happened to it?'

'Who knows?'

'Where is she now?'

'She died a few years ago in a nursing home in Deland, Florida, near Orlando.' They walked down the stair to the third floor.

'Do you have an index to the O & C files?' Harris asked.

'Of course.'

'How about—'

'It's out of the question.'

'But—'

'File an FOIA request, Harris. I've done all I can.'

Harris and Kobie said goodbye to her, put on their raincoats, and took the elevator to the basement garage. Climbing into his jeep, Harris had two questions:

Who was T-22? And where did Kobie get her cool?

They drove out of the garage into a nasty January sleet.

IT WAS AS BALMY A Saturday night in Miami as it was a cold one in Washington, D.C. Ben and Melissa had just finished dinner and were sitting in the study of Ben's Coral Gables house waiting for David to pick her up on his way home from his new *Times* office in downtown Miami. Ben's bow tie was loose and he was swirling two fingers of thirty-year-old Macallan in a crystal tumbler. The conversation turned to his days in the camp.

'The gleeful sadism of the SS was sickening,' he said, 'but you got used to it. You were never unaware of what was happening, but the constant brutality dulled your senses, thank God. Being in a perpetual state of outrage was exhausting, and dangerous.'

Adalwolf had lived in the skin of Benjamin Ben-Zevi for so long he was a convincing Holocaust survivor even to himself. Besides, there were dimly recalled qualities about the real Benjamin Ben-Zevi which he'd genuinely admired, things like the boy's good humor and obedient attitude. Adalwolf had discovered long ago that you could respect certain things about the people you hated. He took a sip and swirled his glass some more.

'There were all manner of atrocities committed by all kinds of so-called doctors,' he said. 'Most of the so-called "science" was bogus, and everything they did violated the principles of medicine.' Another drink. His head tilted back in his leather club chair, his eyes closed. Melissa sat in a rocking chair that had been Myrna Ben-Zevi's favorite and listened.

Ben opened his eyes and shifted in his chair. 'All the doctors were callous, but only Mengele programmed death into all his experiments. He said the only accurate way to measure the effectiveness of his work was with an autopsy.' He was no longer swirling his scotch, just sitting quietly.

'I told the children he called into the dissection room that I had good news, they were going to undergo a harmless physical.' He nodded slightly. 'Chocolate was my main way of winning their confidence. That and lies.' He looked at her. 'I became very good at it.'

Melissa's mouth was dry but she didn't lift her glass.

'I told myself being kind to frightened children was a good thing. Mengele tried all kinds of experiments without anesthesia, so whatever I could do to calm them seemed like a favor. But I was kidding myself. He once grafted twins together to see what would happen if you mixed their blood. By the time they were returned to their barracks they were in such pain their own mother felt impelled to kill them with a dose of hoarded morphine.'

He was starting to re-live the cases. Sometimes he could almost generate sympathy for his victims, although when he tried, it was an intellectual exercise, not true emotion.

'Adalwolf made me teach the children a hymn before bringing them into the room. When they were on the stretcher, he made them sing it.'

Melissa rubbed the rim of her glass, feeling like an eavesdropper now.

'All those blindfolded boys and girls,' he said, 'singing Latin and German lyrics they didn't even understand. All those clear, innocent voices.' He summoned tears the way an actor does by thinking of something awful. In his case, it was easy: he pictured himself at fourteen, his last day at the convent.

'He once told me . . .' He wiped the tears from his cheek. 'He once told me he could insert a needle into a child's heart so smoothly it didn't even know it was there. And it was true, I saw it happen. You'd hear these voices singing, and then he'd inject chloroform into the heart and a voice would just . . . disappear.' He covered his eyes. Melissa wiped hers with the underside of her wrist.

After a while Ben-Zevi lowered his hands and let out a long 'Ahhh,' as a way of dismissing the memory. He looked her in the eye. 'I have worked hard to forget, Melissa.'

'You were only twelve years old,' Melissa said. 'You—'

'I know, I know, I was young and scared, I didn't want to die, the children were going to be killed anyway, I know all that, but it didn't excuse what I did.' He sat staring. 'If it did, why am I so ashamed?'

She said, 'All the Nazis I've prosecuted can't make up for what Adalwolf did.'

'That's not true.' He leaned forward with great effort and got to his feet. Taking her hand, he said, 'I'm so proud of what you do. It's astounding. If you ever get back to the case I'll do anything I can to help you find him. But right now it's time for you to light a candle of your own and get pregnant.'

'You have confidence in Eric, don't you?'

'Completely. He's brilliant, he's educated, and he's an excellent surgeon. Why do you ask?'

She shook her head. 'Just nervous.'

'I've never seen a patient who wasn't.'

'Is there anything I should be doing I'm not?' she said.

'Nothing except stop working so hard and relax. Let others worry about catching Adalwolf, Melissa. Spend time with David. You'll regret it if you don't.'

She gave Ben a long hug goodnight. He asked her to forgive him for not staying up until David arrived, but she told him not to worry, go to bed and get some rest. He said he was going to temple in the morning and invited her and David to go with him, but she said they had other plans. He nodded and headed for the door. She finished her iced tea and opened her laptop. There were two e-mails waiting.

The first was from Barry Sherer telling her some of the details of Jeremy Friedman's death. She rested her forehead in her hand and read it quietly. The second was from Harris saying he'd found a reference to a file called T-22 in Hoover's O & C files but didn't know what to make of it.

She printed out both messages, laid them on Ben's desk, exited the program, and headed for the guest room to pick up the items she'd left behind. Why was she a Nazi hunter? After hearing Ben's story, how could she not be? After hearing how Jeremy Friedman had died, why would she ask?

She opened the medicine cabinet, took out her skin toner, and packed it away. *Where are you. Adalwolf? You've got a bead on me, but I haven't got one on you. Make a mistake. Send up a flare. I'm trying to bring a child into the world and it's not safe with you still out there somewhere.*

OTTO HELLER DONNED HIS biohazard gear and entered the hospital room. Erin O'Reilly, the nurse whose face mask had been broken during the attempted resuscitation of Jeremy Friedman, lay in bed with potato chips, magazines, and a TV remote control on the coverlet. She looked up from her Julia Quinn novel and turned off the TV set.

'How are you feeling?' Otto said.

'Fine,' she said. 'When can I get out of here?'

Otto read her chart, took her temperature, and asked her some more questions. She'd had a twelve-hour headache and a low grade fever for six hours, but nothing more. No coughing, bleeding, sore throat, epithelial sloughing, nothing serious. In fact, if she'd had these symptoms on a weekend, she wouldn't have given them a second thought.

And yet pathology showed that she'd contracted the NTX virus.

Otto took his head gear off – it was hot and cumbersome.

'Am I well?' she asked.

'As a matter of fact, I'd say you are,' Otto said. 'If your internist agrees, you can go home tomorrow.'

'Home? I have to go to work.'

Otto took her pulse, patted her hand, and started to leave. At the door he said, 'Tell me something. You aren't Jewish, are you?'

'With a name like O'Reilly?'

'I thought it might be your married name.'

'I'm single.'

'Any Jewish relatives?'

She smiled at the thought. 'There weren't a lot of Jews in Northern Ireland.'

'Enjoy the rest of the day in bed.' He opened the door and left.

'PARIS, PARIS, PARIS, where the heck is it?' Harris was talking to himself as he sorted through a stack of CDs at the living room console. He finally found the album he was looking for, popped it out of the jewel case, dropped it into the CD tray, and hit Play. A few seconds later Count Basie was doing his classic version of *April in Paris*.

Harris lowered the lights and turned up the volume as high as he could without waking Kobie and Sammy, then walked into the bedroom where Sherrie was sitting on the bed sorting socks and watching *Sex and the City*. Saying nothing, he took her by the hand and pulled her up and brought her into the living room.

'What?' she said.

He took her into his arms and started dancing.

'What's gotten into you?' she said.

'April in Paris,' he said. He sang the lyrics into her ear. She fell into the dance. 'We're going to Paris,' he said.

'We are?'

'As soon as your mom can watch the kids.'

'She's coming in two weeks.'

'Then you'd better start packing.'

She leaned back and looked at him. 'Are you serious?'

'You've been wanting to see Paris for years. Now that I'm off the job, it's time.'

'It's not April, it's January,' she said. She smiled at him, then put her cheek on his shoulder and continued to dance. He sang and she listened. When the song had almost ended, she said, 'How long will it take?'

'How long will what take?' he said.

'The investigation, the real reason for the trip.'

He held her tight and danced. 'One day, two at most.'

She heard the song end in his arms, murmuring, 'Not as bad as I thought.'

NO QUESTION ABOUT IT, she was feeling a little weird.

Melissa was on the examining table again: another day, another ultrasound. It had been ten days since her first hormone injection, and whoever had ridiculed the term 'raging hormones' had never been through a modern fertility procedure. The mood swings were wild. One minute she felt euphoric, the next minute depressed. Turn left and she was Superwoman, turn right and she was the Agent of Doom. When she thought about the future she was self-confident – until she thought about it twice and shook in her boots. Optimistic, pessimistic; up and down. The emotional rollercoaster was starting to wear her out.

Not that the physical ride was any better. She craved candy and olives and chocolate and spareribs, anything with salt and sugar and fat. She gained three pounds and felt as bloated as a hog. She wasn't allowed to jog because she wasn't supposed to get her heart beat above 120 per minute. Her sex life was sporadic, which was a disappointment one day and blessed relief the next. She took expectorants and baby aspirin to thin out the lining of her uterus. Two nights earlier she'd actually poured cherry-flavored cough syrup over vanilla ice cream and eaten it like a sundae, but only after finishing off a plate of nachos and salsa.

At least Harris was going to France to see what he could find. She herself hadn't done anything on the case for a week.

The nurse inserted the sonogram wand into her vagina. Cold

jelly. Beep tones. All eyes on the monitor. Looking for eggs. Privacy? She was so accustomed to people walking around her with legs spread, if she'd had a fingernail file she would have done her nails.

She kept a diary and reported her symptoms to Eric, sometimes laughing as she talked, sometimes crying. He sympathized and said 'Don't worry, it's normal, believe me, I've seen worse.'

Thank God today was the last day.

She stared at the ceiling and waited for the procedure to end. Pictures of her ovaries were blinking on the black-and-white monitor.

David had been great during her hormone jag. Despite having a new beat to cover for the *Times* – financial corruption in Miami – he left home late and got home early and worked as much as possible in his comfortable den. He jogged on the beach every afternoon, swam with her in the ocean – the pool was empty – and took a steam bath every day. Construction was occasionally noisy, but the workmen stopped at three-thirty sharp.

He made late-night runs for her to Blockbuster, the pharmacy, and KFC. He took her temperature and monitored her pulse. The cliché seemed to be true: having a baby brought couples closer together. She loved him more than ever, except when the hormones kicked in and she hated him.

The whirring sound stopped. The nurse helped remove her feet from the stirrups. Eric stepped to her side and lifted her into a sitting position.

'You've got four follicles' – the tiny sacks that held her eggs – 'eighteen to twenty-two millimeters.'

'Is that good?' she said.

'That's excellent,' he said. 'I'm giving you the B-HCG.'

Beta human chorionic gonadotropin – the same chemical home pregnancy tests measured with 'dip sticks' – the stuff a woman's body produced when she was pregnant. Giving her a boost of it would help ripen her eggs. Eric asked her to lift her gown to take the injection, but just then her cell phone rang. He found her shoulder bag and handed it to her. She looked in the message window and saw that it was Harris.

'Hello?'

'Where have I got you?' he said.

'On an operating table.' She lifted her gown.

'Jesus, Melissa, do you live in that place?'

'It's not as bad as it sounds.' Dr. Brandt cleaned a spot on her hip with an alcohol pad.

'I'm headed for France,' Harris said. 'We may need to talk while I'm there.'

'I'll have the cell phone on, and the computer, too. Ouch.'

'What's wrong?'

'Took a shot in the tush.'

'Sherrie says hi.'

'Tell her to bring back pictures.' She hung up and pulled down her gown.

'Was that about your case?' Eric said, disposing of the needle.

'Yes.' She offered nothing more. 'But it's difficult to talk about.'

'I shouldn't be so nosy.' He leaned back on a counter, his feet crossed. 'Are you ready?'

'For what?'

'The day after tomorrow we harvest your eggs.'

For some reason it came as a surprise. 'I'm ready.'

'Have we done a sperm count on David?'

'I don't think so.'

He looked irritated. 'That should have been done by now. Can he come over today?'

'I'll call him.'

'After that he can't have sex until we harvest the eggs. I want a high sperm count.'

He studied her face. 'Are you ready to give up the mood swings?'

She scowled. 'Mood swings? What mood swings?'

Eric Brandt laughed at her and left the room. She laughed, too, until he was gone. Then for no reason whatsoever, she burst into tears.

DAVID WAS SITTING IN an examining room at the clinic waiting to have his sperm tested when the door opened and a nurse stepped in.

'Good evening, Mr. Gale. My name is Eileen Over, and I'm your nurse.'

He set down the dirty magazine they'd given him and looked up. Her voice was well known to him but the outfit wasn't. She wore white spiked heels that elongated her calves, sheer white stockings, and a white nurse's dress so short it barely covered the crease where her legs met her bottom. The waist and midriff were tight, accentuating the fullness of familiar tan breasts that wanted to spill out of her partly unzipped top. Then there was the face he knew so well, beautiful and loaded with big brown eyes.

She wasn't a nurse, and her name wasn't Eileen Over, Forward, or Backward. It was Melissa in a nurse's uniform, and this was her way of finishing the unfinished business of the steam room. He repositioned himself on the white paper of the examining table and straightened his hospital gown. 'Hello, baby,' he said. 'Where'd you get the outfit?'

'Mr. Gale,' she said. 'Despite what you may be thinking I am not your "baby". and I'd appreciate your addressing me as Nurse Eileen.'

'Yes, M'am.'

Melissa opened a shrink-wrapped, pint-sized plastic container and set it next to the sink. 'According to the doctor's instructions,' she said, opening an alcohol pad, 'we're here to collect your sperm for a test, is that right?' She added a couple more items to the tray.

'Guess so.' She glanced at him; he added, 'M'am.'

'Well, then, let's get to it.'

She stepped up to the end of the examining table, set the tray next to him, picked up the magazine, and tossed it onto a wooden chair next to the scale. 'You aren't going to need that,' she said.

'Is that so?' Another disapproving look. 'M'am.'

She put her hand on his chest and pushed him onto his back. He lifted his head and craned his neck to see what she was doing. She gathered up his hospital gown and bunched it on his stomach.

'Hm, what have we here? Is this the donor organ?'

'That's the *donor*'s organ, not the *donor* organ,' he said. 'Jesus.'

'Apparently it's ready to donate,' she said. 'Is it always in such an agitated state?'

'Only in the company of nurses with spiked heels and dresses so short you can see their—'

'Did you *say nurses*?' she said.

'No, M'am. One nurse in particular.'

'Good answer.' Melissa swung a pair of padded leg rests and metal stirrups into place at the end of the table.

'What are those for?' he said, his voice an octave higher.

'You'll see.'

Her reply made him a little less cocky.

'I need to take your temperature now,' she said, lifting a thermometer.

He sat up. 'Whoa, where you planning to put that thing?'

She hesitated long enough to enjoy the moment, then pushed him back down and stuck the thermometer into his mouth.

He said, 'Whucht my temper-chur got to do wif anything?'

'Please don't talk with your mouth full, Mr. Gale.'

He grunted, 'That-ch my line.'

Standing between his legs, she placed her warm hands on his thighs, took some K-Y jelly off the tray, and began her therapeutic massage. A moment later she took the thermometer out of his mouth and laid it on the tray without looking at it.

'Do I have a fever?' he asked.

'I certainly hope so,' she said. She put her hand under her dress and withdrew a warm, glistening finger which she put into his mouth. Then she placed his hand on himself. 'Hold this a minute, I'll be right back.'

'Where are you going?'

She picked up a sterile plastic cup and put his feet into the stirrups.

'Why you doing that?' he said.

'Empathy,' she said. 'Two days from now I'll be in a pair of these things myself.'

'Nurse Eileen—'

'Shush,' she said. 'I have work to do.'

She straightened her little white hat and leaned down, and before long he had something more he wanted to say.

'Oh-oh, Nurse Eileen, I . . .'

She lifted her head and was running an alcohol pad over him for a 'clean catch' when all heaven broke loose. She used the cup in time, then gave him a kiss on the cheek and whispered, 'You're a good patient, Mr. Gale,' and took her harvest to the door. Fun and games were now over. Somebody actually had to count the tadpoles.

Making babies wasn't what it used to be.

IT WAS A FIFTEENTH-CENTURY French convent surrounded by Roman cypress trees, situated on a hill in the Loire Valley. Walking from his rented car to the wooden door, Harris saw a stone foundation that was still strong, its walls cracked by time and weather but not settling. It was unseasonably warm and clear for a January day in the south of France. Maybe it was his imagination, but he thought there was luck in the air.

He knocked and waited, searching for a plaque or inscription showing the Latin phrase that had brought him here. After a minute the door opened and the sister he'd called from town appeared in a blue and gray habit. 'Monsieur Johnson,' she said in lovely French-accented English. 'Come in.'

The convent was laid out in the shape of a squared U. He entered the foyer at the bottom of the U and followed the sister to a reading room that smelled like wooden pews. Thoughts of communion descended on him, but he didn't dwell on them. This was a strictly secular mission.

She led him to a courtyard, then across it to an iron gate at the top of the U where she stood to the side and pointed. Fifty yards away, in a field of uncut grass, a nun in a wool caftan and scarves sat in a canvas-backed chair with a paint brush in hand and an easel between her and a distant valley.

Harris thanked the sister and pushed the cast-iron gate open and tramped out into the field. The air was filled with the musky scent of wet earth. He made sure the old woman heard his footsteps as he approached. Reaching her side, he waited for her to acknowledge him, but she ignored him and continued to paint. A thin winter haze hung across the valley that she was struggling to capture on canvas.

'If you don't mind my saying so,' he said, 'it needs a touch of magenta.'

She finished emptying her brush and nodded ever so slightly, inviting him to step in front of her. Her face, when he saw it, had the look of mild indifference earned by a woman in her nineties.

'It's too green,' he said. 'There's rouge in the mist that's picked up from the afternoon light. A touch of magenta will catch it.'

She stared at him without speaking, making him wonder if she understood English. She turned to the easel tray, pawed through the tubes of paint, and squeezed a line of magenta onto her palate. He waited as she dipped the bristles of a small brush into it, wiped the excess on a dry spot of her palette, and began a light touch on the canvas. With a caricatured French accent, she said, 'Do you paint?'

'Not any more.' He watched as her shaking hand attempted to apply light strokes.

'Now look,' she said. 'Too much.' She took a small rag, tightened it on her index finger, and dipped it into solvent to wipe away the paint. 'And who is my new teacher?'

'My name is Harris Johnson. I'm an investigator with the United States government.'

Her eyes remained focused on the canvas. 'I knew my painting was bad, Mr. Johnson, but I didn't know it was *that* bad.' She dried her brush and tried again.

'Mother Marie-Catherine,' he said, 'I'm looking for someone who may have been one of your students many years ago. A boy by the name of Adalwolf.'

'Adalwolf?' Her brush whisked over the canvas. *'Je ne le connais pas.'*

Harris opened up the leather pouch he was carrying. 'He was

born in nineteen twenty-eight.' He pulled out the photograph of Adalwolf and his prisoner lab assistants standing in front of the lab. 'This was taken in nineteen forty-three, when he was fifteen.'

She thinned the magenta with linseed oil and spread it with a clean brush. This time it caught the mist. Holding her brush, she reached out and took the photograph from Harris and tilted her head back to see it. Her fingers opened and the paint brush fell to the ground. 'Mon Dieu.'

'What is it?' Harris said.

'It is my little Englishman,' she said.

'What Englishman?'

She pointed at Adalwolf. 'Henri,' she said. 'Henri Hallam Brandon.'

THIS TIME IT WASN'T fun and games, it was serious.

Melissa lay on her back with her feet in stirrups – yet again – staring at the ceiling and listening to soft music. She was a reasonably resilient woman, but even Wonder Woman would have been emotionally drained by now. She thought there should be something more romantic about conception than all this machinery, medicine, and light. At least, something a little more solemn. She closed her eyes and said a small prayer begging for conception. If it didn't work, she wasn't sure she had it in her to try again.

She heard the clatter of stainless steel instruments dropped into stainless steel trays and opened her eyes. A nurse bustled over to the side of the room and handed a vacuum-sealed jar through a window to a lab technician on the other side.

'We've got the follicles,' Dr. Brandt said, pulling down his surgeon's mask. To a nurse he said, 'Tell David it's time to make his contribution.'

MOTHER MARIE-CATHERINE and Harris sat in the convent's courtyard surrounded by centuries-old stone walls, their small, square windows giving only a hint of the surrounding vineyards. She couldn't stop looking at the photograph. The rims of her eyelids were magnified by a thin layer of tears.

'They took him away when he was fourteen,' she said.

'Who did?' Harris was taking notes.

'The Gestapo,' she said. 'They wore baggy suits and stupid fedoras. I stood right there' – she pointed at the door to the kitchen – 'and he cried so hard he couldn't speak. He held onto me and begged me not to let them take him.' She dried her eyes. 'What could I do? It was nineteen forty-two. The Nazis ruled the country, Vichy or no Vichy.'

'Did they give an explanation?' He got up and circled right and aimed his digital camera at the door with Mother Marie-Catherine in the foreground.

'They explained nothing. I told them they couldn't touch him without the permission of Monsieur Halliburton, but they wouldn't listen.'

'Who was Mr. Halliburton?' He took a picture of her and set the camera on a stone wall and put it on a ten-second automatic shutter to catch the two of them together.

'The man who brought him here.'

'From England?'

'From London, yes.'

This made no sense. He stooped next to her chair and pointed at the camera. They looked into the lens as it clicked.

'Do you know who Henri's parents were?'

'This was an orphanage, Mr. Johnson, parents were rarely known. When Henry was two years old he was brought here by a nurse and a man named Monsieur Halliburton who said the child's name was Henri Hallam Brandon. Of course, we accepted that.'

He retrieved his camera and sat back in his chair, taking notes again. 'Tell me what kind of boy he was.'

'Quiet and sensitive. When he was five years old he was caught stealing a flower for my birthday. The mother superior's reprimand nearly crushed him.'

'What about his interests?'

'He was very clever, my little Henri. He loved working with the winemakers. A very industrious boy. He had no other particular interests that I recall, other than the choir. He hated to pray but loved to sing.'

'After he was taken away did you ever see him again?' Harris asked.

'Never.'

'Do you have any photographs of him?'

She took a moment to collect herself then said, 'Come with me.'

HARRIS HELD HER CANE and helped her from her chair. Once she was on her feet she moved toward the door gracefully for a woman in her nineties, never stumbling on the grass or stone patio. After walking down a high-ceilinged corridor, they reached a small, starkly simple room containing a bed, a desk, and a wardrobe.

He stood and waited as she walked to the desktop holding a worn bible. She lifted the slanted, hinged lid and ran her fingers through a well of neatly organized contents, eventually coming to a wooden box filled with glossy black-and-white photographs. Shuffling through them, she found the one she wanted.

Harris took it and turned toward the window for light. It showed a group of children roughly the age of his ten-year-old daughter. A nun stood next to them. After studying her face a moment, he could see that it was Mother Marie-Catherine.

Next to her was Henri Hallam Brandon, a gangly boy with a rake in his hand. Harris couldn't take his eyes off him. How had an unassuming young English boy become such a monster? He searched for a clue, a hint of malevolence, a trace of the demon seed, but all he could see was an ordinary young boy's face. It occurred to him that this was only the second time he'd seen Adalwolf's picture.

Harris and the old nun chatted a few minutes more. It was time for vespers and dinner, which she took at five o'clock. The fragile vitality he'd seen an hour before was gone now, her face sad and fatigued. His visit had taken more out of her than he intended; it was time to leave.

'May I borrow the photograph?' he said.

The old woman waved yes and sat on the edge of her tiny bed. He put the photo into his pocket and touched her arm goodbye. He expected her to ask him to write and tell her if he discovered Henri Hallam Brandon, but she didn't. She lived in a different world now, a place where memories meant more than the future and reality was a thing of the past she beheld. She had her young Englishman in her heart, and that was all that mattered.

HARRIS GOT INTO HIS CAR on the convent driveway and drove to a little town nearby to rejoin Sherrie in the café where he'd left her with a guidebook and a cup of French coffee. She told him about a château they could reach in an hour if they left right away.

'I was thinking maybe we should catch a flight to Paris,' he said.

'Tonight?'

'Why not? That's our objective, isn't it?'

'We're not due in Paris for a week. We've got the whole south of France to cover first.'

'Oh, yeah, I forgot.'

She looked him over. 'What's the matter, Harris?'

'Nothing.'

'Tell me.'

'I have to get to London.'

'London's not on the way to Paris.'

'Once you're up there, it's a big sky.'

'What were you going to do, tell me after we boarded the plane?'

He smiled at her. 'Mother Marie-Catherine gave me a lead on Adalwolf. His father was someone named Halliburton. I want to take a detour to London and see what I can find.'

Sherrie finished her coffee. 'Tell you what. Why don't we go to London at the end of the trip?'

'Sounds like a deal.'

She reached out and turned his face to hers and examined it up close.

'What are you doing?' he asked.

'Just checking to see if your nose is okay,' she said.

'Why wouldn't it be?'

'No reason, but since you're going to be paying through it for a long, long time, I want to be sure.'

MELISSA WAS READING IN the morning sun when the call came in.

'Are you sitting down?' It was Eric Brandt.

'I am.'

'We've got an embryo.'

She sat up and lost her place in the book. 'Are you serious?'

'Actually, we've got three.'

'Oh, my God.' She put her hand on the mouthpiece and yelled toward the house. '*Day-vid!*' Back on the phone. 'We don't need triplets, Eric.'

'We'll try to get one to do the job,' he said.

David came outside. She said, 'It's Eric Brandt! We've got three embryos!'

David sat on the end of the chaise and put his hand on her leg. 'What happens next?' she asked the doctor.

'We'll do an implant day after tomorrow.'

'Fantastic!'

'See you Friday.'

She hung up. David put his arms around her. She held on to him and ran her fingers through his hair. 'In two days,' she said, 'I could be pregnant.'

She picked up the phone and dialed Ben to give him the news. He'd be ecstatic.

Ecstatic yes, more than she knew. But surprised, no.

'WE'RE HEADED FOR Provence.' Harris was in their rental car talking by cell phone to Melissa. 'Where are you?'

'At the clinic, where else?'

'Don't tell me you're on an operating table again.'

'I'm fully clothed and working on my laptop in Dr. Brandt's office until he returns. How's the trip?'

'It's raining. I met with an old nun at the convent who knew Adalwolf.'

'You're kidding!' She clicked on her Adalwolf file and began taking notes. 'What did she say?'

'She said he was sensitive and smart and afraid of being unloved and abandoned.'

'Aren't we all.'

'He liked working with the wine bottlers and singing in the choir. I have a photograph of him and her.'

'How did he get from a French convent to Auschwitz?'

'The Gestapo took him in nineteen forty-two.'

'The Gestapo? Why?'

'You tell me. Since we know he was working for Mengele in nineteen forty-three, they must have taken him straight to the camp.'

'How weird. Did you get a name?'

'Yeah. Henry Hallam Brandon.'

'Sounds English.'

'She said he was born in London, and when he was two years old he was brought to the convent by a man named Halliburton.'

'I'll try the internet, although it's probably not his real name. Should we tell Barry and the Task Force and have them run a check on NCIC?' The National Crime Information System was part of the FBI's computerized data bank.

Harris paused. 'Let's see what you and I can come up with first.'

'My feelings exactly,' she said. They both wanted to find Adalwolf themselves and shove it up the Department's ass.

Harris said, 'You haven't found anything on T-22, have you?'

'Nothing. I did a Nexis search and a meta search on the Internet.'

'Okay, talk to you later. I have to go to dinner.'

'Hey, how's the food?'

'Sherrie says it's fabulous.'

'What about you?'

'Acid reflux.'

'There's medicine for that, you know.'

'I've got bottles of it.'

'I was thinking of something called relaxation.'

'Never heard of it.'

'Come to Miami and try it. And tell Sherrie hello.'

Melissa hung up and went home.

Around seven o'clock, the doorbell rang. She went to the door and found Ben.

'What a surprise!' she said, ushering him inside.

'I thought I'd drop by and see your new digs,' he said. 'What a lovely place.'

She showed him around, then brought him into the living room and offered him a drink. She plugged in the laptop to charge it and opened the lid and read him the notes from her conversation with Harris.

'Does the name Henry Hallam Brandon mean anything to you?'

'No, why?'

'Harris found the convent where Adalwolf grew up as a boy,' she said. 'The nun who raised him is still alive and remembered him. She said his name is Henry Hallam Brandon and he was brought to the convent by an Englishman named Halliburton.'

Ben sat quietly a moment, as if he didn't understand what she was saying. His face was slightly flushed. 'An Englishman?'

'That's what she said.'

'We never knew him by any name except Adalwolf, and I never heard him speak English.' He took a drink and pondered. 'If he was English, why was he in a convent in France?'

'I don't know.'

'His father or guardian put him there when he was two years old. When he was fourteen the Gestapo took him and apparently delivered him to the Mengeles.'

'That's strange,' he said. 'Can you check out the name?'

'We'll run it through all the databanks and try.'

He moved to the edge of his chair. 'There's a list of names at Yad Vashem and the U.S. Holocaust Museum you could try.'

'I've got a better idea. Why don't you do it?'

He looked a little surprised, then said, 'Why not? I'd love to. There are Yitzkor books, too – memorial books at YIVO in New York I could check out. Maybe the ADL has something helpful, or the WJC.'

She enjoyed his enthusiasm. 'Try it on anyone who might know.'

'What am I looking for?'

'Anything that might help us track him down. An acquaintance, a family member, a place he lived after the war, his schooling, where he worked. '

'I'll start tomorrow.' He finished his drink and got up to go. 'You look relaxed,' he said. 'How are you feeling?'

'Good,' she said. 'Just waiting for news.'

'About Adalwolf or the pregnancy?'

'Both.'

IT WAS TWELVE DAYS since the *in vitro* implant. Twelve days of sun and relaxation, of worrying about pregnancy more than Adalwolf and the Justice Department's investigation. She was so at ease when the call finally came, she wasn't even expecting it. Dr. Brandt was on the telephone with news.

She listened carefully, then hung up and threw a stack of papers into the air and nearly broke a nail dialing David at the office. She pulled at the phone cord waiting for him to come on. When he did, she said two words neither of them thought they'd ever hear: 'I'm pregnant!'

BEN BEN-ZEVI – ADALWOLF – sat at the monitor in his underground laboratory, reading e-mail, notes, and files from Melissa's laptop. She and Harris Johnson were getting too close, but how to back them off wasn't clear. Everything he'd tried had only committed her more deeply to the case. It was time to send a more convincing message.

He re-read her e-mail. Harris Johnson was the father of two kids in Washington who were staying with their grandmother while Johnson and his wife toured Europe. That presented a distinct possibility. Having worked in Mengele's lab, he had a great deal of experience with children. How to gain their confidence. How to soothe their feelings. How to kill them.

He considered all his options and reluctantly decided what to do. Reluctantly not because he hated to use an innocent bystander to make a point, but because it was risky. He'd have to do it carefully. If he got caught, everything would collapse. With the virus now effective, and with Melissa's pregnancy clock ticking, this was *not* the time to make a mistake.

He got out of his chair and rummaged through a storage chest of biotech apparatus that was part of a well-equipped laboratory. After finding what he wanted, he slipped it over his head and tried it on, then decided to do a bench test of it. If it held up, he knew exactly how to make his point.

He'd warned her more than once. Now, she gave him no choice.

'WE HAVE NOTHING ON A Henry Hallam Brandon,' the ruddy-faced man said. His name was George Spencer, and he was a detective with MI5, the British internal security agency that was the rough equivalent of the FBI. He and Harris sat on the edge of the fountain in Trafalgar Square beneath an enormous cast-iron lion, drinking coffee. 'I turned it into every combination imaginable but didn't find a DOB even close to nineteen twenty-eight.'

'I'm sure the name was invented,' Harris said.

Detective Inspector Spencer pulled a piece of paper out of his pocket. 'When that failed, I plugged in the phrase you gave me on the telephone, T-22.'

On the printout were various phrases, some encrypted, some in the clear. 'I got this from an index of cases Five shares with Six.' 'Six' Harris knew, was shorthand for MI6, the British foreign intelligence agency. 'Look at the bottom of the page.' Spencer had used a yellow marker to highlight a name. 'T-22 was the code name of a German bloke named Thomas Tibalt von Albusser.

'Who's that?'

'He was a member of the Third Reich's foreign service stationed in Buenos Aires during the war. Like a lot of German aristocrats he thought Hitler was a bloody bar-room thug who was wrecking the country. Luckily for us, he loved good gin and long-legged women he couldn't afford, so he became a paid informant code-named T-22. In nineteen forty-three he was caught by the Gestapo selling something to the Allies. They recalled him to Berlin and that was it. *Kaput*.' He cocked his finger like a gun.

'What'd he sell?'

'I don't know. What I saw is unclassified. The good stuff is in Six.'

'Was he working for them or you?'

'Neither. He was snitching for the FBI.'

'Really.'

'You fellows had the money, we had the brains.'

Harris let that pass with a fuck-you smile. 'If he was the Bureau's man, how'd the information end up over here?'

'Any number of ways. Maybe he shopped a British spy. Something in the story he sold must have involved the English.'

'Does the name Halliburton mean anything to you?'

'Lord Halliburton?'

'I don't know. The man who delivered Adalwolf to the convent was named Halliburton.'

'The only Halliburton I'm aware of was the earl who lived in London during the war and was a Nazi sympathizer. According to legend, Churchill was sitting in the loo one day when an aide told him Halliburton was on the phone, and Churchill said, "Tell Lord Halliburton I'll ring him back, I can only deal with one shit at a time." '

'It's hard to imagine an earl personally delivering a child to a convent, isn't it?'

'That depends on whose child it was,' Spencer said. 'If it was his own little bastard he might have handled it himself to avoid being blackmailed.'

Harris had pieces of information floating around in his head like kites on a windy day: Adalwolf born in England and placed in a French orphanage, perhaps by an English aristocrat. Adalwolf taken from the convent by the Gestapo when he was fourteen. A German foreign service officer shot for selling information to the FBI that was so hot it was still classified. Adalwolf as Mengele's acolyte at Auschwitz. It was time to start reeling some of them in.

Spencer looked at his watch and stood up. 'I don't know where this is taking you, but if there's a file in FBI headquarters marked T-22, you don't need me. What you're looking for is in your own backyard.'

'It was cleaned out by Hoover's personal assistant when he died,' Harris said. The two of them walked toward the cab stand. 'What kind of Englishman gives his kid a fake name and dumps him in a French orphanage?'

'A rich, guilty one,' Spencer said. 'Are you headed back to Washington?'

'No, Sherrie and I are going to Paris.' Obviously Harris wasn't all that happy about it.

Spencer stood in front of him. 'You'd rather go to Washington than Paris?'

'You know how it is when a case gets under your skin.'

Spencer laid his hand on Harris's shoulder. 'If this Adalwolf fellow gets to the entire FBI the way he's got to you, the whole bloody bunch of you are buggered.'

IT WAS ANOTHER BEAUTIFUL day in Miami, as pretty as the day before. They'd slept a little late, had a simple breakfast which David made, and then had gone to work, he in his study, Melissa out and about. He was feeling good and writing well. Coming to Miami was the right move for him as much as it was for her.

He knocked off in the afternoon to get some exercise and jogged along the water line, staying where the waves left the sand smooth. His cell phone began vibrating in his fanny pack. He unzipped it and brought the phone to his ear, panting.

'Hello?'

'Hey, baby, it's me,' Melissa said, 'I'm coming up on the market, are you going to be home for dinner?'

'Planning to. I'm having a drink with the bureau chief at seven, but I shouldn't be too late.'

'You sound out of breath.'

'I'm running. Getting shin splints. Are we out of shampoo?'

'I've got it right here.'

'No sweat, I'll use bar soap.'

'On your hair? Cool down and stretch and I'll be there in fifteen minutes. Hello?'

'Just thinking if I have time.'

'Come on, honey, relax. We're in Florida.' A horn. 'Jesus, old people are slow down here.'

'That sounds relaxed.'

'Hang on a sec.'

An engine winding out, then Melissa laughing. 'When I went

around the old lady she gave me the finger. We'll take a short swim
and you can . . . on your way.'

'You're breaking up,' he said.

'Just wait . . . me.'

'Okay, I'll be in the steam room,' he said.

'You're break . . . up, ' she said.

'I'll *meet you in the steam room – the steam room.*'

'Got it,' she said.

DAVID PUT THE CELL PHONE away and ran another minute until he saw the house, then slowed down to cool off, his gray tank top and nylon shorts dark with sweat. He pulled out a plastic bottle of water, drank it, and wiped his mouth with the back of his hand. Looking at the ocean, he thought it was no surprise God covered two-thirds of the earth with this stuff. Look at it out there, all blue and huge and restless.

Usually when he ran he worked out a problem he was having with a story, but today he felt introspective. As a reporter he was always seeing the dark side of life – corruption, mean-spiritedness, bad luck – but the beach offered an upbeat view of things and he wanted to take it in. He was young and healthy, he had Melissa in his life, he had a baby on the way. She was right: he needed to relax and smell the roses.

He reached the house and went to the outdoor shower. It was after three-thirty and the workmen appeared to be gone. He peeled off his clammy running clothes and piled them on a wooden bench, and a moment later was standing under the outdoor shower feeling the sun-baked water turn from hot to cold. He sudsed-up with bar soap – hair included – and rinsed off and took the key to the sliding door from the ledge and went inside wearing nothing but his cell phone. A few seconds later the stereo was on and Sade's voice filled the hallway. He switched on the speakers in the steam room and entered. The thick, insulated door closed on its pneumatic cylinder behind him.

He stepped over to the controls, hit the On button, and turned the Heat lever up. When the coil behind the wall pinged, he hit the switch and turned out the lights. Only the window in the door lit the room like a square moon.

He stretched out naked on the redwood top. The altar, as Melissa called it. It felt good being exhausted from a run. He picked up his cell phone and dialed the office and left a message that he'd be there about five. Taking the pressure off. He lay on the white tile block and listened to another cut of Sade.

Closing his eyes, he pictured Melissa, then the baby, then the three of them posing for the camera on the beach. Melissa smiling with those sensuous full lips. He had no idea he was going to love her this much or be this happy with her. How great it would be if the baby looked just like her.

It was good to be the king.

He took a deep breath and . . . stopped breathing. What was that fragrance? He opened his eyes and breathed in something that smelled like flowers. Wilting rose petals on a hot summer day. He sat up. Perfume? Was Melissa already here?

He got off the redwood tabletop and walked through a cloud of steam to the door, rubbed the glass window and looked out. The hallway was empty. Now the smell wasn't wilted roses, but decaying ones. Heavy and sweet with rot. And – what was that?

He looked at the steam valve and saw clouds of white mist pouring out at intervals. The smell was getting stronger. He reached down and turned the control to Off, but the room was still heavy with fog. Stepping back to his bench, he felt momentarily dizzy. He stumbled, catching himself with an outstretched hand on the tile.

What the fuck?

HE HEARD STEAM FLOWING again and turned toward the control lever on the wall. He'd turned it off, but he could still see vapor coming into the room. A broken pipe? They'd been working on it, maybe that's why. He walked over and checked the Off lever but it was tight. He stooped down and cupped his hand and drew it to his nose. Putrid roses. Another wave of dizziness.

Sade stopped singing.

Huh?

He went to the door and pushed to open it.

It didn't move.

He pushed again, harder, but still it didn't budge. He hit it with the flat of his hand. *Calm down.* The foreman must have told the last guy who left to turn off the lights and shut everything down. 'Hello?' he said. But that smell. He turned and saw the room filling with a pale yellow mist. His pulse picked up.

He turned back to the door and smacked it again. Coughing.

'Hello?' he yelled.

No answer.

He coughed hard, lungs aching. He rubbed steam off the window and put his face against it and looked outside again.

'Anybody there?'

He heard music again – thank God, there's a workman still out there – except now, instead of Sade, it was a boys' choir singing a hymn, Mozart or Handel, he wasn't sure. Who put that on? Singing in English. *'God is our hope and strength . . . in trouble.'* What the hell was *that*?

He strained to see who was outside with his face against the window. 'Who's out there?' he yelled.

Just then a mask – a black gas mask covering an entire head – rose up on the other side of the window three inches from his face.

DAVID JUMPED BACK, HIS heart skipping.

The mask stayed at the window, peering into the room. It was made of smooth, black rubber with tinted plastic eye holes, and behind it was a pair of dark, unblinking eyes and a hose at the mouth that made it look like an ant-eater. It was grotesque. It was monstrous.

David turned toward the redwood platform. *The cell phone. Get the phone!* He stumbled toward it, lost in the fog, alive with fear, fighting the smell and dizziness, still hearing the boys' choir singing: '. . . *though the waters . . . rage and swell . . .'* He dropped to his knees and pawed the area by the tile banquette, feeling nothing but floor. *It has to be here . . . it has to be . . . There it is!*

He lifted the phone to his face. The room was dim and steamy, the phone blurry, but he could see the keypad and . . . coughing . . . knew what to do.

He hit a button, saw the green light blink . . . saw the words *'Waiting to dial.* ' He told himself to use speed dial . . . *Hit number one . . . call Melissa.*

He dropped the phone. *This damn dizziness . . . .* He put his face close to the floor, found the phone lying face up, waiting to be touched. *Touch the number '1' . . . bring up her number . . . touch Send!*

He raised his finger . . . *Hit the key* . . . He coughed again and lowered his fingertip onto the numeral '1.' The phone beeped and up came Melissa's number on the screen, ready to be dialed. The boys were singing louder now, *'the God of Jacob is our refuge . . .'*

He began coughing harder. Tears blurred his vision. He aimed for the Send button . . . *the green one . . . touch the green button!*

The smell of rotting roses was choking him now, and his body was heavy and unresponding, his finger as clumsy as an iron poker. *Don't come without the police, Melissa . . . don 't come without them . . . don't come.* He blinked away tears and the thick, yellowish mist and found the Send button. He lowered his shaking finger toward it carefully.

A black-gloved hand grabbed the cell phone and lifted it away.

DAVID COULD STILL SEE the phone right there in front of his nose, but it might as well have been a thousand miles away. He felt the gloved hand move from his fingers to his armpit. . . a second one beneath his ribs . . . lifting him and rolling him onto his back. He stared upward.

Descending through the haze was the image of the ant-eater. David stared into its eyes. The diaphragm in the rubber mouthpiece moved in and out with its breathing. It was a bad dream, a forever bad dream.

'Hello, David.'

It wasn't a human voice but the mechanical reproduction of a voice. The voice Melissa had described as Adalwolf's.

'This gas is awfully slow, isn't it? Positively agonizing.'

He saw the man turn to his side and lift something . . . a black leather bag. The boys sang on in eerie beauty, '. . . behold the works of the Lord, what destruction he hath brought upon the earth . . .'

'Zyklon-B was much faster and more humane.'

He was opening the bag . . . drawing something out . . . .

'Oh, well. All we can do is our best.'

A syringe . . . he was holding a syringe with a long, stainless steel needle attached to the hub. He felt a welling up inside his chest, his nerves going electric. He tried to speak, surprised that his lips and tongue didn't work.

'Whuh . . .'

Adalwolf lifted a bottle of liquid from his bag and pushed the tip of the needle through the rubber diaphragm. Pulling back the plunger, he drew the fluid in, then removed the needle and expelled a drop that ran down the shaft.

'Nothing personal, David.'

A burst of wild energy filled David's veins. He raised his open hand and tried to grab the rubber mask and rip it off, but Adalwolf caught his hand and crushed it into a fist.

'If you don't fight it, it's painless.'

'Youf . . . .'

'Easy, easy, easy.' He forced David's hand downward. *'I'd let you live, but I need your wife.'*

David's watery eyes widened. His *wife?*

'And your baby.'

Adrenaline and anger split his mind. He tried to rise.

'First she has to quit the case, but she refuses to cooperate.'

Adalwolf turned the syringe around in his hand and pointed the needle downward.

'But she will now.'

DAVID'S RIGHT HAND ROSE fast enough to grab Adalwolf by the throat, feel the rubber straps of the mask and the electrolarynx strapped to his neck.

He grunted with rage. *Melissa. The baby.* He tasted blood. The gas was rupturing the blood vessels in his nose and mouth. It didn't matter, he'd choke Adalwolf anyway. His left hand rose to join the right. He had him now . . . had him by the throat. The choir sang innocently, '. . . *he breaketh the bow . . . and burneth the chariots with fire . . .*'

Adalwolf leaned forward, centering the weight of his body over David's chest, and placed the tip of the needle an inch to the left of his breastbone, between the third and fourth ribs, directly over the heart's anterior chamber. David's hands tried to stop the needle's course. For a moment, four hands trembled like the hands of barroom brawlers in an arm wrestling contest.

Slowly, Adalwolf used his weight to win.

The needle pierced the first layer of David's flesh. He exhaled an involuntary spurt of air and released one hand from the needle. It continued gliding into his chest smoothly . . . until a few inches had disappeared.

David's heart was no longer his own. He exhaled another burst of air and spittle, dotting Adalwolf's gas mask and black nylon windbreaker. Adalwolf was breathing hard now, trying to finish his work. His amplifier clicked on.

'Sing to me.'

David exhaled another puff of air.

Adalwolf brought one hand up to the plunger on the syringe. David's remaining hand weakened. Ghostly voices, pure and angelic, floated through the mist, ruptured by Adalwolf's metallic monotone as he sang along: *'I am exalted among the nations . . . I am exalted in the earth!'*

The boys continued without him: 'Be still then, and know that I am God.'

Adalwolf joined them in German. *'Seid stille und erkennet. . . dass ich Gott bin . . .'* A robot lullabying a child to sleep.

David's eyes softened. Adalwolf raised himself up and pushed down on the plunger of the syringe, squirting chloroform into David's heart. David's hands relaxed and fell to the floor. The boys' choir continued singing the 46th Psalm, now in English. Adalwolf continued to sing with them.

'Be still then, and know that I am God.'

David's eyes turned glassy. His heart was still beating and his last breath was yet to be drawn, but his spirit was already disconnecting.

It was coming too soon for Adalwolf's pleasure. He wanted one more thing.

He leaned down close to David, took a deep breath and held it, then pulled his gas mask to the side to reveal his face. David's heart pounded like a newborn baby's – Adalwolf could actually feel the pumping muscle through the needle – and his eyes were wild. At last, he knew that David knew: Adalwolf was Ben. He wanted to make sure his victim's last moment was filled with profound terror that he was Melissa's most trusted friend, that he could do anything to her and the baby he wanted. His body tingled with the thrill of his power and the horror on David's face.

He replaced his mask, exhaled into the diaphragm, and drew in a lungful of filtered air. Then he let the chloroform he'd injected do its job. Like the little girl in the lab – like all the Jews he killed – he wanted David to stay alive a few seconds more, just long enough to hear those three special words that sparkled like a diamond in the soul, those three words he always made sure his victims heard before they died. It was an essential part of the ritual, the last thing he thought God Himself would say if He could.

　'Goodbye, Christ killer.'

THE CLOSER SHE GOT TO the house the more a steam bath appealed to her. She pulled into the garage, got out of the car and walked around the side to the beach entrance. Obviously David had taken a shower; the wooden pad was wet and his running clothes were heaped on a bench. That bachelor streak in him would never change. Oh, well, if he could live with it, so could she.

She pushed his togs onto the stone patio, stripped off her clothes and laid them more neatly on the wooden bench. She turned on the shower but didn't wait for it to warm – a cold shower followed by hot steam was a nice combination. Dripping wet, she stepped over to the sliding door to the hallway, her nipples firm and goose-flesh rising on her breasts and thighs. She remembered their last time in the room. She felt alive.

She slid the door open and entered the hallway to the steam room. How strange. It sounded like the Vienna Boys' choir singing a Latin mass. So unlike him to play that. Then again, he had these kinky inspirations.

She walked gingerly to the steam room, her anticipation rising. Good grief, what's that? Smells like . . . dead roses? He had a lot to learn about aromatherapy.

She reached the door and cupped her hand at the window to look inside but it was too steamy to see. She pulled the door open and heard the steam hissing and felt the warm, moist air on her skin. The smell of roses was so overpowering it made her eyes water and her lungs hurt. She bent forward and coughed into her hand, dizzy and unable to see.

'David?' No answer. Another cough. He wasn't there, and it was a good thing he wasn't. She backed away from the door and yelled down the hall. 'David, where are you?'

No answer.

Something told her she shouldn't be naked.

Her heart was beating hard. 'David? What's that smell?' She coughed again and retreated to the sliding door and opened it. There was no breeze, but even hot, moist air was better than this rotten smell. She grabbed a bath towel from the stack on the counter and brought it to her face, making herself ready to go back into the room.

No, not quite.

She looked around the hallway and spotted a hammer sitting on a window sill, grabbed it, and returned to the steam room door. Fog was still pumping in.

She went inside and stepped up to the tile island. She didn't have to see the toes twice to know whose they were. She lowered the towel from her face. 'David?'

The heavy door closed behind her with a thud. She turned with a start – told herself it was only the pneumatic mechanisms – and turned back. David was lying there unmoving. She stepped closer and saw his open eyes staring at the ceiling, then the needle protruding from the center of his chest with a thin streak of blood running out of its core and down his side.

'Oh my God.'

SHE DROPPED THE TOWEL and touched his chest with her fingers. There was no heartbeat. She raised her fingers to his neck. None there, either. Her brain split into two: *David!* said one side; *Get out!* said the other.

She walked to the door and looked out the window, brimming with fear. There was no one she could see. Her eyes were stinging and her hands shaking. *The baby – save the baby!* She pushed on the door.

It opened.

She crept outside, looked down the hallway, saw nothing, heard nothing but little boys' voices singing a hymn in Latin.

She found a telephone on the wall, lifted it, and dialed 911. When she'd finished she hung up and walked to the sliding glass door, still undressed. She reached the open door and stuck her head outside, unsure what to expect. The beach was blinding white and as hot as a desert. If there were people in view she didn't see them.

She stepped outside and lifted her clothes from the bench, then sat down and held them on her lap. She wanted to get dressed but she couldn't stay on her feet long enough to do it. She breathed in the stultifying air, trying to clear her head of the putrid gas. Slowly, familiar objects penetrated her mind: the water line, a distant freighter, an elderly couple strolling at the water's edge.

She leaned forward and vomited. When she finished, she held her head in her hands and began to cry.

He was gone. He was gone.

Her thoughts came to her in a strange jumble. Still crying, she thought about the dinner they were supposed to have that night, the peanut butter and pickle sandwiches he loved. She thought about a silver-framed picture of the two of them holding their baby, a photograph she would never see. She worried about the story he was working on and hadn't finished. She noticed that her toenails needed painting. How could she think about something like that now? But the answer was simple: her mind was desperate to escape reality and find a refuge in the safe and normal.

She cried for her baby. She cried over an autumn trip to Vermont she hadn't imagined until this moment. It felt endless, the things they would never do together. All these little, inappropriate thoughts, all branches to grab for on the side of an emotional cliff. *Come back, David. I'm not done loving you. We're not done yet, we're not done.*

Her eyes started to swell and turn dry. She put her hand on her belly, looking for comfort from the baby, her companion, the only thing she had left, but comfort didn't come.

She heard footsteps behind her, the squeak of leather on a policeman's belt, a male voice saying, 'Excuse me, M'am, did you call nine-one-one?'

She didn't even turn to look. Her insides felt like torn tissue paper. She searched for something to restore her bearings but couldn't find it. Bearings? She couldn't even find the ground. She kept rejecting his death but it kept coming back, over and over, surprising her every time. Confusing reality with dream. She understood only one thing, which was as clear as the cloudless sky.

You win, Adalwolf. You win.

IN THE NEXT TWO DAYS Melissa's sorrow descended on her like coagulating blood, rich and dark and tasting of iron. The worst of it was the loss and emptiness, but added to that was her overwhelming conviction that David's death was her fault. If she hadn't been a Nazi hunter, if she hadn't defied Adalwolf, if she'd paid attention to what mattered – her marriage, the baby . . . if, if, if.

She couldn't do it over again, but she could keep David's memory alive with their child. If the baby had been important before, it was the only thing that mattered now. Adalwolf? She hated him and wanted him caught and buried. The mere thought of him enraged her. But it also intruded on her grief, and at the moment, thoughts of David were all that mattered.

When the police arrived at the house, she'd called Ben – his secretary said he wasn't in, so she left word for him to call, it was an emergency – then she called David's older brother, Aaron, a lawyer in San Francisco. After digesting the news, he telephoned Green's Funeral Home on Wisconsin Avenue in Washington. Melissa caught a plane to D.C. the next morning, which was Friday, and took the next step in death's grinding rite of passage: the making of 'arrangements.'

She was inconsolable but not dysfunctional. The business of death didn't allow it. There was a funeral to plan, a casket to choose, a rabbi, music, a burial plot. For those left behind, dying was as much a beginning as it was an end.

Aaron accompanied her to see the funeral director, who laid out her choices. Knowing next to nothing about Jewish custom, she instinctively chose what amounted to an orthodox burial: a dirt grave – no cement encasement – and a simple pine coffin closed with wooden pegs – no nails, nothing that wouldn't disintegrate in the earth. Ashes to ashes, dust to dust. She understood the point.

She asked that his body be dressed in a traditional white linen shroud instead of a suit and instructed that the casket remain closed during viewing, a modern touch. At each turn she did what she thought David would have wanted. Some of that involved guesswork – they'd never discussed their own funerals – but she thought she was on the right track. God, if only he could be here to help.

There was the matter of choosing newspapers for the obituary. The *New York Times*, of course, along with the two Washington dailies and *Jewish Week*. She bought a burial plot in the Maryland suburbs, outside Northeast Washington.

David's body, after an expedited autopsy, was flown to Green's Funeral Home in D.C. on Friday, the day after his death. According to Jewish law the dead were to be buried within twenty-four hours, but given modern distances between friends and family, an additional day for travel was acceptable. That, however, would have put the funeral on the Shabbat, a day exempt from funerals, so it was pushed off yet another day. She was glad to have the time.

David had been a nominal member of the Washington Hebrew Congregation, a large Reform temple. The funeral director contacted the chief rabbi there who assigned a thirty-two-year-old associate to handle the ceremony. Melissa wanted the funeral to take place in the morning, but there were other bodies waiting to be buried first. The earliest they could do it was at two in the afternoon. That at least gave her time to familiarize the young rabbi with enough of David's life to eulogize him passably.

She found the whole process mildly hypocritical until she realized funerals were for the living, not the dead, at which point she relaxed and went with it. She called Ben and ran her decisions

past him and he approved of them all. Thank God for Ben. She
didn't know what she'd do without him. She had never felt more
alone in her life. That was one of the things about ashes and dust.
They were the landscape of loneliness.

SUNDAY AFTERNOON ARRIVED, and friends and family gathered. Melissa sat in the chapel's front pew alongside David's brother and father, a sweet, trembly man in his mid-seventies who lived in San Francisco with David's mother, who was hospitalized and unable to attend. David's father tried to be comforting to Melissa, but he himself needed more comfort than he was able to give. Parents were not supposed to bury their children, he said quietly. It was unnatural.

On Melissa's other side was Ben, who'd flown up with Eric Brandt. David's colleagues from the Washington bureau of the *Times* made up the largest contingent in the chapel. Melissa's students and friends from Justice were also there, including her boss, Barry Sherer, and of course Harris and Sherrie Johnson, who were back from their trip to Europe.

The closed casket rested on a skirt-covered dolly at the front of the chapel. There were tastefully arranged flowers on top, but not many; Jews did not bedeck caskets the way Christians did.

Behind the casket was the *bima*, an elevated stage that held a lectern and a bench with a red velvet cover. Sad, dirge-like organ music played through hidden speakers as the young rabbi took the dais and began the half-hour ceremony. Joe Jacoby, the *Times* bureau chief, and David's brother, Aaron, each spoke on his behalf. It was, Melissa thought, the only truly moving part of the service.

When it was over, the rabbi stepped down and gave Melissa and each of David's relatives a black, fabric-covered button with a few inches of silk ribbon beneath, explaining to the congregation that in the old days the bereaved sat in ashes and expressed their grief by tearing apart their tunics. Today the act was more symbolic, he said, and took a small blade and cut each ribbon vertically.

After the 'renting', gray-gloved pallbearers escorted the dolly-borne casket down the middle aisle toward a hearse while Melissa and the family exited through a side door to two waiting limousines. The assistant funeral director handed her the guest register as she and David's family and Ben climbed into the cars. Soon, a funeral cortège of automobiles with lit headlights and signs in the windshields was headed through the poor, black, northeast section of Washington, then through the poor, white industrial section of Upper Marlboro, Maryland. B'Nai Israel Cemetery was their destination.

THE CARS PULLED ONTO the grass near the gravesite and everyone got out and walked shivering to a tent. Wet snow had turned to freezing rain, which had been replaced by a biting wind. Not even the sound of distant cars disturbed the quiet air.

Melissa, Ben, and David's family walked to folding chairs beneath a canopy and sat in winter coats while the others gathered around. Harris and Sherrie stood close by, and so did Eric Brandt. She found herself staring at him, thinking how kind it was of him to have come, and yet wishing he hadn't. She didn't know why. A widow's instinct, perhaps. She dismissed it as irrational.

The pallbearers removed the casket from the hearse and pushed it onto a set of white straps attached to the arm of an electric winch. Next to the winch was a large mound of dirt dug by a backhoe and covered with green Astroturf. Three stainless steel hand shovels stood neatly in a rack.

Melissa turned to David's brother and whispered, 'I am not going to sit shiva, Aaron. I hope you understand.'

A law partner of Aaron's in the firm's Washington, D.C. office had made his home available for the traditional Jewish mourning ritual that allowed friends to gather together in remembrance of the departed, to say Kaddish – the prayer for the dead – and to talk basketball while little old ladies sneaked dinner rolls into their purses. Melissa knew it would require more diplomacy and less anger than she could muster. It was all she could do to hold it together for the burial. David's brother patted her knee and said okay.

The young rabbi offered perfunctory prayers in Hebrew and English while Melissa stared into the grave. Beneath a frame of silver piping was nothing but the cold, damp earth.

After the reading of scripture, the rabbi closed the Bible and the winch whirred softly as it lifted the casket and swung it over the hole, guided by the hands of two pallbearers. The motor stopped and silence reigned, then the winch shifted gears and the casket began descending into the ground.

Seeing the skimpy, white-pine box, Melissa suddenly wished she'd placed David in a casket of iron after all, and laid it in a vault of steel and surrounded it with concrete walls. She knew he was dead, and yet it was *him* in there, the remains of the man she loved. It felt as if he was still in her care, as if he needed her love and protection now more than ever, as if the safety she'd failed to give him when he was alive could still be given to him now. Tears blurred her vision as she watched the casket drop out of sight. Ben put his arms around her shoulders and pulled her close. She cried with her eyes open. Then she lost it.

She grabbed Ben's hand. 'I feel him!' she whispered.

'Who?'

'Adalwolf!'

He pulled her closer. 'It's your imagination.'

'No, it's not, I can feel it! He's here!'

'But these are David's friends,' Ben whispered.

She craned her neck and took a quick inventory of the guests but saw no one unexpected. The pallbearers began loosening the white straps. The rabbi appeared in front of her with one of the garden spades, inviting her to begin the ceremonial covering of the casket. She stood up and took the handle, expecting to throw a single shovelful of dirt and pass the spade to another mourner. Still, she knew that Adalwolf was there at least in spirit, trying to desecrate David's grave even before it was closed. She could feel that, too.

The rabbi pulled back the green cover on the mound of dirt and she pushed the blade into the dry, loose soil, letting it glide in softly. When it was full she turned and threw it in, raining raw earth onto wood in death's final act. Some people cried, others felt startled at the sound. Seeing dirt on the casket gave her the sense of comfort she longed for. She was shielding him at last.

Instead of handing the shovel to Aaron, she pushed it into the dirt and lifted another load and held it up. *I'll make you safe, David. I will.* She dropped it in.

Mourners stood watching as she went back for a third shovelful, some of them curious, some confused. But not the rabbi. He favored emotional burials; filling the grave was the last earthly gift you could give a loved one. He handed a second spade to Aaron, who dug a shovelful and threw it in. The rain started falling again, turning the ground into a muddy mess.

Harris picked up a shovel and joined the ceremony. Some mourners took a turn, others left in search of cover. Three men who remained at the hole stripped off their overcoats and kept digging. Other than an occasional word that accompanied the passing of a shovel, no one spoke.

Melissa threw in her last shovelful. 'No one will ever lay a hand on you again,' she said quietly. David's father sat under the canopy as teary as the clouds, fingering a painted seashell his son had given him when he was in the second grade.

Melissa's feet were muddy and streaks of dirt spattered her black stockings. Ben dumped in a shovelful and turned to her and said, 'You're overdoing it, Melissa. Don't forget you're pregnant.'

That broke the spell. The casket was nearly covered anyway. The rain stopped again, leaving a red horizon beneath the clouds.

She set her shovel aside and walked over to Harris and spoke to him privately.

'I'm wrecked, Harris. The investigation is all yours now.'

'You'll come back,' he said.

'Don't count on it,' she said. Then, after a moment of reflection, she said, 'But if I do, it'll be with a vengeance.'

AN HOUR LATER, MELISSA was in her Alexandria apartment, slouched in an overstuffed chair with her slippered feet propped up on an ottoman. She'd just come out of a hot shower and had wrapped herself in a huge, fluffy robe. Her hair was still damp and a cup of steaming chicken soup rested untouched on a nearby table. Her eyes were closed, her right arm extended on the arm rest, the robe's sleeve pushed up to make room for the blood pressure cuff. Eric Brandt let the air out slowly and read the gauge.

'I'm okay,' she said. 'Just tired.'

'Fortunately for you and the baby you're a strong woman,' he said.

He peeled the Velcro apart and lifted off the cuff.

'Maybe it's none of my business,' he said, 'but I think you're blaming yourself for something that wasn't your fault.'

'I think you're right,' she said. 'Maybe it's not your business.'

'If it affects you and the baby I intend to make it my business,' he said and laid the cuff in his medical bag. She didn't reply. 'I care about what happens to you, Melissa.'

She looked at him intently, trying to make him blink, but he didn't. She closed her eyes and rested her head on the back of the chair. Why was she being so pissy with him? Without him she wouldn't even be pregnant. Of *course* he cared, what was she thinking?

The problem wasn't him, it was her. This feeling of being at fault. She had to ease up – not just on Eric, but herself.

He reached out and lowered her sleeve and laid her wrist in her lap. She heard a telephone being hung up in the next room and opened her eyes to see Ben come in. He sat on the ottoman at her feet and took her hand in his.

She said, 'Thank you both for coming. It meant a lot to me.'

'I wish we could stay longer,' Ben said.

'I'll be fine,' she said.

'Not by yourself, you won't,' he said. 'I just called the airline. You're coming back to Miami with me.'

'But Ben—'

'You can take the guest room. The sun and sand will do you good. I'll be there when you need company and stay out of sight when you don't.'

Eric said, 'I think that's an excellent idea.'

Melissa looked around the room. Lonely reminders were already haunting the house, and the winter sky was gray. She pulled her robe across her chest. She had friends up here, but she was still suspended at work and didn't want to go back anyway. The clinic was in Miami and so was her dear friend, Ben. No question she'd be happier if she went home with him – and safer, too. After all, Adalwolf was still out there somewhere. If she didn't know it was superstition, she could have sworn he was at the cemetery.

'It won't take me long to pack,' she said.

SHE SETTLED INTO THE soft, downy bed in Ben's guest room. The lamp on the bedside table was too bright to let her sleep, but she wouldn't turn it off. It was still the lamp she kept in the window for her returning sailor.

She got out of bed and walked to the bathroom and returned with a towel and laid it over the lampshade, careful not to let it touch the bulb, softening the light and turning the room dusky.

It took a long time to get to sleep, and when she did, it was fitful at best. Part of her brain kept expecting him to come to bed. She thought if she could get through one whole day without him, the second would be easier, then she'd try for another, a week, a month, until finally she could turn out the light.

Before David's death there were three things that had governed her life: pregnancy, Adalwolf, and her marriage. Now there was only one. The baby wasn't just her dream, it was the only part of David she had left. As careless as she'd been about involving him in her professional life, she'd be careful to keep the baby out of it. It killed her to give up on the case, but if that's what it took, that's what she'd do. Priorities were easier to see when your back was against a wall.

She laid her hand on her pregnant belly and whispered, 'Don't worry, little one, I'm right here.' At last, she dozed.

At three-thirty in the morning she woke up in a fevered fog, wondering if he was home yet, looking over at his side, slowly realizing he wasn't there and never would be. She lay still and let the tears run quietly so they wouldn't wake the baby.

At four o'clock she reached out and pulled the pillow on David's side close and hugged it the way she'd hugged him when he came home. *Let me have him for just one more night. Just one.* She reached up and turned out the light the way he did when he came in and crawled into bed beside her. Then, making believe the pillow was him, she closed her eyes and held on to it long enough to go to sleep.

FEBRUARY AND MARCH WERE like a game of chutes and ladders. A few days would pass and she'd climb a little more out of her sadness only to land on a square that shot her back down again. It was as unpredictable as a roll of the dice. She might be writing a letter and start to yell at David for a word, or she might be walking down the beach and see someone jogging in red shorts. She might be feeling at ease, focused on the baby, climbing another rung or two when she'd hear or smell something that reminded her of him and fall down the slide again.

Nights had their own form of the slippery slope. Because of the pregnancy she couldn't take a sleeping pill or relax with a drink, so she was on her own. Sometimes she woke up and wandered into the kitchen, sometimes she stayed in bed, depending on where she thought she had the best chance of wrestling the devils to the mat. As the weeks wore on she'd learned how to get them in a hammer lock, but now and then they'd flip her on her back and pin her at the neck. That was their specialty – that and making her reach out for David before remembering he was gone.

She stayed in touch with friends even though they soon lost track of her grief. Not that she blamed them; she envied them. Barry e-mailed her regularly saying there was nothing new to report: no Adalwolf, no grand jury, no news on the OPR investigation, no reinstatement of her job. Otto Heller sent a note of condolence and said he'd contact her another time, when she felt up to it. The Miami police and the FBI were both investigating the homicide and made periodic calls to Melissa, either to ask about a lead or give her a status report.

Harris stayed in touch most of all. After his two week vacation he'd gone back to work, although not on the Adalwolf case. Now he was investigating interstate car thefts and running down dead-end leads to Al Qaeda. But he hadn't really given up on the case, and she loved his patient enthusiasm. Hc had ideas. The minute she was ready to get back in harness, he said, he'd be there to join her. He had another week of vacation he could take and he knew exactly how to use it. She wasn't ready yet, but with each passing day she could imagine it a little more. Adalwolf may have been quiet, but not forgotten.

And then there was Ben, who brought her back to life more than anyone. They went to movies and dinner, played gin and backgammon, and took evening strolls on the beach. He tried to keep her mind off Adalwolf, which she considered thoughtful, knowing that he wanted him caught as much as she did. He kept her focused on the baby's development, which he described in detail.

In week five, the embryo was the size of a raisin, he said. In week six, it got a heartbeat and Melissa got sore breasts. Week seven, the embryo was raspberry-sized and facial features became visible. Week eight, the baby was one inch long and officially graduated from embryo to fetus. In week nine, it took a swim in its tiny amniotic sack. Week ten, it looked like a shrimp, its heart almost completely developed.

By the end of week twelve, which is where the baby was now (doctors, he said, counted weeks from the end of the mother's last period, which meant it was 'two weeks old' when it was conceived), certain important thresholds were now being reached. The uterus was still only the size of a large peach, which is why she wasn't showing yet, but the baby's brain was fully formed. It sucked its thumb and stretched and made fists and lifted its head and passed urine. It had its own heart, liver, kidneys, brain, blood type, and lungs. 'It can't survive on its own yet,' he said, 'but the chances of a miscarriage are greatly reduced. It's strong enough for you to start feeling movement soon.'

'Kicks?'

'Kicks, turns, somersaults.'

'I can't wait.'

'In the old days, they called it the "Quickening".'

She liked that. It sounded lively.

Ben said, 'Best of all, it has its own body chemistry now.'

Why that was important she didn't know, but she took his word for it. Who knew better than he what pregnancy was all about? She was so glad he'd convinced her to come back to Miami. What a blessing.

Slowly, something else was happening to her, too: she was getting back into the case. It started with research on the Internet, then progressed to more conversations with Harris. Having taken time away from the files gave her perspective on her notes and cleared her head of the kind of assumptions investigators inevitably made. She was talking more to Otto Heller at CDC, not only about the virus, but about Adalwolf's psychological profile. Adalwolf and Heller were about the same age, had similar medical knowledge, and were both in the business of working with deadly viruses. Sometimes Heller's insights were so good she thought he could have been Adalwolf's brother. Sometimes she even had fantasies that he was.

She decided to treat April Fool's Day as a kind of milestone. The weather was glorious and her attitude good. She read a book and watched the news and took her daily swim. Her recovery program was working well: up a ladder here, up a ladder there. She watched what she ate and sang to the baby – Ben said it would be able to hear her voice any day now. Then she lay in the sun and worked on her tan, thinking, David really loves it when my skin gets—

David really loves it.

Down a chute here, down a chute there.

HARRIS STUCK HIS HEAD into Kobie's room.

'Get ready,' he said, 'we leave in a few minutes.'

She jumped off her bed and lifted her suitcase and brought it to the door. She'd been ready for days.

Harris walked to his bedroom to put on a pair of slacks, loafers, and his usual sport coat. Sherrie was in the bathtub with her eyes closed, up to her neck in a mountain of glistening lavender bubbles.

Harris stepped inside the bathroom and closed the door. 'We're going.'

She raised her arms to him with a sad look.

He said, 'It's only four days, sweetie.' That was all Kobie had left of her spring break.

'I was thinking about Melissa,' Sherrie said. 'Thirty-eight years old, pregnant, out of a job, and now a widow.' She gathered up a handful of bubbles and watched them burst.

Harris sat on the edge of the tub. They'd been through this before. He was an FBI agent, which meant she knew a certain amount of danger went with the job, and yet the older the kids got, the more nervous she became. He took the suds from her and laid them on her shoulder.

She said, 'I don't know what I'd do without you.'

He leaned down and gave her a kiss and breathed in the smell of lavender on her skin. 'Don't worry, baby,' he said, 'I'm not checking out for a long time.'

She meshed her fingers into his. 'It's great watching you spend so much time with Kobie,' she said. 'She adores you, you know.'

Yeah, he knew, she was at that age. 'I couldn't live without you or the kids,' he said.

She tilted her head back and pulled him down and kissed him again. They both stayed with it awhile. It had to last for the next three days. When they were done, Kobie came in wearing a dark blue baseball cap with a bright yellow 'FBI' stitched above the bill and got her own goodbye hug and kiss from her mom.

She and her dad were off to Disney World.

'YOU'RE LOOKING CHIPPER this evening,' Ben said. Melissa stood at the door of his study in a white sun-dress and tan skin. Ben sat in a swivel chair at his computer, listening to a Bach concerto. 'What'd you do today?'

'Spent the afternoon with Otto Heller from CDC,' she said.

'Really. What's he up to?' His voice was even, no hint of concern.

'He's tracing the NTX virus back to the labs that had it in their inventory to see if he can pick up a lead on Adalwolf.'

'How's he doing?'

'It's painstaking work considering how many there are, but if anyone can do it, he can.' She started back out the door. 'We still on for dinner tonight?'

'I've got a lecture tomorrow I haven't prepared yet,' he said. 'Would you mind if I took a rain check?'

'Of course not. Want me to bring you something?'

'I wouldn't say no to a slice.'

'You got it.' She pushed away from the doorjamb and left.

The minute he heard the car pull away, he opened her laptop and read the notes she'd taken on her conversations with Heller. She was right: tracing the virus back to a lab in Miami was a huge job, but even though the odds were long, they weren't impossible. Investigators often got lucky, and the ones with EIS had an instinct that troubled him.

Frankly, it made him nervous.

He turned back to his computer and brought a calendar on screen with the heading 'Action Sequence'. Under each date on the

calendar was a box with a note reminding him what he had to do
that day to reach his ultimate goal with the baby. He found the
word 'Deadline' ten days away, highlighted it, copied it, and pasted
it onto the calendar a week earlier. The schedule he was following
was based on Melissa's pregnancy, which meant he couldn't
change things arbitrarily, but still, he thought he could accelerate
this particular deadline without a problem. He wasn't panicked, he
was just being prudent.

   He converted the computer file into unreadable hieroglyphics –
just in case someone got into it – and for good measure applied a
security code and exited the program. Sitting back in his chair, he
read a review article on nonteratogenic anesthetics – drugs not
harmful to fetuses – and waited for his piece of pizza to arrive. By
his relaxed demeanour, no one would have guessed he was in a race
against time, much less that he was a psychopathic killer. Least of
all Melissa.

KOBIE WAS FAST ASLEEP in the hotel bed when Harris lifted the phone. He dialed and spoke quietly.

'Miss Ford? Harris Johnson. We're in Orlando. I'm talking quietly so I don't wake up my daughter. Late afternoon is perfect, the rest of the day we'll be at Disney World. Yes, I've got the warehouse address. I'll see you there.' He started to hang up. 'Oh, one other thing: will we get soaked on Splash Mountain?' He wrote down her advice: *Stay out of the front seat.*

IT WAS EARLY AFTERNOON by the time Harris and Kobie got to the warehouse in DeLand, half an hour north of Orlando. They'd covered a lot of ground that morning: Splash Mountain, Epcot, the Rock 'n' Roller Coaster, and a hundred foot vertical drop on the Twilight Zone Tower of Terror, Kobie's favorite. Harris was happy to be on four wheels on a highway. Kobie preferred two-wheeled carts on hairpin turns. Mickey and Goofy had no idea what havoc they'd created.

They pulled into the parking lot of Ace Warehouse and Storage and parked in the boiling sun. He got out and stretched conspicuously, and a few seconds later the driver's door on a nearby car opened and a woman in her late thirties got out and approached.

'I'm Janice Ford,' she said.

'Harris Johnson,' he said, shaking hands.

'I see you survived the morning,' she said.

Harris popped a Tums into his mouth.

Kobie got out with her Walkman earphones on, said hello, and the three of them walked toward the front door to the warehouse.

Janice Ford was the daughter of a woman who'd been a clerk for Helen Gandy, the personal assistant to J. Edgar Hoover. When Gandy had gone into a nursing home she'd asked Janice's mother to store some of her personal effects. Harris wanted to take a look.

They entered the warehouse where Janice showed an identification card and filled out a form. After being buzzed through a locked door to the storage area, they were directed to a small room listed on an employee's clipboard.

Janice used a key to enter. Harris flipped on an overhead light. The tiny room was empty except for three banker's boxes stacked against the wall. Janice said she had to leave. Harris thanked her and said he'd call later.

He pulled the first box onto the floor, dusted it off with his handkerchief, and set it on the concrete floor. Kobie helped him remove the lid. It was full of files and papers. He started reading.

THE FIRST GROUP OF FILES were full of memos written between Helen Gandy and her boss, J. Edgar Hoover, having to do with personnel matters – FBI employees the director wanted checked out quietly, others he wanted her to keep track of. Nothing interesting. There was correspondence with friends and family, old mortgage papers, a savings account passbook. He kept looking and Kobie kept stacking the papers. They went through two of the three boxes and found nothing.

In the third box they found Hoover's 'D' list – the list of files to be destroyed upon his death. Each item was checked off with a note at the side indicating what had happened to the file. Harris's eyes ran down the entries. All lines had a checkmark next to them except three: INTERNAL, FINANCIAL, and DOW.

He read the file folder marked INTERNAL, which had to do with an Assistant Director who had a gambling problem. FINANCIAL held records of Hoover's investments. Only DOW remained.

He opened it and found 302s – FBI investigative reports – covering a series of interviews with a confidential source named Thomas Tibalt von Albusser, designation T-22.

Now he was getting somewhere.

He took out his digital camera.

June 21, 1943. World War II. T-22 was described as a Nazi foreign service officer stationed in Buenos Aires. The agent writing the memo was running him for the Allies. Harris lifted his camera, shot the page, and read on.

June 30, 1943. Phrases that described DOW as someone who 'Frequented the Berlin cabaret scene'. DOW's cousin was described as 'a singer', a pretty young woman who'd been 'introduced to Fritz – high level Nazi – by café society colleagues close to DOW'. Huh? Who was Fritz? A pretty English café singer was introduced to a big time Nazi by someone named DOW?

More on DOW. He was an Englishman who spoke fluent German, sometimes called it his 'native tongue'. Spent a lot of time in Berlin. Vacationed in Germany since boyhood. Many relatives lived there, including a German second cousin referred to as KW. Some of KW's children were impressed with AH – had to be Adolf Hitler. Some became supporters and gave money to the Nazi party.

Who was the Englishman named DOW? He photographed the pages and kept reading until another name stopped him cold: Next to the initials FH, in handwriting, was 'Lord F. Halliburton'. The memo described Halliburton as a 'Nazi sympathizer' distantly related to the British royal family but with 'questionable loyalties to the Crown'. Spent vacation time in Germany with his family, was a close friend of DOW.

He opened the next file. There were newspaper articles that had been clipped and marked for filing, and a memo with an FBI logo at the top. What was that?

He read the memo and saw that it was written by 'SOG'. He knew from his days at the FBI Academy that SOG meant 'Seat of Government', the designation J. Edgar Hoover had given himself.

The addressee was POTUS – President of the United States – Franklin Delano Roosevelt. The subject line read, 'T-22'. There were references to DOW again. Hoover was telling President Roosevelt about something the FBI had learned from their snitch, T-22. Something about DOW and Lord Halliburton.

A few lines down he found handwritten words next to DOW that said, 'the Duke'. His eyes darted back and forth and picked up another handwritten explanation: 'Edward'. DOW was the Duke of Windsor – Prince Edward, the crown prince of the British throne, a second cousin to KW, who must have been Germany's Kaiser Wilhelm. Harris saw something coming together: Prince Edward, later crowned King Edward, was known to be a Nazi sympathizer who'd been spurned by the royal family for his proposed marriage to Wallis Simpson, an American divorcee deemed unsuitable to wed the king of England and head of the Anglican Church. Rather than give her up, Edward had abdicated after a year on the throne and quickly retired – some said was exiled – to Bermuda.

Years before that, Prince Edward or one of his cronies had apparently introduced a young woman to a prominent Nazi in a Berlin cabaret. Harris shot photographs of the pages as fast as his camera would go. *Plink*, read, *plink*, read, *plink*.

'Daddy,' Kobie said, 'can we go now?'

'In a few minutes,' he said, wiping sweat from his brow.

He blew the dust off a memorandum marked TOP SECRET – FOR YOUR EYES ONLY – dated September 21, 1943.

The President of the United States, Franklin Delano Roosevelt, was writing to the U.S. ambassador to the Court of St. James, Joseph P. Kennedy, in London. A handwritten note at the bottom of the page read, 'Joe, I need your views on this immediately. Franklin.' Harris shot a picture of it and turned the page.

Next was Kennedy's response to Roosevelt. 'Dear Mr. President: Attached is my report on T-22. The PM's views are verbatim. God-speed. Joe.'

Harris read the attached two-page report. 'PM' was the Prime Minister, Winston Churchill, who was quoted by Ambassador Kennedy in the next paragraph.

Harris read only three lines when he heard himself saying, 'Holy shit.'

HARRIS CALLED MELISSA and said he needed to see her as soon as possible. She told him to come down to Miami, it was only an hour away, so he and Kobie caught the next plane. Melissa picked them up at the airport and headed for the beach. It was five o'clock and still sunny when they arrived.

If you grew up in Seattle as Harris did, you either longed for the sun or considered it a useless relic. Harris was in the latter category. If the soupy air in Washington was bad, the molasses air of Miami was worse. Naturally, his daughter loved it. Kobie was playing on the beach and frolicking knee-deep in the ocean while Harris and Melissa sat in the shade of a cabana, drinking iced teas and digging their feet into the sand.

Sand. That was another thing Harris could do without.

'During World War Two,' he said, 'the FBI had a big operation in Buenos Aires, which was a haven for German spies. The Bureau developed a snitch named Thomas Tibalt von Albusser, code name T-22, a German foreign service officer whose loyalty to booze and women exceeded his loyalty to the Führer. Fortunately for our side, his tastes required cash.' He cupped his hands and yelled at Kobie: 'Don't go in too deep, honey!' She waved and splashed the water with big swings of her arms.

'In the summer of nineteen forty-three,' Harris said, 'von Albusser contacted his FBI control agent and said he had something hot for sale. When our man met him, von Albusser said a well-placed friend told him the Gestapo was planning to arrest a fourteen-year-old boy at a convent in the south of France and take him to Auschwitz – not as a prisoner, but to live with Josef Mengele and his wife.'

'Mengele?'

'Yeah. According to T-22, Himmler himself arranged it.'

'Why?'

'I'll get to that in a second.' He sucked some iced tea through a straw. 'T-22 told his control agent that a beautiful young cabaret singer, stage name Quince, was the daughter of England's Lord Halliburton. Halliburton was a Nazi sympathizer with aristocratic connections and an ambitious politician who saw himself as a rival to Winston Churchill.' A smile crossed Harris's face.

'Did I miss something?' Melissa said.

'No, I was just thinking about a crack Churchill made about him while he was sitting on the can. Anyway, Halliburton's daughter aspired to be the next Greta Garbo, so she hangs out with a fast crowd in Berlin that includes England's Prince Edward, the heir to the throne who speaks German and spends vacations with his German relatives. We're talking Berlin in the roaring twenties, *Cabaret*, smoky rooms, sex, drugs, alcohol, whatever.'

He cupped his hands to yell another warning at Kobie, then thought what the heck, and relaxed.

'What year was it?' Melissa said.

'It was nineteen twenty-seven,' Harris said. 'At this point Hitler is basically a power-hungry wannabe raising rabble with the boys in the beer halls, but some of the guys who eventually signed on with him like to kick back and relax. One night in Berlin one of them meets this pretty young singer from London. The fact that she's Lord Halliburton's daughter must have been an added attraction, although if you saw her photograph you'd know she didn't need any.

'Pretty?'

'Very. She gives this Nazi the code name "Fritz" and they have a fling and she gets pregnant, probably on New Year's Eve nineteen twenty-seven. They correspond a few times, and at one point she takes a train to Düsseldorf to meet him and tell him she's bearing his child. Fritz is not amused and tells her it's out of the question. She is not amused with his response and leaves in a huff. They break off communications, and in September nineteen twenty-eight the Honorable Elizabeth Quincy Halliburton gives birth to the son of a man destined to be a high level Nazi in the Third Reich.'

Melissa's foot stopped digging in the sand.

Harris said, 'Quince's father takes her out of London and puts her on his country estate to give birth to the kid quietly and put it up for adoption. She has a little boy, but once she sees him, she tells daddy she can't give him up. She keeps him for two years, at which point somebody in the royal family gets wind of what's going on and goes bananas. Instead of arguing about it, Lord Halliburton gives the boy a fake name – Henry Hallam Brandon – and puts him in a French convent and orphanage. Quince never sees her son again.'

'Could I have some more iced tea?' Melissa said.

Harris poured.

'Cut to fourteen years later, nineteen forty-three, the middle of World War II, England, America and Russia against the Nazis,' Harris said. 'The FBI agent running von Albusser in Buenos Aires considers T-22's story about Quince and the Nazi to be good enough to report it directly to J. Edgar Hoover, who immediately sees its potential. If they can find out who Fritz is – maybe it's Joseph Goebbels, or Heinrich Himmler, or maybe even Adolf Hitler himself – they can blackmail the Germans into a concession of some kind, or at least embarrass the hell out of them. After all, one of their self-righteous, Aryan symbols of moral purity has fathered an illegitimate child by an English girl and deliberately dumped her and the baby. In those days, that meant something.'

'Go on.'

'J. Edgar tells President Roosevelt he's got a handle on a good rumor, and the President directs Joe Kennedy, his ambassador to

England, to check it out. Kennedy talks to Winston Churchill, who says Lord Halliburton is a royal pain in the ass he'd dearly love to embarrass but they can't use the story because it would damage the country's war effort more than it would hurt Hitler and the Third Reich.

'FDR gets this message from Ambassador Kennedy and tells Hoover to drop it. Hoover puts the information into his Official and Confidential blackmail file, and Helen Gandy, his personal assistant, tucks it away. Meanwhile, our man von Albusser is discovered by the Nazis to be a spy, gets recalled to Berlin, and takes a bullet. So the whole story gets buried.'

'Adalwolf is a big time Nazi's son?'

'He is if T-22's story is accurate. Keep in mind that people who trade information for cash sometimes make things up. On the other hand, the files say T-22 was reliable, and that several people close to Hitler knew about the story and helped cover it up. There's a reported exchange between Himmler and Goebbels about damage control. I can't find anything that knocks the story down.'

'Then maybe it's true. Why else would Himmler go to the trouble of using the Gestapo to take a kid out of a convent?'

'Good question. My guess is they tortured von Albusser before they shot him, discovered that the story of Quince and the baby had leaked, and went straight to the convent and grabbed the kid to put him under wraps.'

'But why send him to Auschwitz?'

'What better place to hide someone?'

She thought about it. 'Why not just kill him?'

'They probably considered it, but he was the son of British aristocrats, and you don't kill an asset like that until you figure out whether keeping him on ice can do you some good later on. Also, maybe the father was reluctant to kill his own flesh and blood. By the way, you know what Adalwolf means?'

'No idea.'

'It's a variation on Adolf.'

'Really. So the kid was named in honor of the Führer?'

Harris said, 'Hard to say whether Adalwolf gave the name to himself or was given it by someone else, but it explains why he doesn't show up in any of the SS records.'

'What about the name he had in the convent, Henry Hallam Brandon?'

'I've got somebody at the Berlin Document Center looking for it right now,' Harris said.

'But how would Adalwolf have known he was the son of a high-ranking Nazi? Surely the SS wouldn't have told him that.'

'When he got to Auschwitz he must have asked Mengele why he'd been kidnapped by the Gestapo and put in a concentration camp,' he said. 'How could he not? Life in Auschwitz wasn't exactly *Fast Times at Ridgemont High*.'

'So Mengele tells him he's the bastard son of a big Nazi?' she said. 'I doubt that. Would you trust a teenager with information that sensitive?'

'While the Third Reich is alive and kicking, no way,' Harris said, 'but once it's in ashes and Mengele's getting ready to make a run for his life, sure, I'd tell him then. Why not?'

Melissa was weighing it.

Harris said, 'I don't find it difficult to imagine Adalwolf knew who his father was. What's missing is what happened to his mother, Quince. I confirmed she had connections with the royal family, but there's no record that she had a child in nineteen twenty-eight.'

'Now that's something *I* find easy to believe,' Melissa said. 'Lord Halliburton wouldn't have left those tracks uncovered.'

Harris dug his feet into the sand in search of coolness. 'How does any of this help us find him?'

Melissa didn't have an answer for that, but somewhere down a corridor of her mind a voice of intuition was saying, '*Of course it's going to be helpful. Don't you see?*'

'By the way,' Harris said, 'I did a background check on Eric Brandt and he comes up clean.'

'You didn't tell me you were doing that.'

'I didn't need to.'

It made her realize how long she'd been out of it. 'Ben and I are having an early dinner tonight,' she said. 'Why don't you and Kobie join us?'

'I would, but after two days of Disney World it's early to bed.'

'For you or Kobie?'

'Me. Kobie's looking for an all-night poker game.'

'We'll get together tomorrow night.' Melissa's face dropped and her hand went to her belly. 'Oh my God,' she said. 'I just felt a kick.'

Harris smiled at that. 'Congratulations.'

'Wait till I tell Ben,' she said. 'Every time it happens it makes him happy.'

BEN ASKED MELISSA TO pour him a glass of wine while he went into the kitchen to get their salad. It was nothing elaborate – Boston lettuce with pear slices, walnuts and a blue cheese dressing – but he had an ingredient to add to it, and considering what it was, he had to do it right.

He used a pair of silver tongs to lift the salad from a large bowl and place it on two plates, keeping an eye on the door. After adding the dressing, he opened a cabinet and took out a metal canister with a label that read TAPIOCA ROOT.

That's what it said, but he knew better.

He unscrewed the lid and removed a white tuber of cassava, a root native to Brazil that was cultivated in Florida. Holding it over the plate on his left, he scraped tiny slivers of it onto the salad, still keeping an eye on the door. Uncooked cassava contained enough prussic acid to cause cyanide poisoning, which is what he wanted. Not too much – too much could cause convulsions, coma, and death – just enough to create some gastro-enteritis and nausea. He'd worked with the root before and knew how much to use.

When he finished scraping, he replaced the root in the canister and, after scrubbing his hands in the sink, picked up the salad plates and carried them to the dining room. The wine had been poured for him, water for her, and Melissa was in her chair.

He served her the cassava-spiked greens, then sat at his place and laid a linen napkin on his lap. He lifted his glass. 'To the baby,' he said, and they both drank. 'So tell me what happened today.'

She outlined what she and Harris had discovered in Orlando.

He listened quietly, careful not to probe too much. There was no need. After tonight, her mind would no longer be on the investigation, it'd be on the baby, and she'd be in his care until it was born.

Everything was still going according to plan.

SHE DIDN'T KNOW WHAT woke her first, the howling rain or the shutter beating against her window. Maybe it was the pain in her abdomen. It felt like the baby had decided to learn how to skip rope.

Melissa turned to see the clock next to the bed, which read five minutes to one. When she turned back, a stab to her midsection brought an audible groan. What was going on? She and Ben had eaten nothing that would cause pain this intense. She waited a moment, hoping it would pass, but it didn't. Then a wave of nausea swept over her.

She got up and walked to the bathroom wearing David's navy blue T-shirt and a pair of his cotton boxers. A night light above the bathroom sink lit her way. She hit the light switch, squinted, and opened the medicine cabinet. There was Pepto-Bismol, Alka-Seltzer, Mylanta, and Phenergan, an anti-nausea medicine safe to use with pregnancy.

She opened the vial, shook out a salmon-colored pill, and held it between her lips as she picked up an empty glass for some water. Another wave of pain punched her in the belly so hard she dropped the glass, shattering it on the marble countertop. Then she doubled over and vomited into the toilet. After a second retch, she leaned against the sink with her head down, breathing hard, trying to compose herself. Her left palm burned from a shard of broken glass; she pulled it out and ran cold water on it, then rinsed her mouth and reached for a towel.

She took another hit in the belly.

Bent over in pain, she shuffled back to the bed and lay on her side. Ben was at the other end of the house but she was too sick to get him. She placed her hands on her abdomen and drew her knees up tight and waited.

The pain got worse.

She saw her Palm Pilot on the nightstand, reached for it and found Eric Brandt's entry. She lifted the receiver and dialed. The phone answered:

'This is Dr. Eric Brandt, I'm not able to take your call at the moment, but if you'll . . . .'

Beep.

'Eric, it's Melissa, I'm in terrible pain, I can't move, call me, please.'

She hung up. If he called back, was the ringer on?

She dialed her own number to test it, thinking she should have done this in the first place. The second line rang three times.

'Hello?' Ben's sleepy voice said from his room.

'Ben . . . It's me . . . I need help.'

THE RINGERS ON ERIC Brandt's telephones were turned off, but the volume setting on his answering machine, down the hall, was on high. He was sleeping easily when Melissa's voice reached him, raising dreamy images of a woman speaking through a megaphone. He couldn't make out the words, which troubled him and stirred him more or less awake. He hovered in semi-consciousness, waiting to wake up or go back to sleep. He went back to sleep.

BEN ENTERED MELISSA'S room in blue silk pajamas and leather slippers, his hair mussed, his beard swirled, and one of the temples on his glasses outside his ear. Melissa lay on the bed with her knees still drawn up to her chest, hyperventilating. She'd managed to turn on the bedside lamp.

'What is it?' Ben said.

'Terrible pain in my belly,' she said.

He rolled her onto her back and lowered her knees far enough to palpate her abdomen. She groaned when he touched her.

'We have to get you to the clinic,' he said.

'What's wrong?'

'You're having premature contractions. I need to get some Terbutaline into your uterus or you'll abort.'

'Good God.' She sat up slowly. 'What's causing it?'

'Stress, most likely,' he said. 'Can you stand?'

She got to her feet.

He said, 'I'll get your raincoat and help you to the car.'

ERIC WOKE UP AND BLINKED against the darkness. The voice he'd heard in his dream sounded as if it might have come from his answering machine. He got out of bed and walked to his study, rubbing his hair. The message light was blinking. He hit Play and listened to Melissa's call: *Terrible pain, I can't move, call me back.* What was going on?

The clock read quarter after one, which was a hell of a time to be calling her, but she sounded bad. He picked up the phone and dailed Ben's number. Never know. The phone rang three times and Ben's voicemail came on. That's weird. Where were they?

'Ben, Melissa, it's me, Eric. I know it's late, but I thought I'd better get back to you. Give me a call.'

He hung up and padded back to bed and lay down thinking that as long as she was with Ben she was in good hands. He rolled over. He had surgery in the morning. He needed some sleep. He closed his eyes.

BEN'S BLACK FOUR-DOOR Mercedes pulled into the underground garage at the clinic like a ship coming in from the sea. Melissa lay quietly on the back seat in the fetal position listening to the windshield wipers beating against the glass. She and Ben had made the trip from the house in fifteen minutes.

Ben opened the back door and helped Melissa to her feet, then through a steel fire door, which he opened with his security card, and over to the elevator. When they reached the fourth floor they walked to the door to the clinic. Ben had his key ready and opened it – the doorbell sounded – and helped her through the reception room, down the hallway, and into the first operating room they came to. He turned on the overhead lights and eased her onto an examining table with stirrups and armrests. Once she was down, he walked to a sink and washed up. After tossing a paper towel into a foot-levered waste can, he pulled on a pale yellow disposable surgeon's gown and returned to the table.

He drew a stainless steel tray of instruments closer to him. 'How are you feeling?' he said, lifting a pair of latex gloves from a box.

'Still in pain.'

He pulled on the gloves, cleaned the back of her right hand with an alcohol pad, and inserted a white plastic catheter into a vein. Moving quickly, he attached dual ports to the catheter and used the first to run a line from a bag of saline, adjusting the plastic clamp to drip every few seconds to keep her vein open. Next he unscrewed the cap on a bottle of Versed, an anesthetic, drew it into a syringe, removed the needle, and stuck the hub of the syringe into the second port leading to her vein. He pushed the plunger down about an eighth of an inch.

'You should feel relaxed any second,' he said.

She felt the room spin a little . . . felt all her muscles turn buttery . . .

She turned her head and saw him walk to a counter, take plastic-covered sterile instruments from drawers, lay them on a paper-lined tray, and set them on a rolling table next to her. He pulled an ultrasound machine into place near her head, on his left, and snapped on the toggle switches. Letting it warm up, he walked to the door and lowered the lights with a rheostat and returned to the table. After pulling a backless stool on casters up to the side, he sat down and sharpened the image and color on the ultrasound machine. It glowed in the soft-lit room.

'How are you doing?' he said.

'Still . . . hurting.'

He stood up and moved to his right, swung the stirrups into place, and set her feet in them. She felt something wrapped around her ankles and lifted her head. When she saw straps, she tensed. 'Why do I have to be . . . tied down?'

'I'm going to inject your uterus wall with Terbutaline,' he said. 'An involuntary twitch with a needle near the fetus could be dangerous.'

He wrapped Velcro straps around her calves, knees, and thighs, then moved the armrests into place and strapped down her wrists, elbows, and biceps. In all the procedures she'd had, she'd never been pinned down like this and didn't understand. She didn't like it. It didn't feel right.

He sat on his stool and poured reddish-brown Betadine into a stainless steel tray, then broke open a half dozen gauze pads and dropped them into the solution. Letting them soak, he lifted her T-shirt and pulled her boxer shorts down, exposing her from her bikini line to her midriff.

She tensed against the straps and told herself to relax. *He's your doctor. Do what he says. He's going to save your baby.*

He lifted a Betadine-soaked gauze pad and cleaned a wide area on her abdomen below the belly button. After tossing it into a kick bucket, he repeated the process four more times.

A plastic bottle appeared in his hand. He squirted a blob of translucent blue jelly above and below her belly button to lubricate the ultrasound wand. It occurred to her that it wasn't easy for him to have to do everything alone, ordinarily there'd be a nurse and an anesthesiologist to assist. *Just get it over with.* She didn't know how much longer she could fight off the rising claustrophobia.

He pulled a condomlike sheath over the white plastic ultrasound probe and laid it on her stomach, then adjusted the dials on the machine. She turned her head to see the monitor. A colorful blizzard disappeared and she could see the outlines of her fetus. *Look at that – the baby's asleep.*

Ben said, 'I think we caught it in time.'

After sharpening the image, he tore open a package containing a sterile drape and laid it over her lower body, then did the same above. He lifted more cellophane packages, tore them open, and let the instruments slide out onto a sterile cover on the tray. She saw syringes. Needles. One of them very long. Longer than any she'd seen before.

'How bad is this . . . going to be?' she asked.

'You'll feel a little discomfort,' he said.

Oh, God.

She watched him turn a small bottle of medication upside down, stick a small gauge needle into the diaphragm, and draw out some fluid.

'It's Lidocaine,' he said, 'to desensitize the needle.' He injected her below the belly button. She felt a sting . . . a burning sensation . . . then numbness. She became aware of pain in her legs. Without realizing it, she was struggling hard against the restraining straps.

'Take the straps off . . . until we're ready, okay?' she said.

'We're ready now,' he said.

HE GOT UP AND WALKED to a refrigerator at the side of the room and came back carrying a gun-metal gray thermos. When he unscrewed the top, wisps of fog from dry ice rose in the air.

'What . . . is that?' she said.

'It's the drug we're injecting into your uterus.'

A drug on ice?

He sat down and pulled a strap across her midriff, then another across her pelvis so that her entire body was totally immobilized. Instinctively, the small of her back arched but went nowhere.

It was all she could do to keep from losing it.

He raised a surgeon's mask, placed a pair of safety glasses on his eyes, and adjusted the elastic strap behind his head.

He drew a pair of sterile surgical gloves over the latex ones.

He lifted the long needle and screwed it onto the hub of an empty syringe, then placed the tip of the needle below her belly button.

He pushed it in.

She nearly fainted.

Steel in my belly – this is crazy – I can't do this!

'Close your eyes and count backwards from a hundred,' he said.

'One hundred. Ninety-nine. Ninety-eight . . .' Breathing like a racehorse.

She felt the pressure of the needle entering her abdomen, more weird than painful. 'Ninety-one, ninety . . . .' She opened her eyes and looked at the monitor.

'Don't move!' Ben said.

She closed her eyes. 'Eighty-nine.' It was like being buried in sand up to her neck. *Don't panic – pretend it's okay – don't panic.*

'Still in pain?'

'Yes."

'You're definitely having contractions,' he said.

He watched on the monitor as the needle moved through her body toward the uterus.

'Keep counting.'

'Eighty-eight, eighty-seven, eighty-six . . .'

'What are you feeling?'

'Claustrophobic.' A sense-memory came flooding back of the time she'd been locked in a closet – the darkness, the smell of wool coats and rubber boots. *I can't breathe – somebody open the door!*

He continued guiding the needle toward its objective.

'Breathe deeply and stay still. We're almost there.'

She opened her eyes again and looked at the monitor and saw the black line of the needle approaching the wall of her uterus. Her pores opened like morning glories. She began to hyperventilate. *I gotta get up a second, Ben, let me up.*

'Take it easy, Melissa.'

'I'm starting to freak out.'

'Talk to me,' he said.

'Oh, God. I . . . I don't . . . I can't do this.' *The claustrophobia's crushing me, I can't breathe.*

'Keep counting.'

'I can't . . .'

'What are you planning to name the baby?'

'I don't know. I don't know. Oh, I'm going crazy—' *My hair must be turning white, I can feel it tingling on my scalp.*

'Tell me what's going on with Harris,' he said.

She began breathing out of control, on the verge of a meltdown. *Harris Harris Harris.* Her legs and arms strained against the straps.

'Don't move!' he said.

I didn't move, if I moved I didn't mean to, I can't help it, I have to move, I'm going crazy!

He reached out and added a sedative to her veins, then returned his focus to the needle on the monitor. A sheen of perspiration covered his forehead.

'Nothing . . . new,' she said. *Save me, drugs, save me, please save me.*

'Any more news from the convent?' he said.

'No.' Dizzy, her heart fluttering against her ribs. *Heart attack any second now, don't think about it, listen, listen and talk to him, answer him and listen.* 'What . . . kinda news?'

'I don't know, another photograph, something Mother Marie-Catherine might have recalled after he left the convent.'

She opened her eyes. The needle was touching the uterus now, she could see it on the monitor. As if sensing it, the baby moved away from the point of contact like a goldfish moving away from a finger dipped in its bowl. Her head was swimming.

Those words . . . she couldn't make sense out of them. *Don't know what that means, I didn't hear that right, why don't I know that name.* Confusion descended.

'Mother . . . Marie . . . who?' she said.

ERIC'S PORSCHE CARRERA pulled around the semi-circular driveway at Ben's house and came to a stop in the driving rain. He turned off the engine and sat looking through the rivulets of water running down the windshield. There were lights on inside. Someone was awake.

He got out and ran in his poncho to the front door, rang the bell and waited. No one came. He banged a heavy brass knocker and waited. Still no answer. Where were they?

He saw the garage door standing open, ran to it, entered. Ben's Mercedes was gone, but Melissa's BMW was there. He walked to the interior door, found it unlocked. He walked into the breezeway, his rain-soaked parka leaving a trail of water on the floor.

'Hello?' He walked into the main hallway. 'It's Eric – anybody home?'

He looked in the unlit living room, then walked to the guest bedroom. The lights were on, the bed unmade, a Palm Pilot lying on the sheet. He picked it up and set it on the bedside table. The adjoining bathroom door was open.

He walked inside, crunching broken glass beneath his feet. Looking down, he saw a plastic bottle of Pepto-Bismol laying in the corner and traces of vomit in the toilet. An overturned vial had scattered salmon-colored pills on the countertop, and there were more shards of glass in the sink. He lifted the vial and read the label. It said Phenergan. He knew what that meant.

'Christ,' he said, and headed for his car.

'I SAID . . . WHO IS . . . Mother Marie-Catherine?' Melissa said.

'You know who she is, the nun Harris interviewed at the convent. Look at that.' He was staring at the monitor. The needle had pierced the uterine wall and was entering the amniotic sac.

Harris never told me the name of the nun, never told me, I'm sure he never told me, so how does Ben know unless Harris told him, but when did he do that, when, when did Harris tell him, he wouldn't have told him, I'm in a fog but I know he wouldn't have told him without telling me, so how does Ben know the name of the nun unless he met her, unless he met her, unless he knew her at the convent, when he was a child, when he lived there, he lived there, he lived with the nun, he lived in the convent with the nun, as a little boy, he lived there as—

Oh, God. Oh, no. Oh, God.

Her face went numb. *I'm hallucinating – no I'm not – oh my God I have to get up, I have to break the straps and get up RIGHT NOW.*

'Don't move!' Ben said. 'I'm into the fluid!'

She lifted her head. 'What are you doing . . . to my baby?' *My baby my baby he's hurting my baby – don't hurt my baby – WHAT ARE YOU DOING TO MY BABY?*

'Look at it!' he said of the sonogram image. 'It's so lively!' His hands were on her belly and the needle was inside the inner sanctum.

'No . . . for God's sake, Ben . . . don't . . .'

'Hold still!'

Her head fell back. *A butterfly on a board, a pin through its belly, pinned to the board, its wings still beating, Mom's polish remover on a Q-tip, touch it to the butterfly's head and its wings stop beating, now it's gone, it's gone, it's still pretty but it's dead and it's pinned down but it's dead, that's me, pinned down with my baby, we're dead, I can't breathe.*

He held the syringe with one hand and wiped his brow with the other. 'You were bound to find out sooner or later,' he said.

Oh, God, he admitted it – the last shred of hope is gone. Oh God, I have to get up, I can't breathe, something heavy's on my chest, I can't breathe, look at all the butterflies flying around the room – those aren't butterflies, you idiot, those are spots in front of your eyes. You're fainting.

ERIC SHIFTED INTO THIRD and got on his cell phone. He dialed the clinic and let it ring. The off-hours announcement came on; he disconnected and dialed Ben's direct line. After three rings it rolled over to the same recording.

He hung up and kept driving toward South Dixie Highway which would take him north to the clinic. Wait a minute: maybe they'd gone to Health South Doctors' Hospital. It was on campus only a mile from Ben's house, and he had privileges. If she was in serious trouble, that's where they'd go.

He fishtailed onto University Drive and wound out toward Heath South Doctors' Hospital.

SHE FELT HERSELF FLOATING off the examining table as if gravity had disappeared from the earth. She stared at Ben in search of the joke, the explanation, the sign that he was still the person she knew, but all she saw was Adalwolf and all her thoughts were jumbled like a dropped deck of cards. David, NTX, dying children, Sergeant Sherwood, Josef Mengele, Grandma Esther, Auschwitz, her baby, her baby, her baby.

He increased her Versed and checked his watch. 'We don't have much time.'

'What are you . . . doing to me?'

He repositioned himself on his stool and concentrated on the needle in her belly. 'Pregnancy runs by a clock,' he said, watching the monitor. 'Midcycle conception, hormone treatment for four-teen days, eighteen hours of incubation, staged fetal development. You're in your fourteenth week, which means we're a little early, but with you and Harris breathing down my neck, I need you now. Okay, it's time to hold still again.'

'Need me . . . for what . . .' *This is a dream . . . no, stop wishing and start coping . . . How? I'm pinned down by the man who killed all those people . . . the man who killed my husband.*

He checked her vital signs. 'I always thought you'd recognize me in the photograph taken at Block Nineteen,' he said. 'I wasn't the young fellow kneeling in front – that was Benjamin Ben-Zevi. I was the one in the lab coat standing off to the side.'

Questions bursting out all over my mind. Stay awake, stay awake, talk and stay awake . . . 'You murdered Ben-Zevi . . . and took his name?'

'Of course I did, but there's no need to be so melodramatic about it. Chloroform was a painless way to die. Good lord, Melissa. We were not barbarians.'

Not barbarians, good, good, not barbarians . . . no, they were worse than barbarians.

He unscrewed the syringe from the long needle sticking out of her belly. 'He'd stolen your grandmother's pendant,' he said, 'which couldn't be overlooked.' He drew liquid from the bottle in the gun-metal gray container, then screwed the syringe to the long needle in her womb.

'The emulsion is full of tiny bubbles so the ultrasound can pick it up,' he said. 'You'll be able to see it enter the amniotic fluid.'

Stay awake.

He pushed the plunger on the large syringe the slightest bit.

'What are you . . . putting in me?'

'If you remember correctly, I told you I killed a child on Christmas Eve, nineteen forty-four,' he said, 'I just didn't say it was Ben-Zevi. The rest of the story was true, though: the little girl I made him kill, the snow falling peacefully. It was a beautiful night.'

He's pushing the plunger in more.

'When the Russians were approaching Auschwitz in nineteen forty-five I thought I was a dead duck, but then it occurred to me if I'd taken Ben-Zevi's life, why not take the rest of him? I had his file and I knew his personality and his story. We had somewhat similar features. He was younger, but in the camp you couldn't tell a twelve-year-old prisoner from a hundred-year-old man. I escaped before the Russians arrived, stayed with Mengele at Gross Rosen for a while, then lived with a family in a town fifty kilometers away for the next year. After that I made my way to France as Benjamin Ben-Zevi, liberated Jew. Look at that.'

She lifted her head and saw the tip of the needle inside her womb. Gray liquid began curling into her amniotic fluid like ink in water. She watched it cloud up. *He's killing my baby.*

He checked his watch again.

'Whenever I learned a new Yiddish word, I thought, isn't this something? Me, the foster son of Dr. Josef Mengele, passing for a Jew!'

He folded his arms and waited.

'Telling you this is a load off my mind, actually. By the way, I never had a tattoo. You heard about that from two eyewitnesses, one of whom was me speaking as Ben-Zevi, the other the survivor's widow in Toronto whom I hired to play the role. We won't have to wait much longer. How's the pain in your abdomen?'

Tattoo . . . Adalwolf has no tattoo.

'It'll be gone shortly,' he said. 'You're not having contractions, my dear. The baby's fine. I put a little cassava in your salad so you'd wake up with a tummy ache, that's all.' He took a drink of water from a plastic bottle and offered her some. She turned her head.

'Jews think they're so clever,' he said. 'They're good with books, but when it comes to understanding the world as it is, they lack *tsaychel*. You know what that is?' He checked his watch, then reached out and injected another small dose. 'It's Yiddish for common sense.'

Still injecting me . . . looking at his watch . . . waiting for something to happen.

'Look at Europe before World War Two,' he said with his arms folded. 'Jews in Germany had more money, education, and success than anybody, and what did they do? They let the Nazis round them up and cart them off to the ovens like sheep. Where did they think those railroad cars were going, to a picnic?'

That thermos holds something sick, oh God.

He placed the bottle back in the canister. When he turned it, she saw an orange and black warning symbol that signified biological hazard.

'If you think they were fools *before* the Holocaust, look what they did afterward,' he said. 'You'd think Holocaust survivors above all would realize that ghettos makes you easy prey, right? So what do they do? They create the mother of all ghettos, Israel! Squeezed themselves into it like fish in a barrel!' He adjusted his surgeon's mask.

What is he talking about?

'Unbelievable,' he said. 'Fifteen years after the Warsaw ghetto, Jews round *themselves* up and put *themselves* in a concentration camp and call it home! They're even building walls around it with barbed wire now, just like the camps! Before you know it they'll be installing guard towers with machine guns and searchlights!' He screwed on the top of the thermos. 'And where do they locate this grand bastion of security? In the middle of a hundred and fifty million goddamned *Arabs*! What idiots! They're Goyishe kops with Jewish blood!'

He reached out and injected another dose of the liquid.

No more, no more, no more.

'Let me tell you something, my dear. Every time a suicide bomber kills another Jew, Hitler dances on their graves. Don't you see, he's still doing it to them! He's still winning! Without him there'd be no Holocaust, and without the Holocaust there'd be no Israel, and without Israel you wouldn't have all those fish in a barrel!'

Fish? What fish . . .

He watched the liquid furl into her womb on the ultrasound screen.

'"Never again" they say, but what they don't realize is that it's never stopped.' His eyes were glued to the monitor. 'We're almost done.'

He pushed the plunger to the bottom.

Break the straps . . . if you don't, you'll go stark raving mad and die.

'YOU'RE SURE SHE'S NOT here?' Eric said to the clerk in hospital admitting.

'Positive,' she said.

'No calls?'

'Nothing. Maybe you should try Mount Zion.'

Eric nodded. 'Right,' he said, tapping the countertop. Frustrated, he pushed away and headed back toward the parking lot.

Relax, she's with Ben. Go home and get some sleep. You've got surgery in five hours.

'IT'S NOT REALLY ABOUT making matzohs out of Christian children's blood or any of those other silly blood libels,' Adalwolf said. 'That's not why everybody hates the Jews.' He moved the ultrasound probe and squinted at the monitor. 'I'll tell you what it is.' He checked his watch. 'Is your stomach feeling better?'

She closed her eyes, spilling tears. *Disconnect until this is over, Melissa. Cut the sanity cord and disconnect.*

'I once heard Mengele tell this brilliant Jewish doctor who was forced to do autopsies that there were two great races on earth – Aryans and Jews – but unfortunately there was room for only one. The problem was, the Jews thought they were chosen to be it.'

He picked up a small light and leaned forward to examine her eyes.

'Chosen by whom, I ask you? And chosen for what? Chosen by God to suffer more than the rest of us? Chosen to turn their precious misery into moral superiority and position? That's how they look at it, you know, as if they are better than the rest of us. Sheer, unadulterated arrogance is the reason the world hates Jews, my dear. You're perspiring a little.'

Her eyelids were leaden. 'No . . . don't . . .' *Please don't hurt my child.*

'Sh, sh, sh,' he said. 'Save your breath, I know what you want to say. Living as Ben-Zevi, believe me, I've heard it a thousand times. You want to tell me how six million Jews created wheat fields and olive groves and orange trees and made the desert bloom. You want to list the names of Jewish Nobel prize winners and universities and medical cures and tell me how Jews have created a military regime so strong no combination of Arabs can crush it. You want to tell me how Germans took the most advanced civilization in the world and reduced it to rubble twice in one generation. But don't you see? Your defense is your indictment, because when you add it all up, what you're saying is you're smarter and better than everyone else. Jews are the ones who see themselves as the master race, not Aryans. And that's just not acceptable.'

He broke out an ice pack and laid it on her forehead.

Cold and heavy . . .

'But none of this banter really matters. The only thing that matters is the lesson I learned from an old Jew many years ago.'

He laid his fingers on her wrist and took her pulse.

'The story goes like this. An emperor was riding his horse one day when he came across an old Jew standing at the side of the road. He stopped and said to his lieutenant, "How dare that man not kneel before me! Cut off his head!" The lieutenant pulled out his sword and did as he was told and rejoined the emperor at his side.'

He lifted the ice pack off her head.

'A few miles down the road they came to another Jew, this one kneeling like a good supplicant with his head bowed. The emperor stopped again and said to his lieutenant, "How dare that old man mock me with false respect! Cut off his head!" The lieutenant pulled out his sword and again did as he was told.'

He dried her face with a paper towel.

'Upon returning to the emperor's side, the lieutenant said, "Pardon me, sire, but I'm a little confused about my orders. If I'm supposed to kill some subjects for kneeling and other subjects for not kneeling, how am I supposed to know who to kill?"

' "Very simple," the emperor said. "If he's a Jew, kill him." '

He moved the kick bucket with his foot. 'In the end, that's all you need to know. If he's a Jew, kill him.' He tossed in the paper towel.

Emperor . . . emperor . . . She began shivering, her teeth clenched.

Jaw hurts . . . cold. . . I'm having a convulsion . . . but how would I know, I've never had one before.

He took hold of the syringe and withdrew the needle smoothly. When it was out he unscrewed it from the hub and dropped it into a sharps box.

'As brilliant and hard working as they are, Jews have created nothing but misery for the human race,' he said. 'In my lifetime alone they gave us World Wars One and Two, and now they're trying to give us Armageddon with a billion Muslims.'

He reached out and brushed her hair away from her face.

Please . . . someone. Anyone. Please.

'No way, my dear. You are going to save us from this scourge right here and now.' He got off his stool and started to walk away, saying, 'I'll get you a blanket. Oh' – he stopped short – 'I forgot to tell you. Congratulations. It's a boy.'

ERIC PULLED INTO THE basement garage and parked in the space next to Ben's black Mercedes. He was glad to see it. If she was here instead of the hospital, she couldn't be in too much trouble.

He got out of his Porsche and hit the remote lock. The head-lights blinked and the car made a small quack. He walked to the steel fire door and reached into his back pocket for his security card. Damn, he'd forgotten to bring his wallet. Now what?

He walked back to his car, unlocked the door, and reached in for his cell phone. After locking the doors again, he walked up the car ramp until his phone found a clear signal, then he headed for the front door of the building as he dialed. A minute later someone answered: 'Clarion Security.'

'This is Dr. Eric Brandt at the Myrna Ben-Zevi Fertility Clinic,' he said. 'I'm afraid I locked myself out.'

'No problem, Dr. Brandt. Bear with me while we run a security check. What's your mother's maiden name?'

ADALWOLF LAID A BLANKET over Melissa and sat on his stool with his arms folded.

'Please . . . untie me,' Melissa said. She was awake and her eyes were open. Her face felt tight, as if all the blood and moisture had been drained out.

'Can't,' he said. He wiped his forehead with a towel. The ultrasound probe was still resting on her stomach beneath the blanket. 'Not yet.'

Not yet? What else is he going to do? Stay awake . . . talk.

'What happened . . . to my grandmother?' she said.

'I told you, she drowned at Coney Island.'

'You said it happened . . . before you got there . . . but that's not true . . . is it?'

'Oh, aren't you alert,' he said. He placed a new syringe of sedative into the port on her catheter. 'I knew she'd recognize me as Adalwolf instead of Ben-Zevi when I got to New York, so I arranged to meet her on the beach at night.' He checked his watch. 'Sadly, there was an accident on the pier and, well. . .'

Melissa closed her eyes. *Keep talking.* 'You married . . . a Jew,' she said.

'Of course I married a Jew, can you imagine Benjamin Ben-Zevi *not*? It wasn't that difficult. Many SS officers had Jewish mistresses.'

'She wasn't your mistress . . . she was your *wife*.'

His head gesture said *Whatever.* 'She annoyed me for years. I finally had to get rid of her.'

Good God, he says it so easily. 'What are you . . . going to do . . . to me?'

'I'd hoped to medicate your false contractions and let you go to term without your knowing who I am, but I'm afraid you finally got lucky.'

Lucky? She wished she didn't know.

He said, 'It doesn't matter. I've always had a backup plan in case you found out.'

Her respiration increased.

'The next five months are going to be very pleasant for you,' he said. 'Blue sky, warm water, good food, books, television, a hammock.'

'What . . . are you talking about?'

'You'll be staying in a lovely house I own until the baby's born,' he said.

Oh, God. She pictured a basement bunker, chains, bread and water, cockroaches—

A chime. Someone opened the door to the reception room.

Adalwolf froze, then put his finger to his lips to shush her and picked up a roll of adhesive tape. Except for the low whir of the sonogram machine, the room was quiet. He ripped off a line and placed it over her mouth.

I can't breathe! I can't breathe! Shaking her head violently from side to side, jerking hard against the restraining straps.

He got off his stool, pulled off his gloves and tossed them away, then lowered his surgeon's mask and walked to the operating room door. He wanted to get into the hallway before the security guard reached the OR. He opened a drawer beneath the counter and pulled out a pair of sharp-tipped surgical scissors, just in case. Hiding them in his palm, he stepped into the hallway to meet the man.

Instead of a guard coming around the corner, it was Eric Brandt.

'Ben – what's going on?'

Adalwolf masked his surprise. 'Premature contractions,' he said. 'What in the world brought you here at this hour?'

'Melissa left a message on my answering machine. Is she all right?'

'She's holding on fine. I was just going for the Terbutaline. Would you mind grabbing it for me?'

'No problem.' Eric walked past him toward the medication room. 'Is Ginny here?' he said over his shoulder, taking keys from his pocket.

'No,' Adalwolf said. He turned back to the OR and pushed the door open.

'How'd you get a nurse at this hour?' Eric said. He unlocked the door and disappeared inside the medication room, walked to the cabinet, unlocked it and found the Terbutaline. After taking it out, he locked the cabinet again, turned out the light, and entered the hallway. When he reached the OR, he pushed the door open and saw Melissa lying on the examining table.

'Hey there, how are you feel—'

He slowed his walk. She was covered by a blanket and there was no nurse in the room. He walked to the side of the examining table and looked down at her and saw – My God – there was a strip of tape across her mouth. He lifted the blanket and saw Velcro restraints, her feet taped to stirrups, her arms strapped down to the rests. He'd never seen anything like it.

Her eyes widened and she began puffing against the tape on her mouth as if signaling him to look out. He wheeled around but the room was empty. He looked back at Melissa and peeled the tape off her mouth.

'Ben . . .' she said.

Ben? Ben what? You mean . . . Ben.

He ran to the door and looked down the hallway, but it was empty.

He ran to the reception room. The front door was locked from the inside, which meant he'd gone the other way. He turned and ran to the other end of the hallway, out the back door, and over to service elevator. The elevator door was closed. He opened the door to the emergency exit stairwell but heard no footsteps.

Ben was gone.

WHEN A HUNTER SHOOTS A papa bear, the mama bear gets depressed. When a hunter shoots a baby bear, the mama bear gets enraged. Melissa was enraged.

It was three in the afternoon when she finally woke up in a hospital room with an anesthesia hangover, but not too fuzzy to be furious. *What has he done to my baby?*

She turned from her side onto her back, letting out a painful groan. Harris, who was sitting in a chair taking notes, heard her stir and looked up. She propped herself on her elbows and pushed her hair out of her eyes. He put down his note pad and reached for the phone.

'What happened?' she said.

Harris spoke into the receiver: 'Tell Dr. Brandt she's awake.'

'Where is Adalwolf?' she asked.

'Don't know,' he said, hanging up.

She lowered herself onto her back slowly, painfully.

'How do you feel?' he said.

'Beat up.'

'You've got bruises on your arms and legs.'

And pain below my belly button. 'What did he inject me with?'

'We'll know soon. The bottles and the needles are at the lab.'

He gave her a glass of water.

She stared at the ceiling tiles. 'How did I miss it, Harris?'

Harris said, 'Not you, we. Eric missed it too.'

She set the glass of water on the table.

Eric Brandt came into the room, closed the door, and went to her bedside. He picked up her wrist to take her pulse. 'How do you feel?'

'That depends on what you have to tell me,' she said.

He examined her eyes, felt for swollen glands under her jaw and neck and placed a thermometer in her mouth. He sat on the bed. 'We did an ultrasound and the baby looks fine. Did you see the needle actually go in?'

She nodded.

'Did it touch the fetus?'

She shrugged and shook her head no.

He took the thermometer out of her mouth. 'No fever,' he said. 'Any chills? Headache? Upset stomach?'

'Nothing,' she said.

'Are you sure the needle pierced the womb?'

'Positive. I don't remember a lot, but I remember that.'

Eric looked calm but worried.

'What did he inject me with?' she said.

'We'll know more about that when we get the lab report.'

The door opened and a nurse came in followed by Dr. Otto Heller, a clipboard in hand. The nurse fussed around and Otto looked unhappy. He asked how she was feeling. She said sore and bruised. He asked if she had a fever, chills, any signs of the flu. She said she had nothing like that. He asked Harris if he'd mind leaving the room, but Melissa said she wanted him to stay. They waited for the nurse to leave and close the door. Melissa knew something bad was about to happen.

OTTO HELLER TURNED A page on his clipboard. 'I have a few facts and a hypothesis. I'll start with the facts. CDC pathology confirms you were injected with the NTX virus. Or to be more specific, a version of it.'

Melissa shouldn't have been surprised, but hearing it drained the blood from her face. 'A version?'

'The micrograph – a picture of the virus taken with a transmission electron microscope – shows a virus that's almost identical to NTX. The PCR – that's a technique that gives us the virus's chemistry – shows a ninety-nine percent DNA match. We're calling it NTX-2.'

'What's it mean?' she said.

'Not clear,' he said. 'The victims who died of NTX-1 began showing symptoms a few hours after they were exposed. So far, you're showing nothing.'

'Maybe it hasn't been long enough to kick in,' she said.

'Maybe, but if that's the case, it's different from NTX-1.'

'And the baby?'

'The amniotic fluid is loaded with it.'

'Good God.'

'On the other hand, he looks fine.'

'Does that strike you as weird?'

'Very.'

'What do you think's going on?'

He looked uncomfortable.

'You may as well tell me,' she said. 'My imagination is worse than anything you can describe.'

'Well, this is conjecture, and doctors hate to guess when—

'Dr. Heller?'

'Yes?'

'Just tell me.'

He shifted his weight from one foot to the other. 'I think Adalwolf has engineered a virus that attacks the Jewish genome.'

She blinked.

'I think he's created a virus that causes a deadly hemorrhagic fever when it encounters cells that contain Jewish genes.'

'Jewish genes? What are Jewish genes?'

He picked up his clipboard and a pen. 'You remember what a virus is, right?'

'I remember the comic book description of the Enza twins, yes.'

'Okay, let's look at the target again – our body's cells. The DNA in our cells determines what they become – nose cells, fingernail cells, livers, hearts, kidneys. Every characteristic we have, including our so-called ethnic traits like the color of our skin, the texture of our hair, or the shape of our eyes, is shaped by our DNA.'

He paused to pull the cap off the pen.

'Some ethnic proclivities we can't see. For example, DNA makes Africans unusually predisposed to sickle cell anemia, Jews to Tay-Sachs disease, white males to cystic fibrosis, and so on. The genetic differences are small and many of them overlap from one group to another, but not completely.'

He started sketching.

'The human genome project identified the typical genetic makeup of every major group in the world, including Ashkenazi and Sephardic Jews. Adalwolf is trying to take advantage of those minute differences by turning the flu into an ethnic killer of both groups.'

He drew two cells, one with a Star of David, the other with a shamrock.

'NTX is toxic enough to make everyone who contracts it sick to some extent, but when it comes into contact with protein markers found on the surface of Jewish cells, it goes wild.'

Melissa stared at the drawings.

'I knew what he'd done when a nurse named Erin O'Reilly accidentally contracted Jeremy Friedman's virus during a resuscitation attempt but showed no serious viral symptoms.'

'Are you sure she got the virus?'

'A micrograph of her nasal washings showed no doubt about it. A virus that killed a Jewish kid gave an Irish woman nothing more than a bad headache.'

Melissa sat staring and thinking. 'What does my baby have to do with it?'

Otto said, 'He's using it as an incubator.'

An incubator? Her child?

'He needs a safe, warm place for the virus to mature over the next few months,' Otto said, 'and when it's ready, he needs someone to transmit it to the population as a whole. Those are the roles he's chosen for your baby.' He let it sink in. 'The flu bug is highly transmissible, Melissa. As I told you before, the nineteen eighteen epidemic killed millions of people in a matter of months. What if he could do that again, but this time with a perverse twist? Non-Jews get a mild touch of the flu, Jews die of massive internal bleeding and shock.'

'An ethnic biological weapon,' Harris said.

Nobody spoke.

Finally, Melissa said, 'What do you know, I was wrong again. Turns out my imagination isn't worse than anything you can describe.'

'I ASSUME YOU REALIZE,' Otto said to Harris, 'that if you can do this with Jews you can do it with any genetically homologous group.'

'Jews today, blacks tomorrow?' Harris said.

Otto said, 'Tomorrow it could be anybody you want. African-Americans, Chinese-Americans, Anglo-Saxons, Irish, Italians, Germans, Poles – there are a handful of genetic markers for virtually every group on the globe. It only takes one marker to set off a properly tailored virus.'

Eric said, 'Jews are the canary in the coal mine of civilization. If it happens to them, the rest of us can't be far behind.'

'It's a terrorist's dream,' H·   id. 'Pick an enemy, design a disease.'

'Since many Jews and Arabs are Semitic,' Otto said, 'I suppose a lot of Arabs would die from NTX, too.' He looked at Melissa. 'What doesn't make sense is that you're not sick, and neither is the baby. We know the virus is in the amniotic fluid, so we have to assume it's in the baby's cells, too, but for some reason it's dormant. If it was the same virus he gave four other victims, you and the baby would be dead by now.'

'Why is this one different?'

'I don't know.'

'But you're telling me I'm going to deliver a child that will destroy the Jewish race?'

'I'm telling you that's my speculation,' Otto said.

'But what if it's true? What am I supposed to do?'

They stared at her.

'Oh, no,' she said, 'don't even think about it. This child is not expendable.'

'I'm not telling you it is,' Otto said. 'I'm not even sure it's infected, much less virulent.' He was trying to give her comfort. 'You certainly don't have to make a decision like that at this point.'

At this point! That sounded like an ax over her baby's neck. She was starting to shake.

Harris said, 'How long does it take to make a vaccine?'

Otto said, 'Depends on the virus. We haven't found a vaccine for HIV in twenty years.'

'Then how come new flu vaccines come out every year?'

'Flu vaccines can be made fast because we know more about the underlying disease. And even then we aren't always right.' That little truth didn't help clear the atmosphere. He turned to Melissa. 'We have to figure out why neither you or the baby is sick. I know Versed causes retrograde amnesia, but can you remember anything more about last night?'

She closed her eyes. 'I remember fighting off panic and trying to escape.' Everyone remained quiet. 'I remember hearing him yammering on about Jews.'

'What else?'

She waited for something to come back to her. 'It's a blur.'

'Do you recall what happened when you first arrived?'

'He worked fast to give me the injection. I remember that because I thought I was having premature contractions and he didn't have much time.'

'That's a little odd,' Eric said. 'Her telephone call came into my answering machine twenty minutes before I heard it, and I didn't get to the clinic for another forty-five minutes after that. If he injected her right away, why was he still there when I arrived? What was he waiting for?'

'An emperor,' she said, her eyes still closed.

Blank stares.

'He told a story about an emperor and an old Jew.'

More silence, time to let her think.

'Not yet,' she said. Her eyes were darting beneath their lids. 'When the injection was finished I told him to untie me, but he said, "Not yet."'

'"Not yet"?' Eric said.

Otto started pacing. 'That suggests he had something more to do. Something important enough to risk getting caught.' He stopped walking. 'I wonder if he couldn't complete the protocol with a single injection.'

Eric looked for an explanation.

Otto said, 'The protocol he set up may require him to give the virus with one injection and animate it with second. If that's the case, he has to inject her *twice*.'

Melissa opened her eyes. 'He kept looking at his watch.'

'And Eric interrupted him before the second injection,' Otto said.

Eric was testing the idea. 'There were no other drugs on the tray.'

'He could have taken it with him,' Otto said. He was running his hand through his gray burr haircut. 'A second injection, a second procedure of some kind. It's a weak virus that becomes virulent only if you catalyze it with another agent. I saw it in Central Africa with the Kowari virus that turned virulent only if you contracted a head cold.'

Harris said, 'If you're right, it means he still needs her.'

'Great,' Melissa said through her teeth. 'I need him so I can find out what he did to me, and he needs me to finish the job.'

Harris turned to Melissa and said, 'From this point forward, I want a bodyguard with you at all times.'

Otto said, 'I'm going back to Atlanta. Call me if you remember anything more, okay?'

'Okay.'

'How do you feel?' Touching her forehead one more time.

'I'm telling you, I'm fine,' she said.

Otto looked at Eric to see if he agreed she could go. He nodded yes.

'So until the baby is born I pose no danger to anyone?' Melissa said.

'As long as you're well, that's right,' Otto said. 'But if you get so much as one shiver or a half degree of fever, we're going to quarantine you until we know what's happening. You understand?'

'Yes, of course,' she said. How could she not? She saw how the other four victims had died. 'Now if you don't mind, I'd like to get dressed.'

HARRIS SHOWED HIS FBI credential to a Miami police officer at Ben-Zevi's house and shepherded Kobie and Melissa under the yellow tape marked 'Crime Scene – Do Not Enter'. Another officer sitting in a squad car in the driveway waved to them as they opened the front door and went inside. Harris and Kobie were moving into Ben's house from their hotel. Melissa wanted the company, Harris wanted to keep an eye on her, and Kobie wanted the excitement. With the place surrounded by Miami PD and the FBI, there was hardly a safer place to be.

They walked down the hallway and entered the study. Every room in the house had been turned upside down, dusted for fingerprints and searched for clues to Adalwolf's whereabouts. By dawn the agents had packed up and shipped out most of the evidence, leaving cabinets, bookshelves, and desk drawers stripped bare. Even the photographs had been taken off the walls. Only a couple of cardboard boxes of file folders sat in the middle of the room. Melissa opened one to look through the papers, but she was too tired to focus.

Harris turned the box around and looked at the description on the side. CASTOR BEANS. 'Who uses castor beans?'

Melissa looked and said, 'Must be from the garage. Ben said he makes a skin cream for stretch marks out of castor oil and lanolin.'

Castor beans for a skin cream? It sounded strange to Harris, but he let it go. They ordered pizza for dinner and she headed for her room and a good night's sleep.

Kobie gave her a hug. 'Night, Melissa, I hope you feel better. I'm gonna miss you.'

'Miss me?'

Harris said, 'She has to go home tomorrow afternoon.'

'Not till *after* the amusement park,' she said for the record.

Harris said, 'Linda Gonzales is taking her and Kevin to a park with rides and miniature golf. Apparently Disney World wasn't enough.'

'Why don't you come with us?' Kobie said to Melissa.

'Maybe I will,' Melissa said.

She gave Kobie a hug and said goodnight.

THE PLACE WAS CALLED Boomer's and it was a kids' paradise. There were go-karts, bumper boats, batting cages, miniature golf, a roller coaster, a climbing wall, and laser tag. Inside an enormous, hangar-sized arcade were Skee-Ball, Max-Fly, Jurassic Park, Police 911, Silent Scope, Road Rage, the Rock, the Jump Zone, Dance-Dance, and seven hundred more games offering endless thrills, spills, and chills. The noise in the room was deafening. Kobie and Kevin Gonzales were in heaven.

It was noon when they arrived, so they decided to give the kids lunch and then let them play. Clad in summer attire, Melissa, Linda Gonzales, and the two kids walked through the game room with Harris and two additional FBI agents at their side. The agents wore chinos, polo shirts, polarized sunglasses, and service revolvers tucked inside their pants. The group entered a glass-enclosed porch with a concession stand at one end and picnic tables lined up along floor-to-ceiling windows overlooking a fish pond and a miniature golf course. Fifty yards away, a wooden roller coaster called the Hurricane loomed against the blue sky.

They set their gear on a table and walked to the food counter and ordered hot dogs, potato chips, and cups of syrupy, shaved-ice 'Icees'. When they came back to the table, they spread out and listened to the din of pinballs, explosions, car wrecks, and motor-cycle crashes in the adjoining arcade. Kobie showed Melissa the embroidered flowers around the edges of her cut-off jeans and said she wanted to go outside and ride The Blender. Hearing that,

Kevin said he'd rather go to the arcade and drive a car on Road Rage.

After downing a hotdog, Harris said he'd check the height requirements on the rides and disappeared into the arcade. Melissa and Linda wiped the kids' faces and cleared the paper and plastic from the table. The FBI agents drank Pepsis and watched. Linda was laying a tray on top of a trash can when a woman nearby called her name.

'It's me,' the woman said, 'Terri Snider.'

'Terri!' Linda said, touching the woman's arm. 'What are you doing here?'

'My sister and her husband are moving to Miami,' she said. 'That's her over there with her two boys.' Pointing at a table at the other end of the room.

'Have they bought a house yet?' Linda asked.

'They're looking now,' Terri said. 'Come on over, I'll introduce you.'

Kevin pulled at his pants and said, 'Mommy, I have to go to the *bathroom.*'

Linda bent down and said, 'I'll be back in two seconds.'

Melissa said to Linda, 'Go ahead, I'll take the kids for a pit stop.'

'Would you mind?' Linda said. 'I'll be right back.' She walked away chatting with her friend.

Melissa shepherded Kevin and Kobie toward the restroom doors, dropping Kobie at the women's room first, then walking Kevin farther down to the men's room. She pushed the door open for him and said, 'I'll be right here, okay?' The FBI agents sat close by.

'Can I have another Icee?' Kevin said before going inside.

'Sure,' Melissa said. 'I'll get it while you go to the bathroom.'

Kevin went inside the men's room and Melissa started for the nearby concession stand. As she walked toward it, she heard her cell phone ring and fished it out of her bag.

'Hello?' she said. There was no answer. She looked at the cell phone window, which said, *No Caller ID.* She brought the phone back to her ear: 'Harris?'

After a long pause, she heard, 'Hello, Melissa.'

No, it wasn't Harris, it was Ben.

No, it wasn't Ben. It was Adalwolf.

OF ALL THE CALLS HE'D made to her over the years, this one took her most by surprise.

Ben – *Adalwolf* – said, 'I had to leave you abruptly the other night, but I'm sure you understand why.'

'I understand nothing,' she said.

'That's why I'm calling,' he said. 'I want to tell you what happened on the examining table.'

There was a long silence. 'So tell me,' she said.

'Not on the telephone,' he said. 'In person.'

'You've got to be joking,' she said.

'If I'd wanted to harm you I would have done it while you were strapped down.'

'Didn't you?'

'That's why we need to talk.'

'If you get within a mile of me you'll be arrested.'

'If that were true I'd be arrested right now.'

She felt a chill. 'Where are you?'

'Close enough to see you're wearing a yellow T-shirt.'

She wheeled around.

'Not that way, Melissa. Up here.'

She turned again, eyes darting.

'Up here by the ticket booth,' he said. 'At the roller coaster.'

She looked through the glass door and saw a foot bridge over a fish pond leading up to a line of people waiting to buy tickets. Could he really be there? She turned and caught the eye of one of the FBI agents and pointed at her cell phone. He stood up.

Adalwolf said, 'Walk up to the ticket booth and I'll explain everything. With all these people around, you couldn't be safer.'

She could see the ticket booth but not him.

'Look to your right,' he said.

She stood on her toes and saw Linda at the end of the room and waved at her to come fast. Linda started walking toward Melissa, who pointed at the door to the men's room, telling her Kevin was in there, okay? Then she walked a few steps toward the windows with the cell phone still at her ear, craning and focused on Adalwolf's location – so focused, in fact, she didn't see two kids with hot dogs nearly run into her, or a hefty woman in gray work pants and a Boomer's work shirt pull up short to keep from hitting Melissa with her trash cart.

'I don't see you,' Melissa said. She heard the rustle of his cell phone against fabric, as if he was taking it from a pocket, or had dropped it.

'What did you say?' he said.

'I said I don't see you,' she said.

She heard him breathing hard. 'Step outside and look to your right.'

Don't go into the open. She looked over at the table. The FBI agents were moving toward her.

Adalwolf said, 'Come on, Melissa, I'm more at risk than you are. I don't have the FBI at my side.'

She held her finger up to the agents, telling them to hold on a second, and pushed open the glass door to the walkway. She stepped outside and stopped, then squinted toward the ticket booth, the phone still at her ear. 'I don't . . .'

'You're staring right at me,' he said.

She was? 'Wave your hand.' The agents came bustling through the door and up to her side. She covered the phone and mouthed the words, *He's on the phone!* and nodded toward the ticket booth. *Up there!*

Adalwolf, breathless again, said, 'See the woman in a pink polo shirt and khaki shorts in the middle of the line? She's standing directly in our line of sight. *Shhh.* Be quiet.'

The agents stood on each side of Melissa, scanning the area through their polarized lenses. She saw the woman in the pink polo shirt, but not Adalwolf. And who was he shushing and telling to be quiet? She tried to step to her left to get a better angle but the agent wouldn't let her move.

Adalwolf said, 'The crowd is for my safety . . . as much as . . . yours.' He sounded very out of breath now. Where was he moving? What was he climbing?

She looked around the ticket booth and the roller coaster cars. As if he was talking to someone else, Adalwolf said, 'That's it, get in.'

'Get in?' she said. 'Who are you talking to?'

No answer.

'Are you still there?' she said.

She heard him panting as if he were walking up hill.

'Where are you?' she said.

One of the agents was searching the area with a small pair of binoculars. He scanned the scaffolding that held the roller coaster.

She heard voices over Adalwolf's phone, people in the background laughing and talking. It sounded as if he was still on the ground in a crowd. She looked at the customers moving from the ticket booth to the roller coaster loading platform. She could see them chatting – so why couldn't she see him? She heard more labored breathing on his cell phone, then loud music and three gongs in rapid succession. Then two more.

Gongs – the sound of a pinball machine. Her face turned prickly. There were no pinball machines up by the roller coaster, the pinball machines were in the arcade. *Behind* her . . .

'Oh God.'

She turned and bolted into the lunch room with the agents on her heels. 'Get the kids!' she said to one of them. They followed her past the picnic tables to the Men's Room door. Kevin was standing outside with his mother, who was drying his hands. Melissa didn't pause but kept running toward the women's room. Kobie was not standing outside the door looking for her. There was an orange plastic cone on the floor in front of the door and a sign that read, CLEANING IN PROGRESS, PLEASE USE ARCADE RESTROOM.

She punched the door open. 'Kobie?' She and the agents entered.

The room was empty.

'Kobie, where are you!'

The three of them bent down and looked under the stalls and pushed the doors open. Nobody there. Melissa stood in the center of the room turning in a circle. One agent was already on his cell phone, the other running out the door with his service revolver drawn.

'Kobie!' she yelled at the top of her voice. 'Where are you?'

Then it hit her: the woman pushing the trash cart! That was him!

She stood aching from head to toe. *Keep your head, they can't be far.*

More FBI agents were joining the first two, talking quietly, dispersing, moving fast. Melissa ran into the game room and saw people strolling around, laughing and having fun. A middle-aged woman in blue shorts caught her eye.

'Excuse me!' Melissa said. 'I'm looking for a little girl with a trash collector!'

'Beg pardon?'

She was sounding nutty. 'Have you seen a woman pushing a trash cart?'

The woman looked at her and said, 'No, do you need help?'

Melissa half ran, half walked deeper into the arcade, past the Dance-Dance machine toward the Skee-Ball lanes. Her cell phone rang. She fumbled in her bag, found it, hit Answer, and brought it to her mouth.

'What have you done with her!' she yelled.

'Say again?' It was Harris.

She crumpled against a cinderblock wall. 'Harris,' she said. 'He's got her.'

'Who's got who?'

'Adalwolf took Kobie out of the ladies' room—'

'Where are you?'

'At the Skee-ball lanes.'

'Don't move.'

BEN'S STUDY LOOKED LIKE a mafia compound in the middle of a turf war. They'd gone to the mattresses waiting for Adalwolf to make his next move, and no matter how often they picked up the room, there were soda cans, plates, printouts, and stuff cluttering the landscape.

Harris used the phone in the bedroom to call Sherrie and tell her what had happened. When he emerged he looked like he'd been sparring with Mike Tyson. Sherrie was taking the next plane to Miami. Melissa sat on the edge of a club chair, devastated, saying nothing. Harris was in a cold fury, pacing silently.

Without knocking, a man in his forties sporting a fifties haircut and calm, piercing eyes entered the room pulling the cellophane wrapper off a pack of cigarettes. He crumpled it up and dropped it on the desk.

'Special Agent Rufus Pickel, Miami FBI,' he said. He looked tough and seasoned, the direct opposite of his name. He shook Harris's hand and took a cigarette out of a pack and lit it before introducing himself to Melissa. 'Care for one?' he said, holding out the pack.

'I'm pregnant,' she said.

He stared through her. 'You believe in second-hand smoke?'

'I wouldn't say I worship it, but yeah, I believe in it.'

He took the cigarette out of his mouth and punched it out against the inside of a Styrofoam coffee cup, then took the pack out of his pocket, shook out a fresh one, and stuck it into his mouth, unlit. 'Tell me if the mere sight of it bothers you,' he said. 'I've been

briefed by WFO' – the Washington Field Office – 'on Adalwolf.
How do you see the situation?'

'Kobie's his bait,' Harris said.

'I'm the one he really wants,' Melissa said.

'What for?'

'A medical procedure of some kind.'

'You don't know?'

'There are several possibilities,' she said.

Harris said, 'He performed a prenatal medical procedure on her
and injected her with a virus that's remained latent so far.'

'I'm not contagious,' she said.

'I got that,' Pickel said.

'We think he wants her so he can activate it,' Harris said.

Pickel sucked on his unlit cancer stick.

'Any communication from him?' he said.

'Nothing,' she said.

'It'll happen soon,' Pickel said.

'I take it you've been through this before,' Melissa said.

'Twice,' Pickel said, 'but those kidnappings were for money, not
a pregnant woman.'

Harris started pacing. 'What do we do next?'

'You're doing it,' he said. 'You wait.'

Harris's face tightened.

Pickel turned to Melissa. 'You knew this guy?'

'Like my father.'

'Did he ever show signs of pedophilia?'

'No,' she said. 'He prefers . . .'

Harris finished for her. 'He prefers to kill his subjects.'

Pickel said, 'If your daughter's bait, killing her won't help him
make a swap for Melissa.'

Harris said, 'He's killed four people in the last two years and
God only knows how many children in Auschwitz.'

'I see,' Pickel said. He sat on the edge of Ben's desk. 'Let's do a
little preparation while we can. If he calls,' he said to Melissa, 'I

want you to keep him talking as long as possible.'

'I'll try,' Melissa said, 'but in five years of telephone calls and e-mail he's never stayed on the line long enough for us to nail his location.'

'Except once,' Harris said.

'Atlantic City,' Pickel said, 'I heard about it.' Looking at Melissa, he said, 'If he wants to meet you face-to-face, try for a rendezvous where we can put a snatch team in place. Somewhere with cover if you can. And try to delay the meeting time long enough for us to deploy.'

'I'll do my best,' Melissa said. 'But if I can't get him to go for that, I'm ready to meet him on my own.'

'What's that supposed to mean?' Pickel said.

'It means I'm her godmother and I'm responsible for her kidnapping.'

'Ayy,' Pickel said under his breath. 'That's all I need.' He dropped his unlit cigarette into the Styrofoam cup. 'All right, rule number one: From this point forward you don't move three steps in any direction without an escort. Understood?'

She didn't agree or disagree.

Agent Pickel said, 'You do something rash, he'll end up with you *and* Kobie and I'll end up with shit on toast.'

Melissa said, 'It's time to check my e-mail.' She took her laptop out of her bag, plugged in the AC adapter and the telephone line, and booted up.

'One other thing,' Pickel said. 'We need to decide when to go public.'

Melissa clicked on her e-mail and saw a message waiting from an address she didn't recognize, *FreeVitamins@Send.com*.

Be prepared to meet me at a time and place of my choosing. No police, no FBI, no Harris, no one but you. And no publicity. If you put Kobie's picture on the side of a milk carton make it a pretty one because it's the last one you'll ever see. Keep three lines of communication open: your cell phone, your e-mail, and the telephone at my house. If you are not already there, go there now. I will contact you half an hour before it's time to meet me and give you further instructions. Hit your reply button to indicate you've received and understand.

A

Melissa said, 'Look at this.'

Harris and Rufus read over her shoulder. They had to reply, but not without a strategy. Three minds, three approaches. Now the un-fun part began.

RUFUS PICKEL SAID, 'TELL me what you know about his vulnerabilities.'

'What kind of vulnerabilities?' Melissa said.

'Whatever you can think of. Physical, emotional, psychological. He's seventy-five, right?'

'Yes, but he's strong as an ox,' Melissa said. 'Works out, jogs, eats well, no illnesses.'

Pickel picked up a deck of cards. 'Mentally?'

Harris said, 'He's a chess player who's been one move ahead us every step of the way.'

'Money?'

'Take a look around,' Melissa said. 'He's got all he needs.'

Pickel tossed a card toward a waste basket and missed. It was his way of relaxing and thinking. 'What's the deal with his childhood?' he said. 'Anything that could help explain his mindset?'

Harris said, 'There's too much, not too little. An unknown Nazi father, a mother who abandons him at two, life in a convent till he's fourteen, a lab assistant in Auschwitz after that. Who knows how this stuff shaped his life?' Then, to himself, he said, 'For that matter, who cares?'

'I do if it give us a clue to his behavior,' Pickel said.

Melissa watched a playing card flutter in the air. 'He once told me – speaking as Ben-Zevi, that is – he once told me Adalwolf had a fixation with the families of the children in the camp and was always asking the kids what it was like to have parents, what they did together, and how wonderful it must have been. Obviously, he was talking about himself.'

Pickel leaned forward and spun a card toward the can. It wobbled and dropped in.

'He doesn't know why he was put in an orphanage as a baby,' Melissa said. 'He doesn't know why he was dumped in Auschwitz as a teenager. Even at his present age, those questions still have to be under his skin.'

'Very possibly,' Pickel said. 'Psychopathic killers are often sentimental about their own lives even though they're heartless about their victims'.'

'Sentimental?' Harris said, peeling the covering off a fresh roll of Tums. 'He's a sadistic animal who wants to do to Melissa's baby what he did to her husband.'

She touched her belly. 'If he touches my baby again, I'll kill him.'

Harris tossed a handful of Tums into his mouth. 'You're not going to get close enough to him to have the chance.'

Agent Pickel said, 'Here's what we know: he's a killer who wants to meet you alone. Everything else is speculation.' He stopped tossing cards.

Melissa stood up. 'I think my response should be I agree to meet his terms whatever they are. He calls me half an hour before it's time to meet and gives me the location of the rendezvous. If you can get a snatch team in place before I get there, I go to the meeting, and if not, I don't.'

'It's too obvious,' Harris said. 'He's already thought of that and devised a counter ploy.'

'Anything we do is a risk,' she said, 'but if he's willing to meet me, that's a risk for him, too. I'm tired of him always being the cat and us the mouse.'

'We need to catch a break,' Harris said. 'Wait for him to make a mistake we can exploit.'

'How long can we afford to do that?' she said.

'Not long,' Harris said. 'We have to force it.'

'How?'

'By going public. TV, press, radio.'

'But you saw his instructions. He said no publicity.'

'If you want to be the cat, you have to act like one.'

'But if we go public we'll scare him and drive him underground and make him desperate.'

'And if we don't go public we'll deny ourselves the eyes and ears of half a million people who see his face and Kobie's on TV and know who we're looking for. A fuzzy-haired, bearded seventy-five-year-old white man with a ten-year-old black girl in pigtails isn't what you call an inconspicuous couple.'

'I say we try the meeting first,' she said.

'We haven't got time,' Harris said. 'It's already been twenty-four hours. What are the statistics, Rufus?'

'*America's Most Wanted* says if you don't get a kid back in the first four hours, there's an eighty percent chance she's been killed.'

Harris looked grim. He was doing his best to stay professional, but this was his daughter, for God's sake.

Melissa said, 'But those are anonymous kidnappers with sex on the brain.'

'Mostly.'

Harris said, 'Doesn't matter. After forty-eight hours a kidnap victim of any age or sex is rarely found alive. The faster we get her picture out there, the quicker we get people working for us.'

'But we already know who the kidnapper is and we already know what he wants,' Melissa said. 'I say we play ball and catch him our way. Hide a snatch team and hook him.'

'And I say we don't.'

'Harris—'

'Goddamn it, Melissa, we're doing this by the book!'

'But this one isn't in the book! And she's my goddaughter!'

'You should have thought about that before you turned your back on her and let him grab her right out from under your nose!'

Her face drained to white.

Harris heard his words. 'I didn't mean that.'

She picked up a can of soda, found it empty, threw it toward the wastebasket, picked up another.

Harris was cool now. 'Nobody's a better friend of Kobie's than you are,' he said. He found a fresh can of soda, opened it, handed it to her. 'Now I know why they don't let agents work their own cases.'

She looked at her reflection in the window. 'I feel responsible for her,' she said. Her eyes were puffy and dark, her hair beyond hope, and she needed sleep. 'I'd feel that way no matter what, but with all this maternalism going on inside me, I feel it even more.' She turned away. Harris was sitting on a chair with his head down and his elbows on his knees, rubbing the back of his neck. She laid a hand on his shoulder.

'If we let him get between us, we're sunk,' she said.

He straightened up and nodded.

'Here's the deal,' she said. 'I'll back you up on going public if you help me put together the story of his childhood. Something I can use to make him curious.' She grabbed a pad and pencil from the coffee table and sat down.

Harris said, 'What have you got in mind?'

'I need documents to hook him,' she said, writing. 'I'd like copies of the stuff you got on Adalwolf from the Bureau and MI5.' She continued writing. 'I need your interview with Mother Marie-Catherine and the photographs you took of her at the convent.'

Harris got up and looked over her shoulder.

She said, 'I also need some documents you don't have.' She tore off one page and handed it to him and kept writing. 'Everything from the Berlin Document Center showing what the SS compiled on Henry Hallam Brandon.' BDC had an office with duplicate microfiche in College Park, Maryland, not far from FBI headquarters in Washington.

He read the list of what she wanted. 'I'm not sure I understand this one.'

She said, 'I'll explain it in a sec.' Still writing. 'Here's the tough part. I need them by tomorrow.'

'Not easy,' Harris said.

'If you'll e-mail a request to MI5 and MI6 and telephone the Bureau,' she said, 'I'll ask Barry to cover the rest from the files in my office and anything he finds at the BDC.' She finished writing, tore off the next two pages, and handed them to him.

'I'll give it my best shot,' he said.

She squeezed his arm.

'Time to send our reply,' Rufus Pickel said. 'I think you should tell him you agree to his terms but Harris doesn't. If he has a television set he's going to see the publicity on this anyway.'

'That's fine with me as long as the three of us understand each other and work as a team,' Melissa said. The two of them nodded and she opened her laptop.

THE LIGHTS WERE BRIGHT in the media room at the Miami office of the FBI. Sherrie and Harris Johnson stood in front of the TV cameras and a small bundle of microphones, finishing their televised statement.

'You're accused of terrible crimes,' Sherrie said, speaking to Adalwolf with a strained face, 'but no man's heart is without mercy. I beg you not to harm our daughter.'

The lights dimmed. Sherrie turned to Harris and put her head on his shoulder. The field producer of WMIA-TV told the crew they could get it on the eleven o-clock if they cut and ran.

Sherrie pulled away from Harris and put a tissue to her eyes. He said he'd be back in a few minutes, right now he had to pay a visit to the crime lab downstairs.

WHEN HARRIS ARRIVED AT the FBI lab everyone was gone but the man he wanted to see, a technician named Jake Winzerman, otherwise known as Jake the Wizard. They had become friends in Washington years earlier, but now that Jake was living in Miami, his primary job was to create fake documents the Bureau used in bank fraud stings. Harris leaned over his shoulder and watched him examine a document from Melissa's file using intense light and a pair of magnifying glasses with loupes.

'Don't stand so close, you're bugging me,' Jake said.

Harris backed off. After a few minutes, the man lifted his head, placed the loupes on his forehead, and turned off the halogen lamp. He swiveled around in his chair. 'I can give you duplicate originals of this stuff, but only if you tell me what they're going to be used for.'

'Getting back my daughter.'

Jake the Wizard lit a cigarette. 'So you're not selling something illegal?'

'Come on,' Harris said.

Jake tapped his cigarette ash into an empty ink bottle. 'Must be a nightmare, having a kid swiped.' He drew on his cigarette and squinted as he exhaled.

Harris said, 'If you do me this favor, I'll do you one in return.'

'What's that?'

'I won't tell IAD you're counterfeiting hundred dollar bills.'

Jake the Wizard smiled. 'Don't think it hasn't occurred to me,' he said, holding out his hand for the rest of the documents. 'I've got a few more questions. Give me the right answers and I'll do what I can.'

ADALWOLF SAT IN HIS La-Z-Boy lounger with his feet up and his head back a notch, waiting for the eleven o'clock news. Kobie was asleep in the next room, covered with a cotton blanket. Out here on the water the breeze was warm, but he didn't want her to catch cold.

On the little round table next to his chair was a *glasl tae*, a tall glass of hot tea with lots of sugar and milk, the tea bag still inside, a spoon handle sticking out. Next to it was a piece of *babka*, the apple cake he'd become addicted to over the years. Tea and *babka* made the eleven o'clock news tolerable, although exactly how tolerable he'd know in a minute.

Even though he expected it, when he first saw his face on the TV screen – actually, it was the face of Professor Ben-Zevi with his beard and glasses and unkempt hair – he was not amused. Then a photograph of Kobie appeared, and then an FBI composite drawing of Adalwolf as he might look without Ben-Zevi's beard and glasses. Behind the three faces were the newscaster's words, '. . . FBI manhunt tonight . . . kidnapper of ten-year-old Kobie Johnson . . . taken by a man named Adalwolf . . . shown here in the guise of Professor Benjamin Ben-Zevi . . . if you see him, call this number . . . do not attempt . . .' Not that he didn't want to see his face on TV. He hoped he would, because that meant he could stick with Plan A which assumed they'd refuse to follow his e-mail instructions. They were so predictable, those FBI types. Still, the audacity of it, the sheer *disobedience* of it was outrageous.

It only made what he had to do that much easier.

He watched the TV set as Harris Johnson and his wife told the world their pathetic tale about their little girl lost, appealing to Adalwolf's sentiment – God how he hated sentiment – turning every TV watcher in Miami into a lookout for himself and Kobie. What fools.

When it was over he got up and walked to the kitchen for another piece of *babka*, but it was all gone. Even the tin of butter cookies was empty. He made a note to pick some up tomorrow when he took his boat into town. He had to do that anyway because it was the first step of Plan A.

He opened his laptop and went on line, then found the Coast Guard website and the chart of the tides in Biscayne Bay. He wanted to make sure he had the high and low tides right. He did.

After closing the computer, he walked into his bedroom and picked up his tan trousers and dropped them into a laundry bag. When he finally made contact with Melissa she would almost certainly ask him why he wanted her to meet him at midnight instead of an earlier hour. He didn't need to cook up a fake answer, he didn't need to answer at all. She didn't have a clue. After all, who'd expect a wanted kidnapper to attend a public concert at eight o'clock on the very same night he was going to meet the object of another kidnapping at twelve? After the Johnsons' little TV press conference, everyone including the FBI expected Adalwolf not to show his face in public. As usual, they were wrong.

A clean white shirt, polished brown shoes, and freshly pressed tan trousers would work fine. Nothing flashy, nothing noticeable. Given the FBI composite he just saw on the tube, no one would identify him anyway. Besides, how many people who watched the eleven o'clock news would be at a university concert featuring Johann Ritter von Herbeck's *Pueri concinite*? Not bloody many. How he loved that piece of music. So spiritual and soothing. Such perfect preparation for what he had to do at midnight.

He put some Mozart on the stereo, turned the volume down low, and looked in the mirror. What he saw was the antithesis of

Ben-Zevi: a smooth face, a bald, shaved head, blue contact lenses in place of glasses, brown skin tinted with self-tanning cream. He looked like a million retired Florida golfers. At least ten years younger than Ben-Zevi. He put on a pair of sunglasses and his fishing hat and looked at himself again. If he handled it right, he'd be in and out of the dry cleaners without a hitch. Sure, there was a risk of being recognized, but not much. It was well calculated.

He walked to Kobie's room, opened the door, and saw her asleep on her side with the covers kicked off. After entering, he tiptoed past the bassinette he'd bought for Melissa's baby. Hanging above it was a cute mobile of stars and planets and a cow jumping over the moon. Very sweet. In the corner of the room were boxes of unopened medical supplies: forceps, scalpels, sutures, clamps, an incubator, a heart monitor, a surgical lamp – everything he needed to deliver Melissa's baby. Nearby were cans of paint and boxes of brushes and rollers to paint the room pastel blue. He'd get to that soon.

When he reached Kobie's bed he pulled the cotton blanket back over her, then found what he was looking for: her cut-off jeans. He picked them up and looked at the chain of pink and purple flowers embroidered around the legs. They were distinctive, clearly hers, just what he wanted. They weren't dirty, but that wasn't the point, he'd have them laundered anyway. Then, after the concert, around eleven-thirty, he'd call Melissa and tell her where to meet him.

But not before picking up a tin of butter cookies.

IT WAS SEVEN IN THE morning when Melissa came out of her bedroom wearing a pair of jeans, a white shirt, and sandals. Outside were two policemen in a car, keeping an eye on the house. Sitting in the kitchen was an FBI agent with a tap on the telephone and communications gear that helped trace a cell phone call. She walked into the study and picked up the phone and called Harris at FBI headquarters, where he and Rufus Pickel were fielding calls from people who'd seen the news and thought they had a clue about Adalwolf's whereabouts.

'I'm about to look at Ben's files,' she said. 'Any leads at your end?'

'Nothing so far.'

She hung up and opened an evidence box marked 'B-Z Desk Contents.' Inside were folders of paid bills, income tax returns, and housekeeper-candidates' resumes. At some point Adalwolf's and Ben-Zevi's lives must have intersected, but where?

She looked at bank deposit slips and read the names of med students he'd taught over the years. At noon she called Harris and got Agent Rufus Pickel who said Harris was on the other line. Yes, they were still receiving calls, he said; no, they had nothing to report.

At two p.m. she microwaved some left-over Chinese food and ate it. At three she got a call from Harris saying he was coming back to Ben's house to comb through the files with her.

She was glad he was on his way. Two could fail at this as easily as one.

Her cell phone rang. 'Hello?'

'Midnight tonight.'

It was Adalwolf.

He said, 'I'll call you at eleven thirty and tell you where.'

'You bastard, what have you done with her?'

'She's fine.'

'I don't believe you.'

There was a rustling of the cell phone, then a little girl's voice. 'Melissa?'

'Kobie! Are you okay?'

'I want to come home.'

'Where are you, honey?'

'I don't know!'

'Kobie, listen, look around and tell me what you see!'

'I see—'

Broken off.

Adalwolf came on the line and said, 'Midnight. If you show up with the police Kobie will die.'

'Ben, for God's sake.' She heard Kobie crying. *Keep talking.* The tapes were rolling and a trace was underway. 'Tell me what you injected into my uterus.'

'I'll explain everything tonight.'

'Why not tell me now?'

'Because it's going to take more than an explanation.'

'What's that mean?'

'I have medication you and your baby need. If you don't get it, it'll be a disaster for both of you.'

'That's bullshit! I'm not sick and neither is the baby. Eric interrupted what you were doing, and now you want to get your hands on me so you can finish the job.'

'You understand so little.'

'Then explain it to me!'

'I will. At midnight.'

'Why so late? Why not nine or ten?'

'Don't ask stupid questions.'

Keep him on the line.

'I have something you need, too,' she said.

'I'm hanging up now,' he said.

'Your childhood.'

Silence. 'What about my childhood?'

'I know the truth about it. Trust me, it's shocking.'

More silence. 'If you're expecting me to faint you're going to be disappointed.'

'Not when you find out what I have.'

'Nice try, Melissa. I have to go now.'

Keep him on the line. 'How do I know we'll get Kobie back?'

A pause. 'If you do as I say you'll have her back at exactly twelve-fifty-seven a.m.'

'Twelve-fifty-seven? What's so special about twelve-fifty-seven?'

'Play ball and you'll see. Don't forget to keep your cell phone turned on. And one other thing: Kobie wants some red licorice. If you do exactly as I say you can bring her some, and if you don't, don't bother, she'll be in no condition to enjoy it anyway.'

'How do I know she—'

Disconnection.

'IF YOU WERE DESIGNING it, how would you create a biological weapon that would wipe out a particular ethnic group?'

The question was asked by Dr. Otto Heller, one of three wise men who had gathered in a small conference room at the University of Texas Medical School in Galveston. Another was a researcher from CDC, and the third the host of the meeting, Dr. C. J. Pevlov, a virologist and expert on biological terrorism. The known facts were easy: four people had come down with flu symptoms within ten hours of exposure to a virus called NTX and died shortly thereafter of a hemorrhagic fever. Melissa and her baby were injected over forty-eight hours earlier with a variation of the virus, called NTX-2, but showed no symptoms of disease whatsoever. What was going on?

Pevlov took a bite of his sandwich and said, 'Let's assume this guy Adalwolf has managed to identify genetic markers that are prevalent in Ashkenazi and Sephardic Jews.'

'Prevalent or exclusive?'

'Ninety-eight percent homologous to Jews, two percent scattered in non-Jewish populations. The same distribution you'd expect to find in Swedish, African, Chinese and other populations.'

'Go on,' Heller said.

'Let's say he manages to make the virus robust enough to spread it as an aerosol and manipulates a docking protein that binds with the Jewish host surface markers. Non-Jews get nothing more than a runny nose and chills, Jews get virulence and clinical VHF.' Shorthand for viral hemorrhagic fever.

'Which is what we've seen in four cases so far,' Heller said.

'So what is the terrorist's problem?' Pevlov asked himself. 'Speed. The virus kills so fast there's no time for a contagion. It's like Ebola: the infected victims die so quickly there are no vectors left to spread it.'

He took a bite of his sandwich.

'To create a Jewish plague you have to slow down the onset of the disease. First I'd give the prototype time to incubate and mature, then I'd make sure it has latency in the general population. Only after a large percentage of the target population – in this case, Jews – has contracted it do you want it to start killing or showing symptoms. That way, it's too late to contain. HIV, the bubonic plague – the models are out there.'

'How would you slow it down?' Heller said.

Pevlov opened a notebook and turned some pages. 'I think I'd construct it to stay dormant until I catalyzed it with a toxin.' He looked at his notes. 'BDUR has been known to set off a latent virus. So could the A chain of ricin.'

Otto Heller said, 'Maybe that's what he was doing when Eric Brandt interrupted him. Maybe he was injecting her with a slow-acting toxin that kicks in after the baby's born.' He turned to Pevlov. 'You know of anything that would do that?'

Pevlov said, 'No. The agents I'm aware of would act immediately after being injected.'

Heller said, 'Could he have been trying to inject a capsule of the toxin in the fetus that dissolves twelve months later, after the virus had incubated and matured?'

'Wouldn't work,' the researcher said. 'A capsule would show up in a routine sonogram, and there's no sign of one in Mrs. Gale.'

Back to square one. 'Whatever catalyst he had in mind,' Heller said, 'he missed his chance. So where's that leave him?'

'You mean where's that leave us?' Pevlov said.

After finishing their sandwiches, Heller and the researcher got up to leave.

'By the way,' Heller said to Pevlov, 'where do you get these catalysts?'

'BDUR can be made with a handful of chemicals.'

'And ricin?'

'Ricin is an extract of castor beans.'

IT WAS FOUR O'CLOCK IN the afternoon. Wearing a fishing hat and sunglasses, Adalwolf stood at the counter of the Quik-Fix cleaners at an RK strip mall in Hallandale waiting for the customer in front of him to lift the dry cleaning off a hook and leave.

Finally, it was Adalwolf's turn.

'Can I help you?' the girl behind the counter said.

'I'd like to have these cleaned,' he said, laying a pair of tan men's pants on the counter. 'These, too,' he said, laying down Kobie's denim shorts.

'Cleaned or laundered?'

'Whatever. I need them as soon as possible.'

'You can have them in three hours,' the girl said, tearing off a receipt.

'The sign outside says one hour.'

'I know, but it takes three.' She handed him half the receipt and laid the other half on the shorts.

Adalwolf took back the trousers. 'Three hours is too late for these,' he said.

'It might be a little sooner.'

'Afraid that won't do. What time do you close?'

'Nine-thirty.'

'If I don't pick up the shorts tonight I'll pick them up tomorrow.'

He got out of there before anyone had a chance to get a good look at him.

HARRIS CAME INTO THE study at Ben's house and found Melissa sitting on the floor going through a file. She had called Harris and told him she'd talked to Kobie the moment Adalwolf hung up.

'How'd she sound?' he asked.

'Scared.'

'No clue where she is?'

'He didn't give her a chance to say.'

Harris sat in the club chair, his leg bouncing nervously, his jaw muscles rippling. 'Why's he want to meet at midnight?'

'No idea.'

'We'll probably know more about that when we find out where he wants to meet you,' he said. He rubbed his face and dropped his hands. 'Find anything in the files?'

'Nothing interesting. How about you?'

He shook his head and handed her a plastic envelope. 'Here are the copies of the documents you wanted, courtesy of Jake the Wizard.'

She took them and sat up straight, stretching her back, then unwound the string on the envelope flap and laid the contents on the floor. She looked at them as if they were photographs from a vacation. 'These look great.' But now that Adalwolf had scheduled a meeting, they seemed worthless. She gathered them up and put them back in the envelope and got off the floor. 'How's Sherrie holding up?'

'Better than I expected,' he said.

She went to the kitchen, said hello to the agent manning the recorders, opened the refrigerator and brought two cans of root beer back to the study. Harris took one without looking up from a document he was reading from Ben-Zevi's files. She opened a new folder and started reading.

Wait, Rufus Pickel had told them. *You have to know how to wait.*

'I'D LIKE TO TALK TO someone about the kidnapping,' the caller said.

The switchboard operator at Miami FBI knew exactly where to transfer the call. It went down the hall to the situation room.

'Agent Rufus Pickel here.'

The caller, a man, said, 'I'm calling about the report on TV of an old man who kidnapped a little girl?'

'Yes, sir?'

'I think I just saw him.'

'You think you saw the kidnapper?'

'His name is wolf something, right?'

'Adalwolf, that's right. Also known as Professor Benjamin Ben-Zevi.'

'Yeah, I saw his picture on the news. Mid- to late-seventies, about five-eleven.'

'Where did you see him?'

'At the Quik-Fix Cleaners at the RK strip mall in Hallandale.'

'When?'

'Ten, fifteen minutes ago.'

'At a dry cleaners?'

'Yes, sir. I came in to pick up my laundry and this old man was standing in front of me holding a pair of shorts he wanted cleaned. I heard him ask the girl at the counter how soon he could get them back.'

'What did they look like?'

'You know, cut-off jeans with a string of pink and purple flowers around the legs. And I'm thinking, who dry cleans jeans instead of laundering them? That's when I took a closer look and recognized him from the news.'

'Go ahead.'

'When he left I followed him out to the parking lot and saw him get into a blue Ford sedan and drive away.'

'Did you get his license plate number?'

'You know – I was too excited to think straight. I ran over to my car and tried to follow him, but by the time I got to the exit he was gone. How dumb was that?'

'Not dumb at all. You're sure it was a blue Ford sedan?'

'Yes, sir, about three or four years old. I overheard him tell the girl at the cleaners he'd come back later.'

'Today?'

'Yeah. He asked what time they closed and said he'd be back if he could, otherwise tomorrow.'

'What's she look like?'

'The kidnapped girl?'

'The girl behind the counter.'

'Oh. She was Asian, short dark hair, early twenties.'

'What else can you tell me about the man?'

'That's about it. He was wearing a fishing hat and sunglasses, but I'm sure it was him.'

'Do you have a telephone number where you can be reached?'

'To be honest, I really don't have anything more to tell you. Talk to the girl at the cleaners, she'll tell you what happened. And good luck. I hope you catch this guy before he does something awful to that little girl.'

The caller disconnected his cell phone and set it in the cradle by his dashboard on his car. He turned left at the next light and headed south-west toward Biscayne Bay. The information he'd given the FBI agent was mostly right, but not completely. The man at the cleaners was definitely Adalwolf, no question about that, but he wasn't driving a blue Ford sedan, he was driving a green Chevy station wagon.

The caller knew this to be true because the caller was Adalwolf.

Telling the FBI he'd dropped off Kobie's shorts at the Quik-Fix Cleaners was part of Plan A, and so was the false description of the car he was driving. No way could he describe his own green station wagon and risk getting picked up by the highway patrol. As for the rest of the story, it was accurate because he was counting on the FBI to check it out. That was the whole point of the call, to get them out to the cleaners' as fast as possible.

It was a strategy of misdirection, as old as Sun-Tzu and *The Art of War*.

HARRIS'S CELL PHONE RANG. He put down a file and answered.

Melissa continued reading.

Harris listened quietly, saying nothing but 'Mm-hm,' and 'Got it.' He hung up and talked as he went to the door. 'Rufus Pickel just received an anonymous call that an old man fitting Adalwolf's description dropped off a pair of shorts at a cleaners'.'

'Kobie's?'

'Yeah, they're cut-off jeans with a chain of flowers around the legs.'

A break at last. Harris was right: the television publicity was helping.

'He told the clerk he's coming back,' Harris said. 'We're staking out the place.'

'Why is he having her shorts cleaned?'

'Don't know, but I'm glad it caught someone's attention.'

He was out the door before she could ask him if she could come along.

'LOOK WHAT I BROUGHT you.' Adalwolf pulled a long strand of red licorice from a paper grocery bag. Kobie tore off a piece and put the end of it into her mouth.

'Are you going to kill me now?'

'No, sweetie, we're just playing a game.'

'Why doesn't the house sink?' she said.

'It's on pilings,' Adalwolf said.

'What are pilings?'

'Telephone poles sunk into the ground below the water. Do you want to see what they look like?'

'No.'

'They're pretty interesting.'

He walked to the door of the house and opened it and waited for Kobie to join him. She held back.

'Come along now,' he said.

'I don't want to.'

'There's no reason to be scared.'

'Daddy said you were bad.'

He opened his arms and gave her a big smile. 'Kobie. Do I seem like a bad man to you?'

She wasn't sure. 'Why did you shave off your hair and whiskers?'

'Why do you braid your hair some days?'

He stepped back into the house and found a turquoise nylon jacket and held it out.

She said, 'It's too hot to wear a jacket.'

'You have to, we're going for a boat ride.'

'Where to?'

'Back to shore and then home. Put it on.'

'But it's too hot.'

He threw the jacket at her. 'I said put it on!'

Her face froze at the sudden outburst.

He stepped out the door onto the deck surrounding the house. She followed him taking small, cautious steps.

The blue Atlantic surrounded them in all directions as far as the eye could see. The house was in a place called Stiltsville, one of seven houses that rose like clowns on pilings in the middle of the Atlantic Ocean. About two miles away they could see the condos and office buildings of Key Biscayne Village, and ten miles beyond that the skyline of Miami Beach. Most of the thirty-some houses had been blown away over the years by hurricanes, but these seven remained, separated from each other by a quarter mile of water. Isolated. Private. Concealed in full view.

Adalwolf's sleek fiberglass boat sat at the bottom of a long ladder that ran down from the deck to the water. The boat rocked and bobbed against rubber tires screwed to a small dock attached to the pilings.

The tide was out. The pilings and ladder were discolored from sea water that covered them at flood tide, which was three feet above ebb. Barnacles grew where the water covered the wood, green and gnarled with sharp edges. Adalwolf started down the ladder carrying a canvas bag on his shoulder.

'Are you going to let me go now?' Kobie said.

He reached the lowest rung of the ladder that remained dry, a foot or so above the tops of the waves that rolled in endlessly. He looked up. 'Come on, Kobie. Climb down.'

She looked over her shoulder and started down, then stopped, fear etched on her face.

'Come on,' Adalwolf said. 'I'm taking you home.'

She lowered herself another rung and froze. 'I'm scared,' she said.

A tall wave swept over Adalwolf's shins, soaking his shoes, socks, and pants. 'Damn it!' he said, looking down. How was he going to sneak into a concert with wet pants? It was risky enough showing up at all. He'd have to dry them with the station wagon's air-conditioning vent. There were two and a half hours till the concert started, but with everything he had to do, there was no time to waste.

He reached into the canvas bag on his shoulder and pulled out a white paper package with a medical insignia on it. Placing the edge of the package in his teeth, he tore it open and spit out the top, sending it fluttering to the water. Inside the package were rolls of white adhesive tape.

'Kobie! Get down here! Now!'

'I can't!' Kobie said. She was crying and hugging the ladder tightly and looking down through wide, teary eyes. 'I'm scared!'

MELISSA WAS TRYING TO remember comments she'd heard from both Adalwolf and Ben-Zevi that coincided. Even Clark Kent and Superman shared a phone booth. What overlap was there between these two separate lives that might offer a clue about where he was?

She was dropping Ben's files back into the evidence box when she heard a commotion at the front door. Walking into the foyer, she found Eric Brandt at the door telling a skeptical police officer that he was Melissa's doctor and had to come in. She vouched for him and thanked the officer. 'I'm working in the study,' she said to Eric, heading back to it.

Eric handed her the mail he'd collected from the mailbox, took off his coat, and followed her down the hall, asking her how she felt. 'Fine,' she said, reading envelopes addressed to Professor Benjamin Ben-Zevi. The return addresses revealed a Salomon Smith Barney financial statement, an AT&T phone bill, some Valu-Pac coupons, and a letter from the University of Miami Choral Society.

They entered the study and Eric sat on the sofa, still quizzing her about her health as she opened the university letter. It was addressed to Professor Benjamin Ben-Zevi as a member of the Choral Society board of directors, confirming that his tickets to a performance of the Boys' Air Choir would be held at the box office. An accompanying flyer said the concert was being held at the Gusman Concert Hall on the University campus. Tonight. At eight o'clock.

She read the letter again.

'What is it?' Eric said.

'Ticket confirmation to a concert.' She looked up. 'It's being held tonight.' She stared at Eric as she wondered about it. 'You think there's a chance he'd show up?'

'No way,' Eric said.

She re-read the letter, wondering what to make of a simple courtesy notification Adalwolf didn't know he'd receive.

Eric said, 'His picture is all over town.'

'You mean Ben-Zevi's picture is. No one knows what Adalwolf looks like.'

'What about the FBI drawing?'

'It's too far off center,' she said.

'How do you know?'

'Harris got a description of him from a girl at a laundry. He was bald, clean shaven, and tan.'

'I still don't think he'd risk being seen at a public concert,' Eric said.

'No, probably not.' *But if he showed up at a dry cleaners' in broad daylight, is showing up at an evening concert that much worse?* He had the arrogance and the track record to try it. He'd lived a double life successfully for fifty years. Harris had said it long ago: even the smartest criminals eventually make a mistake. This concert was going to be Adalwolf's. She could feel it.

She stood up. 'I'm going to the concert.'

'No you're not. You can't go anywhere without a bodyguard.'

'You're coming with me.'

'Me? I'm not a bodyguard,' Eric said, 'and I hate choral music.'

'If he's not there we'll dump the concert and get something to eat.' Pulling him to his feet.

'I don't think—'

'Come on, I'm going stir crazy sitting around here all day.'

He checked his watch. 'But it's only six thirty.'

'I know, but I have a couple of things to pick up first.'

MELISSA PARKED HER BMW convertible, top up, in an angled parking space in front of Gusman Hall. Eric sat in the passenger seat looking at the entrance. Concert-goers with tickets had parked in a large lot off to the side of the building.

It was eight-thirty by the time they got there and the concert had already begun. Melissa had wanted to arrive before it started so she could eavesdrop on the box office, but, worried that Adalwolf would recognize her, she'd taken time to stop at Nicki's Play Pen in Coconut Grove and buy a disguise.

She looked in the rear view mirror. 'How do I look?' She wore a shoulder-length, honey-blonde wig and horn-rimmed glasses, makeup foundation that was two shades lighter than normal, lip liner that changed the shape of her mouth, and a natural shade of lipstick she'd never worn before. The black slacks and white shirt were her own.

'You look fine,' he said.

'But do I look like me?'

'Not so he'd notice,' he said. 'Besides, you're not getting within twenty feet of him or anyone else.'

'Don't worry,' she said. 'I won't be out of your sight.'

Her best defense was surprise, assuming he was there. Everyone with a ticket had already gone inside the hall, leaving a handful of people sitting on wooden benches and the steps listening to the music on outdoor speakers. Now she wondered if the disguise was worth the effort. By the time the concert ended it would be dark, and Adalwolf probably wouldn't be there anyway, and she and

Eric would go to dinner and the wig would look ridiculous. She told herself to stop figuring the odds and take a look.

'Okay, I'm ready,' she said.

She got out of the car and walked in the dwindling light to the front of the hall. The night air was hot and the choir boys' voices as pure as icicles. Under different circumstances she would have enjoyed the music, but as it was, she was jumping out of her skin.

She opened the doors to the foyer, turned around so she could see the faces of the people sitting on the benches, and started back for the car.

I know he can see me, I can feel it. She'd felt him at David's funeral, too, and she was right: he was sitting next to her the whole time.

She looked from side to side, trying not to mimic a radar dish, but she saw no one remotely resembling Ben-Zevi or Adalwolf. When she reached the car she climbed into the passenger seat. Eric looked at her from the driver's seat.

'Anybody interesting?' he said.

'Nothing.'

'Let's go get something to eat.'

'I'm too nervous,' she said. 'Let's wait a couple more minutes.'

THEY WERE KOBIE'S CUT-OFF jeans, no question about it. Harris and Rufus Pickel sat in a room behind the laundry's counter, armed and waiting. Two other agents dressed as mall clean-up men emptied trash baskets outside the door. More agents waited in cars in the parking lot. A communications van sat nearby.

Adalwolf hadn't shown yet. The young Asian girl behind the counter and her father were doing a great job acting normal and being brave.

It was almost nine-thirty and he still wasn't there. But that was the thing about stakeouts. You had to be patient. You had to wait.

IT WAS NINE-THIRTY AND the concert was over, and still Adalwolf hadn't shown. No surprise. When the usher kicked the door stop to close the concert hall front doors, Melissa knew it was time to leave.

'Let's go to dinner,' she said.

Eric started the engine while Melissa flipped down the visor to start disassembling her disguise. She felt silly in her wig and dumb for thinking he'd be there. The mirror picked up stragglers walking to the parking lot in small groups or couples.

Except one.

She was about to pull off her wig when she saw the silhouette of a man thirty yards away, which was too far to see any of his features but one: his limp.

'Wait!' she said, and turned to look out the rear window.

She watched him continue toward the lot. It was a pale imitation of Ben-Zevi's limp, but it was a limp nevertheless, and it was on the right leg, too. Then it hit her: as Ben-Zevi he had exaggerated the hobble, and as Adalwolf he had minimized it. It was one of the differences he used to mask a double life, but it wasn't quite different enough. She'd finally spotted something that linked one persona to the other.

'It's him!' she said, and opened the door and got out.

'Melissa!'

'I'll be right back! Turn the car around! I don't want to lose him!'

She followed him down the sidewalk, not letting him out of her sight. He walked past a fence and entered the parking lot next to the concert hall. When he was halfway down one of the aisles she realized that any second now he'd get into a car and drive away and leave her standing there on foot.

She watched him – she turned back to see if Eric was behind her yet; he wasn't – then looked back at him limping down the lane. She turned again and saw Eric pull up at the curb, signaled him to drive into the lot – then turned back to see Adalwolf.

He was gone.

Damn!

Eric pulled up next to her and she jumped in. 'He's somewhere up ahead!'

Eric came to the end of the first aisle and turned down the next.

'Where are you?' she said. They drove down the lane, watching people get into their cars and pull out and head for the exit. They couldn't find him.

'Nuts!' she said. They'd come that close.

Eric turned down the last lane of the lot, which was nearly empty now, and stopped behind a parked car in order to keep their BMW hidden. At the end of the row, illuminated by another car's headlights, was a man standing next to a nondescript green Chevrolet station wagon with his car key in hand.

It was Adalwolf.

They had him.

'HARRIS, IT'S ME!' Melissa said into her cell phone.

'Hang on a sec,' Harris said. His voice was low and urgent.

'Harris, listen—'

She heard the rustling of the phone against his body. He was moving – walking or running, she couldn't tell – but the phone wasn't at his ear. She waited.

Adalwolf's green Chevy station wagon was two cars ahead. They were on Route 1 headed toward Miami Beach, moving along in the right lane just under the speed limit. She memorized the configuration of his tail lights – size, shape, brightness – so they could keep track of him if he got too far ahead.

Harris came back on the line. 'I can't talk, we're about to bust a Ford.'

'Forget it, we've got him!'

'Not sure I heard that.'

'Eric and I have Adalwolf in view right now! We're on Route 1 about two miles from UM.'

'What's he driving?'

'A green Chevrolet station wagon, Florida plates Four ZR two-two-two.'

'Hold on,' Harris said. She heard him talking to someone in the car. 'Okay,' he said, 'we're about twenty minutes away. I'll contact Miami-Dade PD and see if they can pick up your location. What's your license plate?'

'I don't know, DG something.'

'The silver BMW convertible?'

'Yeah, with the top up, black.'

'I'll tell them to use an unmarked car. Don't spook him. He could be going to Kobie.'

'Got it.' She pulled off her hot, itchy wig and fake horn-rimmed glasses.

'Keep talking to me,' Harris said.

She could hear his siren through the phone. Then a small tone in her ear. She checked the message window and put it back to her ear. 'My battery's running low,' she said.

'Eric got a phone?'

She asked. 'No, he left it in his car.'

'How much juice you got left?'

'I don't know, a fourth maybe.'

'Leave the line open,' he said. 'Turning the phone on and off eats up more energy.'

'I'll give you my markers as we go.'

MELISSA COULD HEAR HARRIS ask agent Rufus Pickel how far they were from I-95. He came back on and said, 'We're two minutes from the interstate.' He was in a cobalt gray unmarked FBI sedan with a magnetic rotating beacon on the roof. 'You still got him in sight?'

'Two cars away,' Melissa said.

'Don't get too close!'

'Don't worry, we're staying back and if he looks in the mirror our headlights are in his eyes.'

'We're coming up on the I-95 on-ramp now. What's your twenty?'

Melissa asked Eric, 'Where are we?'

'Coconut Grove.'

'Coconut Grove, in the southwest thirties,' she told Harris.

Adalwolf's brake lights lit up.

'Wait a sec. He's slowing down. He's pulling into a Walgreens.'

'Be careful.'

'We're moving past him and pulling into a Maaco parking lot.'

Adalwolf pulled into a slot outside the store and got out, leaving his headlights on. Eric pulled into a parking space on the next corner and turned off his lights, but kept the engine running.

'He's going into the store,' Melissa said.

'You sure he can't see you?' Harris said.

'He hasn't even looked in this direction.'

'What's he look like?'

'Just as the girl at the cleaners described him. Bald, clean shaven, no glasses.'

'Can you see him through the store window?'

'No. You think he went out the back door?'

'Just asking.'

They waited. She heard the siren on Harris's car.

'Why does someone stop at a Walgreens at this hour?' she said.

'What d'ya mean?' Harris said.

'You stop at a convenience store when you're close to home.'

'Maybe.'

'Did you hear that?' she said.

'What?'

'I'm getting another call. Hang on a second.'

She hit the 'flash' button. 'Hello?'

'Hello, Melissa.'

It was Adalwolf. She looked at Eric with saucer eyes and mouthed, *It's him!*

'Hello.'

'Where are you?' Adalwolf asked.

'In my car a couple of blocks from your house,' she lied.

'Okay, here's the situation. At exactly eleven-thirty you're going to leave the house and take Route 1 north to the Rickenbacker Causeway and drive out to Virginia Key. With me?'

'Go on.'

'When you get to Virginia Key you'll see a large marina on your right just before you get to the Seaquarium. It's well lit with plenty of boats and people, so you'll be safe.'

'Keep going.'

'When you get into the parking lot turn right and go to the far end. When you get to the dock you'll see a blue and white trawler with the name *Sea-Duction* on the transom. Park nearby and walk to the boat. Alone.'

'I understand.'

'It's half an hour from the house so leave at eleven-thirty sharp. I want you there at midnight on the dot.'

'I thought you were going to call me at eleven-thirty.'

'I've got something to do first. Just do as I say.'

'What about Kobie?'

'She's waiting for you to come and get her.'

'So she'll be on the boat—'

He hung up. She punched the flash button. Harris was waiting. 'That was him!'

'What did he want?'

'He gave me the directions to a boat at a marina on Virginia Key and told me to be there at midnight! I think he's – he's coming out of the store!'

'Is he looking your way?'

'No, he's looking at a plastic bag he's carrying.'

'Keep your head down!'

'He's got his keys out to unlock the door. Can't find the keyhole. Uh, oh – the bag slipped and spilled everything on the pavement. He's picking them up. A carton of milk, a tin of cookies, some — what's that?'

'What's what?'

'He's stuffing something back in the bag. Oh, wow, we're on the right track, Harris!'

'What is it?'

'Red licorice.'

'HE'S BACK ON ROUTE ONE headed to the right,' Melissa said.

'You mean northeast?'

'Please, Harris.' Compasses were such a male thing. She asked Eric which direction they were going. 'Yeah, toward I-95 north.'

'Good, we're coming south on I-95. How's your battery?'

'Hang a sec.' She looked. 'Down to an eighth.'

Eric said, 'Tell Harris he's turning onto Brickell Avenue and by-passing I-95.'

'He's not taking I-95,' Melissa said.

Eric said, 'He's headed for the Rickenbacker Causeway.'

She relayed that to Harris.

'I see it on the map,' Harris said. 'He's going to Virginia Key.'

'Maybe he's going to the boat now instead of midnight. It's a blue and white trawler at the right end of the parking lot called *Sea-Duction*.'

'We're on it.'

She could hear Rufus Pickel talking to base on the car radio.

Eric kept one or two cars between their BMW and Adalwolf's station wagon, which trundled along with the flow of traffic, up the bridge over Biscayne Bay, then down onto Crandon Boulevard toward Virginia Key. Melissa relayed markers to Harris as they went: a small marina on the left, a beach on the right, Madfish House restaurant and the Mast Academy High School. 'The Seaquarium is coming up on the right,' she said. 'I see the marina. He's slowing down.'

Adalwolf's car moved into the left lane with its turn signal blinking. Huh? 'He's turning left instead of right.'

Eric slowed but couldn't make a left turn without being conspicuous. He turned right instead, drove into the Seaquarium parking lot, made a slow U turn, and came back to Crandon Boulevard, a four-lane highway. Adalwolf had turned left off Crandon and was headed down a road directly across from Eric and Melissa, his taillights moving into darkness. Eric waited for a car to pass on Crandon then crossed the highway and followed.

'We're on an unlit macadam road . . . looks like it's called Arthur Lamb Jr. Road,' Melissa said into the phone. 'There's a guard house and a sign that says Central District Wastewater Treatment Plant.'

'I see it on the map,' Harris said. 'That's weird. It's a dead end road.'

'He said he had to do something before our midnight meeting.'

Eric said, 'Maybe he's going to pick up Kobie.'

'Hold a sec.' Harris talked to Rufus Pickel, then came back on. 'Rufus says there's a bar at the end of the road.'

'I just saw a sign for it,' Melissa said. 'It's called Jimbo's.' They hit a speed bump.

'You sure he can't see you?'

'No, we're hanging back,' she said. 'We look like just another car headed for Jimbo's.'

'Don't get too close, but don't lose him, either.'

'Got the picture, Harris.' The closer they got to Kobie, the more desperation she could hear in his voice. They drove down a road with pine trees set back on both sides and a thin ground fog over the road. Adalwolf's taillights were easily visible, brightening as he braked for speed bumps, disappearing on the gentle curves, reappearing on the straight-aways.

'Think he sees us?' Eric asked Melissa.

'He wouldn't be going down a dead end road if he did.'

They passed an enormous stack of rusty pipes lying by the side of the road and a barbed wire fence around a huge sewage plant lit with flood lights.

Harris said, 'Miami-Dade PD has an unmarked car on the way. Coast Guard's ETA is twenty minutes. They know the lagoon at Jimbo's, they'll sit behind a mangrove across from the dock. We've got another FBI car corning. Chopper's no help because of the noise.'

'He's on the brakes again,' Eric said.

'Looks like the restaurant up ahead,' Melissa said to Harris and Eric.

Harris came back: 'Park as far away from him as you can and wait.'

They drove up to a dirt entrance on the right and watched as Adalwolf's station wagon came to a stop among cars parked amid sea grape trees.

'It's an open air bar, no walls, tin roof,' Melissa said into the phone. 'There's a beat-up abandoned house on the left, another one about fifty feet away. Junk all over the place.'

'Is he headed for one of the houses?' Harris asked.

'Not yet. He's going into the bar.'

Eric parked as far from the bar as possible and turned off the headlights.

Melissa said, 'I see a dock off to the left. A couple of fishing boats.'

'Don't move till you see Miami-Dade PD, okay?'

'Did you hear that?' she said.

'Hear what?'

'That beep. My battery's cutting out.'

'Stay . . . your car!'

'Say again? I can't hear . . .'

He was gone.

ERIC AND MELISSA SAT and waited. Jimbo's looked like a backwater bar straight out of an Elmore Leonard novel, full of fishermen, boaters, drunks, and talkers. Sitting around the structure were the artifacts of a future archeologist's dream: a rusted-out, multi-colored VW bug, broken chaise-longues, bedraggled coco palms, an abandoned school bus, picnic tables, trash cans, umbrella stands, rusty oil drums, an old fireplug, stolen road signs, bottles – if heaven was a dump, this would be it. There were a few old shacks nearby nestled beneath root-exposed trees on the perimeter of the parking area. Over to the left were two fishing boats sitting at a small dock, their superstructures rising out of a marine fog. Inside the bar patrons sat drinking Old Milwaukee beer and eating grilled salmon and laughing and listening to Tammy Wynette.

'Think we should get out and follow him?' Melissa said.

'No way,' Eric said. 'He sees us, it's all over.'

Melissa's eyes roamed the landscape. The fog obscured some of her view but gave them cover. 'You think Kobie's in one of these shacks?'

'Maybe. We have to see where he goes.'

They looked over at the bar.

'I can't see him, can you?' Melissa said.

'No, but he's in there.'

'Unless he slipped out the back. This fog, he could have.'

'Regardless, we're staying put.'

They heard tires on gravel and turned to see a police car drive into the entrance. There was no siren or lights, but it was – what the heck, it was a *marked* police cruiser, the Miami-Dade PD logo on the door and a light bridge on the roof.

'What's going on?' Melissa said.

The doors opened and two policemen got out slowly, pulled up their belts, and sauntered over to the BMW the way cops do when they arrive at a scene.

'They're wearing uniforms!' she said.

One of the officers checked the license plate and leaned down on the driver's side. 'You call about a kidnapping?' he said.

'Not us, the FBI,' Eric said.

Another marked squad car pulled into the driveway and parked next to the first. Two more uniformed officers got out and moseyed toward the BMW.

'The Kobie Johnson case?' the policeman said.

Melissa said, 'The kidnapper's in the bar. I thought you guys were supposed to be in unmarked cars! If he sees you, he'll bolt!'

'Nobody said anything to us about being unmarked.' A police dispatcher's voice blared out the open window from the cruiser's radio. Despite the music in the bar, Adalwolf might have heard it. Melissa thought, *What a screw up*.

A cobalt-gray sedan pulled up with Harris and Rufus inside. 'That's the FBI now,' Eric said to the policeman.

Melissa said, 'One more car and we'll be a used car lot.'

Harris got out and walked to the BMW. 'What's with the cruisers and uniforms?' he said, showing his FBI credential.

'I don't know anything about that,' the police officer said.

Over at the bar there was commotion. 'Hey!' a guy with a beer belly yelled. 'That's my damn boat!' Thumping toward the water with an object in his hand.

Harris, the cops, and Melissa saw a fishing boat pull away from the dock.

More yelling down at the dock, then two shots fired.

'Sounds like a ·38,' one of the cops said. He and the others started running toward the boat, fingers unsnapping their holster straps.

Harris pointed at Melissa – 'Stay in the car!' – moving backward. To the policeman standing by the BMW he yelled, 'Don't let her out of your sight!' Rufus Pickel joined him and they sprinted for the dock with the cops.

Patrons too drunk to know better emptied out of the bar and ran toward the action while the more sober ones stood and watched. The boat continued moving slowly away from the dock into the misty lagoon. Melissa sat high in her seat and craned her neck to see what was going on. Someone at the dock had climbed a moored boat's fishing tower, turned on its spotlights, and cast them out onto the water. In a few seconds he picked up a blue bimini moving across the top of the fog like a kite strafing a cloud.

Sitting in the driver's seat, Eric's eye picked up something else. 'Who's that?' he said.

'What?' Melissa said.

'Somebody walking toward that shack!'

Melissa and the police officer looked and saw a figure moving in the distance. Keeping his eyes focused, Eric opened the door and got out. 'I'm gonna check. I'll be right back!'

'Eric!' Melissa yelled, but he was already off and running. 'Nuts,' she said to herself, 'I feel like a prisoner in my own car!'

The Miami-Dade policeman Harris told to watch Melissa climbed into the BMW's driver's seat, introduced himself, and hit the button locking the doors. Eric's silhouette moved through the ground fog toward a red shack forty yards away. The searchlights at the dock stayed on the boat's canvas bimini as it headed toward mangroves across the lagoon. Male voices in the bar and on the dock yelled at it across the water.

A Florida State Highway patrolman with a wide-brimmed hat and a chin strap knocked on the driver's side window of the BMW. The Miami-Dade policeman sitting next to Melissa turned, put his finger on an electric button, and lowered the window. It hadn't dropped more than a couple of inches before Melissa saw a spray can nozzle come through the crack . . . a mist whoosh in. Her police bodyguard reached for it, grabbed it, pushed it away, his eyes closed, grimacing, now coughing. She saw his head drop forward quietly and thought, *Adalwolf's good with gas.* Then she passed out.

MELISSA WOKE TO THE sound of tires hitting a speed bump and her head jolting against the window on the passenger side of a car. She opened her eyes and recognized the dashboard, the hood, and the charcoal gray leather of her BMW. She also recognized the driver. Her lips and cheeks were pinched by adhesive tape covering her mouth. When her hands rose to pull it off she discovered they were bound at the wrists, sloppily, and taped to the metal frame beneath the seat.

She couldn't have been unconscious long; they were still on Arthur Lamb, Jr. Road, on the way back from Jimbo's. She sat up straight and turned back to see if Harris was on the road behind her. There were no headlights. Adalwolf said nothing.

They passed the empty guardhouse and stopped at Crandon Boulevard. The Rickenbacker Causeway and the city of Miami were to the right; the town of Key Biscayne and the ocean to the left. Adalwolf waited for a truck to pass on the four-lane boulevard and turned left.

The car accelerated smoothly and followed a set of tail lights in the distance. Adalwolf turned on the radio and found some classical music. A few minutes later they entered Key Biscayne Village and drove past restaurants, a KFC, and a Citibank. They stopped at a traffic light and waited. She looked around but the streets were empty. When the light turned green they moved slowly down the main drag. On the radio a Beethoven sonata ended and a weather report began.

'. . . *partly cloudy skies under a full moon* . . .'

Adalwolf had sent Harris on a wild goose chase to the cleaners to split him away from her.

'. . . *temperature seventy-six degrees* . . .'

He'd sent a fake letter from the Chorale Society to himself, knowing she'd read it.

'. . . *the barometric pressure at thirty point four and rising* . . .'

He'd given her his signature limp at the concert hall, even waited for her to get into the BMW and drive into the parking lot so they wouldn't lose him.

'. . . *calm seas with high tide at twelve-fifty-seven a.m., low tide at six-fifty-seven a.m.*'

He'd called the cops to Jimbo's, which is why they showed up in uniform. He'd sent the boat into the lagoon and snagged her like a . . . did the radio say, '*high tide at twelve-fifty-seven a.m.?*'

Kobie was being given up at 12.57, and high tide was at 12.57?

Good God. She felt sick to her stomach. She told herself to calm down. If she vomited with her mouth taped shut, she'd suffocate.

THE ADHESIVE TAPE covering Kobie's mouth had gotten so soaked with sea water it was sliding toward her chin. She'd managed to poke it loose with her tongue so she could breathe a little easier. Her crying had stopped but her nose was still stuffed up. The barnacles on the wooden ladder were jabbing her in the back. She couldn't move.

She sat on a foot rest at the bottom of the wooden ladder at Ben's Stiltsville house. The deck was about fifteen feet above her; behind her was a dock. Her hands were tied together in her lap and her feet were taped together and dangling over the edge of the platform. Rolls of adhesive tape pinned her arms and torso to the ladder. She was on the inside of the wooden frame, facing the pilings beneath the house, not outward where a passing boat might see her in the moonlight.

The barnacle gouging her back was a small problem. The big problem was the rising tide. Before the sun set she'd found a barnacle at the high water mark on a piling in front of her, just above her line of sight. She didn't know how long it would take, but when the water reached it, she knew her eyes would be under water.

The sea was already waist high. It was warm but she was getting cold. When she turned her head to the right she could see the lights of the Miami Beach skyline. She wanted her daddy.

She looked at the pilings in the moonlight and named all the flowers she could think of.

ADALWOLF DROVE TO THE center of the village and pulled into the driveway of a two-story building with *Loring Pharmaceuticals* written on a brass plaque by the front door. Next to it was a sprawling, three-story medical center. He lowered the window and punched in a code and waited while a metal gate rose. When it was high enough, he drove into an empty parking lot in back, turned off the engine, and looked at Melissa. 'Your head will clear when we get inside.'

HARRIS SAT AT THE intersection of Arthur Lamb, Jr. Road and Crandon Boulevard, trying to decide which way to turn.

'He went to the city,' Rufus Pickel said. 'Easier to hide.'

'What's to the left?' Harris asked.

'Key Biscayne Village, a state park, and the Atlantic Ocean. Essentially a dead end.'

Sitting in the back seat, Eric Brandt said, 'Jimbo's was a dead end, but he took it.'

Harris rolled down the window and stuck his arm out and signaled the police cars behind him to turn right and head for Miami. When they'd gone around him, he pulled into the median and turned left toward Key Biscayne Village. The expanse of Miami was hopeless. At least the village was small enough to give them a chance.

THE DOOR OPENED ON A laboratory lit by red bulbs in the ceiling. In front of Melissa were computer-driven analyzers, sinks, beakers, Bunsen burners, and books. There was a water purification system to the left, and against the wall, an autoclave to sterilize instruments. Next to that was a stainless steel refrigerator with double glass doors revealing 'egg crates' of bottled medicine and containers.

Adalwolf closed the door behind them and turned on the overhead lights. Melissa stood with her hands tied and a line of tape across her mouth. *I've entered an insane asylum.*

'Follow me,' he said, and walked toward a red velvet curtain strung across a doorway at the side of the room.

She stood still, her eyes sweeping the room. So this was his private lab. To the right of the refrigerator was a centrifuge the size of a washing machine. There were graduated cylinders and dozens of glass and acrylic test tubes in plastic racks. Sitting on shelves were bottles of chemicals in light-resistant brown glass, and against the wall was a work area with a chair and a knee-well and two desktop computers, two monitors, two keyboards. There were hoses everywhere.

He turned. 'Melissa?'

She saw stainless steel sinks and acrylic gel trays with electrical wires attached. On the walls were whiteboards with colored magic-marker notes and diagrams and maps sequencing viral DNA. Computer printouts tacked to a cork wallboard. Stacks of notebooks. A large glass case with a roller hood and ultraviolet lamps to kill bacteria, and a large fan to suck out volatile fumes. Mounted on an ultraviolet light box was a digital camera linked to a computer that could show gels stained with ethidium bromide, a chemical that labeled DNA under fluorescent light. There were X-ray cassettes and incubators. More than one.

She started walking, passing a stainless steel freezer the size of a casket, looking for a knife, a tool, anything that might serve as a weapon. The only thing she found was a glass beaker, which she picked up.

He stood waiting for her, holding a coil of tan rubber tubing and a knife. He took the beaker from her hands – it was useless anyway – and lifted them as if to cut the tape on her wrists. Instead, he looped the rubber tubing around them, tied a knot, and reached up and laid the rubber coil over a chin-up bar between the door jambs. Pulling down on the other end, he strung her hands above her head and tied the tubing to the bar. Then he walked back into the lab.

'I know what you're thinking, but you're wrong,' he said.

She looked through the doorway into his private lair and saw his bed, a night stand, and framed photographs on the wall. The tape across her mouth was making her skin raw.

'You're thinking I'm going to give you something that will activate the virus,' he said.

She heard him open a drawer behind her, but her eyes were still fixed on the photos: a long-lens shot of her and David walking arm-in-arm on the beach, another of herself at a political rally on the Washington mall. She felt new chills.

'I'm not going to activate the virus,' he said. 'I'm going to do the exact opposite.'

Above the photos was a portrait of Adolf Hitler with a leather belt across his chest, his hair angled diagonally, his mustache trim, his eyes boring into the lens. Music filled the air – a Mozart mass, beautiful, eerie, and inappropriate. She spun around on the rubber tubing and faced the lab. He was walking toward her carrying a small bottle of liquid in one hand, a syringe and needle in the other.

'I saw you looking at the photographs,' he said, unscrewing the cap from the bottle. He set it on a table and walked to the night stand and lifted the book of photographs and opened it to a worn page. Then he turned it and showed her his favorite picture of her grandmother. 'Beautiful, wasn't she?' To himself he said, 'I was so in love with her.'

He set the book down and opened a drawer in the night stand and lifted out a black leather box. After opening it, he lifted a silver chain with a white pendant dangling at the bottom. It was her grandmother's, the one that had cost Ben-Zevi his life. He stepped over to Melissa and placed it around her neck. 'But no more beautiful than you are, my dear.' He admired her a moment, then picked up the bottle of liquid.

'I traced three generations of your family in search of Jewish genes,' he said. 'Fifty years of work and I couldn't find them. Then one day I didn't need to. The genome project did it for me.' He pointed at a poster on the wall near the end of the bed. 'See that chart? The lines on the left are the chromosomes unique to Ashkenazi Jews, and the ones on the right are Sephardic.'

He stuck the needle through the rubber diaphragm on the bottle's mouth and drew out a carefully measured amount. 'Those handful of genes are like little fuses. When they come into contact with my virus, *whoosh!* Bleeding, convulsions, disorientation, coma. Viral hemorrhagic fever that makes the gas chambers look kind.'

He set the bottle on a tray.

'I named the version you're carrying "FSV", by the way. FS for final solution, V for virus. Don't be so nervous, there's not going to be an ultrasound this time.'

He snapped the syringe with his finger, eliminating any bubbles.

'The problem with NTX was that it killed so fast there was no time to spread it. The Friedman boy and the other beta testers proved that conclusively.'

He picked up an alcohol pad in an envelope.

'FSV solves that problem. Once the prototype matures in your baby – which should happen by the time it's born – the virus will be robust enough to spread as an aerosol. When someone is exposed to him by a cough or sneeze the virus will stay dormant for forty-five to sixty days, then wham, you're gone. If you're Jewish, that is.'

He tore open the envelope.

'You want to know something interesting? If your baby spreads the virus to one person a day, and each of them spreads it to one person a day, in forty-five days – before the first symptoms appear to the first epidemiologist – every man, woman, and child on earth will have the virus. That's right. Two to the forty-fifth power is ten billion.'

He took out the alcohol pad.

'With modern travel it'll spread around the globe faster than the nineteen eighteen flu, and that one killed over twenty million people. It's easy. There are only thirteen million Jews in the world.'

He raised the syringe. She shook her head no, her eyes wild and pleading.

'Don't worry, this drug isn't going to set off the virus,' he said, trying to calm her. 'The virus is *already* active and maturing in the baby.

She puffed at the tape. Was this possible?

'The problem is,' Adalwolf said, 'as it grows, it can cross over the placenta barrier into the mother. Too many of my pregnant rats caught the virus from their fetuses and died before their babies were born.' He tossed the alcohol pad onto the floor.

'So you see, you don't want to stop me from giving you this injection. It's going to save your life.'

She watched him helplessly.

'I'm ready to inject it now. With your permission.'

She shook her head and her nostrils flared above the duct tape gag.

'I want your permission, Melissa. I want you to beg for your life.'

Sweat ran into her eyes.

'I want you to beg for your baby's life, too.'

Now tears.

'David did.'

She closed her eyes.

'Beg for it! Now!'

'Mmm-mmm!'

'What?'

'Mmm-mmm!'

He reached up and pulled the tape off her mouth. 'I couldn't understand what you said.'

She spoke in a hoarse whisper. 'I said, fuck you.'

His face turned red – then softened into a smile.

'Melissa, Melissa, Melissa. That is *so* you.'

He unbuttoned her shorts and pulled them down at her hip.

'You should be proud to call yourself a Jew.'

He used the alcohol pad to clean a spot on her skin.

'Just like another Jewish woman, you've been chosen, Melissa.'

He tossed aside the pad and raised the needle.

'And just as her son gave his life to save the world, yours will give his to save it again.'

He inserted the needle smoothly and pushed down the plunger.

'Melissa, the Chosen One. Chosen to be the Nazi Madonna.'

He pulled out the needle, then lifted the pendant from around her neck.

'It's time for you to see your new home, my dear. You'll love the baby's room. I'm painting it blue.'

HARRIS JOHNSON, RUFUS Pickel, and Eric Brandt drove through Key Biscayne Village looking for Melissa's BMW. They got on the radio to FBI Miami, but there was no news, no sighting by their own agents, Miami-Dade PD, the highway patrol, the Coast Guard.

Harris decided to return to headquarters. He pulled into a driveway, turned around, and headed north toward the Rickenbacker and Interstate 95 north. The building next to the driveway had a small brass sign by the door that read *Loring Pharmaceuticals.* Not that he noticed it, and not that it would have meant anything if he had.

They sped away.

MELISSA'S BMW LEFT THE laboratory parking lot and turned right, which was south, and headed toward the dead end of Key Biscayne. Adalwolf was driving. Now that it didn't matter, she was conscious of the compass and their directions.

Adalwolf had put her in the backseat and laid her on her side with her hands tied and fresh tape on her mouth. Moving along the main street, she pulled herself into a sitting position and looked around. Adalwolf saw her do it but didn't object. She was hidden in back by the convertible's canvas top, and at eleven thirty at night, there was no one around to see her anyway.

He drove carefully through the village to a remote area and came to a set of white metal gates across the road. A sign to the right said *Bill Baggs Cape Florida State Recreation Park*, and one hanging on the gate said *Road Closed At Sunset – Do Not Enter*. There was no one in sight.

He pulled up to the gates with his headlights on, got out, and walked to the center where the crossbars met. Using a pair of wire cutters, he snipped a thin cable that held them together, swung them open, and came back to the car and drove through. On the other side he stopped and closed the gates, then got in the car and continued on.

They drove past a closed ranger station into the abandoned park, passing signs to a lighthouse café and beach rentals. A mile or so down the road they came to a sign that read *No Name Harbor and Boater's Grill*. He turned right and took the road until it ended in an empty parking lot. To the left, partly hidden behind trees, was a closed restaurant, and in front of the car was the stern of a sleek white boat which she guessed was about twenty-five or thirty feet long. Beyond it, the harbor's smooth water shimmered in the moonlight where four or five boats sat quietly at anchor – a mast light on some, softly lit portholes on others. He cut the engine and headlights and turned back to her.

'The situation is simple,' he said. 'If you want to see Kobie alive you must do exactly as I say.'

She looked at him.

'Disobedience will get her killed, Melissa. I trust David's experience makes that point?'

She nodded. She heard distant music – rock and roll – and an occasional burst of laughter.

'I'm going to make the boat ready now. Sit quietly and relax.'

She nodded.

He taped her hands to one of the metal ribs supporting the convertible top and got out of the car. Carrying his leather doctor's bag and a flashlight, he crossed a patch of sandy crab grass and walked up to the stern of the boat. He looked to his left, toward the source of the music. She could hear it and assumed it was coming from a boat, although her view was blocked by the low foliage of sea grape trees.

He'll kill me the minute the baby is born.

Adalwolf stepped from a concrete abutment onto the boat's foot-wide aft deck, then down onto what must have been a seat and onto the cockpit floor. She could see him from the waist up as he worked.

The virus will kill the baby soon after the disease spreads.

He set his medical bag down and stepped over to the boat's steering wheel. Next to it in the moonlight, she could see pairs of throttles, gear shift levers for twin engines, and a panel of gauges. Holding on to a tall chair, he inserted a key in the ignition, lit up the instrument panel, and started the engines. The rumble of twin Mercruiser 360s blended with the music from the party.

He stepped on the deck above the cockpit and walked along the side of the cabin to the bow. She heard the clank of a heavy chain as he hoisted the anchor. He returned to the cockpit, bent down, and straightened up with two flat, foam-filled cushions that he laid on the floor. With the engines still grumbling, he climbed onto the foot-wide aft deck, stepped onto the cement abutment, and walked back to the passenger side of the car.

'Remember, exactly as I say,' he said.

He pulled the tape off her mouth and cut the tape that tethered her bound hands to the metal rib and helped her out of the car. With his arm in hers and her wrists still taped in front of her, he walked her across the grass toward the boat. About fifty feet to the left, tied to a cleat on the abutment, was a large yacht with a flying bridge and fishing poles and complicated rigging. Music, laughter, and the occasional whoop of a card game came from a well-lit salon along with the pungent smell of pot. But no one in sight.

He guided her to the stern of his boat. Up close, the engines rumbled loudly and sump pumps spit water from the hull into the bay. He helped her step from the abutment onto the foot-wide aft deck. Five feet below the deck, just above the water line, was a swim platform that kept the boat away from the concrete wall. The platform's swim ladder was stowed in the up position.

He followed her onto the narrow aft deck, stepped ahead of her onto a cockpit bench, and down to the floor. Taking her by her bound hands, he helped her down. The moment both her feet were planted, he said, 'On your knees.'

She knelt on the cockpit floor as slowly as she could. When she was almost down she looked over the gunwales for a party-goer, a sailor, anyone who might help. There was no one.

He pushed her head down, then reached out and loosened the two stern lines and tossed them onto the deck near her feet. With the boat now floating free, he walked to the helm and sat in the skipper's chair and pushed the gear shift levers forward, engaging the propellers with a clunk. The boat began moving at idle speed. When they'd cleared the boats sitting at anchor, he increased power slightly and headed toward the cut leading to the Atlantic Ocean. Once they got there, she knew it was all over.

He placed the two throttles in his palm and pushed them forward an inch. The sound of the engines turned from a rumble to a purr and the boat started gliding through shallow waves.

Melissa heard a loud banging noise behind her. The swim plat-form ladder had fallen backward on its hinges and was dragging in the water and bobbing up and down. Adalwolf pulled the throttles back to idle, got out of his chair, and stepped around her to the stern. Leaning over the aft deck, he grabbed a small line and pulled the ladder out of the water into the up position, then stretched out to secure it with a bungee cord.

Now, Melissa told herself.

SHE ROLLED ON HER BACK, raised her feet, and shoved Adalwolf just below the seat of his pants. He lurched over the foot-wide deck, arms flailing, and fell head-first onto the swim platform. His body crumpled behind his outstretched hands – his torso slid over the edge of the platform – and his hands pawed the smooth, wet fiberglass in search of a handle, a line, anything to keep him from falling into the water.

Melissa heard the thud when he hit the platform – but no splash, which meant he was still on board. She rolled to her hands and knees and used the edge of the molded fiberglass bench to raise herself to her feet. The boat continued moving at idle speed, heading for the channel.

She looked over the edge of the aft deck and saw Adalwolf's left hand splashing in the water, and his right hand gripping a rubber shower hose he'd stretched to the limit struggling to pull himself back.

She turned and looked for a sharp edge to cut the tape on her wrists, but boat cockpits, by design, had few sharp edges.

She saw his black medical bag on the bench, grabbed it, opened the mouth, and turned it upside down, spilling the contents onto the white cushion. She glanced over the transom again. Adalwolf had pulled his torso onto the platform and lay on it catching his breath.

She pawed through the paraphernalia and saw a glint of steel, a pair of scissors. She turned one of blades back between her wrists, slipped her fingers into the handle, and began sawing at the adhesive tape. With her wrists bound, the stroke was too short to be effective.

Adalwolf got to one knee, breathing hard.

She continued sawing at the tape as hard as she could. The edge frayed but didn't tear. She wasn't going to make it. They were in the middle of the harbor now with a wide expanse of water on all sides.

Hit the throttles and make him slide off the platform!

She stepped up to the levers and looked back. One of his hands came over the aft deck just as she jammed the throttles forward. The boat lurched ahead but it was too late: he managed to hold on. She pulled back to idle and turned the wheel hard left, putting the vessel into a wide, slow circle, hoping someone would notice.

She looked around frantically. On the side of the boat was a row of 'rocket launchers,' the metal tubes that held fishing poles. She opened the scissors wide, dropped the handle of a blade into one of the tubes, and laid the other blade across the mouth to keep the pair from falling in. Then she drove the sharp edge of the protruding blade between her wrists, trapping it in the tape. She lifted the scissors out.

Adalwolf stood on the swim platform and looked at her through snaky eyes.

Picturing a severed artery, she brought the scissors handle down hard against the fiberglass bench. The blade cut the tape half way through before falling to the floor.

Adalwolf started climbing over the transom.

She was out of time. Adalwolf put his foot on the fiberglass bench in the cockpit. She saw a long aluminum pole wedged between a pair of clamps on the outside of the cabin wall in front of the helm – a gaff for pulling fish on board or reaching the loop on mooring balls.

Adalwolf stepped on the floor of the cockpit. Furious.

She reached up with bound hands and pulled the gaff out of the prongs and in one continuous motion swung it around, clipping

Adalwolf above the eyes, snapping his head back. He touched his forehead where the pole had hit him, looking for blood. She raised the weapon and brought it down on top of his shaved head, feeling the impact vibrate up the aluminum shaft into her hands. He squinted and raised his hand to his skull.

She hit him again. And again. And again.

He grabbed the pole and tried to pull it away from her, but his inner ear was already confused and struggling. His legs buckled and he fell to his knees and toppled forward onto his face, mumbling incoherently.

She raised her hands and brought the tape between her wrists down hard on the edge of the rocket launcher. The adhesive binding split and her hands went free.

Adalwolf rolled on his back.

She pawed through the spilled contents of his doctor's bag, found a plastic-wrapped syringe and a capped needle – found a bottle with a red and blue label that looked like the sedative he'd used on her in the clinic – the Versed – and unscrewed the cap.

Adalwolf reached for the bench to pull himself up.

Her hands were shaking too hard to get the needle screwed on the hub of the syringe. *Come on, all those hormone pregnancy shots you gave yourself, you know what to do.* She finally felt it snap into place and pulled the cap off the needle.

Adalwolf looked up and saw what she was doing.

She drove the needle through the rubber diaphragm, pulled back the plunger, and yanked the needle out. Adalwolf got to his knees to rise. She pushed him back onto his side and put her foot on his cheek and pinned his head to the floor. Leaning over, she drove the needle into the side of his neck – *Hit a vessel, please, God, hit a vessel!* – and jammed the plunger down.

He grabbed her hand with an iron fist and pulled the needle out. 'Jew bitch.'

He bent her hand backwards, bringing her to her knees in a silent scream. Just as he was about to break it, his grasp eased, his eyelids went to half-mast, and his eyeballs rolled up. His lips were parted as if he was in the middle of a sentence he couldn't quite finish.

God must have heard her prayer.

A BOAT. KOBIE HEARD THE growling engine of a speed boat. She turned her head as far as she could but she couldn't see it, so she listened. *Over here.* She sent the strongest thoughts she could. *Over here, over here, over here!*

The sound of twin engines grew louder, alternating their pitch with the pounding of the hull against the waves and the whine of cavitating propellers. Louder and louder they came . . . held their volume . . . then turned softer and softer, fading until they were drowned out by the sound of waves lapping against the pilings.

Water lapping at the ladder, and her chest, and the telephone poles that held the house above her head. Stupid, dumb water. Stupid like Jimmy Whitacre who sat behind her and kicked her chair all day, kicked and kicked no matter how many times she turned around and said Stop it, Jimmy. Wave after wave, lapping at her chest, lapping and lapping no matter how many times she told it to stop.

'Daddy!' she cried.

Lapping and lapping.

Worse, rising.

THE MOMENT THE BOW eased back toward the cement abutment Melissa pulled back the throttles and threw the props into reverse. For someone who didn't know much about boats she had the right idea, just not the best timing. The boat's momentum carried it into the cement, crunching the fiberglass bow and jolting her against the wheel.

The crash moved like a shock wave down the abutment to the party boat. The laughter below decks stopped, then the music, and a moment later three young men emerged with bare feet, tank tops and boozy eyes and walked along the abutment to her boat.

'Hey, nice job,' a guy with a bottle of beer said, looking at the damage.

'I need help!' Melissa said.

'No shit,' a guy with a joint said.

The guy in the tank top said, 'Hey, I know you! You park cars in my garage.'

'It's my grandfather!' Melissa said. 'He hit his head!'

Mr. Beer Bottle and Mr. Tank Top jumped aboard and walked down the side of the boat to the cockpit. 'How bad is it?' Tank Top said.

'It knocked him out,' she said.

'Wow, you better get him to a doctor,' Beer Bottle said.

'I'll call an ambulance,' Tank Top said, patting his shirt, 'soon's I find my cell phone.'

Melissa said, 'Just help me get him into my car and I'll take him myself.'

Tank Top stepped into the cockpit and looked at Adalwolf more closely. 'I don't know, man, he looks pretty bad.'

Melissa said, 'If you call EMS it's going to mean police reports, medical forms—'

'Hey, Alphonse!' Mr. Beer Bottle yelled at Mr. Joint. 'Give us a hand! We gotta put this lady's grandpa in her car!'

MELISSA HEADED NORTH in her BMW with Adalwolf on the passenger side, his head resting in the crook of the seat and the door. He'd be awake in half an hour, forty-five minutes max. Now that she finally had him she didn't know what to do with him.

Ask Harris.

She lifted her cell phone and hit the speed dial before remembering the battery was gone. He couldn't help her now. She was on her own.

Take him to the nearest police station.

But the police had rules, and rules took time. Eventually they might get the truth out of him about Kobie's whereabouts, but eventually wasn't good enough. And what about the virus? His lab notes? A vaccine? The police would never get that information out of him, not without a rubber hose. But they didn't do that anymore. At least, not when you needed it.

My God, listen to what you're saying.

She was getting ideas.

She pawed through her shoulder bag and found the red sneaker on her key chain. Lifting it in front of the rear view mirror to catch the light from headlights behind her, she saw the key to their beach house still on the chain. She put it back in her bag.

Get hold of yourself.

Wait a second: she had a DC adaptor for her cell phone. She could plug it into the cigarette lighter and call Harris. She fished it out of the console and plugged it in and stuck the jack into her phone. It gave her a power-on beep. She lifted it and found the speed dial button to Harris. Her finger pressed lightly – and backed off.

She looked over at Adalwolf. He was still unconscious with a knot on his head. Farther up I-95 was FBI headquarters, and coming up on the right was the turn-off to Golden Beach. *There are rules for everybody else, and then there are rules for monsters.* He'd taught her that himself. But there was also her own voice, the one she used in the classroom to each legal ethics. 'Do what's right,' she said out loud. 'Turn him in.' Then, *You're already the subject of one grand jury investigation, why not two?* The exit sign flashed in the corner of her eye.

She veered right and headed for the beach.

SHE DROVE SLOWLY INTO the driveway, turned off the headlights, and reached into the glove compartment for the garage door opener. When the door rose, she drove in, hit the button to close it, then turned off the engine and sat still until the door banged shut. The garage was silent. Only her heart was making noise. It had a beat she'd never felt before, simultaneously cool and angry.

She got out of the car and flipped the switch to turn on a fluorescent ceiling light. Walking around the front bumper, she looked at the steel door leading inside the house and saw Mr. Butterfield's collapsed wheelchair sitting by the wall. She walked to it, unfolded it, and pushed it to the BMW's passenger side.

Nothing about this was going to be easy.

She opened the door and caught Adalwolf's torso before it fell onto the floor, then jostled his butt into the wheelchair seat. Leaving the passenger door open – she needed both hands to keep his body from falling   she pushed the chair to the hallway door and unlocked it with the key on her red sneaker chain. Once it was open, she pushed him inside onto the smooth tile and stopped to catch her breath. She flicked on the hallway light and stood thinking. *Am I really going to do this?*

She looked down the hallway and saw the door to the steam room. She pictured David standing there with towel, opening the door . . . then pictured him lying on the redwood platform with a needle in his heart.

Yes, she was going to do this.

She got behind the wheelchair and pushed it onto the automatic chair lift, raised the safety bar, took a breath, and hit the 'up' button. The electric motor came to life, turning the gears with a quiet whir. The elevator with Adalwolf's crumpled body rose to the second floor as Melissa climbed the steps next to it, one hand on his shoulder to keep him steady.

When the lift reached the top she lowered the safety bar and pushed the wheelchair onto the hallway carpet. Leaving Adalwolf slumped in the chair, she walked down the darkened hallway to the master bedroom.

She entered the bedroom by feel and put her hand on the light switch to turn it on – then changed her mind. There was enough moonlight coming through the picture window to let her navigate where she needed to go. She wanted no curiosity from the security company that patrolled the beach. The curtains were open; she drew them closed with a pull cord, putting herself in total blackness, then felt her way to a lamp next to the bed and turned it on.

She lifted the bedside telephone. It was dead, the service cut off when she'd moved out. The clock said it was nearly midnight. An hour to high tide.

She walked into David's office and pulled a book off the shelf and scanned the tidal chart. Biscayne Bay rose and fell three feet every twelve hours. Three inches an hour. If Kobie's nose was near the high water mark, she was only inches away from drowning. Maybe she already had.

There was no time to waste.

She estimated the distance between the door and the side of the bed, then returned to the wheelchair. She approached Adalwolf cautiously. His eyes were still closed, but so were a possum's. She reached out and poked at him. He didn't move. She poked him again, this time a little more confidently. He didn't grab for her.

She got behind the wheel chair and pushed him down the hall into the bedroom. When she was inside, she turned the chair toward the side of the bed and held her forehead in the palm of her hand. *Think about this first. Once you get started, there's no turning back.*

'But there's no time,' she said out loud, 'he'll wake up any moment.'

She leaned into the chair as if she were pushing a car and stepped forward. The well-lubricated wheels picked up speed and the chair's footrest hit the bed frame about shin-high with an enormous crash. The momentum sent Adalwolf's body forward with a lurch and plopped his torso onto the bed with his knees on the floor. The wheelchair fell onto its side, its upper wheel spinning. The weight of his body was starting to pull him over the edge of the mattress onto the floor.

She pushed the chair out of the way and grabbed his belt and held him up. With her other hand she reached out and grabbed the bedside lamp and ripped the electrical cord out of the socket. Feeling her way in the dark, she ran the end of the cord under his belt, tied a quick knot, and wound the lamp and the cord around the bedpost on the opposite side.

Letting the lamp dangle over the foot of the bed, she went to the other bedside lamp and turned it on. Adalwolf's upper body was still face down on the mattress, held in place by the electrical cord.

She walked to the near side of the bed and lifted his legs, grunting under their weight. Once they were on the mattress she pushed them toward the middle of the bed and twisted his body onto its side. She stood up and caught her breath and heard Eric's warning: too much effort could cause a miscarriage. She talked to the baby a moment, telling him to stay with her, and checked the time. It was midnight. The thought of Kobie gave her new energy.

She tugged at Adalwolf s clothes until he was lying on his back in the center of the bed. His head moved from side to side. He was waking up.

She ran into the bathroom, opened the cabinet under the sink, and read the labels on the containers: hairspray, shaving cream, shampoo, everything except what she needed. She ran out of the bedroom and down the steps to the utility room and pulled bottles and pressurized cans off the shelves, reading, tossing, and reading.

Finally, a possibility: *Carbonette.* She read the label out loud.

'Spot cleaner . . . main ingredient carbon tetrachloride. That'll do.'
She threw it into a plastic garbage bag and pulled the ironing board
out of the closet and found the iron behind it. She grabbed it and
ran out the hallway door into the garage. The ceiling light was still
on, the passenger door of her car still open.

She unplugged her cell phone and dropped it into the garbage
bag, then pushed the passenger seat forward and reached into the
back seat and grabbed Adalwolf s medical bag. She saw the plastic
envelope containing the documents she'd gotten from Jake the
Wizard lying on the floor. Acting on instinct, she threw them into
the garbage bag, too.

She dumped the contents of the medical bag onto the back seat,
picked up rolls of adhesive tape, and tossed them into the bag. After
backing out of the car door, she closed it, turned out the light at a
wall switch, and re-entered the house. She sprinted up the steps
and down the hallway and entered the bedroom cautiously, the
clothes iron in one hand, the garbage bag in the other.

Adalwolf was lying on the bed, groaning.

She gave herself exactly five minutes to get ready.

HARRIS SAT IN THE dispatcher's room at FBI Miami, hanging on
every telephone call and police report that came in over the radio.
Lots of chaff, not a kernel of wheat.

Special Agent Pickel set a cup of coffee in front of Harris. Harris
took a drink, grimaced, and unrolled his Rolaids.

Rufus said, 'We've got Miami-Dade on alert, and we've got
every car we own out there on a grid ready to roll at a moment's
notice. The chopper's on the pad.'

Harris nodded. He started to say something, but decided to cut
himself off with a drink of nasty coffee instead.

SHE'D NEVER SEEN ANYTHING like it. Never even imagined it. Her breathing was short and her mouth as dry as a desert.

Melissa stood at the side of the bed looking at her handiwork. Adalwolf s eyes were open, his head clearing. He turned his face toward her.

'What . . .'

He tried to get up but his hands tugged against the adhesive tape holding his wrists to the bedposts. He looked surprised, although she couldn't imagine why. His knees rose instinctively, but not far: his feet were taped to bedposts, too. His face showed confusion, then dawning awareness.

Straining his neck muscles, he lifted his head and looked down at his spread-eagled body. His shoes and socks and shirt were off, his pants and white undershirt on. His eyes asked the obvious: *What is that thing in the middle of my body?* It looked like an iron – a household iron – sitting on his stomach – no, not sitting on it, *taped* to it. Her version of an ultrasound probe. His eyes followed the electrical cord from the back of the handle to an extension cord to an outlet in the wall.

Melissa pulled a chair up to the side of the bed and stood leaning on the back the way she did when she taught her class. A class on ethics and the law, not, as she'd once pointed out, a class on the Marquis de Sade. *Torture is no more justified than killing*, she recalled lecturing her students. And what had Maria Tressler said about that after class? *I hope you never have to face the choice.* Oh, Maria, if only you knew.

'Where is she?' Melissa said. She took a drink of water from a glass. Her hand was surprisingly steady.

He lowered his head and closed his eyes and started laughing. 'What do you think you're doing?'

She felt fury rising in her cheeks. *Thank you, Adalwolf. That helps.* She reached out and turned the heat setting on the iron to LOW and came around and sat on the chair and waited.

He stopped laughing slowly, tears running down his temples. 'Oh, my dear. Now you really are in a pickle, aren't you?'

'*Me* in a pickle? You're the one tied to a bedpost with a hot iron on your stomach. You said I could have Kobie at twelve-fifty-seven, which is high tide.'

'I did?' Adalwolf said. 'Inadvertent disclosure is one of the short-comings of the highly specific mind.' To himself, he mumbled, 'Like giving you that stupid Latin phrase.'

She reached out and turned the dial up a notch. 'We don't have much time, Adalwolf.'

'Call me Ben,' he said.

'You aren't Ben. You don't even look like him.'

'Your iron is getting warm.'

She leaned over and looked at the dial. 'We've got plenty of settings to go.'

'Let's stop this charade,' he said. 'Look at you, behaving like some Colombian drug lord. We both know you're not a torturer. Besides, you have to cut me loose if you want to find her.'

'Where is she?'

He let out a weary sigh. 'You want to play a game? All right, but every minute we lose the water gets higher.'

'Where is she?'

'The problem isn't Kobie, Melissa, it's you. If you'd just accept your fate none of this would be necessary.'

'I don't believe in fate. I prefer action.' She turned up the heat to polyester-rayon. 'Where is she?'

He grimaced and began to sweat.

She looked at her watch. Ten after midnight. She reached out and turned up the dial two notches.

'We're at Wool,' she said. 'Cotton and Linen to go.'

The iron clicked as the steel surface expanded. She could smell his undershirt scorching and see it turning brown at the edges.

'This is so good,' he said in a hoarse voice. 'The child of an Auschwitz survivor . . . full of moral indignation about the ovens . . . the Nazi hunter behaving like the hunted. So . . . absolutely . . . good.'

Wisps of smoke rose from the burned shirt.

He screamed.

'Where is Kobie?' she said. Her hands shaking.

'I'll tell you what you need to know,' he whispered. He was breathing hard, rocking from side to side in pain. She leaned in close to hear what he had to say. What he said was, 'Go to hell, you goddamned Jew.'

She reached out and turned the dial up a notch – then pushed it all the way to number seven, the highest setting.

'Where is she?' she said. She was trembling and felt outside herself. She gave herself a pep talk under her breath: 'Stay with it, Lissa, it's him or you. Him or Kobie.'

He breathed like a sprinter. The iron burned through the shirt and seared the skin on his nerve-rich stomach. The stench of burning flesh filled the air. He began yelling harder.

Melissa began crying. 'Where is she!' she yelled. It was her voice but she didn't recognize it. 'Answer me or I'll let it melt right down to your spine!'

More crying by her, more yelling by him, more stink of roasted skin. Adalwolf s body began shaking and writhing and his face turned reddish-purple and shiny with sweat.

Melissa reached out for the iron – Adalwolf raised his trembling head to see. 'Take it off!' he screamed. His head craned backward, his eyes smashed closed.

Her hand hovered above the handle. 'Where is she!' She told herself not to lose her nerve. 'Where *is she*!'

He didn't answer. She put her hand on the iron as if to lift it and cut the tape . . . then pressed down instead. The searing heat sent Adalwolf into a new spasm. His back jerked and she heard his neck pop.

'Where is she?' she yelled in a crying slur.

'Take it off! Take it off! Take it off!'

'Tell me!' – 'Take it off!' – 'Where is she?' They were both yelling at the same time. 'I'll tell you!,' he said. 'Oh, God . . .'

'Tell me and I'll stop!' She cried harder.

'Oh, Jesus, Jesus, Jesus, stop it, Jesus . . .'

'Tell me!'

He'd cried himself into silent heaves. '*Stits* . . . vi.'

'What?'

'*Aahhh!* Take-it-off-take-it-off-take-it-off . . .'

'I couldn't hear you!'

He took a breath in and used it to expel a word. 'Stilts . . . ville!'

'What's Stiltsville?'

He began a new round of weeping.

'Did you say Stiltsville?'

'*Yesssss!*' he screamed. *'Yes, yes, yes, yes, yes . . .'*

She raised the scissors and slid the blades around the tape holding the iron and was starting to cut it when it occurred to her that Stiltsville was a whole town.

'*Where* in Stiltsville?' she said.

'Oh, God, stop it, please . . .'

'Where in Stiltsville!!?'

He gathered a breath. '. . . house . . . by the channel marker . . . oh, *God, God, God* . . .'

She cut the tape on one side of the iron and pulled it off his stomach and laid it onto its side. Burned flesh stuck to the bottom; she couldn't bear to look at it, much less see his stomach. The moment she lifted the hot metal surface, air hit his exposed nerves and sent a new electric-chair jolt through his body. He began screaming.

She had to get word to Harris. She picked up the telephone by the bed, forgetting the service was dead. She pulled her cell phone out of the garbage bag hoping the battery had recharged in the car. It lit up.

She couldn't remember the number at the FBI. Her hands were shaking. She wiped her eyes and hit the speed dial button to Harris. His phone rang. She turned her back to Adalwolf, who was still whimpering, and covered her other ear with her hand.

'Melissa?' Harris said. A helicopter engine nearly drowned out his voice.

'She's in Stiltsville!' she yelled.

'Say again?'

'Kobie's in a place called Stiltsville! Stiltsville! Do you read me?'

She heard Harris talking to the pilot, heard the word 'Stiltsville.' Then back to Melissa. 'We're on our way!'

'The house by the channel marker!' she said.

'By the channel marker,' he shouted.

'Call me on my cell phone the second you find her!'

THE CHOPPER SWOOPED down low over the water. The pilot knew where Stiltsville was, and at 140 miles an hour, it was only a minute before the channel marker appeared blinking in the moonlight.

He angled toward a house with a large antenna but no lights or signs of life. Harris turned on the powerful 1300 watt spotlight as the helicopter descended gently and hovered off to the side of house. The spotlight moved across the deck, then the water line at the pilings.

They saw no sign of her.

'Closer!' Harris yelled, pumping his finger.

The chopper dropped until it was three feet above the water and began circling the house. Harris moved the spotlight up and down, searching the deck, the boarded-up windows. There was nothing.

'Put me down!' he yelled, pulling on his gloves.

The helicopter rose above the house as Harris gathered up a fast rope coiled behind his seat. He opened the door and dropped it over the side, then unbuckled his seat belt. The crest of the roof was only a few feet below, the deck a story below that.

He checked the equipment strapped to his jumpsuit to make sure everything was in place. Facing the pilot, he went out the door and slid down the fast rope like a fireman's pole. When he reached the deck, he yelled 'Kobie!' but the sound of the chopper's engine drowned him out.

Shining a flashlight through an unboarded window, he made a quick search of the cabin interior, saw nothing, then walked to the top of a wooden ladder leading down to the boat dock. His watch said 12:30.

He climbed down and searched the pilings beneath the house. Then, for some reason – call it instinct – he stuck his head through the rungs and looked down. Below his feet was the face of his daughter, her head tilted back, her eyes closed, water washing over them.

'Kobie!'

He lowered himself until he was waist deep in the sea. She was coughing up water and trying to catch her breath between the waves. The gag that circled her head was around her neck. She opened her eyes and saw her daddy but showed no sign of recognition. She was almost gone.

He pulled the snorkel from his jumpsuit and stuck the mouthpiece between her lips. It didn't fit; she swallowed water and coughed. He tore the rubber mouthpiece off and stuck the bare tube back into her mouth. She closed her lips around it and breathed.

After setting the flashlight on the deck above his head to free his hands, he cut the tape viciously, freeing her. He lifted her out of the water so fast she dropped the snorkel. But she was still breathing. He laid her on his shoulder and climbed up to the deck. After sitting her down, he cut the tape around her wrists and smothered her shivering body in his own.

Pulling away, he told her to open her eyes and talk to him. She said, 'I'm cold.' He was ecstatic. He asked her if she had any cuts or wounds. She didn't answer, just lifted her arms and put them around his neck.

He held her in one arm with her head on his shoulder and looked toward Miami. A pair of flashing red lights were approaching, Miami P.D. or the Coast Guard, it didn't matter. He pulled his cell phone from his pocket and hit two buttons. Melissa answered.

'I've got her!' Harris yelled over the din of the helicopter. 'She's alive and . . .

... IN MY ARMS!'

Melissa felt her muscles relax.

'How did you know she was here?' Harris yelled.

'Tell you later.'

She hit the end call button and laid her cell phone on the bed.

Adalwolf was still taped to the bed posts with his head back and his eyes closed, breathing more calmly now, his face drawn and wet. Melissa had laid a cold washcloth on his burned stomach to help cover the exposed nerves. The iron was lying on the bed next to his side, the handle still taped to his body, the other side cut free.

She reached out and lifted it. Adalwolf opened his eyes and strained to raise his head.

'You're in luck,' she said. 'They found her.'

He laid his head back.

She said, 'Now tell me the rest.'

He raised his head again and watched her cut the tape on the iron and set the cold surface on his chest.

'What . . . are you . . . doing?' he said. His eyes were wild and red-rimmed, his voice so soft and hoarse it would have benefited from an electronic amplifier.

'Where is the antidote?' she said. 'The vaccine? The serum?'

He gave her a look that said he didn't understand the question. 'There isn't any,' he said.

She reached out and put her fingers on the heat control dial. 'This time we're going straight to steam.' Her voice was calm and assured. If she had to do it again she would, and he knew it. 'Where is it?'

'The vaccine isn't made yet – and the serum is gone.'

She looked into his eyes. They were pleading.

'I'm not going to ask you again,' she said. She laid her hand on the iron.

'They're at the clinic!' he said.

'Where in the clinic?'

'In the medication room! Cabinet five, the bottom tray! The

vaccine labeled Meclizine XPL, the serum XPL-2.'

'How do I know you're not lying?' she said.

'Call the clinic! They'll tell you they're in the cabinet.'

Not at this hour. She lifted the iron off his chest.

He stared at her waiting for another shoe to drop. 'You're going to kill me now, aren't you?' he said.

She got up and dragged the chair back to the writing desk.

He said, 'You've got the taste for it, I can see it in your eyes.'

She unplugged the iron and wrapped the electrical cord around the handle as she walked it to the bathroom.

'It's the same look I saw in Mengele's eyes,' he said.

She opened a closet door, set it inside, closed the door and returned to the bedroom. She wound up the extension cord and put it into a drawer in the bedside cabinet.

He said, 'All that stuff about ethics and the law you taught your students means nothing. If you hate someone enough, you can justify anything.'

She made sure all the contents of his medical bag were in place except the scissors, then looked around the room to be sure everything was in order. The curtains – she needed to open the curtains.

She turned off the lights in the room except for a small bedside lamp, then walked to the huge window overlooking the beach and pulled the drawstring to open the drapes. A full moon shimmered on the water, and across the beach a bonfire lit the faces of a group of college students who'd gathered around to talk and drink beer.

She returned to the bed and picked up the scissors and sat down on the edge of the mattress. Adalwolf opened his eyes and followed her like a child.

'You're no better than the rest of us,' he said, pleased to say it.

She reached out with the scissors. As they approached his face, he pulled his head back in a flinch, then watched them move toward his left wrist.

She slid blades over the tape and snipped his hand free, letting it fall to his side. She lifted his wrist and ripped the tape off, taking his hair with it. He didn't mind, he was too grateful and amazed.

Next she removed the adhesive tape bonds from his feet, so that only his right hand remained bound to a bedpost. Staying clear of his freed left hand, she picked up the plastic envelope containing the documents she'd asked Harris to get for her and unwound the string on the flap.

'You're right, I'm no better than anyone else,' she said, pulling the documents from the envelope. 'But there's one thing I absolutely won't do. I won't kill a Jew.'

SHE HELD UP THE FIRST document.

'You are the bastard son of a high-level Nazi, that much you know.' She arranged the documents in order, reshuffling them like cards. 'But your mother, Elizabeth Quincy Halliburton, was not the biological daughter of Lord Halliburton. She was his *adopted* daughter.'

She laid the document on the bed.

'Let me see that,' he said, reaching.

'In a minute,' she said. 'The name you had as a child, Henry Hallam Brandon, was derived from your mother's birth name, which wasn't Brandon, but something close.'

'What was it?'

'Brandeis.'

She handed him another document. 'Do you understand what I'm saying? Your mother was the daughter of a London banker named Isaac Brandeis and his wife Laila. Both Jews.'

She laid another document in front of him.

'Isaac and Laila Brandeis died in a boating accident, and Lord Halliburton, who did his banking with Brandeis, took in their daughter, your eventual mother. Everyone thought she was Lord Halliburton's biological daughter, but she wasn't. She was born a Jew.'

His hand held the document she gave him. The edge of it was quivering.

'According to your mother's diary,' Melissa said, 'your Nazi father discovered she was a Jew on her last visit to Düsseldorf, when she was pregnant with you. He said fathering a Jew was out of the question and told her to abort, but she refused, which sent him into a fit of rage. He said he would have no contact with her or the child, which sent *her* into a rage. She left Düsseldorf and never saw him again. It's all here in these pages.'

She turned to the next document.

'But your father's last meeting with your mother wasn't the end of the matter. As he rose to power, he considered you not only an abomination but a potentially terrible political embarrassment. Fearing the Gestapo would come after you, your mother hid you in a French convent. It worked for twelve years, but eventually Himmler's men found you. For all we know, Himmler was your father. Or maybe it was Goebbels, or Heydrich, or maybe even the Führer himself.'

Another document.

'You thought the SS took you away from Mother Marie-Catherine so Hitler's enemies couldn't find you and humiliate him and his elite staff with your birth, but you were wrong. They didn't send you to Auschwitz to hide you, they sent you there to die like the Jew you were. Look at the transfer document.'

She showed him a piece of parchment with a swastika at the top, beneath it the name *Heinrich Himmler, Reichsführer-Schutzsiaffel (SS), Minister of the Interior.* The year was 1943. Instructions in German were followed by rubber-stamped authorizations and the unmistakable signature of Heinrich Himmler, Hitler's close aide, head of the Gestapo and the Waffen-SS. Next to it was the signature of Adolf Hitler.

'Your transfer was authorized by Hitler himself.'

He read quietly.

'When you got to Auschwitz Josef Mengele took you in, but he never intended to protect you. He knew whose son you were, and he knew the SS was watching him. He received temporary permission to use you as a lab assistant not because you were special, but because you were expendable. Viruses, bacteria, chemicals, deadly organisms – he used Jews to handle these things. I know because you told me so. Here is his letter of request and the authorization from *Reichsführer* Rudolf Höss, the commandant of the camp.'

She handed him another document with another swastika at the top, another authorization from the SS.

'These are from the Berlin Document Center, which means they come from the SS itself. Notice the conditions attached to the permission to use you in the lab. It stipulates that like all of Mengele's Jewish lab assistants, you were to be killed before the end of nineteen forty-five.' She handed him another letter. 'That's when Mengele's laboratories were scheduled to be moved from Auschwitz to the Kaiser-Wilhelm-Institüt in Berlin-Dahlem.'

Melissa watched Adalwolf read. His face was white.

'So now you know,' Melissa said. 'The man you adored and served all these years – the man you honored by taking his name – this man, the Führer himself, thought so little of you he sent you to the gas chamber.'

She laid the last few documents on the bed next to him.

'It's your worst nightmare, Adalwolf. Your entire life has been a sham. You are the thing you despise most, the object of your own Final Solution. The documents don't lie, but never mind that. Look inside your heart and you'll know what you've always known.'

She reached out and lifted the can of cleaning fluid.

'Everything you hate about Jews you are obliged to hate about yourself. Their arrogance is your arrogance. Their disgrace is your disgrace. These things can't be erased because they're in your blood. Which means the only thing you can do as an honorable man is . . . what?'

His eyes were full of tears, his psychic pain deeper than the pain of the hot iron.

'What's the only thing you can do with shame this deep?' she said calmly.

He finally said in a whisper: 'Destroy it.'

She unscrewed the lid on the can of cleaning fluid and set it on the bed next to him. 'Destroying Jews is what your Nazi father did best, Adalwolf, whoever he was. It's in your genes. It's your *destiny*.' She lifted the box of matches before his eyes. Tears ran down his cheeks. 'You don't want to wait for your own virus to kill you, do you? It's such an ugly death.'

He said 'No,' so softly she could hardly hear.

She leaned in dangerously close to him and said, 'What is the first rule an obedient Nazi lives by?'

He stared at her pathetically, pleading for a way out.

'Come on, Adalwolf, you know what it is. You told me long ago, remember? Fire is for . . .'

He began crying.

'Come on say it. 'Fire is for . . .'

'Ovens,' he whispered.

'That's right. And ovens are for . . .'

He was crying too hard to answer.

'Come on, Adalwolf, you can say it. Ovens are for . . .'

He stifled his sobs, trying to do his duty. Finally, he whispered it: 'Jews.'

She patted his arm, then picked up the scissors and walked to the other side of the bed and cut loose his right hand, leaving him completely unfettered. She wasn't troubled by his freedom. He was in no condition to fight.

His shaking hand lifted the can of cleaning fluid. He turned it upside down and doused his body from his neck to his legs, then dropped it and reached out to her persistently.

Her heart was beating wildly. She handed him the box of matches. *This is for my husband, Adalwolf . . . and for all the others you killed.*

He opened the box, spilling the matches. He lifted one off his chest and laid its head against the sandpaper strip. He looked at her with pathetic eyes, begging for guidance. She nodded it was all right, it was time, go ahead and do it. He struck the match and instantly was engulfed in flames.

She stepped back, her hands raised against the heat. His skin disappeared in the swirling licks. He rose off the bed like a human torch and ran wildly toward the window and crashed through it and fell to the sand below. She stepped over to the broken glass and looked down and saw him on fire. The college kids across the way ran over and kicked sand on him trying to put it out. They looked up at her for help. She said, 'Stop kicking the sand! Let him burn!'

She blinked away the image. Her throat closed. The match was still in his hand – the real one, not the one in her daydream – still poised against the strike strip, ready to light, shaking. He drew it across—

She knocked it away and grabbed the box and threw it across the room. She stared at him, flushed and hot. He lay there quietly, grief-stricken and crying, filled with the despair and self-pity of an anti-Semite trapped in the body of a Jew. Saving him had been more instinctive than deliberate, but now that she'd done it she knew it was right. She caught her breath and picked up her cell phone and dialed 911 and asked the police to come. The dispatcher said they were on their way. When she disconnected she was calmer than she'd been for days.

She sat there watching him. Didn't kill Jews? She didn't want to kill anybody, not even someone as despicable as this. Not that he didn't deserve it, but killing him would have made her too much like him, and she wanted no part of that. Besides, there were alternatives. Letting him burn as a killer was her own satisfying fantasy; letting him live as a Jew was his own brutal reality.

His, she thought, was better.

NEVER HAD SHE BEEN given a better hug.

Melissa stood in a room at the fertility clinic waiting for Eric Brandt to come in with a verdict. They'd found the vaccine bottle Adalwolf had told her about, and Eric and the lab were analyzing the contents before sending it off to the CDC. Kobie had her arms around Melissa's waist, hugging her tightly.

'Thank you, Melissa,' she said in a sing-song voice.

Harris ended a cell phone call and turned to Melissa. 'That was WFO. The grand jury no-billed the investigation of Sergeant Sherwood's death.' They exchanged looks of mild disgust. It was good news, but after all they'd been through, no big deal.

Harris picked up Kobie's suitcase and laid his hand on her shoulder, telling her it was time to catch their plane home. Looking at Melissa, he said, 'Let me know when you're ready to give me the whole story and I'll fly down to hear it.'

The door opened and a nurse stuck her head inside. 'Dr. Brandt is in the lab, Ms. Gale. He's ready to see you now.'

Melissa, Kobie, and Harris walked down the hallway to the lab door where Melissa said goodbye. Harris gave her a one-handed hug – the other held a suitcase – and said, 'When are you coming back to Washington?'

She pushed the door open. 'Soon. I have a new ethical problem I want to try out on my next class.'

'Try me.'

She held the door. 'Hypothetically speaking, would you say it's wrong to tell a man a lie so convincing it makes him try to kill himself?'

'What kind of a lie?'

'Say, like, telling him he's a Jew even though he's not?'

'It would bother him that much?'

'Afraid so. His father was a big time Nazi.'

'Which one?'

'If I had to guess I'd say Himmler or Goebbels, although it could have been Hitler himself, there's no way to tell. Anyway, his father's identity is irrelevant to the ethical issue at hand.'

'Let me ask you this: was this guy shown documents to make him think he was a Jew?'

'Yes, but they were forgeries.'

'Convincing ones?'

'The best you've ever seen. Worthy of Jake the Wizard.'

'And he believed them?'

'Every last one.'

'Hm. But you say this is a hypothetical case?'

'Purely hypothetical,' she said.

'Sorry, but I can't answer without more facts.'

'More facts for a classroom discussion, or more facts in real life?'

'For a classroom discussion,' he said. 'In real life it's the coolest thing I ever heard of.'

THE MINUTE MELISSA walked into the lab she saw the answer on Eric's face.

'It's glucose,' he said.

She heard the words but didn't understand. 'Glucose?'

'Sugar water,' Eric said. 'There's no vaccine in the bottle labeled Meclizine XPL.' The disappointment was written on his face. 'There's no vaccine or serum in any of the containers. We've tested every one.'

Melissa felt an old, familiar weight descend onto her shoulders.

He handed her a piece of note paper. 'This was taped to the one he identified.'

She unfolded it. Written in Adalwolf s hand was a single sentence:

The game goes on.

Melissa sat in a chair and held her forehead in the palm of her hand. Eric stooped next to her. She looked at him, then reached out for him. He took her hands and held them in his own.

'What am I going to do?' she whispered. 'As much as I love this child, I can't give birth to a genocidal monster.'

'But you can't assume it will be,' Eric said.

'I can't assume it *won't* be,' she said. 'How can I take the chance?'

'You don't have to,' Eric said. 'If he turns out to have the virus, we'll know before he becomes contagious, just as we did with the other victims. And that gives us time to contain it.'

'How?'

'We can quarantine him while we search for a serum. We can

find a way to boost his immune system to kill it. Point is, we can prevent an epidemic.'

'And if we can't cure him, he lives his life in a bubble?' she said.

'Until we find an answer, yes. But it could be worse.'

'Like what?'

'You could abort him thinking he was sick when he's not. Imagine how you'd feel if Adalwolf revealed that this baby you wanted so much – this one-in-a-million conception and the last living part of David – was actually as normal and healthy as could be.'

She thought about it a moment, then pulled her hands out of his and leaned back in the chair and stared at him as if she had something profound to say. He didn't blink.

'Stay with it, Melissa. I'll be at your side every step of the way, I promise.'

'Thanks, Eric,' she said, 'but that's not my problem.'

'What is?'

'My blood sugar. Would you like to get some dinner?'

MELISSA WAS LOADED FOR bear when she entered the courtroom. She found a seat on the aisle in the second row, as far forward as she could get, and sat down. Arraignments usually drew a small crowd, but word of Adalwolf s appearance had circulated the courthouse all morning and the room was nearly filled.

She looked around nervously, stoking up her nerve. Finally, the clerk of the court called the case and the side door opened. She heard the ankle chains, then saw him come through the door with two guards behind him. He was dressed in the clothes he'd worn the night before, unshaven and disheveled and heavy-lidded and bruised from the injuries he'd sustained on the boat. He walked bent forward, trying to protect the bandaged burns on his stomach from touching his clothes. His lawyer, a young woman from Legal Aid appointed to represent him, came down the center aisle and stepped through the swinging doors and joined him at the defendants' table.

Adalwolf still hadn't seen Melissa.

Everything in her head told her that the law was the only way to resolve a conflict like this, but everything in her gut told her the law was too good for him. There were still rules for everyone else, and there were still rules for monsters. It was the frustration of having superior knowledge that drove her now: she knew about the lives he'd taken and the genocide he'd planned, and she knew about his overwhelming, undeniable guilt. Balancing that knowledge against the abstract good of honoring a defendant's rights wasn't easy. She told herself to be calm and wait, her opportunity would come in a moment.

The judge read the booking report and confirmed various matters for the record: the defendant's name – his counsel said it was Professor Benjamin Ben-Zevi, aka Henry Hallam Brandon, aka Adalwolf – his address, and his consent to being represented by his lawyer. After other administrative matters had been handled, the judge turned to the question of bail. The prosecution resisted it strenuously, claiming the subject was a violent man and a substantial flight risk and that the safety of the community depended on his remaining behind bars. If she'd had the chance, Melissa would have added that the safety of Adalwolf depended on his staying in jail, too.

After listening to Adalwolf s counsel, the judge denied bail and the next arraignment was called. A plea would be entered by Adalwolf after his indictment. The guards took him by the elbows and turned him around to escort him back to his holding cell.

That's when Melissa made her move.

'What have you done to my baby?' she shouted, standing up and stepping into the aisle. Heads turned and the judge motioned toward the guard at the rear of the room, who was already moving toward her. Adalwolf turned and looked at her with a blank expression.

Melissa opened the swinging door that separated her from the well and went through it. One of the guards at Adalwolf s side stepped forward just as the guard from the back of the room reached her. She lunged toward Adalwolf with her arms outstretched.

'Tell me how to save my baby!'

The guards grabbed her before her fingernails reached his face. The judge was on his feet, the audience sitting transfixed. When it finally became clear to Adalwolf that he was beyond her reach, he relaxed and a smirk crossed his lips.

'I'll be watching you with great interest, Melissa,' he said. 'You and your baby both.'

Melissa felt her face redden, then made herself calm. 'Don't watch for me,' she said as the guards tugged her toward the aisle. 'Watch for the angel of death.' She saw a puzzled look on his face. 'You won't have trouble recognizing him – some days he looks like David Gale, some days like Jeremy Friedman, some like twelve-year-old Benjamin Ben-Zevi.'

The guards pushed her toward the door, but she turned her head and kept her eyes on Adalwolf as she went. He still hadn't blinked by the time she lost sight of him. But the smirk, she noticed, was gone.

ADALWOLF WAS RIGHT about one thing: it was a baby boy.

He was crying. Melissa liked that. A nurse wrapped him in a blanket and was about to hand him to her when one of the doctors stopped her. 'Here, let me,' he said, taking the baby in his arms. He stepped to Melissa's side.

'Here he is,' Eric said. 'Isn't he beautiful?'

She took him and held him on her chest. She was flushed and exhausted but happy to see him. 'Hey, there, little fella. At last we meet.'

He stopped crying and his wrinkled, old-man's face came to life. He opened his eyes and looked for her, saw nothing but felt her presence, heard her voice. He yawned and closed his eyes. His features were perfect. Perfect lips, perfect nose, perfect little fingers with perfect tiny nails. A perfect swirl of hair on his head, very auburn, his great-grandmother Esther's way of making her presence known. Everything about him was just . . . perfect.

Now they'd have to wait and see if he stayed that way, or whether the NTX virus would rear its ugly head. It was a matter of time, and no one knew how much.

Eric took a dab of Vaseline from a jar and drew it over Melissa's lips. She caught his hand and held it to her cheek a moment.

'Thank you for all you've done, Eric.'

'What are you going to name him?' he said.

'David,' she said.

'David Gale,' Eric said. 'Are you giving him a middle name?'

'Yes,' she said. 'Eric. David Eric Gale.'

Four Years Later
A picnic ground in suburban
Washington, D.C.

THERE WAS NOTHING IN the air to hint that a disaster was in the making. The day was full of Fourth of July sunshine and laughter, the smell of roasting hot dogs and sweet relish and kids' damp hair, the sound of parents cheering at each swing of a plastic bat.

There were two outs in the bottom of the fifth, the last inning of the game. A four-year-old boy with auburn hair and brown eyes and a face stolen off a shampoo ad stepped up to the whiffle ball sitting atop a waist-high rubber tee.

A man coaching a little girl standing on third base cupped his hands and yelled at the batter, 'You can win it all, David! A hit wins the game!'

The batter's adoptive father, Dr. Eric Brandt, stood with the spectators with an arm draped over his wife's shoulder, a cold beer in hand, yelling, 'Put your hands closer together, Dave!' The little boy heard his dad's instructions and closed the gap on the bat. His mother, Melissa Gale Brandt, clapped and yelled, 'Come on, David!'

The families on the picnic ground quieted as David Eric Gale got ready to hit. His tongue came out as he swung the feather-light bat – and missed the ball. There were a few groans, more whistling and clapping, but the boy heard none of it. He may have been more Babe than Ruth, but he knew what he had to do.

He swung again and the white plastic sphere sailed off the tee onto the grass. The picnickers erupted. 'Run!' Eric yelled, spilling his beer.

David started running toward first base, all feet and no speed. It took forever, but when it was over, he'd won by a step.

Everyone cheered and hopped up and down and danced and laughed. Dads wandered onto the field to gather up the bewildered players on both teams and lift them onto their shoulders.

Everyone, that is, except David.

Melissa saw him first. 'Oh, my God!' Her hand went to her mouth and she started running toward first base with Eric close behind. The silence of a crisis slowly rippled over the stunned crowd.

Melissa reached him and kneeled at his side. His eyes were open, his face flushed, his head drenched with sweat. Clear fluid ran out of his nose and glistened on his upper lip.

'What's wrong?' Melissa asked.

The boy didn't answer.

Eric kneeled on the other side of him and saw him shaking with chills. A woman handed Melissa a towel soaked with water from a cooler and she wiped his cheeks and neck and forehead. Someone else handed Eric a blanket which he wrapped around his son before picking him up and carrying him toward the car in a half run, half walk, Melissa at his side.

Opening the door to the back seat, she said, 'This is it, isn't it?'

Eric didn't answer. He knew what his wife wanted him to say – 'It's nothing, just too much sun and ice cream' – but he didn't say it because he couldn't. She might have been right. It might have finally kicked in.

MELISSA SAT IN THE waiting room of the hospital. Eric paced, rubbing the back of his neck.

'Maybe it's a coincidence,' she said.

Eric didn't answer.

She answered herself, out loud. 'It's not a coincidence, it's the same symptoms Jeremy Friedman had.'

Eric shook his head, telling her to stop speculating.

A doctor came into the room. 'Come with me,' he said.

They followed him through a swinging door and down the hospital hallway. He opened the door and ushered them in. David was sitting on a bed playing with a rubber dinosaur. Melissa and Eric both looked at the doctor for an explanation.

'He's fine,' the doctor said.

'No NTX?' Eric said.

The doctor shrugged. 'Not that we can find.'

'What does that mean?' Melissa said. She felt uncertainty wash over her and heard frustration in her voice.

'It means,' the doctor said gently, 'that he has a touch of ordinary flu, that's all. It's not NTX. Your immune system seems to have defeated the virus, so maybe his will, too. We just don't know.'

Melissa looked over at David and spoke softly. 'How do we live with something like this hanging over our heads?'

Eric said, 'We do it one day at a time. We're not alone, you know. Everybody has a touch of terrorism hanging over their heads these days.'

She looked into his blue eyes. Whenever he was sure of something, they didn't blink, and they didn't blink now. Reassured, she relaxed, then turned to David and scooped him up in her arms. 'Let's go home, Tiger.'

'I'm not a tiger, I'm a Tyrannosaurus Rex,' he said, reaching back for his rubber dinosaur.

Eric picked it off the bed and handed it to him as they said their goodbyes to the doctor. Then they went home and cleaned up the mess from the picnic. David got over his flu in a few days, and soon they were back to their normal state of low level, semi-controlled, domestic chaos. They liked it. They got used to it. It was their life.

One day at a time.

Acknowledgements

NO ONE HAS BEEN A better friend to this book, or to me, than my friend of many years, Warren Dennis. If I were eligible for it, he would be my rabbi. He is anyway.

I want to thank my son, Dr. Paul Pottinger, for his encouragement and sharp mind, not only with the medical information, but with my writing.

Joe Lisi was, as usual, a great technical advisor. Without Jennifer Malki, I couldn't have done my Miami research. What a find she was. Thanks as well to Rex Tomb, Judy Orihuela, and Ken Crosby of the FBI for their excellent and precise help.

Dr. C.J. Peters of the University of Texas Medical Branch – Galveston was remarkably generous with his time, advice and imagination, for which I am equally impressed and grateful.

Without Hilary Goren of the Columbia Presbyterian Medical Center For Women's Reproductive Care, Melissa Gale never would have gotten pregnant. Way to go, Hilary.

Thanks to my friend Chris Parker, a marvelous screenwriter whose knowledge of story and character would also make him a first-rate novelist, but who's smart enough to know better.

Appreciation goes to Tina Schwartz at *America's Most Wanted* and to Dr. Harry Gruber for his fine technical reading. And the deepest of gratitude goes to my agents and friends, Joni Evans and Owen Laster.

Flowers galore go to Sue Fletcher, my UK publisher, who is not only a world-class publisher, but a world-class editor and friend. What a pleasure it is to know her.

And to my test readers, Richard C, Eleanor F, Fredi F, Liz F, Alicia G, Ellery G, Rena G, Verna H, Rafa J, T. Barry K, Adam M, Judy M, Bruce N, son Matt P, daughter Katie P, thanks for being my early warning system. Most of all, thank you, Kathleen. I have enough words to write a book, but not enough to express the depth of my love and gratitude for all you've meant to me and this novel.

To John and Sally and everyone at St. Martin's Press, thanks not only for your professional skill, but your enthusiastic collaboration. This is what publishing should always be about.

Finally, I'd like to thank my editor, Charlie Spicer, for his perceptive eye and persistent effort to make this a better book. It must have been a daunting moment, the day it hit his desk.